BLACK DEATH IN A NEW AGE:

A Novel

Kathy T. Kale

Black Death in a New Age: A Novel

First published April 22, 2003

Copyright © 2003 by Kathy T. Kale

Published by
Pollux Press,
Fort Pierce, Florida

ISBN 978-0-9836866-5-1

DISCLAIMER

This is a work of fiction. Names, characters, places, and incidents are either the product of the author's imagination or are used fictitiously. Any resemblance to actual persons, living or dead, events or locales is entirely coincidental.

ACKNOWLEDGEMENTS

Many thanks to those who helped in this endeavor. This book was made possible by the support of my husband. Joan Baxter's guidance was also instrumental. I am grateful to my parents for their endless enthusiasm for my projects. I am especially appreciative of my children, Will and Luc, who inspire hope for a better future and a world that will know peace. Thanks to Joan Farrell, Jan Dawson, and Jake Logsdon for editing the manuscript. Also many thanks to my early readers: Ann Marie Montgomery, Mary Ferguson, Claudette Wingell, Ann Viljoen, Frances Kavanagh, and Clarice Giffen. Thanks also to Mimi Alonso of Arista Graphics for the cover design. I am especially grateful to Beverly Pietlicki for all of her help.

To vaccine developers, my apologies for making complex research look easy. This is truly fiction. The cover photo is from CDC/ Science Source and shows the plague bacterium *Yersinia pestis* illuminated by direct fluorescent antibodies in a light micrograph at 40X magnification.

In memory of those affected by the August 1998 bombing of the American Embassy in Nairobi, Kenya.

For Bill

Returning violence for violence multiplies violence, adding deeper darkness to a night already devoid of stars...

—Martin Luther King Jr.

APRIL 24TH

CHAPTER ONE

On the Friday before embarking on the grandest adventure of his life, Dudley Shaw woke up sick. He watched the morning news on CNN and felt worse. During the night, the United States had bombed Mogadishu and bodies lay like driftwood in the sand. The dawn skies were smoking. Dudley read a warning that the pictures were graphic and could be disturbing. He turned off the TV and patted his dog. "Ready to go, boy?"

On Monday, Dudley and Bingo were taking a road trip. They were going off the grid, checking out. He smiled in anticipation, despite the rhythmic pounding inside his skull. His skin felt tight and clammy and he guessed he was running a fever. He didn't want to know. He checked his to-do list. The first item was to wash the car. He glanced through the living room window and saw the '57 Thunderbird gleaming in the sunlight. He took Ladybird to the car wash last week to get her ready for the road, but since then it had rained and she was splattered with mud. He had to wash her before it got too hot.

Dudley stood up. He felt dizzy and put a hand to the wall to steady himself. He was weak and his vision was blurred. He hauled himself to the kitchen, where he swallowed three aspirin with orange juice fortified with added vitamin C and hoped that would take care of the problem. He called Bingo and went outside.

He stood for a moment on the porch to acclimatize to the heat. It must have been eighty degrees already, though it was not yet nine, not yet May. Summer had come early to Texas. The weather was changing. The winter was too hot and the spring had too much rain. Already the fleas were bad. Beside him, Bingo propelled a hind leg, scratching his ear.

"Come on, boy." Dudley grabbed a bucket, turned on the faucet, and Bingo headed for the woods. He hated water, hated to be bathed. "Not you, Ladybird," Dudley shouted, but Bingo didn't look back.

When the bucket was full, Dudley lugged it across the mucky lawn. The long arms of the sun stretched across the field and strangled him. The bucket was heavy and his breathing was hard. The day was just getting started and already he felt exhausted and worn out.

He reached the car and dropped the bucket. Water slopped over the side. He ran his hand across Ladybird's sleek back fin and felt better. She was lemon yellow and gleaming with chrome. He rested his cheek on the sun-warmed roof. Her surface was smooth and hot, and she felt solid and strong beneath his weight; a beauty aging well. He loved his car— something that had exacerbated his ex-wife to no end. *You've got more feeling for that car than me*, she used to say, and he guessed it was so.

He set to work, swabbing Ladybird down. There was a lump under his arm and it ached. He laid down the sponge and gingerly felt the swelling in his left armpit that was the size of an egg. It had grown larger and harder overnight. Whatever it was, was growing fast—a high rate of growth. That was what the doctors told his father when he had lung cancer. He had been sixty-five, the same age Dudley was now. Three months later he was dead. His father refused to go to the doctor, and Dudley was just like him. It was best not to know.

He went back to work, trying to keep his mind on the job. He squeezed out the sponge and rubbed the windshield. Tracks of mud streaked down the glass. Bright sunlight bounced off the chrome and hurt his eyes. It was too hot. No gulf wind blew. His head hammered and his underarm burned.

Dudley dropped the sponge and shrugged off his shirt. Perspiration soaked his skin. He pressed his palms to his forehead to counteract the building pressure. Bingo reappeared with the fur on his back raised. He growled a low growl.

"What is it, boy?"

Bingo turned and stared at the woods.

Dudley shivered. There were no clouds, but the sun seemed dim and far away. He was too sick to finish the job. He would do it later. He bent down to grab his shirt and his head screamed. When he stood, the ground tilted under his feet. His body shook with cold and his teeth chattered. Ahead the house shimmered. The pecan tree was a hundred feet from the house but the distance seemed like miles. He took a step, then a rest, then another step, and minute by minute he inched his way to the house.

Bingo was waiting by the door and they went inside. Past the kitchen, the hallway leading to his bedroom looked endless. Dudley tottered to the couch, flopped down, and gasped for breath. He felt a choking heat on his face and tried to pry open his eyes. The room was turning. From far away, he heard a dog's mournful howl.

CHAPTER TWO

Three hours later and three miles away in the veterinary building at Duane University, Dana Sparks was finishing a paper for the Journal of Immunology when the telephone rang. Her new boss needed to see her immediately. It was an order, not a request. Of course TJ McCoy couldn't send her an email or say what he wanted over the phone; he had to waste her time in person.

The military man was new to the Department of Infectious Disease and used to getting his way. In the month since he arrived, he'd been busy making unnecessary changes and issuing new regulations that inconvenienced everyone. He was getting harder to take by the day, and Dana's patience was wearing thin. She put up with him because she needed tenure.

She left her lab and went down the hall to the main office. It was lunchtime and the secretary was gone, but the new chairman was waiting. He stood in the doorway of his office, dressed as usual in military attire, minus his many medals.

"Dr. Sparks, I'm glad you could make it." TJ McCoy was a gray man, with gray eyes, gray skin, and a gray crew cut. He was Dana's height, five-ten, and their eyes were level. He was sixty years old and looked every day of it. He'd suffered a heart attack in the fall and was forced from the Pentagon where he had spent forty years planning wars. "Come in. Sit down." Always the imperative. Commands Dana hated to follow, even as she did so.

In the room it was winter, dark and cold. The curtains were drawn, a floor fan blew, and a window air conditioning unit hummed. She sat down and they faced one another across his clean and polished desk. "I'm reassigning parking spaces," he said.

Of course he was. He liked to throw his weight around, abuse his position.

"I wanted to tell you in person. So there would be no misunderstanding." He tapped his fingers on his desk. His nails were meticulously filed. A silver bracelet engraved with the misspelled word 'Dady' slipped down his thick wrist. His wedding ring was the size and color of a thimble.

"I have a new parking space. What is there to misunderstand?"

"It's a ways away."

"Okay."

"On the other side of the building."

She raised her eyebrows.

"Near the farm."

That was a half mile away, a space as far from the building as possible. He was letting her know how difficult he could make her life. "Perfect," she said, refusing to show any ire. "I can leave my car at home and walk."

"Up to you. Parking is tight. We need to make more room for clients at the veterinary clinic. Everyone has to move. Well, not tenured staff, of course."

He spoke without making eye contact. He was staring over her shoulder, past her, as if her chair was empty and she was already gone. She needed tenure by the end of the year, or she was out.

Was he trying to tell her something? Could he let her go after tenure had already been promised? Though, as he liked to remind her, not by him but by his predecessor, Brian Boswell, who died suddenly on Christmas Eve. McCoy had been dragged out of retirement to take his place.

He'd been a nightmare from the start. He ran the department as if it were the army. McCoy had some nebulous doctorate but had been an administrator for most of his life. His specialty was war and fiscal efficiency. His post was supposed to be temporary, but he didn't act as a place-holder; a fleeting replacement for someone more qualified. For a figurehead, he answered to no one and did as he pleased.

She knew it was pointless to argue with him. "Okay, fine, I have a new parking space. If that's all, I have work to do." She glanced at his clean and empty desktop. "I know you're busy, but have you signed off on the grant proposal?" She had written a proposal for a three year, one million dollar army grant to research an active plague vaccine. Brian had signed off on the proposal, but McCoy was dragging his feet.

"I have a problem with it," he said.

"Excuse me?"

"I'm not sure the research is necessary."

"You're not sure." Who was he to decide? She sat forward in her chair. "A resurgence of the plague could present enormous problems. There—"

He cut her off. "There are antibiotics against the plague."

"The plague bacteria are becoming resistant. Last year, a six-teen-year-old boy in Madagascar nearly died because the antibiotics didn't work."

"You have your monoclonal vaccine. That should work."

"It's a passive vaccine. With a little more research, we can get an active vaccine. Something that endures. One shot, that's it."

"There are more relevant health concerns. The money could be better spent elsewhere."

"Dr. McCoy, the research was already approved."

He tapped his fingers. "Not by me."

"The army requested the research. I've already found a promising antigen."

"I'll talk to them. Perhaps it's time to move on."

Another threat. She stood up. He was so obtuse that he didn't get the distinction between an active and passive vaccine. There was no point explaining it again. She would have to find a way around him. If she got the grant, he couldn't deny her tenure.

McCoy stood too, at ease, hands slung around his back, straining the shiny brass buttons on his blazer. "By the way," he said, as he eyed her with a sweeping glance. "Where is your lab coat?"

It was the last day of the semester and she was dressed casually in beige jeans, a button-down shirt, and cowboy boots. "My lab coat's in the lab."

"According to the compendium, Section 16, lab coats are mandatory whilst at work." McCoy reached down, opened a desk drawer, and retrieved his heavy compendium that outlined his new rules in excruciating detail. He flipped through the pages, stopped near the end, and jabbed a line with his finger. "A lab coat must be worn in the lab at all times by all faculty."

"I'm not in a lab," Dana said, as she walked to the door.

"Dismissed," McCoy called out.

She closed his door way too loud, betraying her indignation. She strode to her lab, internally raging. He had too much power. He could get rid of her. At the moment, he was the chair of the tenure committee that decided her future. Grant or not, he could shake his head and she'd be gone. It was too unfair.

She reached the end of the hallway and entered her lab. Maybe it was a sign. Perhaps it was time to leave. Go somewhere new, start over, shut the door on the past.

She went to her office and sat down at her desk. No, this was her place. She was an assistant professor and had been in the department seven years. She'd been in Duane eighteen years, half of her life, and she belonged here. He didn't. He was the one that should leave.

She wouldn't go easily. She would make it as difficult for him as she could. She stared up at the Van Gogh print on the wall that served in the place of a window. *Starry Night* was the painter's view from an asylum window. Even locked up, going crazy, losing his mind, he had hope. He saw a bright night, invisible force fields, order in chaos. She liked the print because it was unscientific. There was more going on than the eye could see; invisible connections linking disparate things together.

She leaned back and stared at the stars. McCoy didn't get to decide her future. He may not realize it, but if she found the active vaccine, it would be a huge deal and would not go unnoticed. It would draw attention, and in her dreams re-catch an eye that was caught long ago. She jumped up, went to the fridge, and grabbed a small ampule containing clear amber fluid. She held her future in her hand.

CHAPTER THREE

McCoy was recovering from the most disagreeable encounter when his telephone rang. He picked up and heard the frantic voice of the manager of the Lone Star Heritage Hotel. "Did you hear about the bombing of Mogadishu?" the manager asked.

"Of course," McCoy said. He got up early to watch the story on the morning news. It pained him greatly that he was not a part of the response, for he knew the four-star general who briefed the press. On TV, McCoy caught a glimpse of his old life that was gone forever.

"There's talk of retaliation," the manager said. "Some Islamic factions have issued a decree. What if they bomb my hotel? I'm expecting two hundred guests."

Including the United States Vice President, Rich Rutherford, who was coming in less than a week to deliver the convocation address. Rutherford was an old friend from West Point and McCoy was head of the team planning his visit. Though he wasn't personally in charge of security, it was never far from McCoy's mind. "Did the hotel receive a specific threat against the VP?"

"Threats have been made," the manager said, in a high whine. "It's no secret the VP will be here. What if they hit the hotel?"

What if. Hysterical words in McCoy's view. "Look, we'll get together with the FBI and discuss security. I'll set it up." Already an advance team from Virginia was in town and McCoy was working closely with Barry Ackerman, the FBI agent in charge. Ackerman was too young in McCoy's view to handle the responsibility, and McCoy was holding his hand. If there was a credible threat, they'd get more agents. If Ackerman didn't have the clout to authorize it, McCoy would make some calls and it would be done. He hung up the phone, called Ackerman, and set up a two o'clock meeting.

Only now there was a conflict. At two o'clock McCoy was scheduled to deliver a lecture on biological warfare to seniors in Molecular Biology. McCoy wanted new blood in his department and was seeking promising graduate students. He wanted anyone interested in war.

McCoy tapped his fingers on his desk, wondering who would give the lecture. The problem was that no one in the department was capable of it. The Department of Infectious Disease dealt primarily with infectious diseases, and his expertise was war. He'd been promised his own department. As soon as the university's finances improved, Infectious Disease would merge with Microbiology, and McCoy would build the Department of Human Health—that would specialize in biological and chemical warfare. It was the carrot that dragged him from retirement. When McCoy left the Veterinary College he would take with him those researchers who could contribute to his vision.

In the meantime, McCoy's personal mandate was to restore discipline to a department run amuck. He would turn the department around and get rid of 'dead wood' as he saw fit. The department was in economic ruin. The former chairman may have been a pleasant, happy-go-lucky guy, but the department had suffered under his tutelage. Brian Boswell spent money he did not have. He lived off grants not yet approved. He allowed his staff to run wild.

Dana Sparks was a case in point. She could be good. She had a strong publishing record and a demonstrated ability to secure funding. By most accounts, she was hard working and well liked. Yet her attitude was insufferable. She refused to recognize his authority. McCoy had dealt with people like her before. It was like breaking a horse. The beast had to know who was boss. You had to hit hard, over and over, until the spirit broke, and submitted to outside direction. If that didn't work, you had to shoot the horse.

He reached for the phone. Dr. Sparks would give the lecture on his behalf. He called her office and got no answer. After scrawling a short note explaining his directive, he carried it down to her lab. He was in a full sweat by the time he reached the end of the hallway. Cutting down on air conditioning was a cost-cutting measure McCoy was forced to take that he did not like. He had endured the treeless swamps of Quang Tri, the steaming deserts of Kuwait, and now this. He mopped the back of his neck. Texas was too damn hot.

He entered Spark's lab and was taken aback when he saw her in her office, eating an apple, though consumption of food in laboratories was strictly forbidden. "Dr. Sparks, did you not hear your phone?"

"I heard it."

He entered her office and walked around her cluttered desk. She had a picture on her wall McCoy could only describe as disturbing. Weird buildings, weirder clouds. Margaret, his youngest daughter, could paint better pictures than that. He averted his eyes and looked down. Sparks seemed to be working out a dose. For an animal that weighed sixty kilograms! "What are you doing?"

She covered the paper with her hand. "A calculation."

"I see that. Is it a dose? For what?"

"A big rat." She scrunched up the paper and tossed it at the garbage can. She missed, but left the wadded paper where it fell.

Her office was a mess. Papers everywhere, binders stacked haphazardly on the floor, and reprints towering in a corner. Her screen saver was enough to induce an epileptic fit—rolling dice tumbling over and over. McCoy was mystified by her success. She was emotional and reactive, qualities unbecoming a scientist. She lacked the sober, plodding, reasonable, rational temperament he equated with scientific accomplishment. He picked a vial up off her desk. "What's this? There's no label."

She stood up and took the vial from him. "I know what's inside. Can I help you with something?"

She deliberately kept him in the dark about her activities. "You will deliver a lecture for me."

"A lecture? School's finished."

"Not quite. The fourth year Molecular Biology students expect instruction this afternoon."

"This afternoon? Today?" Her tone was querulous. She shook her head, blond hair flying in her face. Her eyes were too blue and her gaze too direct. She was too pretty—and it made him uncomfortable. She did not fit his image of a scientific researcher. She favored blue jeans and pointy-toed cowboy boots that turned heads when she clomped down the hall. She was thirty-six, never married, and McCoy had heard rumors about her personal life that he refused to consider, and did his best to ignore. She would have to shape up if she didn't want to ship out.

He stared her down. "The lecture is today, that is correct. In the biology building, in the main lecture hall, fourteen to seventeen hundred hours."

"Two till five? Three hours?" She put down her apple.

"The subject is biological warfare. Make it interesting."

She frowned. "I don't know anything about warfare."

"Talk about the plague and your vaccine work. How it was developed to save millions in the event of a biological war."

"There are natural infections," she said. "At the moment prairie dogs are the biggest culprits in spreading the plague."

What was this talk of prairie dogs? Sparks' military grant would not be used to cure sick prairie dogs, that was for sure. McCoy held out an envelope. "When you're finished, there will be a teacher evaluation. Betty will collect the forms at five."

She stared at the envelope. "On the last day of the semester?" She folded her arms. "You're joking."

"I don't joke," McCoy dropped the envelope on the desk. "We need these evaluations for your file, for the consideration of your tenure."

"My teaching has already been evaluated."

"Not by me. We'll repeat the exercise." McCoy had been puzzled by her previous evaluations. Her overall rating was too good to believe. Did she discard the negative replies while the previous chairman winked and looked the other way? "Today's process will be strictly supervised."

"As it was the last time."

"This is not open for discussion." He wanted to add, it was a goddamn order and like it or not, she'd do as he said—but he held himself back.

She clucked her teeth with displeasure, tapped the toe of her boot, and glanced at her watch.

McCoy would not be hurried. "By the way, I neglected to mention that we're having a visitor next week."

She raised her eyes to the ceiling. "Yes, I know, your friend, the Vice President of the United States."

McCoy realized his mistake. "I'm talking about Michael Smith."

"Who?"

There was a bite to her tone and an angry look in her eyes. She was easily provoked.

"Dr. Smith is a bacteriologist," McCoy said. "His specialty is anthrax. He is a West Point graduate like myself."

"Why is he coming?" Dana asked.

She questioned everything he said; it was most unpleasant. "Because I invited him."

"Great." She picked up the apple.

"There is no eating in the laboratory."

"This is an office."

"Where is your lab coat?"

"I'm not in the lab."

They could go around and around in circles like this indefinitely. If she was deliberately trying to drive him crazy, she was succeeding. He returned to his office wondering about the wisdom of returning to work. Perhaps he was too old. His vigor and love of the fight seemed to have ebbed. He found the civilian setting bewildering, and the lack of respect for superiors infuriating. If his aim to head the specialized unit was to come to pass, his authority had to be recognized. He was the commanding officer. It was him. He was in charge. Either get the message or get out. McCoy was fully aware that some horses could never be broken.

CHAPTER FOUR

Dana arrived at Halbourn Hall fifteen minutes before the lecture was due to begin. Usually parking on main campus was a nightmare, but today there were many empty spots. She'd worked in the building before she moved to the vet school—before the university fell on hard fiscal times, and before the biology department had been split in two. The part relating to human and animal health had been relegated to the Veterinary College, and the other part became the Department of Environmental Biology. Although Dana was unhappy with the mandatory relocation, it turned out for the best. If she'd had her way and stayed put, she would have missed out on the love of a lifetime.

She shrugged off the thought as she entered the building. The lobby was freezing, and the lecture hall was even colder. There was a row of high windows that would let in bright light, but they could not be opened. Dana wished she'd brought a sweater. Texans were nuts about their air-conditioning and she could live without it. Growing up in Buffalo, she'd had enough cold weather to last a lifetime.

Dana opened her briefcase, pulled out her laptop, and opened a PowerPoint presentation on the plague. McCoy may not know it, but she could effortlessly give a three-hour lecture. She would talk about biological warfare and get it out of the way. Then she would address the history of the plague, its biology, and the diseases it caused. After handing out the evaluations, she'd get back to work. She'd left a message for her technician, asking her to wait. Dana needed help.

She was ready before the students arrived and stood by the door waiting for them. The lecture hall was set up like a movie theatre with ascending rows and seats for two hundred. At the front there was a podium and a long counter. Behind that there was a huge blackboard, and above it, a retractable screen. With the floors covered in thick gray carpet, the acoustics were perfect and sound carried well throughout the room.

At five past two, the first student strolled in—a young man of about twenty-two, sporting hair dyed white and green. He had a razorblade necklace and a ring through his eyebrow. He was soon followed by a girl in a halter, and then a young man in sunglasses and a muscle shirt. Then students streamed in steadily, dressed as if for the beach.

Five minutes later, when twenty students in the class of thirty-two were present, Dana began. "I suspect you don't want to be here any more than I do."

A student yawned.

"Don't worry about taking notes," Dana said. There was no point anyway, for there would be no test. Graduating seniors did not take finals. Nonetheless, a girl in a flowered dress sitting in the front row took out a pad and a pen. Dana picked up the attendance sheet McCoy had thoughtfully provided.

"Not only do you have to be here, you have to sign in." Dana added that it was not her doing and if she had her way, she would cancel the class and they could go.

The students woke up.

"Unfortunately, someone is coming at five to hand out teacher evaluation forms, so you have to stay."

There were scattered cries of protest.

"I don't like it either," Dana said, though it wasn't strictly true. She liked a challenge and would do her best to hook the kids and reel them in.

She began the lecture. "This afternoon we're going to talk about biological warfare." She pushed a button and lowered the projector screen.

For the next thirty minutes, Dana spoke about emulsions, delivery systems, bombs, and warheads. She ran through slides showing invisible organisms and toxins so deadly that one teaspoon could kill ten million people at the cost of one dollar.

The students remained unimpressed.

Dana switched gears and talked about the plague. "The disease is caused by the bacterium *Yersinia pestis*, which is spread by fleas. The fleas commonly feed on rats and other rodents. They can also feed on cats, dogs, and humans."

A girl at the back began to brush her hair.

"There was a nursery rhyme written about it. 'Ring around the Rosie' was about the plague."

The note taker scribbled madly, but the others sent Dana blank stares. It would be a hard crowd to turn.

"The bacterium itself is very old and dates back to centuries before Christ. In the last two centuries, there have been three pandemics. The first in 540 AD caused the fall of the Roman Empire. The second in 1346 wiped out twenty to thirty million people. The third in 1665 swept through London and killed a fifth of the population."

She showed a slide of a man dressed like a penguin and wearing a black cape, top hat, and mask in the shape of a beak. It was the quarantine clothes worn by fourteenth century physicians. "They filled the beak with camphor, vinegar, and other noxious scents to ward off the aroma of putrefaction: the smell of death."

A kid took out his cell phone.

She went on to the next slide. This one showed the dead—people lying prone on the ground, stacked on top of each other like pick-up sticks. Above, angels with bows rained down poisoned arrows. "In the fourteenth century, people used to blame their misery on a punitive God. They thought bad things happened when God wasn't happy." She described the flagellates, traveling Christian men who went from town to town whipping themselves into a frenzy, trying to buy God's favor. "They wished to atone for the sins they thought they must have committed to earn God's wrath, but to no avail. Most of them died anyway."

There was some stirring in the room. This was Baptist country and the students had no trouble combining religion with science and retribution.

"Some people think the plague ushered in the Renaissance. Because wealthy Christians died as easily and quickly as destitute non-believers, some believed that God didn't play the active role they had thought. For the first time, people sought answers outside of God. The disease caused a shift away from religious explanations."

Dana paused and stared at the pupils. She found this fascinating and could usually pass on her excitement, but not today. Not on the last day of school, not to students who would likely never sit in a classroom again, nor take another test. She was wasting her time and theirs. Was forcing the students to listen to a lecture any different from McCoy forcing her to deliver it? Was taking attendance any different from the threat of a visiting West Point recruit whose specialty was war, and was likely looking for a job? No, there was no difference at all.

Dana climbed the stairs and collected the attendance sheet from the girl with just-brushed gleaming hair. Dana crumpled the attendance sheet into a ball and threw it at the garbage pail, missing by a mile. "If you all want to leave, you can."

Now she had the students' attention. The guy with sunglasses lowered them. A girl eating lunch stopped chewing. The girl in front taking notes gasped. No one made a move for the door.

Dana returned to the front. When you gave people a choice, they usually chose the right thing. It was a subtle point McCoy missed. Dana smiled warmly at the class and hoisted herself up on the front counter and continued. "Right now in the U.S., there are about ten cases of the plague a year. Some people believe the plague occurs in three-hundred-year cycles and that we're imminently heading for another pandemic."

There was a question from the girl taking notes. "Where do the bacteria go between cycles?"

An excellent question, and a major mystery. "We don't know," Dana said. "The disease is a zoonosis. It's an animal disease, and presumably the bacteria hide out in animals that are resistant to the plague. We know that for months, the bacteria disappear. Then, without warning, a sick animal tests positive for infection, or a human falls ill. There are a few mammals, like cats and some species of mice, which aren't sensitive to the plague and may act as a reservoir. The bacteria can hide in these species."

The girl nodded and scribbled away.

Dana explained how the disease was spread. "It wasn't until the end of the nineteenth century that a scientist named Yersin realized the disease was associated with rats. Before any humans were afflicted with the plague, rats would die off in great numbers. Later, when people began to die, Yersin found safety-pin shaped objects in the blood of the dead. He took this blood and injected it into healthy mice, and a few days later they were dead. When he looked in the blood of the dead mice, he found the safety-pin objects there too. A few years later, another scientist realized it wasn't the rats that caused the disease, but rather their fleas. It took many more years to figure out the culprit wasn't a flea—but a bacterium."

Dana pulled up a slide of the bacillus. *Yersinia pestis* was a gram-negative, rod-shaped bacterium. While it resembled a safety pin in the light microscope, in some growing conditions it formed long chains and curled like a question mark. When tagged with a fluorescent antibody at forty-fold magnification, the bacteria glowed a brilliant green.

Dana hopped off the counter and moved on to the next slide, which was a blown-up picture of a flea. "The flea is the vector. It transmits the bacteria from animal to animal. A common host is the rat. When fleas feed on rats, they inject bacteria into the blood, about four hundred with every bite. When the rats die, the fleas abscond."

The next slide was a picture of her technician's cat. "If an infected flea bites a domestic cat, the cat can serve as a host. If an infected flea bites a person, they get the bubonic plague."

She paused and eyed the class. She seemed to have their attention. They were focused. There was no eating, no hair combing—just the girl in front taking notes.

Dana went on. "There are three different forms of the disease. Bubonic plague is caused by a flea bite. The bacteria are picked up by the lymph system and concentrate in lymph glands, which swell as the bacteria proliferate. Lymph glands in the neck, groin, or armpit, get as big as an egg, as hard as stone. It's called a bubo."

She described the symptoms. "As with most bacterial infections, there is fever, malaise, headache, and fatigue. The symptoms appear within two to eight days after exposure. Without treatment, a person can die ten to fourteen days after being bitten."

She progressed to the next slide, which showed two people coughing and bacteria moving in an arc in the air from one mouth to the other. "The second form of the disease is pneumonic plague. It's the most serious, because it's the most contagious. It's transmitted like a cold and causes severe pneumonia. Without treatment, death occurs two to four days after exposure."

The next slide showed an autopsy of a person who died from septicemic plague. The internal organs were swimming in blood. "Septicemic plague is a blood infection acquired by direct contact with the bacteria." Dana swept her finger along the front counter. "If the bacteria were here and I had a cut on my finger, or if I put my finger in my mouth, I would internalize the bug, and be dead within a day."

Wide-open eyes were fixed upon her. The girl taking notes turned to a new page. Dana went through a series of slides that showed the pathology of the disease. Particularly disturbing were the black fingernails on the hands of the corpses.

The bacteria killed by pumping out a toxin that impaired red blood cells from picking up oxygen. Even though the oxygen was present, the cells couldn't use it. "Deoxygenated blood looks blue," she said. "With the plague, all blood vessels turn so blue the skin looks purple or black. Look at the veins on the back of your hands." When the students did so, she knew she had them.

She moved on to treatment. The next slide showed three bottles of antibiotics lined up in a row: tetracycline, streptomycin, and chloramphenicol. "What can we do to treat the disease?" She didn't wait for a response. "We use antibiotics. We have to use three of them. The bacteria are becoming harder and harder to kill."

She explained antibiotic resistance. "Bacteria reproduce rapidly and have a quick generation time. They adapt to changes in their environment by changing their DNA. They mutate. One mutation is acquiring the ability to breakdown poisons. From their point of view, antibiotics are poisons. When they break the drug down, it no longer works. You can add as much as you like and it doesn't matter. The resistant bacteria will continue to multiply and spawn more resistant bacteria."

She turned off the projector, but kept the fan running. She raised the screen and turned on the overhead lights. In the next section, she would cover immunology and wanted to go slow.

"Our immune system is our internal defense against disease. We make antibodies that combine with bacteria to neutralize them." At the blackboard, she picked up a piece of chalk and drew a stick person with a round head, ping-pong paddle hands, and big feet. "Bacteria, like humans, are asymmetrical. We have a head, arms, hands, legs, and feet. Think of antibodies like articles of clothing—a hat, gloves, shoes; they fit certain shapes and go in certain places. A hat goes on the head, not the feet. My boots fit me, not you."

She put down the chalk and wiped her hands on her jeans. "An antibody clothes a piece of the bacterium and serves as a handle. It's like using a pair of tongs to catch a snake. Antibodies deliver bacteria to immune cells, which neutralize them."

She described the last three years of her research. "Due to antibiotic resistance, we've been looking at vaccines. These boost the immune system. They get it primed and ready to fight in advance of a future invasion." She explained how they found the passive vaccine. They used two different strains of mice; one strain was resistant to the plague and never got sick, while the other strain was extremely sensitive. They compared the antibodies in each strain, and after a lengthy search, found one antibody that gave protection. They isolated the antibody, injected it into sensitive mice, and the mice became resistant. "We genetically engineered a human analogue of the antibody and this is the passive vaccine. There's a problem with this, though."

The class saw immediately what McCoy failed to get. Someone from the back shouted out, "It doesn't last."

"Very good," Dana said. "That's precisely the problem. The antibody is a protein and it breaks down. It lasts about three weeks." She did not mention that there was a complication with the guinea pig, which had proved to be inordinately sensitive to the vaccine and had died in response to it. The possibility remained that some people could react like the guinea pig. At the moment the question of human lethality was a serious one—and a question left for the army to resolve, for they were the ones who would conduct the large-scale clinical testing. Dana moved on to active vaccines.

"Ideally, we want to find the piece of the bacterium that stimulates the production of the protective antibody. Then we give that piece of the bacteria as a vaccine, and you manufacture your own antibody. One shot and you're done."

This was the gist of the research of her next grant, which she'd already been working on for six months. Her strategy was to do the research first, and then write the grant. Once you knew the answer, you knew the right question to ask. You didn't waste money on research that went nowhere.

Out in the audience, an alarm beeped and Dana glanced at her watch. It was five o'clock and the seminar was over. She walked to the door and looked out. There was no sign of Betty, McCoy's secretary. Breaking protocol, Dana handed out the evaluation forms. "Just two more minutes of your time, please."

Five minutes later the class was cleared, except for the girl in the front who seemed to take the evaluation seriously. Too seriously. What was she writing? What was so important she had to go on and on about? How long did it take to write the word: great? Dana watched her turn the form over and scribble on the back.

Dana began packing up. Without looking at the filled-in forms or fixing the form that had been folded into an airplane, she stuffed them into the envelope. She closed her laptop, packed her briefcase, and erased the chalkboard. The girl finally put down her pen.

"I gave you all 'excellent'," she said, handing Dana the form.

"Well, thank you. And good comments, I hope?"

The girl nodded.

Dana took her form. "Don't tell me any more." She closed her eyes and shoved the form in the envelope.

The girl stood before her, waiting. "Can I ask you a question?"

"Sure." Dana picked up her briefcase.

The studious note-taker introduced herself. Carol Dupuis had a problem. "I'm doing a fourth year project and I've been collecting rats for DNA analysis. This week I collected twenty, and four died." Carol wrung her hands. "They were bleeding internally, and some had fleas. I wonder if they had the plague."

Was that why she took such careful notes? Did she think she had the plague? Still, the combination of rats and fleas did not automatically equal an infection of *Yersinia*. "The rats were probably poisoned. It could be warfarin. That stops the blood from clotting and can cause internal bleeding."

"What if I get sick?" Carol said.

"You don't have to worry. Duane is too far south for *Yersinia*. The bacteria can't stand the heat."

"Really?" Carol sounded skeptical.

"I'll test the rats, if you want."

"I'll go get them."

CHAPTER FIVE

Dana left the main campus with a biohazard bag containing four dead frozen rats. She drove west on University Drive, past a row of bars. The campus was dry—no alcohol allowed—and the student drinking happened here. Music blared and the sidewalk overflowed with students celebrating the end of the semester.

Privately, Dana was celebrating as well. Her research was finally bearing fruit. She had almost given up and feared her career would end before it ever got going. Then she had a dream. She held something in her hand she could not see. A voice that didn't sound like hers whispered the word: research, which means look again. The dream told her that she'd overlooked something very small. *Yersinia* induced a number of major antibodies, as well as a number of minor antibodies. The major antibodies were in high concentration and easy to study. The antibodies that were in low concentration were much harder to study, and while she didn't discard them, she lumped them together. She injected them into mice, they gave no resistance, and she forgot about them. Until the dream.

That was a year ago. She went back and spent six months making a monoclonal to match each minor antibody. It was then that she found what she was looking for. There was another setback when she discovered the problem with guinea pigs. Once again Dana thought the research was finished, but the army already had the monoclonal and had tested it on rats, dogs, and monkeys, and were thrilled with the response. They decided to continue on with the next phase and were scheduled to begin human testing in June. Meanwhile, she was working on the active vaccine.

Ten minutes later, Dana was back at the Veterinary College. She parked in her old spot, happy to see that McCoy was gone, his parking space empty. She tore upstairs. In the main lab, Sheryl was washing glassware. She wore yellow gloves and was up to her soapy elbows in test tubes. Per McCoy's orders, she was in a lab coat. As always, her brown frizzy hair was pulled back in a tight ponytail.

Sheryl was Dana's age and a single mother of three. They had been roommates during their first year of college and friends ever since. Dana was the maid of honor at Sheryl's wedding and the godmother of her youngest child. Sheryl was an English major—a thesis short of a Master's—and a stay-at-home mom until her husband ran off with his secretary. Despite a hiring freeze in the fall, Dana gave her a job.

"Where were you?" Sheryl said, as she lifted a soapy test tube rack out of the sink. "What's in the bag?"

"Rats." Dana locked the lab door, went to the Revco freezer, and deposited the bag. "I had to give a lecture for McCoy."

Sheryl shook excess water out of the test tubes. She turned on the tap and filled the sink. Over the sound of running water, she said, "What's going on? Betty said McCoy wanted to see you."

"He changed my parking space."

"I hope you were nice about it."

"Of course."

"When you say it like that, I know you weren't. You're never nice to him. I don't know why you can't try harder to get along." She immersed the test tube rack in the sink and the tubes tinkled against each other.

"McCoy's unreasonable," Dana said. "He shouldn't have the position he has."

Sheryl drained the tubes, which would now be autoclaved to kill any remaining bacteria. She snapped off the gloves. She was short, five-foot-three, and the white lab coat went below her knees. She was big-boned, and though often dieting, not overweight. "McCoy's the boss. He's in charge."

"Not of me."

Sheryl shook her head and the ponytail swung back and forth. "He can make things difficult for you, and he is. Can't you go along with him? Do what he wants?"

"No," Dana said, more stridently than she wanted.

Sheryl glanced at her watch. "Why did you want me to wait?" Her boys got home from school at three, and Penny—who was almost a year old—had to be picked up at day care by six. How she managed it all, Dana didn't know.

"I need your help. A favor."

"Of course," Sheryl said. "Anything. What?"

"Could you take some blood?"

"From you? Sure. Why?" Sheryl looked suspicious. "Are you worried you're exposed to *Yersinia*? That you're sick?"

"No. I want to look at my antibodies."

"Why?"

"Check their level."

"But why?" Sheryl's eyes were light brown and in some light, looked red. She may have been an English major, but she was a quick study when it came to research.

"I just want to do it. What's wrong with that?" Dana opened a drawer and grabbed a tourniquet, needle and syringe. She unbuttoned her cuff, rolled up her sleeve, and sprayed alcohol on her inner elbow. She handed Sheryl the tourniquet.

Sheryl shook her head, but took the tourniquet and tied it around Dana's deltoid. "Make a fist."

Dana did so.

Sheryl advanced with the needle. There was a slight prick and blood flowed immediately. While Sheryl filled the syringe, Dana closed her eyes. The sight of blood made her queasy.

Sheryl unsnapped the tourniquet, finally withdrew the needle, and slapped the tube down on the counter. "Now what?"

"You can go."

Sheryl shoved her hands in the pockets of her lab coat. "What really happened with McCoy?"

"He doesn't see the need for the active vaccine. That's how obtuse he is."

"He knows you've found it?"

"Of course not. And he's not going to know. What happens here is none of his business." Dana went to the fridge where she kept her lunch and cold drinks and pulled out the unlabeled vial. She slowly inverted it three times to mix the solution. The potential active vaccine was a section of the bacterial cell wall that induced the protective antibody in mice.

"You're going to take that?" Sheryl cried. "You can't! It's never been tried on humans. What if you respond like the guinea pig?"

"This is an antigen, not a protein. I tried it on guinea pigs and they were fine." Though one died under mysterious circumstances, the other three responded well. Dana grabbed another needle and syringe. She would be able to inject herself, pierce her deltoid, close her eyes, and depress the plunger.

"Human testing is the end stage, not the beginning," Sheryl said.

"I need to see if it works," Dana said. "Save us from going down a long road from which we can never get back."

"You don't have to do this."

"I know, but I have a good feeling about it."

"That sounds like solid science," Sheryl said.

"I'm going to do it. You can go."

Sheryl held out her hand. "If you've made up your mind, allow me."

Dana handed her the syringe.

"If you feel sick, call me."

"I will."

"And you owe me."

"Many times over."

Sheryl took the vial, drew the vaccine up into a syringe and neatly jabbed Dana's deltoid, injecting amber liquid into her muscle. There was a localized burning and Dana held her breath. Sheryl threw the empty syringe on the counter. "When will you know?"

"Monday," Dana said. In three days, she would take more blood and see if she produced the protective antibody.

Sheryl took off her lab coat. "If this gets out, I wasn't here. I know nothing. You did it yourself."

"Thank you."

They locked up the lab and left, heading downstairs. With classes over, the hallways were empty and it was unusually quiet. They reached the ground floor and Dana paused. "I've got to pick up Frank."

"How's he doing?' Sheryl asked, as she worked her car keys out of her purse.

Dana shrugged. Frank was her fourteen-year old black Labrador, currently being treated in the vet clinic for arthritis and lung cancer.

"And Tim?" Sheryl asked.

He was the veterinarian in charge of Frank's care. "Doing his best."

"That's not what I meant. I don't know why you won't go out with him."

Dana pushed open the door. "I did go out with him. It didn't work out."

"He's good-looking, successful, rich, smart, and single." She emphasized the last word. "Make it work."

"It won't. Beyond the realm of possibility."

Sheryl sighed as if with exasperation. "Give him a chance. He's not like you. He won't wait forever for someone who said he would never be back."

Sheryl left the building and Dana went to get Frank. Maybe Sheryl had a point, maybe it was time to stop waiting, to give up, to shut the door on the past, and move on. The problem was, she could think this way all she liked, but her heart refused to listen. No amount of logic or reason would it heed. The men she knew these days fell short. Rather than settle, Dana preferred to be alone.

And she wasn't alone; she had her dogs. Tim wanted to keep Frank over the weekend, but that wasn't happening. She was taking him home. He'd been in the clinic all week while Tim tried one treatment after another. Unfortunately, the drugs used to treat arthritis worked against the drugs used to treat cancer. To treat arthritis you had to stop the immune system, while to treat cancer you needed an active immune system. Which disease did you treat? What did you do?

Dana had done nothing until Frank stopped walking. By then, his prognosis was so poor that no veterinarian would touch him. Only after great coercion, and as a personal favor, did Tim finally agree. Now she owed him but had nothing to give in return.

Dana went down the back hallway of the clinic, happy to see it empty. She scanned the chalkboard that listed the names of the veterinarians on duty. Phew—Tim Sweeny had checked out. Breathing easier, Dana headed toward his animal room.

A clipboard dangled from a hook on the door. Dana paused and read Tim's notes. He was the best clinician in the vet school, a troubleshooter, and challenging cases throughout the state came to him. He was treating an eight-week-old puppy from Lubbock for parvo, a poodle from West Texas eviscerated by a cougar, a cat in need of a leg amputation, and Frank.

Dana saw Frank had been taken for a lung scan that afternoon. The IV infusion of methotrexate, an anti-arthritic drug, had been discontinued. Was Tim stopping the treatment? Was Frank's cancer back? Dana inhaled sharply, drawing air past her tight heart. What if she put him through a week of hell just to have him die?

Dana took another breath and entered the animal room. A row of cages lined one wall. The young parvo puppy was curled in a ball. There was an orange cat with a stump wrapped in a bloody cloth where a front paw should have been. Frank's cage was at the end of the row, and she heard his tail thumping before she saw him.

His body shook with excitement. She lifted the latch and swung open the door. Panting hard, Frank stiffly pulled himself out, dragging his wagging backside on the ground. He weighed almost a hundred pounds.

Dana knelt down and threw her arms around his back. He fell against her, nearly knocking her over. She rubbed his gray fur. His breathing was labored and quick. His nose was dry and he looked at her with cloudy blue eyes. Maybe she should have done nothing. A lame dog was better than no dog.

Dana grabbed a gurney and with difficulty, heaved Frank up. He lay on his side with his tongue lolling out. His tail slapped the stainless steel surface as she rolled him from the room. They went down the deserted hall and out the automatic doors into the heat and bright sunshine. On the way to the car, Dana stopped short. She wouldn't escape so easily after all. The veterinarian she wished to avoid stood by her car.

CHAPTER SIX

Tim Sweeny crossed the parking lot in an easy bow-legged stride. He was lean, six-foot three, and thirty-five years old. His hair was blond and he wore it long. Behind him, traffic whizzed past and a horn blared. Dana refused to look, but Tim spun around and waved. The horn honked again, and Dana saw a pickup filled with laughing girls go barreling by.

Tim reached the curb and hopped up beside her, his blue eyes shining. A giant smile lit up his tanned face. She broke eye contact and stared over his shoulder at his car. He hadn't lost his parking space, and his cherry red corvette with the vanity license plate K9-DOC was parked in his spot.

Tim lowered his head, craned his neck and blocked her view. "I was going to keep Frank over the weekend. If I can't keep you." He flicked his eyebrows up and down.

He'd been trying to get her out on a second date for months. He incorrectly believed she was playing hard to get and was aggressively making sure his intentions were clear. She sunk her hand into Frank's sun-warmed pelt and looked into Tim's eager eyes. "I'm taking Frank home."

"I could come watch him."

"I'm sure you have more productive things to do." She changed the subject. "How's he doing?"

"I took him off the methotrexate."

"How come?"

"His respiration is poor." That much was obvious. Frank's chest heaved in and out as he struggled to breathe. "I took a pulmonary X-ray and his lungs are cloudy. I didn't see any tumors. There are signs of inflammation. It could be nothing more than a cold. Then again, it could be pneumonia." Tim coughed into a fist.

Dana exhaled and stared up at the sky. She had hoped this treatment would fix everything, not make things worse. "Now what?"

"I think you should put him down."

And this from a man who said his secret of success was to never give up.

She shook her head. "What about colchicine?"

Tim clicked his teeth. "Is that what you want?"

She nodded her head. When he stared in her eyes, she stared back.

"All right. I'll do it." He raised his hand and brushed a dog hair off her sleeve. "For you."

Dana felt a lump in her throat. Once again she wondered if she was being rash—if he would grow on her in time if she gave him a chance.

"Bring him in on Monday. I'm off to D.C. Sheila can handle it."

Tim insisted on lugging Frank to the car and carried him effortlessly. Dana threw open the door and Tim carefully arranged Frank on the passenger seat. Dana rolled down the window.

There was a gardener nearby on a mower and the scent of cut grass hung heavily in the air. He was indiscriminately mowing down the wildflowers, obliterating the pink primroses and yellow coreopsis. Dana never cut her grass until the wildflowers were dead. She closed the car door. Frank poked his head out the window and licked her hand.

"I'll see you," Tim said, staring into her eyes.

She wondered if he would kiss her, and while the sunlight streamed across them and the oak leaves waved, she wondered how she would react if he did.

He did not. Abruptly he stepped away, cleared his throat, and rearranged his hair with a shake of his head. "I'm late, I've got places to go, people to see." He yanked sunglasses from his pocket and shoved them on his face. Walking jauntily to his convertible, he vaulted over the side. The tires squealed as he tore out of the parking lot.

Dana watched him go. He was letting her know that he wasn't waiting for her, and she got the message.

Dana was backing out of her parking spot when McCoy roared into the lot and blocked her car. He flung open his door, and leaped from his bullet-proof Mercedes. Sweat drenched his hair, and his cheeks were florid.

"I told you, those parking places are for clinic clients only."

She got out of her car. "The clinic is closed."

"That's not the point. If I see your car here again, I'll have it towed." He frowned at Frank whose head hung out the window. "And pets are not allowed in the building during office hours."

"He's sick. He's been at the clinic. Technically I'm a client."

He dismissed her explanation with a slash of his arm. "I have just come from main campus. Betty could not monitor the evaluation exercise and I went in her stead. Where were you? Where are the evaluations?"

Only then did Dana remember the evaluations she neglected to leave on Betty's desk. She retrieved the envelope from her briefcase and handed it to McCoy.

She willed him to take it and leave, but he opened the flap and pulled out the forms. The one folded into the airplane was on top. McCoy frowned at the form.

"I didn't touch them," she said. "I didn't look at them."

McCoy unfolded the airplane and squinted at the form. "Humph."

Holding the evaluations close to his heart, he perused the stack. Brian, the former chairman, always showed them to her, but McCoy did not. Usually the student responses were good, and she wondered what happened to the evaluation conducted in the fall. Did McCoy, not liking the response, toss it out?

He looked up, stared for a moment across the parking lot at the clinic where a painting crew was fashioning a scaffold. Finally he sighed and held up a form. "All excellent." He picked up another. "All excellent." He stared at her with cold, gray eyes. "How do you explain this?"

"It was an excellent lecture."

"I'll bet." The sun slipped behind a cloud and she felt cold. McCoy lowered his head, licked an index finger, and began counting the evaluations. Dana backed up against her car. She could hear Frank's labored breathing and the rhythmic ticking of her watch.

"Twenty evaluations," he said finally. "Twenty evaluations only, yet there are thirty-two students registered in the class."

"Only twenty students came."

"And the attendance sheet is where?" Shifting the evaluations in his hand, McCoy peered into the envelope.

Dana could see it in her mind, crumpled in a ball in the corner of the lecture hall. "I handed it out," she said. "I must have forgotten it."

McCoy threw her another long hard stare. Balancing the evaluations under his arm, he shoved his hand in his trouser pocket and extracted the balled-up attendance sheet.

Dana opened her mouth to explain, but no words came.

Nonetheless, McCoy raised his hand for silence. "We'll talk about this Monday. I hope you realize this is a serious breach of protocol." With a vivid shake of his head, McCoy stalked to his Mercedes and disappeared behind the darkly tinted windows. He slowly pulled away.

Dana stood by her car until he disappeared. *A serious breach of protocol?* She didn't know whether to laugh or to scream. Was he collecting violations to present to the tenure committee? Did he think she could be dismissed for forgetting an attendance sheet? For parking in the wrong place? For having a sick dog? She thought not. But why did he always catch her? She couldn't break a rule without him knowing. A malevolent force was on his side.

The sun came out from behind its cloud, and Dana got in her car and headed for home. She lived in the country on the south side of town and took the west bypass. She ran the air conditioner and rolled down the windows. The air was heavy, hot, and humid. Frank hung his head out the window and the wind lifted his ears, blew back his fur.

The bypass curved south and Dana sped past vast flat fields. The forest to the west fringed the right horizon. To the left stood a ranch where cows grazed on emerald-colored grass. Dana drove past the tree that her old boss hit on Christmas Eve. The tree was wounded still, the soft pulp splintered and shiny with dark sap or dried blood. After Brian's accident, she bought a four-wheel drive Raider that could mow down a tree.

If only she could go back in time and change what happened; break one link in the chain that delivered Brian to his death. If only the weather had been balmy and there was no ice on the road, no Christ's birth to celebrate, no party to go to, no flimsy fence, no solid tree. Would Brian still be here, would Phase 2 of the grant be in the bag, and tenure in her pocket?

She would never know. Instead, there was a fatal collision and McCoy was pulled from retirement. He shouldn't be here. He broke an orderly chain of causality—where a cause induced an effect, which served as a cause that elicited another effect, which was its own cause—and on and on down the line. Except for accidents. What were they? Random events? A cause that was fated to happen, or an effect that had no discernible cause? Were events fated or avoidable? Who knew?

Until Brian's car crash, Dana didn't believe in accidents. She thought things happened for a reason. She came to Duane because she didn't like Buffalo's cold weather. All her life she wanted to be a doctor and Duane had a pre-med program with low tuition. She didn't know until her sophomore year that she couldn't stand the sight of blood. If it didn't make her sick, it made her faint. She switched to biology, a close cousin, and ended up in immunology.

When she graduated, an oil boom went bust and the job market crashed. With limited options, she went to graduate school and got a Master's, then a PhD, and went on for a post-doc. Midway through that, money ran out. Departments were juggled, programs were modified, and Dana was relocated to the vet school. Her supervisor resigned in a fury and she was stuck with a new boss.

At first she saw him as a burden—cold and aloof. When she got to know him, he was the polar opposite of what he had seemed. She wouldn't be where she was without him. Everything she had she owed to him: everything she achieved, everything she became, everything she aspired to, everything she dreamed of, had bloomed under his influence. He had been gone seven long years, but his presence remained as if he never left. She thought if she held on to him with her mind, it would bring him back.

Dana shook off the memory and drove on. He didn't feel the same as she did. He swore when he left that he would never return.

The bypass circled east and she took the first right that led onto a dirt road. A mile down the shaded lane she reached the border of her land. She paid a fortune for it, buying at the hilt of the housing boom, just before the market fell. But it didn't matter—it was worth it. She belonged here. She didn't feel she owned the land, but that it owned her. There was no way she could leave. She was locked in, a piece of the place.

She reached her driveway, turned right and bounced down a muddy decline. She had five acres of land, and her nearest neighbor was a mile down the road. At night when she turned off the lights, she could see the stars. During the day, her dogs ran free.

They were running toward the car now; a small one racing in a blur and a large one loping like a pony. Dana parked and jumped out. Anthony jumped up, resting his paws on her shoulders. He was a border collie-lab mix with black fur and three white paws. An off-center white stripe ran down his face. Beside him, Judy barked shrilly, leaping into the air. Dana helped Anthony down and caught Judy mid-flight. She was a poodle-terrier mix and a bag of fur. Dana put her down gently. She went around the car and lifted Frank out. The other dogs knocked him over. He struggled shakily to his feet.

They walked together down the driveway to the house. Frank needed help climbing the porch steps, which Anthony cleared in a bound. He nudged the screen door open with his nose.

Inside it was cool, though it was over eighty outside. The house was small and square and bright with sunlight. There was a kitchen-dining room-living room combination, with a bathroom and bedroom off the back. A cross-breeze blew across the house through open windows. The walls were paneled with light pine, and a wall-to-wall turquoise carpet hid the dirt.

Dana grabbed a Lone Star from the fridge, sat at the kitchen table, and kicked off her boots. Wilted petals lay on the table and she looked up. On the ceiling support beams she had pinned flower bouquets. There were the dozen red roses Tim sent after their only date. There were many sprays of wildflowers she had collected in long-ago springs. The petals on the table were yellow, and came from lilies her PhD student gave her earlier that week. The flower that meant the most would last forever. It was a plastic Remembrance Day poppy pinned to a bandana Frank once stole and Dana once wore to cover small bites of love on her neck a long time ago.

She shook off the memory, stepped into sandals, and called the dogs for their walk. Judy and Anthony burst outside, but Frank refused to move. He lay in bed, gazing at the door through clouded eyes. How long could she wait for him to get better? When was it time to let hope die? Not in the spring, she thought.

She left him and went outside. Bluebonnets and Indian paint-brushes grew in the long grass. A hundred feet across the field stood thick woods that spread south and west for miles. The dogs were already out of sight. She headed for the trees. The sun slipped behind a cloud and a dark shadow fell across the land. Usually the air was filled with the cacophony of bugs and birds and squirrels, but today silence boomed. The quiet made her uneasy. The land seemed foreign and disturbed, as if something was wrong.

APRIL 25TH

CHAPTER SEVEN

Late Saturday afternoon, McCoy was in the Mercedes teaching his youngest daughter how to start the car, when the front door opened and his wife called out that he had a phone call. "I'll be right back," he told Margaret who was ensconced in the driver's seat. "Leave the car in park and don't touch anything."

"Okay, Daddy." She smiled at him and McCoy's heart lurched. The move to Texas had been unspeakably hard for her. He had dragged her away from D.C. in the middle of her senior year of high school and she had cried bitterly for weeks. These driving lessons were bridging the divide between them.

McCoy hurried to the house. For him, unexpected phone calls meant an emergency. He had five daughters, ten grandchildren, and received calls in times of crisis. Was a hundred-and-four fever high enough to take James to the doctor? How did you pop Phillip's dislocated shoulder into place? Did an inch-long cut on Hanna's chin warrant stitches? God, how he missed his children. How he would miss Margaret, who at sixteen was too young to drive, too young to go to college the following year. He wondered why he ever allowed her to skip grade five. If he knew then what he knew now, he would never have given his consent.

In the house, Marge said, "Mitchell Marshall is on the line."

What did the university president want now, McCoy wondered. Everything for the VP's visit was on track. The kink at the Lone Star Heritage Hotel had been ironed out—security would be tightened and additional secret service agents were on their way. He grabbed the receiver.

"We've got a problem," Marshall said. "The FBI don't like the security in the stadium. They want to move the graduation ceremony to the auditorium."

"It's too small," McCoy said.

"You don't have to tell me," Marshall said. "Tell them."

McCoy sighed. Organizing the VP's visit was an endless headache. Glancing through the vestibule window, he saw the car lights blaze. The windshield wipers started and stopped. The emergency flashers flickered. "I'll call Ackerman," McCoy said. "Brackton Hall has seating for two hundred and we've sent out twelve hundred tickets. We're going to have to hold it in Johnson Field."

"What about the rain?" Marshall said. "There may be a deluge. A tropical storm's building in the gulf."

McCoy said nothing. Three weeks ago he had raised the issue of rain, but Marshall wanted the extra tickets and dismissed his concerns.

"It won't be very pleasant outdoors if there's a tropical storm," Marshall said.

"We'll get tents," McCoy said.

Outside the horn blared. Margaret's patience had worn thin.

"Don't spend too much money," Marshall said. "We don't need tents for the whole hundred yards. Just enough to cover the VP and his entourage."

"Yes sir," McCoy said, imagining the remaining guests standing in the rain in the midst of a tropical storm.

The university president hung up, and McCoy called FBI agent Barry Ackerman to schedule another emergency meeting. Which presented a new conflict. Not only would McCoy have to postpone Margaret's driving lesson, he would have to find someone to entertain Michael Smith, his West Point visitor.

McCoy pondered his options as Margaret stormed from the car. She looked angry, her jaw was set. She had been so unhappy lately. McCoy had promised himself he'd spend more time with her, but so far he was breaking all his promises.

The front door slammed. McCoy winced and faced his daughter. "Something's come up. I'm sorry baby. We'll do this—"

She didn't give him time to finish. She ran crying up the stairs. McCoy's weak heart tightened. When this was over, he'd make it up to her. He gripped the bracelet she gave him for Father's Day when she was six years old. It seemed like yesterday. She was growing up too fast.

McCoy sighed again and reached for the phone. Since he couldn't keep his dinner appointment, Dana Sparks would have to go in his place. But her cell phone went unanswered. He tried her lab and got voice mail. He tried her cell again and waited to leave a message. He wondered if she'd turned her phone off. She refused to be on call. If she behaved like this now, how would she behave with tenure? She set a bad precedent for others in the department who struggled to toe McCoy's line.

McCoy threw down the phone and went upstairs to talk with Margaret. She was locked in her room and would not answer his pleading knock. He tried bribing her with a shopping trip next Saturday to Houston, but his overtures went unanswered. McCoy finally gave up and slumped back to the phone.

CHAPTER EIGHT

Saturday afternoon, Dana was returning home from a walk in the woods when her phone rang. She hurried up the slope but missed the call. She was helping Frank up out of bed when her cell phone rang. McCoy was on the line.

"Dr. Sparks," he said, using her title, as was his way. He never called her Dana, and no one ever called him anything but Dr. McCoy or sir. "I'm afraid there's an emergency."

"Emergency?" Had a student died? Did someone break into her lab and steal lethal bacteria? Was there a deadly car crash?

"Michael Smith and I have a dinner appointment. Something came up and I will not be able to attend. You will have to go in my place."

"What's the emergency?"

"I would not ask unless it was absolutely necessary. It is not a request."

Dana made a face. She wasn't averse to meeting Michael Smith. It would give her an opportunity to check out the West Point man first-hand, but she wouldn't make it easy for McCoy. "I have a favor to ask of my own."

There was a long silence. "Dr. Sparks, I will not be blackmailed."

"Keep my latest teacher evaluation forms. There is no reason to discard them."

"The exercise was unobserved, and therefore invalid."

"Nonetheless it was conducted correctly."

McCoy sighed. "Dr. Smith is at the Motel Eight. He'll expect you at seven."

***

Dana was at the hotel early. If there was a bright side to Michael Smith's visit, it was his residency at the cheap motel. In Dana's mind, it was an insult to be kept at the Motel Eight. Most visiting scientists stayed at the Lone Star Heritage Hotel or the Tremblant Apartments. It was an added insult that the boss had cancelled at the last minute and sent an underling instead.

But in the faded dingy lobby, the visitor was all smiles, refusing to appear insulted. Michael Smith was her age, a slight man with short dark hair. He had dark brown eyes, an olive complexion, and a thick, wiry moustache. He was a head shorter than Dana and reeked of after-shave and Scope.

She extended a hand and Michael looked at it a moment before taking her palm lightly in his. His fingers were soft, his handshake weak. He said, "Hello," with a hint of an accent Dana couldn't place.

"McCoy is sorry he couldn't be here. He was doing something else tonight," she said, deliberately vague.

"He called me. He has an important meeting with the president about security plans for the vice president." Michael Smith smiled a smug smile. He smoothed the wrinkled lapels of his beige blazer.

"We can go," Dana said, coldly.

He followed her to the car. He wore open-toed sandals that slapped on the concrete. He walked in a slouch, staring up at the sky. His moustache resembled the bristled end of a toothbrush.

They drove along Texas Avenue and Dana recited a brief history of the town. Located between Houston and Dallas, Duane had a population of fifty thousand. About half the people were associated with the college, which had twenty thousand full-time students. Duane University was over a hundred years old. It had started out as an annex to the state university, and was now funded primarily by land grants. Its reputation was in the arts, but the university president was trying to change its image. Thirty years ago the veterinary college opened, and if the president had his way, they would soon have a medical school and law school as well.

Turning west on University Drive, Dana shot past the row of student bars that were packed early on Saturday night. They whizzed by the University Plaza, the outdoor plaza for one-stop student shopping. It had a car wash, K-Mart, movie theater, Giant supermarket, and laundromat. Beyond that, the Lone Star Heritage Hotel shone like a castle. A fleet of dark limousines lined the forecourt and dark-suited men wearing sunglasses huddled on the steps. FBI agents scoping out the hotel where the VP would stay, Dana guessed. She pulled into the parking lot. McCoy's reservation was at the Pizza Garden, the outdoor bistro behind the hotel.

A doorman in a tux opened the front door. The lobby was busy. It seemed many parents had arrived early for the graduation ceremonies the following weekend. A small crowd of people milled outside the Caprice Bistro, the hotel's five-star restaurant. There was a line up at the bar and people gripping drinks stood aimlessly in the lobby.

The Pizza Garden was out back by the pool. The perimeter was demarcated with a string of gold, red, and green hanging lanterns. Despite a reservation, they had to wait.

Michael went to wash his hands, and Dana read notices pinned to the thorns of a large Sequoia cactus. Someone was looking for a roommate, someone wanted a ride to Austin, and someone had lost a cat. There was a color photo of a young boy with red hair and freckles clutching a calico that looked bigger than Judy. *Please bring Pumpkin home*, said the sign written in a childish scrawl. *Call Travis Levine.* Dana wondered if the cat had been found, if Travis got his call. Poor kid. She knew what it was like to lose a pet. Anthony ran away soon after she got him, and she easily imagined a thousand horrible deaths for him—drowning, murder, car accident, or a mountain lion attack. But none of her fears transpired. Two days later, he limped home and hadn't run away again.

A short vivacious waitress with a stack of menus indicated the table was ready. Dana followed her to the pool and sat down facing the bistro. The enormous glass doors were open, and muslin curtains billowed with the night breeze. The bistro was Dana's favorite restaurant, but she didn't eat here often. This year she had been once, with Tim. He was extravagant, she remembered, and unbidden the memory of their dinner returned. They had danced as a violinist played.

Michael was back and shrugging off his wrinkled blazer. "Quite a place," he said. He stared at the pool, complete with underwater stools aside a poolside bar. Two voluptuous women relaxed in a Jacuzzi and Michael averted his eyes. The waitress bounced back, pad in hand. She wore a short skirt and a tight tube-top. Michael stared at the menu.

Dana recommended a large pizza with everything, but Michael objected to the sausage. Dana wondered if he didn't eat pork. Was he Jewish? "Okay, we'll skip the sausage. What about jalapenos? Do you eat hot food?"

Michael did.

Dana placed the order. She wanted a glass of wine and recommended the house wine.

"I don't drink." Michael said.

McCoy would like that, Dana thought. He was almost a teetotaler himself. She ordered a glass of wine and Michael ordered a coke. But when the drinks came, he sent his back. He didn't want ice.

Fussy, Dana saw, though he tried to explain it. "Most people don't realize warm drinks are more refreshing than cold."

"Is that so," Dana said, drinking cold wine. Trickles of condensation ran down the glass. "Are you from a warm climate?"

He wasn't. He grew up in London.

"I thought I detected an accent," she said.

Michael said nothing. She sipped more wine and watched a crowd of students stream into the bistro. Trying to deter the college crowd, the hotel had jacked up its prices, but to no avail. The loud and boisterous beer-swilling students still came.

The waitress brought Michael a new coke. He took a long pull and nodded his approval. Then to Dana's happy surprise he pulled a box of Winston cigarettes from his pocket. McCoy detested smokers.

"Mind if I smoke?" Michael asked.

"Mind? Be my guest," Dana said. He struck a match and exhaled a puff of smoke. How could a biologist smoke?

Michael finished his lukewarm coke and ordered another. He wiped sweat from his brow and put down his cigarette. He rolled up his sleeves. She noticed three lines of deep scratches running up his forearm.

"I went for a walk in the woods and was caught in a thorny vine," he said, as he rolled his sleeves back down. He sucked on his cigarette intently. "What research do you do?" he asked.

"I work on the plague," Dana said.

"You are the one who found a vaccine. Is it available?"

"The clinical trials won't start until June."

"Did you try it against resistant bacteria?"

"A number of wild type strains."

"How effective is it?"

"On mice, ninety-seven percent." She did not mention the dismal response of the guinea pig.

He blew a large round smoke ring that grew larger in the air. "How much money do you have?"

His boundaries were a little loose, Dana thought. Would he next ask how much she made? Still, she answered his question. "I'm looking at a grant for one million dollars."

"To study what?"

"An active vaccine. A one shot deal that will last a lifetime."

"Any chance of success?"

Dana picked up her wine and watched a long line of students march to an adjacent table. "Maybe."

"TJ said the research may not be funded."

Dana narrowed her eyes. "TJ is wrong."

"He gave me a tour of your lab," Michael said. "Very impressive."

"When?"

"Friday afternoon. You were not there."

"I was giving a lecture," Dana said, wondering if this was why it had been thrust upon her.

"There was no one in the lab. You have no students?"

"I have four. A post-doc, PhD, Master's, and fourth-year student, plus a technician," Dana said, sounding defensive. There was no reason to go into all these details. What she didn't say was that the students would soon leave—and she had no replacements. Until she knew she had tenure, she could take on no new people.

"It is a very big lab," Michael said. "With much equipment."

Dana was tired of answering questions. "What about you? TJ said you graduated from West Point."

"I did my undergraduate there. West Point has no graduate school."

"What brings you to Texas?"

"A job interview."

She choked on the wine. It was as she suspected. McCoy was interviewing people for her position.

"TJ said he may have an opening. He asked me to give a seminar."

"On what?"

"Anthrax."

"What are you researching?"

"The research is classified," he said, and smoked on.

He was secretive. McCoy would like that. After a few minutes
of silence, Dana asked him about his personal life. He didn't wear a
wedding ring and she hoped he wasn't married, for McCoy believed
strongly in the sanctity of marriage.

"Yes, I have a family," Michael said. He worked a photograph out
of his wallet and passed it across the table. Dana saw a beaming dark-
haired mother cradling two infant babies.

"Twins," Michael said, and there was a catch in his throat, as if he
missed them. He turned, wiped his face, distracted by the din from a
nearby table. Ten students were standing, glasses raised. They chugged
their glasses. A guy drinking from a pitcher belched loudly, then ran to
the bushes. Michael crushed out his cigarette.

"Does your wife work?" Dana asked, when the adjacent table settled down.

"No," Michael said. "She was—is—happy being a wife and a mother."

McCoy would love that too—men who had wives who stayed at
home and raised the children. Except for the chain-smoking, Michael
was winning on all grounds, Dana thought as the waitress brought the
steaming pizza. Michael ordered his third coke.

They ate the pizza. The jalapenos brought tears to Dana's eyes, and
she watched incredulously as Michael shook crushed cayenne pepper
over his slice. He chomped loudly as pizza juice dripped down his fingers. Unlike McCoy, he had not maintained his table manners after
leaving West Point. McCoy's manners were fastidious.

As they ate, Michael asked about her personal life and seemed surprised she wasn't married. "You live with your parents?"

An odd question. "No. I live alone. I have a house just outside town."

"In the country?" Michael said. He wanted to live in the country,
thought it would be healthy for the twins. "May I see your place?"

"Sure. Anytime," Dana said vaguely. "Not tonight."

They talked about the weather, the heat in Duane, the snow in Iowa, and the twins and their mother who were cooped up all winter long. "Here they'd be cooped up all summer," Dana said. "The sun is a major problem." She mentioned the high incidence of malignant melanoma and childhood leukemia, fire ants, and killer bees.

"The world is a dangerous place," Michael said.

They discussed the bombing of Mogadishu. The VP was coming at a bad time, for the government was taking heat for the attack. There was evidence to suggest that the U.S. had bombed a hospital and a mosque, and twenty innocent civilians had died. The Secretaries of State and Defense had launched dual investigations to learn the truth.

Finally, the meal was done and the waitress came with the check and left with the plates. Michael went for more cigarettes. Dana paid the bill and asked for a receipt. McCoy would pay for this dinner. She wondered if he had set it up on purpose. Was he more conniving than she thought? Was he sending her a covert message? Did he want her to know he considered her position open and available?

Dana stared across the lawn at the Caprice. A couple sat near the window. The woman's blond hair was pulled up in an elegant French twist. Heavy gold dangled from her ears. She looked about twenty-five. The man across from her with the bronze tan stared deeply in her eyes. Tim Sweeny on the move.

Michael was back, followed by the waitress. Dana was ready to go. Hoping to evade Tim, she led Michael across the grass toward the parking lot. She stopped short when a woman in the restaurant screamed. Dana turned around and watched through the open window as Tim jumped up and hauled a writhing man with a purple face to his feet. Tim wrapped his arms around the man's back and pulled up hard under his thorax. The Heimlich Maneuver, designed to stop choking, was effective. The man gagged and spluttered and began to cough.

"Let's go," Dana said.

She was quiet on the way home, thinking about Tim and wasted opportunity. She said nothing until she bid Michael goodbye.

He got out. "Will I see you tomorrow? At TJ's? For the party?"

A party she wasn't invited to. "Unlikely," she said.

APRIL 26TH

CHAPTER NINE

The garden party began right after church. McCoy had hoped the barbecue would ease Margaret's loneliness and help her find new and appropriate friends, but she wouldn't cooperate. As the guests arrived, Margaret sulked upstairs. She had refused to attend church that morning and wouldn't talk to him.

McCoy escorted a blue-haired lady through the house to the garden. The kitchen smelled sweet, of just-baked biscuits. The counter was filled with smoking baked potatoes and steaming beans. Brass bowls collected in the Middle East brimmed with nachos, cheese dip, and corn chips. Standard Texan party food according to the cookbooks.

In the backyard, clumps of people holding cups of fruit punch milled under a striped awning. McCoy sat the dowager down next to Drake Duncan, the Dean of the Veterinary College. His wife, Nellie, shook the old woman's hand. The doorbell rang and McCoy hastened to the door. Father Bob loomed in the entrance, gripping a crate of Lone Star beer, though McCoy had not planned to serve alcohol at his party. Father Bob dropped the case, opened his arms, and suffocated McCoy in a strong embrace.

"A great idea, a fine idea," Father Bob said. He released McCoy, grabbed his beer, and headed to the garden.

Michael Smith came next, dressed in white and moving shyly. McCoy apologized for his absence the previous night.

"It is no problem," Michael Smith said.

McCoy was happy to hear it. This was the kind of man he needed on his team. One who could take last minute setbacks without having a nervous breakdown. "We'll talk later." McCoy pointed him to the yard as a flock of young girls walked up the drive.

They were Margaret's age and their clean appearance pleased him. They wore long dresses and happy smiles. If only Margaret could make new friends. But how to coax her from her room? McCoy aimed the young ladies at the garden and climbed the stairs.

He reached Margaret's door as the phone began to ring. "Margaret, dear," he said, fingering his bracelet. "Can you get that?"

No answer. God, why did children have to grow up? McCoy grabbed the phone. Someone must be lost and looking for directions.

There was an introduction and a name he didn't catch. Then, "Is this Dr. TJ McCoy, head of the Department of Infectious Disease?"

"Yes, yes," McCoy said, as the doorbell rang.

"This is Greenlee Hospital," said the caller.

"One minute." McCoy called to Margaret. "Baby, get the door. I'm on the phone."

No answer.

"We need help," said the caller.

"What is it?" When McCoy had first arrived, he informed both local hospitals that if they ever needed any assistance, they had only to ask. McCoy's plan was to provide cutting-edge diagnostics to both local hospitals.

Downstairs the doorbell clanged again. McCoy stared helplessly at his daughter's closed door. The caller continued. "A man came in this morning with what looks like a bacterial infection. His white blood cell count is two hundred thousand per ml with a predominance of immature and mature neutrophils. He's got enlarged lymph nodes but cultures haven't shown anything. We don't know what he's got and our treatment isn't working."

"Where's your infectious disease specialist?" McCoy asked, as the doorbell went again.

"Dr. Taversham is out of town for the weekend. We're trying to reach him. Any assistance you could provide would be much appreciated."

"Draw the patient's blood," McCoy said. "Have it waiting at the admissions desk. I'll send someone immediately."

McCoy hung up and called to his daughter again, "Margaret, honey, could you please get the door?" Still no answer. He yelled, "Come on in," as he dialed the phone.

CHAPTER TEN

The call brought Dana in from the yard where she had been bathing Anthony. He was overrun with fleas and ticks, and she left him soaking in flea lotion and snaking on his side across the grass. She leapt over Frank, who lay in a patch of sunlight by the door. She picked up her cell phone. McCoy again.

"Dr. Sparks, I've got a problem. A blood sample is waiting at the front desk of Greenlee Hospital. I need you to run an ELISA with a full panel of your bacterial antigens. Get back to me ASAP."

Dana frowned and didn't answer. In the background she heard much whoopla and high voices calling hello. A doorbell rang and rang—McCoy apparently indisposed at his party. Even on Sunday he would tell her what to do? She wanted to hang up, but curiosity won out. Why couldn't the hospital run the test? "Is there an unusual bacterial infection?"

"I'm hoping you'll confirm it."

McCoy never gave anything away. He always spoke as if he were at war and information was restricted. Dana pressed him. "What are the patient's symptoms?"

But McCoy distributed information on a need to know basis only. "Let his doctor worry about that. Get the blood sample, take it to the lab, run the test. Call me with the results."

"Aye-aye, sir." She called him that when she was angry—not that he noticed. The word usually pacified him.

Dana finished rinsing Anthony and took a shower. She was worried about Frank and hated to leave him at home by himself, but there was no way around it. During the weekend his condition had grown worse, and he'd acquired a rasping cough. Dana had called Tim earlier that morning, but he hadn't answered his phone.

She took the east bypass and arrived at Greenlee Hospital in ten minutes. The south hospital catered primarily to university students and staff, while St. Joseph's Hospital on the north side of town served the general population. Neither hospital was equipped for exotic diagnostics or major emergencies, and critically ill patients were flown to Houston for treatment.

Dana headed for the emergency entrance on Texas Avenue. She knew the layout of the hospital because she'd served as Sheryl's labor coach, and in one of the Lamaze classes there had been a hospital tour.

The waiting area in the emergency room was empty, except for two doctors dressed in scrub suits playing checkers. A young receptionist with curly red hair sat at the information desk filing her nails. Dana introduced herself, and was handed a small plastic vial that contained about a half-milliliter of blood. There was no biohazard bag—no written indication that the tube may contain an infectious organism. Despite McCoy's orders, Dana inquired about the patient.

The receptionist consulted her computer. "That belongs to Dudley Shaw, room 202."

Dana left the receptionist to her nails and rode a quiet yet brisk elevator to the second floor. Room 202 was across the hall. The patient's chart hung on the back of the door, and Dana scanned the report.

Dudley Shaw was sixty-five years old, and like her had a post office box address. He had been brought by ambulance at ten the previous morning. He was dehydrated and confused. His temperature was 104 degrees. His blood pressure was 90/50—seriously low. His neutrophil and lymphocyte count were three times higher than the norm, indicative of a bacterial infection. Routine antibody tests were negative. Dudley's blood had been cultured for bacteria and nothing unusual was found.

Dana checked Dudley's treatment schedule. He was taking acetaminophen for fever, oxymorphine for pain, and three different antibiotics effective against a wide spectrum of bacteria. He was on an IV drip and receiving plasma intravenously to boost his blood volume. The clinical observations did little to shed light on the nature of his infection.

As Dana replaced the chart in the slot in the door, a heavy hand clapped her shoulder. She spun around to find a hulking health care attendant with a face as black as old coffee. "I'm sorry ma'am," he said, "that's a restricted room." His nametag read Sam.

"Oh." She smiled sheepishly. "That's okay. I'm a doctor." She didn't explain what kind. She groped in her purse for the tube of blood and held it up. "I was sent to assay Dudley Shaw's blood."

"I hope you find out what he's got," Sam said. "The doctor here is stumped. When Shaw came in he looked dead, but he's doing better. We got him on morphine and he's off his rocker."

"Have you talked to him?" she asked.

"We're fixing to. He wasn't talking when he came in, and now he's so stoned he's not making much sense."

"Do you mind if I ask him a few questions?" Dana asked.

Sam thought it would be all right.

She left him in the hall and went into the room. It was dark and the drapes were drawn. Dudley Shaw was sleeping. His hair was white and swept across his scalp to hide a bald spot. He cried out in his troubled sleep and Dana froze, not wanting to disturb him.

She eyed the room, her eyes growing accustomed to the dark. The room was decorated in shades of pastel. There was a pink flowered quilt on the bed, pale-yellow curtains on the windows, and caricatures of baby blue birds on the walls. But all the soothing colors in the world could not camouflage the odor of the ill, or muffle the drip, drip, drip of the IV that sounded like a clock winding down.

Dudley stirred, flailing his arms. He blinked his eyes, stared up at her, and then struggled to sit up. His eyes were a washed-out brown, the irises floating in a soupy opaque sea. "Who are you?" Dudley said. His voice was soft, his words coming out on wisps of air. His breathing was raspy and labored.

Dana introduced herself. "I came to check your blood. How are you feeling?" A ridiculous question given the circumstances.

Dudley shook his head. His skin was pale and his five o'clock shadow was white and looked like snow sprinkled on his chin. "Been better."

She pulled a chair up to the bed and sat down. After a few questions, she learned he had worked as a gardener at the university and had recently retired. He was taking a big trip. He snapped his fingers. "Bingo."

She wondered if he was talking about the game.

"My dog. He'll be hungry. I've got to go."

"I'll feed him."

Dudley cast his watery gaze upon her. "You would?"

"I have three dogs of my own. I don't mind. Where do you live?"

He gave complicated directions that left her confused, and she finally asked him to draw a map. His wallet was on the bedside table and he pulled out a receipt and scribbled a map on the back. He lived by the forest not far from her house.

He handed her the paper. The receipt was from the car wash next to campus. Thirty bucks for a wash and wax. Unbelievable! She folded the receipt and crammed it in her back pocket. Texans were nuts about their cars.

"When will they let me out?" Dudley said.

"Soon, I'm sure. You've got some bug. The antibiotics will make you feel better real soon."

"You're sure? It's just a regular infection. Nothing more?" He touched the flesh under his left armpit and winced.

"Is there a pain in your underarm?" Dana asked.

"No."

He answered too quickly. "The lymph drains into nodes under the left arm," Dana said. "Not the right, just the left. If you have a bacterial infection, sometimes the nodes can swell and the pressure can cause significant pain."

He seemed to consider this. "Do the nodes feel like a lump?"

"If they're swollen. You mind if I feel?"

"My father died of cancer when he was my age." Dudley held out his hand.

Dana looked at his hand and gasped. The base of his fingernails were black. A classic sign of the plague—something she had only seen in textbooks.

"What's wrong?" he said.

She took his hand. "How long have you been sick?"

"It's Sunday, right? I've been feeling off for a few days. Since Thursday, I reckon."

"So not too long."

"No," he said, sounding hopeful.

She pushed up the sleeve of the hospital gown and felt gingerly under his right armpit. He didn't flinch or react. She let go of his arm, and lifted the other. When she felt under this arm, he jumped. The lymph node was hard and solid. The size of a chicken egg.

"What is it?" he said.

A bubo, she wondered? A swollen lymph gland teaming with plague bacteria? The hair on the back of her neck stood on end. "A swollen gland," she said. The attending physician missed it somehow.

"Not a tumor?" Dudley said.

She shook her head and sat back down. If he did have the plague, she had to find out where he was infected. He couldn't get the plague in Duane—it was too far south. The *Yersinia* bacteria maintained a strict geographical range. "Have you been away?"

"To New Orleans, to see my sister."

That was the same latitude as Duane. "When was that?"

"Easter."

Four weeks ago. The incubation for bubonic plague was seven to ten days. He couldn't have been infected there. "Have you had any visitors?"

"No."

"Are you married?"

"No."

"Any rats at your house?"

"Pardon?"

"I meant fleas. Does Bingo have fleas?"

"Sure. He hates water. Whatever you do, don't turn on the hose. He'll run away. Is it a problem?"

She didn't want to worry him. "My dogs have fleas too. It's the rain and the mild winter." She wanted to ask him more questions but didn't want to upset him by giving him the third degree. Not until she knew what he had. It may not be the plague. An acute or chronic bacterial infection could explain swollen glands, and there were other explanations for hypoxia. The blue color meant a lack of oxygen—it could be a sign of failing respiration, shock, or poor circulation. As McCoy would be the first to tell her, she shouldn't jump to conclusions.

"I'll go feed Bingo and do the blood work. I'll come back tomorrow."

"Am I really going to be okay?"

"You'll be fine."

"Thank you." He lay back in his pillow as if she had bequeathed him good health.

She drove to his house—found it without difficulty. She located the key under the mat and unlocked the door. The dog was nowhere to be found. She filled up his water bowl and his food bowl and left them on the front porch. She would have to check back later. Given the presence of fleas and the possible diagnosis, the missing dog was worrisome.

She reached her office and the phone was ringing. McCoy again. "What have you got?"

"A blood sample," Dana said. "I was about to start."

"Start? We talked an hour ago."

"I realize that," she said sharply. "And the sooner I start, the sooner I'll get back to you."

                                    ***

The quarantine room at the back of the lab was claustrophobic and windowless. The walls were white and the fluorescent light was blinding bright. The floor was gray and the room smelled of acetone and Lysol.

Dana washed her hands, and then pulled on a lab coat and disposable gloves. She opened the freezer and retrieved a biohazard box that contained bacterial standards. She thawed eighteen vials in a beaker of warm water. She took the standards and Dudley's blood sample to a laminar flow hood and sat down. She flipped a switch and the fan turned on, creating negative pressure that drew air and any airborne pathogens up and out of the room. The bacterial standards were dead and no longer infectious. It was Shaw's blood that demanded care.

She began the assay, labeling an immunological plate. It looked like a miniature egg carton that contained ninety-six depressions. She added a drop of known bacteria to each depression: *Staphylococci, Streptococci, Pneumococci, Neisseria, Erysipelothrix, Bacillus, Listeria, Nocardia, Escherichia, Shigella, Klebsiella, Proteus, Salmonella, Brucella, Francisella, Vibrio, Pseudomonas* and lastly, *Yersinia*. Next, she added to each well a drop of Dudley's blood; the assay required all that the hospital had given her.

The ELISA was a method of identifying an unknown pathogen. The assay used bacterial standards to fish out complementary antibodies from the blood. If the blood reacted with one of the known bacterial standards, that meant it contained specific antibodies—the blood had been exposed to a given bacteria.

The assay took forty minutes to run. In the final step, a marker that fluoresced in UV light was added that recognized antibodies bound to bacteria. Dana added the marker, waited five minutes, and then turned on an ultraviolet light. There was a glowing spot—a positive match for *Yersinia pestis*. Dudley Shaw had the plague.

Dana sunk onto the stool. There was no mistaking the result, but the diagnosis didn't make sense. Where was Dudley infected? She thought of Bingo lost in the forest. Did the dog have fleas infected with *Yersinia*?

Hold on, she cautioned herself. Back up. Wait one minute. Antibodies alone only confirmed a presumptive diagnosis. To make a positive diagnosis, the infecting bacterium had to be grown and identified. The bacteria could be seen in the blood under a microscope, and according to the hospital report, no untoward bacteria were found in Dudley's blood. Still, when it came to the plague, blood work to detect the bug was notoriously unreliable. With bubonic plague, they would have better luck directly aspirating the bubo.

Dana took off her gloves and washed her hands. She went to her office and called McCoy. "There was a positive response for *Yersinia pestis*."

He said nothing.

"Should I call the hospital and let them know?" she asked. The U.S. Public Health Service policy was for doctors to report all suspected cases of the plague to the local and state health departments, the Centers for Disease Control, and the World Health Organization.

"Don't do anything," McCoy said.

"If Dudley Shaw has the plague, he's on the wrong medication. He should be taking streptomycin, tetracycline and chloramphenicol. If he—"

McCoy interrupted her. "I'm well aware of what he should be taking. I'll handle this."

"All I'm saying is that the hospital needs to be alerted. His lymph node fluid needs to be tested. Dudley should be in quarantine, he could be contagious, and—"

"Thank you for that information. It may surprise you to know that I am familiar with infectious disease." There was a long silence and then McCoy added stridently, "Don't say a word about this to anyone."

"But—"

"I'll handle it. With the VP's visit, this could present a precarious complication. Good day."

Dana heard the dial tone in her ear. McCoy had hung up before she could tell him about the missing dog.

APRIL 27TH

CHAPTER ELEVEN

After a fitful night, Dana lay in bed waiting for the sun to rise. It was a cool morning and she felt on edge, worrying about Dudley Shaw left to TJ McCoy, who was going to handle things. Dana had tried calling the previous night to tell him about Bingo, but according to his wife he was out for a drive. McCoy had a strange way of handling things.

Anyhow, if she had found out about Bingo, he could too. After the presumptive diagnosis of the plague, someone with experience would conduct a proper interview. But who was that someone? In the small town of Duane, she was the plague specialist. The university hadn't had a resident epidemiologist for seven years. Even if McCoy didn't know it, he needed her help. If he thought he could exclude her from investigating the case, he was wrong. It was her specialty, her diagnosis, and she wasn't about to let him run an investigation that should be hers. As soon as it was light, she was going back to the hospital to ask Dudley more questions. The most important thing right now was his dog. She needed a description of him and a means to track him down.

When the sky turned orange, Dana rose from bed. She fed the dogs and Frank refused to eat. He had eaten nothing in twenty-four hours. Overnight his condition seemed to have deteriorated. He refused to get out bed and she had to pull him up. Then he started coughing and couldn't stop. It was a difficult struggle to get him to the car.

She stopped at the hospital on her way to work. Outside Dudley's room hung a bright orange sign with the words: QUARANTINE AREA. STRICTLY NO ADMITTANCE. In the hallway, next to the door was a chair piled high with packages of protective clothing. Dana ripped open a bag and donned a yellow paper suit, gloves, and booties. There was a paper toque for her hair and a mask for her face.

She went into the room. The bed was empty. The windows were shut and the drapes were pulled. She heard water running in the bathroom and breathed more easily. If Dudley was up and using the bathroom, his condition had improved.

The bathroom door opened, but it wasn't Dudley. It was Sam, also dressed in protective clothing. All Dana could see was his white teeth, dark eyes, and black skin. "Where's Dudley?" she asked.

"Gone."

"Home?"

Sam lifted his eyes to the ceiling. "You might say that."

"When did he leave?"

Sam walked over to the bed and picked up the pillow. He removed the case and tossed it on the floor. He tore the bedspread and sheets off the bed. "Middle of the night. He kept getting worse and worse and the drugs didn't help. At the end he couldn't breathe. His skin was blue. He was convulsing. He couldn't get enough air. Electroshock couldn't start his heart."

Dudley was dead. Dana leaned against the wall, needing support. *What the hell happened?* The bubonic plague could be treated with antibiotics. Yet, Dudley had died.

She watched in silence as Sam stuffed the pillow, sheets, towels, clothes, and comforter into a biohazard bag. Dudley died from a flea bite. *A flea!* There was something very wrong when an insignificant occurrence could have such a far-reaching effect. It was a tenet of chaos theory: a small initial cause exerting a great distal influence—like a butterfly beating its wings in India causing a typhoon in Madagascar. A breakdown of predictability.

She caught Sam looking at her. "Are you all right?" he said. "I thought doctors were pretty much used to death."

"Most," she said.

Sam swung the biohazard bag in a circle to seal the open end. He knotted the bag, placed it inside another biohazard bag, and then tossed the bundle at a corner. "I heard the old gent had bubonic plague." He straightened and looked Dana in the eye.

She confirmed the diagnosis. "What antibiotics was he taking?"

Sam listed the three usually used for the plague. At least Dudley had been treated correctly.

"You should take prophylactics," Sam said. "Oral antibiotics. Dr. Taversham said they'd protect anyone who may have come in contact with the man."

Dana nodded again. The antibiotic tetracycline provided post-exposure protection against the plague. She didn't need oral antibiotics though. For the last eight years she'd been vaccinated against the disease. As recently as Friday, she hoped. She rubbed her deltoid. Later today she could check the antibodies in her blood.

"I heard agents from the CDC were on their way," Sam said. "The hospital called for help."

The CDC couldn't come unless they were invited and Dana was unhappy to hear that they were involved. Once they arrived, they'd take over. She wanted a chance to prove herself. This was the point of her research, what made her work meaningful—real life application.

Sam picked up a large canister that looked like a fire extinguisher. "You'd better go. I've got to fumigate the room."

"What should I do with the suit?" Under normal quarantine regulations, after working in a hot zone, any person exposed to a highly contagious organism would decontaminate their clothes and body in a sealed room. But the small town hospital had no such room.

Sam pointed to the biohazard bag. "Leave the suit there."

The orange biohazard bag reminded Dana of the orange bag Carol Dupuis had given her on Friday afternoon. Four rats that died under mysterious circumstances were sitting in the Revco freezer awaiting testing.

Dana left the hospital at a jog. The sun had cleared the trees and the air was hot. Frank was standing in the back seat, panting hard, head thrust out the window. His nose was dry and salt-stained.

She jumped in, started the car, turned the air-conditioning to high, and lowered the windows. "Hold on, Frank, hold on." She aimed the vents at the back.

She reached the vet school and parked near the clinic. She would move her car later. Theoretically, she was still a clinic client.

But the clinic wasn't open, and Dana took Frank upstairs in the service elevator. She left him in her office while she went to the quarantine lab to test the rats' blood.

She got the biohazard bag from the freezer. The Revco maintained a minus seventy degree Celsius temperature, which preserved biological samples nearly indefinitely. At that temperature there was little molecular movement, little decay. She placed the bag in the microwave and set the machine on defrost. While she waited, she put on a lab coat, gloves, and a mask, and prepped for the assay.

In forty-five minutes she had the answer she sought. All four rats were infected with the plague. Regardless of whether it was possible, the fact was that the plague bacteria were in Duane. A man had died from bubonic plague, a student was likely exposed, and a dog that may be carrying infected fleas was lost. McCoy had to be told.

Dana removed her protective gear quickly. She was already late for the weekly staff meeting that began at eight o'clock sharp. Nonetheless, she washed her hands with antibiotic soap for the requisite two minutes. Racing from the quarantine room, past her office, she stopped short when she saw Frank. How could she forget about him? It was as if he were already gone.

She left him heaving and sprinted across the hall and pounded loudly on Tim Sweeny's door. No answer. His resident, Sheila, often used his office, but she wasn't there. The door was locked.

"Tim isn't there."

Dana spun around and saw the last person she wanted to see— Nellie Duncan, wife of the Dean of the Veterinary College. She was fifty years old and dressed like she was thirty. She dyed her hair an unnatural shade of honey brown and had it cut in a pageboy that was flipped under at her chin. She was an unaccredited department histologist who was paid a fortune to prepare slides she never found time to make. By virtue of marriage, she held a position she didn't deserve and had power she didn't earn. When Brian Boswell was alive he kept her in line, but with the coming of McCoy, Nellie was a rising star. She was using two decades of experience and history at the vet school to 'help' him find his way around the department.

"I know Tim isn't here," Dana said. She turned and began walking down the hall toward the conference room adjacent to McCoy's office.

Nellie was on her heels. "I hate to be the one to tell you, but Tim was out with another woman on the weekend."

"He can go out with whomever he wants."

"Oh." Nellie clicked her teeth. "You broke up. I'm so sorry," she said, not sounding sorry at all. "But there is a visitor. Michael Smith. Maybe he's available."

"Don't worry about me. Anyway, he's married."

"I didn't think that was a problem for you."

Dana increased her pace. Nellie was never one to let her forget the past.

Nellie was jogging to keep up and pulling on her lab coat as she went. "At least I'm not the only one late."

Nellie had no reason to be worried. If she was late to the weekly meeting, McCoy never said a word, but when Dana was late, he took grave offense.

They reached the main office, and Dana waved to Betty, who was on the phone. Behind her, Nellie said, "I guess you know about the case of bubonic plague in town."

Dana said nothing. She reached the conference room and opened the door.

Nellie wasn't finished. "Oh, wait. I take it back. It's confidential and McCoy's going to handle it."

CHAPTER TWELVE

By the time the eight a.m. meeting rolled around, McCoy was already exhausted. The day began with the news that the man infected with the plague had died, and CDC agents were on their way. God damn it! Greenlee Hospital had called them, requesting help. The State Health Department had also been notified. They were taking over. They would survey hospitals across Texas in search of patients with similar symptoms to Dudley Shaw's. The State Extension Service would commence trapping wild animals throughout the region. Local health officials would interview the contacts of the infected man and dispense prophylactic antibiotics as necessary. McCoy, who last night told the dean he needed no help handling the problem, was left with nothing to handle. The pieces of the investigation he wished to control had been divided already. McCoy pounded his fist on the desk.

To make matters worse, the infected man died before he could be interviewed. No one knew where he'd been, or where he could have been exposed. Certainly not in Duane. In McCoy's view, the state health officials, the hospital, and the CDC were overreacting, and he would have told them as much had they consulted him, but they had not.

At least all parties concerned had agreed to keep the details of the case out of the public eye. All inquires would be discreet. The last thing they needed was an influx of hypochondriacs who would zap their energy and muddy their focus the week of the VP's visit.

McCoy was determined to stay ahead of the ball. He wanted his own expert on the case. He had called Washington, but the man he wanted was out on an emergency. Thankfully, he convinced the CDC to set up headquarters at the vet school. Since the hospital had no space, McCoy offered a spare office for the two agents. He would keep his eye on them, prod them in the right direction, and get them out of town before Friday.

That settled, McCoy headed for the conference room and his weekly meeting. The door was unlocked and he threw it open. Christ, some lunatic had turned off the air conditioning. He gasped for breath and stepped back. Despite McCoy's strict instructions that no one touch the thermostat but him, the order had been ignored. He cranked it on high, went to the table, and took the lone seat at its head.

Before he arrived at the university, the conference room had been set up as a lounge and resembled a bordello. There were couches, a stereo, dart board, microwave, even a coffee machine. McCoy had cleared out the junk and moved in a long rectangular table, hard-backed chairs, and a chalkboard. He filled a large bookshelf with the latest scientific annals. Despite all the grumbling, the room now resembled a place of serious business.

The door opened and the first researcher clumped in. McCoy noticed the high-strung Charlotte Lane was gaining weight. Was she pregnant? Was it possible? She was forty and had four children already. She wasn't planning to take maternity leave, was she? McCoy had barely enough staff as it was.

Bob Fairway came in next, wearing a ridiculous bow tie. He stooped beside McCoy to discuss a jam in the scintillation counter. McCoy was not listening. He watched Michael Smith step into the room and realized he had forgotten all about his guest. Unable to extricate himself from Fairway, McCoy was relieved to see Smith sit down without much ado.

Next, Phillip Becker hobbled in. He had a badly hunched back that grew worse by the day. The man was eighty-five and should have retired, but he wouldn't go willingly. Unlike the army, the university lacked the policy to force him out.

At precisely oh-eight-hundred hours, McCoy stood up, effectively dismissing Bob Fairway. Though Nellie Duncan and Dana Sparks were late, McCoy would wait no longer. Dr. Sparks was often late. He was well aware of her complaint that the weekly meeting was a waste of her precious time. In McCoy's mind, the meeting was the most efficient way to monitor the department's activities. His staff provided services to the veterinary clinic, which in turn provided a small percentage of the department's core funding. The clinic wanted to know what it was getting for its money, and McCoy held these weekly meetings to find out.

Shaking off fatigue, McCoy welcomed his staff. He asked Dr. Charlotte Lane for an update on the veterinary cases she'd handled the previous week. She was in the midst of an arbovirus case when Sparks finally arrived.

McCoy eyed her coldly. He held up his hand to silence Dr. Lane. "Good afternoon, Dr. Sparks. Glad you could join us." She started to speak, but he waved her to silence. "Dr. Lane, you were talking about the arbovirus." McCoy nodded to his virologist.

"I'm finished."

Nellie Duncan arrived and McCoy waited for her to take her seat. He was grateful to the dean's wife for her support and advice. She'd been around the department a long time and knew it inside and out. She sat down and he waved to the verbose Bob Fairway, who launched into a full history about his recent parasitology cases.

Fairway was fifty, a tenured professor, who liked to toot his own horn. He had an air of self-importance McCoy found unsubstantiated. Incredibly, Fairway spoke about a case of babiosis he treated six months ago as if it were current. All he had to report was that the cow recovered, yet it took him twenty minutes to do so.

Next the hunched Phillip Becker had his say. The pathologist spent most of his day huddled over carcasses and microscopic slides. His favorite pastime was to conduct autopsies. As long as there was death, and unless it was Becker's own, it was unlikely the pathologist would ever leave the university on his own accord. Becker said he was about to autopsy a cat. On Friday, Tim Sweeny had amputated the cat's foreleg. Saturday, the cat fell seriously ill, and Sunday it had died.

"Was the illness a result of surgery?" McCoy asked. The last thing the veterinary school needed was a malpractice lawsuit to tarnish its image.

"I don't know," Becker said. "I haven't started the autopsy. But the cat was a hit-and-run so there's no owner and no fear of a lawsuit."

So why the hell was Becker doing an autopsy? It was a flagrant waste of time and money. "Incinerate the cat," McCoy said. He moved on to Nellie Duncan.

She asked permission to order a projector she had not budgeted for.

"We'll discuss it later," McCoy said. She would have her projector, despite his warning that once budgets were written, they were set.

McCoy turned to Sparks. "If you could give us an update on the veterinary cases you handled last week."

"I tested about twenty sera samples and identified a cow infected with *Brucella* and a bird infected with *Chlamydia.*"

McCoy stared at her. "*About* twenty samples? Is it possible to be more specific, so that when I let Dean Duncan know *exactly* the value of our service, *I* know it?"

"The information is in my office. I could get it. This morning I did a *Yersinia* ELISA and—"

"If you have nothing else of relevance to add, we'll move on."

McCoy was determined to introduce the current complication his way. As the boss, that was his prerogative. As he rose from his chair, Dr. Sparks' raised her hand, and he waved it away. In his most somber tone, he said, "At this juncture, it appears we have a presumptive infection of *Yersinia pestis* in Duane. Of course, given its location, the source is not here. Nevertheless, two CDC agents are on their way. No doubt they'll complete their investigation in one or two days. To this end, I've assured Dean Duncan and the president that we shall provide all the assistance they require."

He began pacing. "From this moment on, you will avail yourselves to the CDC. We've given them an office down the hall and we'll call it Headquarters. The CDC is in charge and we'll provide laboratory assistance. Our goal is to get them out of here as soon as possible. I don't think that will be a problem."

At the far end of the table, Dana Sparks' hand was waving spastically again.

He ignored her. "Because of the sensitivity of the situation, I insist this information remain in this room. We do not want a panic on our hands. Indeed, there is no justification for one. We have an isolated case of bubonic plague and that is it. There is no doubt the bacteria came from somewhere, but that somewhere is not here."

There was a rap at the door and McCoy marched toward it. He was feeling immensely better. The room was finally cool and McCoy was no longer sweating. The explanation that the bacteria originated elsewhere was logical, reasonable, and sobering. There was nothing to worry about. The bacteria could not thrive in Duane—it was that simple.

McCoy threw open the door.

One look at his federal assistance and McCoy was sweating again. *These were the agents?* Who was the government hiring these days? The older man wore a ponytail and a clump of moss on his chin. His mouth was too wide and his smile was too big. The younger man looked like a college kid and wore a diamond in his ear. *God help us all*, McCoy thought, as he shook hands with the ponytailed Karl King and the youthful Jeffery Tuttle.

"I was in Houston," King said. "This was kind of on my way."

He was smiling broadly, like a lunatic, while McCoy felt faint. In a room that suddenly seemed much smaller and hotter, McCoy introduced the agents to his staff. He pulled two chairs to the front and invited the visitors to share his head of the table. He was about to repeat his overview when Karl King jumped in.

Not knowing McCoy's proclivity for titles and formality, King made his second mistake. "TJ, Jeff and I appreciate your cooperation and the cooperation of your people. We've verified your suspicion of the plague. Unfortunately, the index case, Dudley Shaw, died this morning. We don't know where he was infected, or who he may have infected. It's only a matter of time before more cases surface."

McCoy frowned as his chest constricted tightly. It hurt to breathe and his ears were plugged as if there had been an abrupt change in air pressure. This was the last thing he wanted to hear. *More cases?* "This is an isolated incident," he said stridently. "The source of the plague is not here."

"Maybe, maybe not," King said. "That is something for us to determine."

"Look," McCoy said, aiming to be reasonable. "It's too far south. It's too hot. There's no evidence whatsoever of a wildlife infection that always precedes—"

Dr. Sparks interrupted him. She raised her hand and spoke without permission. "It appears rats from this area *are* infected with *Yersinia* and—"

"*What?*" McCoy forced his fists to unclench. He took a deep breath, a method suggested by his cardiologist as a means to control his blood pressure. What the hell was she talking about?

"Rats?" King said, as he smiled at Dr. Sparks for far too long.

She ignored McCoy's warning tone. "I received four rats Friday afternoon and just finished an ELISA. The lymph nodes of all four tested positive for *Yersinia*."

"Where did you get the rats?" Karl asked.

It appeared someone had given them to her. *The previous goddamn week*. Yet, she was only testing them now. McCoy's deep breathing did little to contain his mounting anger.

"Where is the student?" Karl asked.

Of course, Sparks didn't know where the student was. Nor did she know where the rats had been trapped. What she did know was that four of twenty rats trapped had died. "If twenty percent of the rodents near town are infected with the plague, that means—"

McCoy exhaled loudly. His hands were fists again. He took grave exception to her statistics. "There is no scientific basis for that statement. Maybe only sick rats were trapped. Did you type the bacteria? Can you say with a hundred percent certainty these rats are diseased? Rats are a reservoir. Some species host the bacteria and don't get sick. Do you know precisely what killed these particular rats?"

She backed down. Of course she didn't have the answers to any of his questions. Just as he was getting a grip of the situation, she opened her mouth and nearly sent him into cardiac arrest.

"I'm concerned because Dudley Shaw's dog is missing. He could be carrying infected fleas."

McCoy felt blood rush to his head. Despite his specific emphatic instructions to retrieve the sample and leave the patient alone, she had not complied with his request. "What do you mean? How do you know Shaw had a dog that's missing? How do you know?"

She stared at the tabletop. "I talked to him."

The CDC man was on his feet. "Great. What did he say?"

Sparks spoke directly to Karl King. In a few sentences she dashed all McCoy's hopes that Dudley Shaw was infected elsewhere.

"Dudley hasn't been anywhere except to New Orleans one month ago. He visited his sister at Easter. Given the timing and the elevation, I don't see how he could have acquired *Yersinia* there. It wasn't clear to me how he was exposed. Unless *Yersinia* has moved to a lower altitude and—"

McCoy cut her off. He would not tolerate idle speculation. At this point, all they had were possibilities and hypotheses. "The bacterium has been around for thousands of years. It has never moved to a lower altitude."

King ignored this. "What do you know about the dog?"

"His name is Bingo," Sparks said. "He's not at his house."

"We have to find him. Take a closer look at those rats."

McCoy stepped into the conversation. "Dr. Becker will do the autopsies."

Becker rubbed his liver-spotted hands together.

King looked at McCoy. "Fine. We'll trace this student. Jeff can liaison with your staff and the university registrar to track her down. I'll head out to the field and find this dog. We'll lay trap cages and check the wildlife. See if *Yersinia* has moved south. Find out how and where Shaw was infected. Stop the epidemic cold."

"Any assistance you need is yours," McCoy said.

"I have no doubt we'll have the situation cleared up in one or two weeks," King said.

"One or two weeks?" McCoy almost choked. "I'm afraid we'll have it cleared up before Friday, which is when the VP is scheduled to arrive."

Karl King rubbed his goatee. "In lieu of the possible rodent infection and the fatality, we'll advise the VP to cancel his trip."

"Impossible!" McCoy barked, feeling like he was about to explode. "One person is infected. We have a single, isolated case. Surely this is not your recommendation."

It surely was. "We will begin our investigation and inform the Bureau of our progress."

McCoy's face fell. It never failed to amaze him how fast things could spiral out of control. The Feebs now? The town was crawling with special agents—Ackerman and the like. The stuffed shirts from

Washington had completed FBI training and thought they were ready for war. No, no, no! Ackerman and his men would be informed of nothing if McCoy had his way. If the CDC agents couldn't handle this on their own, he'd call the army and help would be his before the end of the day.

"Do you think it wise at this juncture to call Washington?" he said, speaking in a tone that made his feelings on the matter clear. "At this early stage, I would expect discretion is the order of the day. People are coming to Duane to see the VP. It is an election year."

"I'm aware of that," Karl said. "There is no need to scare the general populace without cause. Mention an infectious disease and before you know it, everyone thinks they're sick." He laughed heartily at a joke McCoy did not find at all funny.

"Let's get to work," McCoy said. "Let me know when you find that dog and we'll find a vet to examine it."

Karl checked his watch. "I'm awaiting a specialist. He should be here any time. He's a veterinarian and can assist with the dog."

McCoy exhaled his frustration. Karl King was bringing in a veterinarian epidemiologist? When a human was already infected and dead? What kind of joker was this CDC man? "A veterinarian?" McCoy asked with palpable disbelief.

Karl smiled on. "He's a professor of epidemiology and a medical doctor. He knows the terrain. He lived here. I don't know if you know him: Nick Biget?"

McCoy finally smiled. His chest relaxed and he felt a weight lift from his heart. This was McCoy's expert who was off on an emergency. Now that Nick was coming, McCoy felt better. It was good news, good news indeed. Here was a man who could do a job effectively and quietly. For a civilian, McCoy held him in the highest esteem. McCoy was just surprised that Nick hadn't informed him he was coming. Dr. Sparks looked surprised too, which reminded McCoy of rumors he refused to consider. He concluded the meeting. "We'll adjourn for now and meet back at fourteen hundred hours."

Karl threw him an exaggerated salute.

CHAPTER THIRTEEN

The room cleared. Dana sat at the table, unable to move. Her heart thumped in her ears as if it had moved into her head. Her body pulsed in and out, as if something inside her was trying to grow. Hope, nearly given up for dead, was blooming. Nick was coming back.

She got up, walked to the window, and drew back a curtain McCoy always kept closed. The sky looked bluer, the leaves more green, and the bluebonnets more purple. The sun and everything under it seemed brighter. She caught her reflection in the glass smiling back at her. Anticipation, disbelief, hope, and desire coursed through her. Another accident—an outbreak of the plague—brought Nick back. She'd been granted a wish she had not dared to voice.

Not that in the past her hopes hadn't been raised. She was certain after he left that he would miss her and call, but he never did. She envisioned meeting by chance, at a scientific meeting, an immunology conference—but no. When Brian died, she looked for Nick in the crowded auditorium during the memorial, and later in the graveyard under a cold December drizzle, but there was no sign of him. Later, Dana heard Nick would be offered Brian's job, and she held her breath and waited. The next thing she knew, McCoy was coming and Nick's name was no longer mentioned. Until today.

She turned from the window. At the far end of the room in the corner sat an empty chair. At the table was an empty place, saved for a man who was seven years in coming. Nick was back. Dana walked the length of the room and moved the chair to the table.

The next plane from Houston landed at the small Duane airfield at nine. She glanced at her watch. He would be at the vet school imminently. He could be here now. Dana floated from the conference room. Her boots felt light, her body weightless, as if her feet weren't touching the ground.

The secretary brought her back to earth. "Sheryl called," Betty said, looking up from her desk. She spoke in a thick Texan accent, elongating every vowel. She was forty-something, single and not happy about it. She wore a rainbow of blue and mauve eye shadow. Her hair was flouncy, though stiff. She favored bright dresses with stripes that camouflaged her weight. She was good and kind-hearted—but too desperate when it came to men. "Penny's sick. Sheryl's not coming in."

Dana nodded, unhappy at the news. Sheryl was supposed to take blood today. Dana was anxious to check her antibodies and there was no way she could do it herself.

McCoy's office door opened. "Dr. Sparks. My office. Now."

Dana grimaced at Betty, who lifted her eyebrows. Dana went to his office.

He closed the door. Though the room was dark and cold, McCoy was sweating. He stood at ease with his arms folded across his chest. "What the hell were you thinking?" he asked, in an abnormally high-pitched voice. "Why didn't you tell me about those rats?"

"I just found out myself. I tried to tell you at the start of the meeting."

"You weren't there at the start of the meeting." McCoy narrowed his beady gray eyes. "Why didn't you tell me about the dog?"

"I called you last night. You were out for a drive."

McCoy dismissed her explanation with a swipe of his arm. "This stops right now. I am in charge of the investigation. Anything you think the CDC should know, comes through me."

She tried to argue. "This is *my* specialty. I can type the bacteria. I have the antibodies and monoclonals. I'm the one experienced in dealing with plague-infected blood. If anyone can help the CDC, it's me."

"I am in charge. Period." McCoy ran the heel of his hand across his forehead. "One more thing." His tone dropped and he spoke in a normal voice. "Check your vaccine data and make sure everyone is up-to-date on their shots. If the CDC checks, I want our department in full compliance with federal policy." McCoy threw open the door.

Dana left his office. She nodded to Betty and strode into the hall. Nellie Duncan's shadow fell across her. "You looked surprised when you heard Nick was coming," Nellie said, dancing by her side. "You mean you didn't know?"

Dana increased her speed. This was a conversation she would not have.

"You don't keep in touch?" Nellie sounded incredulous.

Either way, it was a loaded question and one Dana wouldn't answer. Up ahead on the right was her lab, three doors away.

Nellie skipped down the hall. "I'm as surprised as you, frankly. After Brian passed, Drake offered Nick the position. We offered a lucrative deal and he refused to even consider it. I thought this place had too many bad memories for him."

Feeling dizzy and faint, Dana kept going.

"You can't blame him though, can you," Nellie said. "His poor wife. His dead baby. It's enough to make anyone lose their mind. Do things they wouldn't otherwise do. Things they may later regret." She clucked her teeth and shook her head.

Dana ignored her. She had reached her lab and the refuge she sought. She entered her office and shut the door, relieved to be alone. Then she saw her abandoned and forgotten dog.

CHAPTER FOURTEEN

The pilot announced the descent to Duane, and Nick Biget tightened his seatbelt. He leaned forward and peered out the small window, watching the tiny houses and tinker-toy cars come into focus. He was already having second thoughts. He felt uneasy about the assignment the moment the Secretary of Homeland Security requested his help. After the Mogadishu bombing, threats from Islamic extremists were pouring in. Rumors of a biological attack were running rampant. Then, a man died in Duane from a rare and deadly infectious disease outside the pathogen's range—on the exact week of the VP's visit. Nick was supposed to check it out, serve as the liaison between the CDC and Homeland Security. He had the background and clearance to do the job, and refusing would have required a lengthy explanation Nick could barely formulate, let alone understand. Even after all this time.

He left behind a mess, an affair that should have never happened. He had been out of control. He couldn't stop himself, no matter how hard he tried. Leaving was the only way to get free. It was unspeakably hard but the right thing to do. Now, seven years had passed and it finally felt over. It had taken a long time. A verse from a Robin Wheeler song played unbidden in his head: *I had to go, I couldn't stay; though it was hell, I went away and left myself. I'm coming now to claim what I have lost.*

Nick shook his head, shifted in his seat, and cleared his mind. He was too tall to sit comfortably in the small space. There was no place to put his legs or rest his arms. He preferred an aisle seat, but at this late notice he had to settle for what was left. He stared out the window. The ground flew up at him, the plane's engine roared louder. He hated flying.

The pilot landed smoothly. The wheels grazed the runway, the brakes squealed sharply, and the plane came to a shuddering stop. A click of seatbelts and passengers jumped up. No stewardess accompanied the short flight and the copilot manned the door, bidding passengers farewell.

Nick stepped out into a wave of heat. The humidity reminded him of Washington, D.C. in August. His hands were sticky and clammy. He heaved his overnight bag onto his shoulder and wiped his hands on his slacks. The sun blazed and Nick slipped on his sunglasses. The pilot said the ambient temperature in Duane was seventy-eight, but it seemed hotter. Nick guessed it was the shock of leaving snow at Dulles Airport only hours ago.

Karl King met him in the terminal. They had known each other for over twenty years, ever since medical school. They had been each other's best man. Karl married at twenty, Nick at twenty-one—both ridiculously young. They were now forty-two.

"I'm sorry about your wife," Karl said.

"I'm sorry about yours." Nick had been shocked to hear Karl was divorced. He always thought Karl and Helena were happily married. She fussed over Karl like a child, choosing his clothes, fixing his hair, cautioning him on his drinking and his weight. He now looked a mess. He'd lost weight and his clothes no longer fit. His hair was long and tied back in a ponytail. Though in the past he was clean-shaven, he was sporting a goatee.

"I'm glad you came," Karl said. "Frankly, I'm surprised you agreed. It looked to me like you've been avoiding Texas. When was the last time you were here?"

"A while," Nick said, vaguely.

Karl pressed on. "You haven't made it to one Texas meeting. When there was that Hanta virus scare in El Paso, you sent a replacement."

"There was an emergency. I went to Uganda." Nick lifted his sunglasses. The terminal was cool and the artificial light was bright.

"Why come now?" Karl asked. He raised an eyebrow and looked at Nick askance. "Anything to do with the VP's trip?"

Nick nodded, shrugging. His mission was confidential and he could not reveal its real purpose, not even to Karl. Still, Nick wouldn't lie to his friend. "I can't say much. Don Stodgecraft asked me to come. With the VP's visit, Washington wants to be in the loop. I'm here as an observer. Don't worry, the investigation is yours." He changed the subject. "What do we have? One man dead?"

As they walked to the exit, Karl filled him in. "The dead man hadn't left town in a month. Four rats were infected. So far, no bacterial source has been found.

Nick didn't like it. If the dead man acquired *Yersinia pestis* in Duane, it would be the first time the bacterium was found at sea level. Typically, *Yersinia* was not found at an elevation below forty-five hundred feet. It had also never been found so far south.

They left the terminal and crossed the parking lot. The sky was a brilliant blue. Nick had forgotten the big Texan sky. Also the thick, heavy heat Dana adored. He pushed her from his mind. "Do we know the species of rat?"

"*Rattus rattus*," Karl said.

Nick whistled. The black rat was the worst species for harboring *Yersinia pestis* and spreading bubonic plague. "Any infected fleas?"

"Not that we've found. Yet."

At least there were infected rats. It would be untoward to have a disease carried by rodents appear in an environment where rodents weren't infected.

They reached the car, a navy Buick with a Hertz sticker on the windshield. "There's a problem," Karl said, as he opened the trunk. "A missing dog. The dead guy's hound Bingo took off."

Nick pulled on his shades and whistled again. Calling that 'a problem' was a substantial understatement.

"I thought we'd go to Dudley Shaw's house, search for Bingo and secure the site," Karl said.

Nick tossed his overnight bag in the trunk. "It's a pity no one interviewed him before he died."

"Someone did. The plague specialist." Karl slid into the driver's seat and threw open Nick's door. "She's pretty sharp and looks it too. Dana Sparks."

Hearing the name made Nick's heart race. He changed the subject. "Any idea of origin?"

"She didn't speak with a Texan accent. I guess she's from up north."

"I'm talking about the bacteria."

"Don't know the origin of the bacteria, no." Karl cranked the key. "Dana's been around a long time. You know her?"

"She developed the plague vaccine."

Karl whistled.

Nick was uncomfortable and wasn't expecting this reaction. He wished Karl would shut up.

Karl backed out of the space. "Who did she work with? Nellie Duncan said she did her Masters, PhD and post-doc research here."

"Robert Jones. Until he retired."

"The molecular immunologist."

"Him. Yes."

"And she took his place?"

"No, she finished her post-doc."

"Who'd she finish with?"

"Well. Me."

Karl braked the car to a full stop and stared at Nick.

In the wing mirror, Nick saw a car pull up behind them. Karl was blocking the road. "There's someone behind you."

Karl started moving again. "You never told me."

"It wasn't long. More on paper than anything else. She knew what she was doing. She just needed a supervisor and I got the job. I didn't have a choice," Nick said, protesting too much.

"I'm surprised you didn't mention her." Karl pulled onto the airport access road and increased his speed. The wind blew through the car as the air conditioning fan hummed and chilled the air.

"I left the year she came," Nick said.

"You left quite suddenly." Karl glanced at him again.

Nick pointed ahead. "There was a new treatment for Rachel-Anne. We went to D.C."

"Nellie said she's single."

What was Nick supposed to say to that? They reached the bypass and he told Karl to turn left. Nick leaned forward and fiddled with the radio. The news was on, and once again Somalia was the lead story.

The U.S. was adamant that a military target had been struck, but a French physician who had been in Mogadishu on the evening of the strike maintained that a hospital and mosque were hit. Arab communities were united in their call for the formation of a UN team to investigate the tragedy.

The news clip ended and classical music began. Nick leaned back in his seat and watched the trees go by. They were heading south along the bypass. It was eleven o'clock and traffic was light—though unlike D.C., Duane traffic was always light. They passed a six-story high apartment building, a new condominium complex, and a billboard for a coming mall. When Nick lived here, there was nothing in this area but the airport. He was appalled by the development that had turned the fallow land to concrete.

He relaxed when he saw the forest, with its thick post oak, cottonwood, and white pine. He had forgotten how flat the land was, how humid the air, how strong the south coastal wind. It swept brutally across the land, flattening the grass, and stirring the low leaves of the mulberry, hickory, and sweet gum.

The dead man lived in the country, and soon Karl turned off the highway and they were bouncing down a pitted road that was more dirt than asphalt. The houses were isolated, far from the road, mostly unmarked, and Karl got lost. He pulled over to the shoulder, got out his cell phone, and pulled up a map. He jabbed his finger at the screen. "Here's Dudley's house. Do you know where we're at?"

Nick knew exactly. They were on a rural road not far from Dana's house. "Take the second right ahead." When they passed the turnoff to Dana's, Nick closed his eyes. He would not travel down that road.

Beside him, Karl said, "Everything all right?"

Nick looked at him. "Fine. Everything is fine. Just fine. Why do you ask?"

"There's no need to tell me three times you're fine," Karl said.

He had a point.

"McCoy's going to be a problem," Karl said, apropos nothing. "You can tell he wants this swept under the carpet. He was trying to convince me I should be somewhere else. Anywhere but here would suit him just fine. All he cares about is keeping the VP's trip on schedule."

Nick had worked with McCoy on a number of occasions and knew he would never jeopardize an investigation or place human lives at unnecessary risk. More than once, McCoy had risked his own life to save others. In Vietnam, he carried a wounded colleague for three days. When the man died, McCoy would not leave the body behind. Later, in Iraq, near the end of the Gulf War, when the oil refineries were torched and fires were raging, McCoy shared his gas mask with a soldier whose own mask had melted. In Yugoslavia, he gave his MRE rations to starving refugees fleeing Kosovo. Nick knew there was nothing McCoy's men wouldn't do for him. He wasn't a general because he kissed the right boots or said the right thing. He deserved his four stars. In the army, he was a man of awed distinction.

"McCoy is all right once you get to know him," Nick said. "He plays by the rules. Likely had an arrhythmia when he saw your ponytail."

Karl patted the back of his head. "The ladies seem to like it."

They reached Dudley Shaw's house. Karl parked in front of a mailbox labeled with the dead man's name. He had no mail. Dudley lived on a corner lot ringed with cedar. The grass was cut short and resembled Astroturf. Rows of white and pink petunias lined the driveway. Above the small bungalow stood a spreading pecan tree, and under the tree, an old car.

"Would you look at that," Karl said, pointing to a vintage yellow Thunderbird. The car had extended tail fins, a nose grill, and headlights that looked like eyes. Karl made a beeline across the lawn toward it.

Nick followed him through the grass. Since it was cut short, it would not be a good harbor for fleas. Nick saw no butterflies, no moths, no grasshoppers, and wondered if Dudley used insecticides.

Karl reached the car and ran his hand across a fin. "What a beauty. I wonder if it's for sale."

Nick said nothing. He examined his slacks for fleas and saw none. He whistled for the dog and there was no response, only the sound of the wind in the leaves. He walked toward the house that appeared freshly painted and edged with bluebonnets.

That was another thing Nick had forgotten—the wildflowers. Highway dividers were brimming with them. He remembered a ceiling full of them.

Nick shook the image from his mind and surveyed the land. It looked good. No corn fields, no barn, no seed, no grain, no bird feeder that would interest *Rattus rattus*. There was no overt sign of fleas.

He walked around the house. The screen door banged lightly in the wind. While there was no garbage lying around that would attract rats, on the back porch, Nick saw dog kibble crumbs in a bowl infested with fire ants. Someone was feeding the dog.

Karl found a key under the entrance mat and they unlocked the door and went inside. The house was clean and in good shape—no evidence of rodent feces. Nick shook out a blanket left on the floor. No jumping fleas.

Nick checked the fridge and saw little food. From the freezer, he picked up a package of frozen meat. The previous year in New Mexico, a hunter had acquired bubonic plague from a rabbit he had shot and skinned. Nick saw a rifle hanging on the kitchen wall. Was Shaw a hunter? Had he killed something that had fleas infested with *Yersinia*? Would they find *Yersinia* in the wild around Duane if they looked? But what were the bacteria doing so far south?

On the back of the kitchen door was a calendar turned to April. The squares were mostly blank. Nick thought of his own covered calendar and felt a twinge of envy for the quiet, private, uncomplicated life Dudley seemed to have led. Nick saw at the beginning of the month that Dudley had returned from New Orleans. On April 20th, Dudley had written *L'bird bath*. Whatever that meant. On April 27th—today—a big star covered the square. It was obviously a significant date.

The day of his death. Marked in advance? No, Nick didn't buy that.

They finished examining the house, drew the drapes, closed the windows, and locked the front door. Karl taped a notice to the door stating the house was under quarantine. Using a yellow ribbon inscribed repeatedly with the words DO NOT ENTER, they ran the ribbon around the circumference of the house. They draped the tape across the car. Until they knew where Shaw had contracted bubonic plague, everything he had been in recent contact with had to be isolated.

Nick walked to the verge of the forest and called the dog. "Here Bingo, here Bingo, come on boy," he yelled. A crow cawed from the woods, but no dog came. Karl clapped his hands loudly, to no avail.

Thick smilax vine covered the trees at the edge of the woods and there was no access to the forest.

Nick frowned at the woods. If the dog was carrying infected fleas, it could spread the disease through the wildlife population. The risk of human exposure was proportional to the exposure of the wildlife. "We have to find that dog," Nick said.

Karl pointed across the road to a dilapidated house and a lady who pushed a baby on a cockeyed swing. "Let's talk to her. See what she knows."

They walked down the newly paved driveway, crossed the dirt road, and headed up a bumpy drive that was littered with trash. The neighbor was Suzie, in her mid-twenties. When asked about Bingo, she said, "I ain't seen him. I'd kill him if I did." She was braless and wore a dirty faded shirt and short shorts that showed white bumpy thighs.

The baby began to cry. Behind the house, a dog barked. Nick craned his neck and saw a thin, mangy beast chained to the back porch.

"Shut up, Dog," Susie yelled. Dog barked louder. He charged at the end of his chain so hard that he jerked himself backwards with each jump. Dog was a black Labrador, and reminded Nick of Frank, also a lab, who Rachel-Anne tried to drown in a swimming pool. He would be dead by now.

Susie yanked the crying baby from the swing and jostled it on her hip. The baby looked about six months old and wore a filthy pink sleeper with built-in feet. The baby grabbed a hank of Susie's matted hair and shoved it in her mouth. Susie was telling Karl all about Dudley Shaw.

"He was mean," Susie said. "He never had no kids. He'd go bananas if Marty's ball got in his flowerbed. He terrified poor Terry when she climbed on his precious car. He had a temper, for sure."

"Was he away a lot?" Karl asked.

Susie shook her head.

"Did he have a lot of visitors?" Karl asked.

"Um, nope." As far as Susie was concerned, that was self-evident. "As I was sayin', he wasn't so nice."

There was a loud cry from inside the house. Another child had begun to cry. The dog, who had been quiet, was barking again. "Quit yer yapping," Susie yelled.

Susie shifted the baby to her other hip and continued. It was too much for Nick. He interrupted Susie's tale about her absent drunken husband. "Excuse me. If you want to get that child, we can wait."

"Coming, Terry," Susie bellowed in an ear-splitting scream that silenced the dog and started the baby crying anew. "Come on in, come on in."

With a sweep of her hand, Susie invited the men into a house that smelled of cats and urine. While Susie padded down the hallway, Nick poked his head in the kitchen. Breakfast dishes remained on the table. A sink overflowed with dishes. The floor was sticky under his shoes. Dust balls and dried cornflakes spotted the graying linoleum. At least there were no rodent droppings. He went outside.

Karl went after him, followed him around the side of the house. Nick examined Dog. His eyes were too large for his skull. His ears were red and irritated and he had dry scabs on his head. His gums were pale and his teeth were rotting. He was undernourished and his abdomen was distended with worms. When Nick parted the mangy fur by the dog's tail, he saw running fleas. He picked off three and dropped them in a vial.

He looked around. The grass was long and unkempt. Nick took a few strides through the grass and examined his pants. He attracted burrs and a ladybug.

"Hey, where are you? Where you at?" Susie came looking for them and seemed happy to see them. She was carrying the baby, and was trailed by a toddler who was wearing a droopy diaper and tripping over untied laces of tennis shoes many sizes too large.

Nick said, "Look, this dog is suffering from malnutrition and needs treatment for fleas, ear mites, and worms."

Susie blinked and Karl laid a restraining hand on Nick's arm.

Nick pulled out his wallet, extracted a twenty-dollar bill, and thrust it in Susie's hand. "Buy him some food. Get flea shampoo. I'll come back and check on him."

Karl angled in front of Nick, shouldering him out of the way. "Ma'am, we'd like to ask you some questions. Am I correct in assuming you did not feed Dudley Shaw's dog?"

Nick wandered away, listening to the conversation transpiring behind him.

Susie thought Bingo was mean like his owner. "He was meaner than a snake. You couldn't walk on that property if that dog was home, or he'd nip at your knees. He almost tore Marty's head off."

"I see," Karl said. "Now, Mrs., um, Susie, do you know anyone who would be feeding him?"

"No."

"Would you mind if we took a drop of blood from Dog?"

Susie didn't mind, and Nick took the blood. He pierced the base of the dog's tail with a lance and filled a capillary tube with blood.

The toddler was watching intently, picking at a scab on his arm. His nose was running and his face was filthy. Nick bent down and tied the laces of his shoes, remembering a night when someone tied his laces—and his stomach up in knots. He stood up, momentarily dizzy and unbalanced.

Karl passed Susie a business card. "If you see Bingo, call me. You can call the university, and my personal cell phone number is on the back."

"What about Dudley? If I see him?"

Karl and Nick looked at each other. Karl said, "He's at the hospital."

Susie's mouth dropped open. "What's wrong with him? Why are you asking all these questions? Does Dudley got a disease? You thinkin' Dog might have it too? Is that why you want his blood?"

"Dudley had an infection," Karl said, vaguely. "We're not sure where he acquired it."

Susie's eyes were suddenly bright. "Is it something like AIDS? Can you get that from dogs?"

"It's bacterial, not viral," Karl explained.

The terms were lost on Susie. "Well, go figure. I knew there was something strange about that man. Who could reckon? And you think he might have given Dog something? Or us?"

"Very slim chance of that," Karl said. "We just want to make sure Dog's fine." He pointed to the business card bent in her fist. "If you or any one in your family gets a fever, call me. Or, if you see Bingo. You can call anytime."

Susie said she would. Nick reminded her to feed her starving dog. Karl grabbed hold of Nick's arm and escorted him down the pitted driveway and across the road to the car. "We need that lady's help," Karl said. "Where's your bedside manner?"

Nick knew Karl had a point. Returning to Duane had been more stressful than he imagined. Being out in the woods stirred old memories better left dead. What happened was over. He had to watch himself, keep in the present. He was here on a case, and Karl was right, he was being less than professional. "It won't happen again. Let's go see the dog-catcher."

The animal pound was on Texas Avenue. It was a small white building in the middle of a large and empty parking lot. Inside, a tall blond man in cowboy boots waited on them. Nick thought it would be a simple matter to ask him to find the dog, but Jim the dog-catcher was busy with other things.

"I've already looked for him," Jim said.

"Today?" Nick asked.

Jim shook his head. "We've been busy." He spoke in a quick southern twang. "The end of the semester is always like this. Students leaving and abandoning their pets. I didn't know it was an emergency."

"It is," Nick said,

Karl immediately contradicted him. "There is no emergency."

It was Nick's error. Officially, there was no crisis. He stepped away from the counter, letting Karl take over. Nick absently studied posters of lost pets that were tacked to the white-washed wall. He saw a poster written in a childish hand begging for the return of Pumpkin, a huge orange cat the kid could hardly hold. There was a lost canary. A lost turtle. A lost diamond ring.

Karl was giving Jim his business card. "If you find the dog, give me a call."

Nick turned around.

Jim frowned at the card. "Why is the CDC looking for a dog?"

"We're not," Karl said. "The next of kin are. The dog's owner is dead, the dog is lost."

Jim shoved Karl's card in the front pocket of his jeans.

"The family is actually quite distressed about losing him," Karl said.

"I'm real sorry," Jim said. "But you know, I've got four calls to make this afternoon and I don't know I have time to look for a dog that's not causing trouble."

Nick cleared his throat. They weren't getting through to this man and he was out of patience. "If I were you, I'd make the time."

Jim folded his arms across his chest. "Is that so."

Karl laid a restraining hand on Nick's arm. "What my friend means is that we've had a complaint from a neighbor that the dog is vicious."

Jim looked at Karl. "In that case, I'll see what I can do."

"We appreciate it," Karl said. Then he turned around and shepherded Nick out the door. Outside in the sweltering, muggy air, Karl said, "Well, that went well."

Nick didn't reply. He had handled the situation poorly and was appalled at how easily he lost his temper. Usually, no matter how hard he was pushed or provoked, he stayed calm. Growing angry never accomplished anything. In the past, under the worst circumstances, Nick kept his cool. This morning though, control seemed to elude him.

"We've got time for a burger before a two o'clock meeting," Karl said. "Shall we get a bite to eat?"

"Sure," Nick said, though he had no appetite. "Who are we meeting?"

"The whole department. Dana Sparks included. How long has it been since you've seen her?"

"A while," Nick said, though he was beginning to wonder if it had been long enough.

CHAPTER FIFTEEN

Twenty-one people in the Veterinary College were deemed to be at high risk for accidental exposure to *Yersinia* and received a prophylactic vaccine dispensed by the army. Their vaccine was over twenty years old and consisted of dead *Yersinia* bacteria. Its effectiveness was unknown, as USAMRIID labeled all data related to the vaccine as top secret. Everyone in Dana's lab, two other professors in the department, various clinicians in the veterinary school, and assorted support staff received routine shots.

Dana found the current vaccine wanting, and nowhere near as good as the two vaccines she was working on. The army's vaccine had to be taken repeatedly. Six injections were required over a two-year period before the vaccine was considered effective. Then there was a shot every other month for six months, followed by a shot every six months for eighteen months, and finally a booster once a year. With staff and students coming and going, maintaining the correct vaccine status of personnel was a complicated business.

Sitting at her computer, Dana matched people with dates of vaccination and verified correct time intervals. At the end of the morning, she concluded everyone was up-to-date except for Sheryl, who was still breast-feeding.

She double-checked the data. She was having a hard time concentrating. More often than not, the timed activation of the screen-saver told her that she was daydreaming again. Nick was coming back. She couldn't stop looking at her watch, stop listening for footsteps in the hall. When would he arrive? Would he come see her when he did? How would it feel to see him again? Why had he really come back?

Time seemed to have slowed; the seconds were strolling. Even the dice tumbling on the screen saver appeared to move slower than usual. There was no second hand on Dana's watch, just a minute hand that looked as if it were stuck. Somehow it managed to keep time with the computer's clock. What was taking Nick so long? Where was he? Avoiding her? Over the years, she thought he must have been. Now he was back, something he swore he would never do. And she never saw him coming. He did not cast a shadow before him.

An accident brought him back. What were the odds against a local outbreak of the plague appearing during the week of the VP's visit? She stared at the invisible forces in the van Gogh print. There was more to things than the eye could see. If there was an invisible force, like gravity, that held the planets and stars in place, another force that governed chemical reactions, and another that worked across great distances—why not a force that worked across time? A force that governed chance, and brought together two things that shouldn't be apart? A force that made coincidences happen.

Dana heard footsteps in the hall, and for the hundredth time she took a deep breath and steeled herself. The footsteps drew nearer. Her heart pounded and her stomach tightened. She faced the monitor as the footsteps came closer, into her lab. She bent over the keyboard, peering at the screen and a stream of words and numbers as if they commanded all her attention. There was a knock on her open door and she slowly turned her head.

Phillip Becker. He stood stooped in the doorway holding a bio-hazard bag. "I brought a lymph sample from Dudley Shaw for you to culture."

She stood up, disappointment and relief simultaneously flooding through her. Her heart was racing and her face was flushed. She didn't want Nick to see her like this. "Great." She took the bag from the octogenarian.

He seemed to study her from afar, squinting his eyes to see her better. He was a widower and looked like the Pope, only he had more hair. He dressed comfortably, favoring khaki slacks and brightly colored polo shirts. "I looked at the rats," he said. "They have symptoms compatible with bubonic plague. I'd say they had the disease."

His autopsy confirmed her blood analysis. "Thanks, Phillip." He'd been Brian's mentor and has been in the department longer than anyone. Any support she had in the department came from him. Now, and even back then, when Nick was around and she was still a post-doc.

"You did right," he said. "Seize opportunity when you can."

She wondered what he was referring to.

"What kind of specialist goes halfway?" he asked. "Deliberately shuts one eye? It was only right you talked to Mr. Shaw."

"Thanks, Phillip." She noticed he was sweating. "Are you okay?"

"I seem to have the flu. I'm going home."

"Sure it's not the plague?" she asked.

"Plain old flu, I'm afraid. I already checked my blood. My white blood cell count negates a bacterial infection. It appears to be viral in origin."

"I don't know how we're going to do this without you," she said. She was referring to herself. He was always there to back her up.

"Perhaps that's the point," he said with a twinkle in his eye. "With me out of the way, you'll have to use other resources." He smiled a benefic smile. "Say hello to Nick for me." He bowed slightly and shuffled away.

Dana took the biohazard bag to the quarantine room. Years ago she had tried to be discreet, but the affair was no secret. Not that anyone asked, and few were told; it was just too hard to hide. Like burying a bright light under a dark blanket—their transgression was out there for the whole world to see.

Nick could not bear it. It was one reason, though not the only reason, he left. She forced herself not to think of it, to focus on the task at hand. The definitive diagnosis of the plague was to grow the bacteria. *Yersinia* was easy to grow in the lab. All the bacteria needed was a little food and the right temperature. Dana prepared agar, which contained the nutrients. She weighed out the powder and dumped it in a flask along with a liter of distilled water. She sat the flask on a stirrer, dropped in a magnetic stir bar, and watched the liquid swirl round and round.

Once the agar was mixed, she poured it onto five round culture plates. The agar began to solidify immediately. She moved to the laminar flow hood, lit a Bunsen burner, and sterilized the hooped end of a long thin wand. Using the hoop, she scooped out a sample of Dudley's lymph node, which she smeared lightly across the top of the agar. She repeated the same process for the rat biopsies, and then placed the culture plates in the incubator. Left at twenty-eight degrees Celsius, the bacteria would divide and fill the plate within twenty-four hours.

She returned to her office. No sign of Nick. She sat down at her chair and couldn't stay seated. She jumped up. She couldn't just sit and wait for him—it would drive her insane. It was lunch time and she grabbed her car keys and headed to Sheryl's.

She turned on the radio. It was tuned to a Rock station, and the Stones were belting out a tune. In the last few years, Rock was the only music she could listen to; it was the only type of music Nick didn't care for. He was a musician, a guitarist, and he preferred folk music. Robin Wheeler was his favorite and Nick knew every lyric, every song. After Nick left, she had listened to Wheeler nonstop, reliving memories that now hurt too much to remember.

Dana reached Sheryl's house and pulled into the drive, inadvertently knocking over one of the boys' bikes. It crashed into a red wagon with a loud clank. Sheryl flung open the front door.

"Sorry, sorry," Dana got out of the car, hands raised as if Sheryl held a gun.

Sheryl put a finger to her mouth. "Penny's sleeping. I just got her down."

Dana followed her into the house, accepted the offer of iced tea, which they drank in the living room. "She's cutting a tooth," Sheryl said, leaning back on the couch. "She's okay. Miserable though. It shouldn't last."

"No fever?" Dana was seeing the plague everywhere.

"No."

Dana sipped the iced tea. Lemony and cold. No sugar, just the way she liked it. "Where are Ricky and Paul?" The boys were usually home for lunch. "You got them gagged and bound somewhere?"

"They're in Houston with my mother. I took them for the weekend and was supposed to get them yesterday, but with Penny sick, I couldn't go. They can stay for the week."

Dana picked up a Dr. Seuss book from the couch and flipped through it. *Green Eggs and Ham.* "I do not like them, Sam-I-Am."

"What is it? What's wrong?" Sheryl asked.

Dana closed the book. She stared at her hand and a line on her palm. A fortune-teller once told her she had a strong love line. "Nick's here."

"Nick who?" Sheryl sipped iced tea and crossed her legs.

Dana was astounded she didn't get it immediately. "Nick Biget."

Sheryl coughed, spilling iced tea down her chin. She dropped the glass on the table. "My God."

Dana put down the book and stood up. She couldn't stand to be still and circled Sheryl's living room. "There's a case of the plague in town. A senior doing a project collected four infected rats. The CDC is here and asked for Nick's help."

"Have you seen him?"

Dana stopped behind the couch and stared out the front window. "No."

"Good."

"I always knew he would come back."

"You need to stay away from him."

Sheryl never approved of the affair, and during its time, Dana and Sheryl had become estranged. Dana accepted what happened, gave in to the inevitable, and Sheryl thought she should fight it. Dana could not. Though a married man was the last person she would choose, what happened with Nick was never a choice. She was drawn to him, as if an invisible hand had pushed her at him. It was not something she could stop, always something beyond her control. The only good thing about Nick leaving was that her friendship with Sheryl was back on track.

Now Dana regretted coming. She knew Sheryl's advice before she opened her mouth. *Find someone else. A man who runs around on his wife will run around on you.* Maybe that was the real reason Dana had come. To hear the objection voiced out loud. She said, "I can't stay away. This is my disease."

"You're not an epidemiologist. Let the CDC take care of it. Stay out."

"Who will do the immunology? Run the assays?"

"I'll be back tomorrow. I'll do them. You should go away. Go see your parents. This is the worst thing that could happen to you."

Dana thought it was the best.

"He's married," Sheryl added. "You can't ignore that."

But Dana could. Had. Rachel-Anne was terminally ill and in an asylum indefinitely. Forever, as far as Dana was concerned.

"Maybe Rachel-Anne is better," Sheryl said. "Maybe he brought her with him."

Dana felt like she'd been punched. She hadn't thought of it. What if it were true? What if she had to see them together?

Sheryl struck again. "Even if he didn't bring her, maybe you should have the mindset that he did. They're the couple. Not you. Maybe they had more kids. Maybe they're finally happy."

Dana couldn't stand to hear any more. She walked to the door. "I've got to go. We have a two-o'clock meeting."

Sheryl got up and joined her. "Remember what he does to you. The effect he has on you. He's like a drug. You get obsessed. Leave him alone. For your own good. For his. Go while you have a chance."

In the car, heading back to campus, Dana railed against the advice. Staying away wasn't for her own good. Maybe it was good for their friendship, but not for her and Nick. This was an opportunity to settle something that had to be settled. Hadn't Becker intimated as much?

But Sheryl was right, too. This was dangerous territory. Seeing Nick was like opening a flood gate. He did something to her, took over her brain, commandeering her mind. Seven years had changed nothing. There was no chance of her staying away. Like a black hole, Nick was drawing her irrevocably towards him. She felt the pull as strong as ever. She had to be near him; already it was too late to stop herself.

Back at the vet school, Dana grabbed her lab coat. She could play McCoy's game and put on the coat, as she headed for the bathroom. Staring in the mirror, she combed her hair with her fingers and despaired of her hair. It was frizzed with the humidity and she wetted it down, yanked out a few strands of gray. She washed her face that looked too pale. She licked her lips that were chapped from the air conditioning. She didn't wear makeup and wished she had something now. She needed more time to prepare. Time to cut her hair, get in shape. How could she get up in the morning and have no clue today was the day he'd come back? Even her dreams had betrayed her.

Not that it mattered, she told herself as she washed her hands again. He was still married. Nothing had changed. That was why he had left and why he swore he would never be back. He thought it was best for them both and she gave her word she would never contact him. Though she didn't share his guilt, she understood it. His wife was sick. She was mentally ill and locked away in an asylum. For Dana, she had been easy to forget.

Rachel-Anne could be better now. Psychiatrists at the National Institute of Mental Health in Washington, D.C. were experts in treating schizophrenia, which was why Nick had moved north. She could be cured, happily married. For some, a lot could happen in seven years.

Dana buttoned the lab coat and washed her face again. The bathroom door banged open and Nellie swept in. She sashayed across the floor and dumped her oversized purse on the ledge over the sink, then studied Dana through the mirror.

"Getting all gussied up?" Nellie grabbed a tube of lipstick from her bag.

"I had to pee." Dana turned off the tap.

Nellie held out her lipstick. "Would you like some?"

"No."

"It would help. Add some color to your palette. You wouldn't look quite so grim."

Dana looked at her reflection. Did it show? Her face was white, as if her sickness was written all over her face.

"The lab coat isn't your color," Nellie said. "All that white washes you out. I can see why you don't wear one." She spritzed perfume on either side of her neck and then offered the bottle to Dana.

Dana shook her head. Nellie smelled like musk—something found in an Indian incense shop.

"Go on and smell like dead rats then."

Dana had to stop herself from raising her arm and checking her scent.

Nellie grabbed her bag and slung it over her arm. "Shall we go? Isn't it exciting—I just can't wait to see Nick."

Dana took a breath and steeled herself as she walked across the hall and into the main office. They were five minutes early and Dana thought they would be the first to arrive, but they were not. The conference room smelled of onions, and Karl sat at the end of the table in the chair she got for Nick. He was stuffing a burger into his mouth.

Nick had his back to her. She recognized his long torso, broad shoulders, and thick wavy brown hair. He turned his head and she saw her own discomfort and anguish in his face. His eyes met hers and she felt him inside her mind, as if he were touching her soul, bridging a long span of years. Then Nellie moved between them, and the connection was broken again.

CHAPTER SIXTEEN

McCoy arrived flushed, out of breath, and unpardonably late for his afternoon meeting. He had hoped to be early, had wished to speak with Nick privately, but it was not possible. The dean and university president kept him late at lunch. They wanted an update on the crisis. McCoy assured them everything was under control; the VP's trip would proceed as scheduled. They spent an hour discussing the graduation tents, and the order of guests and faculty as they entered the stadium, and now he was late. He had only a moment to greet Nick and to wave sheepishly at Michael Smith who had graciously accepted another cancelled meal. He walked to the head of the table and opened the meeting. He wanted to hear that the CDC had broken the case, that the four rats weren't infected with *Yersinia,* that Dudley Shaw had acquired his infection far, far away.

He began by introducing Nick Biget to his staff. Mid-sentence he was interrupted by loud hammering. McCoy strode to the window and yanked open the curtains. Outside, by the window ledge on a narrow scaffold, stood a painter hacking at chipped paint with a chisel and hammer.

McCoy jacked up the window. Hot, humid air assaulted him. "We're in the middle of a meeting here."

"That's all right," the painter said. "You won't disturb me."

"Come back later," McCoy barked. He slammed the window closed and thrust the curtains together. He went to the table, sat down, and offered Nick the floor.

The epidemiologist went to the chalkboard. In his mind, the outbreak was not that unusual. Over the past two decades, five to ten cases of bubonic plague appeared in the U.S. every year. Isolated cases, such as Dudley Shaw's, did not pose a serious threat.

McCoy's heart stopped racing. This was common. There was nothing unusual—nothing to interfere with the VP's trip.

Nick described the progression of plague epidemics. Bubonic plague, spread by fleas, usually appeared first. If an infected person lived long enough, the bacteria could move through the lymph to the lung and cause pneumonic plague. This was an infection of the lung that spread like a cold and was extremely contagious. "Right now, we're at an early stage and the prognosis looks good," Nick said. "So far we have four infected rats and one person infected with bubonic plague. With early diagnostics and treatment, we should stop the bacteria's spread. Our goal is to keep this from progressing past the bubonic phase."

News of the four infected rats gave McCoy pause. That was a definite setback. But apparently isolated cases of the plague were annual events. They happened every year and posed no serious danger. No one had pneumonic plague. The prognosis looked good. The VP's trip could proceed. He was settling back into his chair, a heavy load lifting off his mind, when there was a loud crack followed by the sound of breaking glass. Large chunks rained onto the carpet.

McCoy was back at the window. He jerked the curtains apart and saw the workman's stupid grin.

"Guess I missed," the workman said.

McCoy could only stare at the man.

"Not to worry. I'll have it fixed in a jiffy." The painter shoved the hammer through a loop in his overalls and climbed down the scaffold.

Hot air billowed into the room, lifting the curtains and letting in the light. McCoy, out of breath again, returned to his seat.

Nick continued as if interruptions like these were routine. "The question we need to answer is, where did the bacteria come from? The key, of course, is Dudley Shaw. Where was he infected?"

New Mexico, McCoy silently prayed. California. New Orleans.

"Since infected rats were found in Duane, we'll assume for now the bacteria are here," Nick said.

McCoy squeezed his hands together and felt his heart tighten.

Nick unfolded a map of Duane and spread it out on the middle of the table. Heads craned forward. With an index finger, Nick pointed to the southwest side of town where Dudley Shaw lived. "We know that ninety percent of the people infected with *Yersinia* are infected within a mile of their home. Perhaps Dudley was infected in the forest near his house."

McCoy mopped his head. His hair was soaking wet. Despite the air conditioner, with the broken window the room was growing hot. Nick, with a hand in his pocket, looked cool and comfortable as he continued.

"We know the plague is not a disease associated with hot climates. Since outbreaks are correlated with high rainfall, this could explain the appearance of *Yersinia* in Duane. There was a lot of rain this spring. More rain means more plants; more food means more animals. Due to an increased population, animals increase their range. They travel where they have not been before, and bring with them bacteria that aren't native to here."

A reasonable explanation, McCoy thought, and one that would satisfy the FBI, who were constitutionally suspicious of everything.

"What about bacterial resistance?" Dana Sparks inquired. "Why did Dudley die?"

Christ, she always said the last thing McCoy wanted to hear.

"Bacterial resistance is always a factor," Nick said, answering without looking at her.

McCoy groaned out loud. "But it's unlikely to be a factor in this case. Shaw didn't come in for treatment soon enough. He left it too late."

Nick agreed. "Antibiotic treatment has to be started early. Within twenty-four hours after infection. There's no telling how long the man was sick before he was admitted to the hospital."

"He said he started feeling sick Thursday," Sparks said. "He was admitted to the hospital on Saturday."

"We don't know when he was first exposed," McCoy said, but Sparks could not let it rest.

"*Yersinia* resistance could be a problem," she said.

Nick returned to his seat. "That's true," he said, addressing McCoy. "We've encountered highly resistant strains in the past."

McCoy shot his colleague a pleading glance. "There's no scientific evidence showing we're dealing with resistance, is there?"

"Dana has a valid point," Karl King said, interrupting. "We should test for it." He smiled at Sparks and she smiled back at him.

McCoy leaned on the table. Under his jacket, his shirt was soaking. There was a bright patch of light on the wall that hurt his eyes. When he was in the tropics, his pupils had been burned by the sun and he could not tolerate the light. He found it irritating. Himself, irritated. The older he got, the less patience he seemed to have. "Test for resistance then," he said. "Have you examined the dog?"

"Examined it?" King laughed. "We haven't found it."

McCoy felt his heart squeeze tight. He had assured Dean Duncan that problem was solved.

"We're working on it," King added. "We should locate the animal shortly."

McCoy shot Nick a worried glance. The apprehension on Nick's face did little to assuage his unease. They couldn't find the dog? That should have been the least of their problems.

"We can't find Carol Dupuis either," Jeff Tuttle piped in.

McCoy groaned aloud. The two CDC men were the most incompetent agents he'd ever met. Here was another simple problem that should have been easily solved.

"Carol is the student who trapped the infected rats," Jeff continued, as if no one could recall who she was. "She's not answering her home phone and no one from her lab knows where she lives. She was in contact with the infected rats and may be infected herself. She didn't show up at the lab today and wasn't there on the weekend. Anyway, her professor just returned from an overseas trip on Saturday. He has no idea where she trapped the rats. No one in the lab knows. But none of the other researchers have had similar problems with rodents' dying. Though, no one has collected any rodents recently. Anyway, we have to find her."

McCoy could not believe what he was hearing. A lengthy list of negative results and statements of the obvious. "Why don't you go through the university records," he suggested frostily. "Find her local address. If she's not there, try her parents."

Tuttle looked offended. "We're working on it," he said with great affront. "We should have that information soon."

He should have had it hours ago, McCoy thought. He glanced at his watch. It was fourteen-thirty. If he was going to get out of this inferno with his sanity, he would stop here. He stood up. "Anything else?"

It appeared there was. King felt he had to give a long and detailed explanation of his morning trip to Dudley Shaw's house that turned up absolutely nothing.

"His house was clean and tidy," Karl said. "There were no obvious signs of a flea or rodent infestation. Shaw lived alone. In any case, his sister's en route and we'll talk with her later. Perhaps she can shed more light on Shaw's last days. Help locate the dog."

"When is she expected?" McCoy asked.

"Three o'clock."

"Good." McCoy would wrap up this meeting and go see her himself. The last thing he needed was a grieving relative blabbing to the press.

King wouldn't stop. "We went through Dudley's refrigerator and freezer and removed samples of what appears to be wild meat. We saw a rifle and suspect Dudley's a hunter. Maybe he killed something infected with *Yersinia*."

A logical explanation, McCoy thought. Lots of rain and an increase in wildlife expanding their territory and moving to Duane. Dudley was most likely a hunter. He went out in the woods and shot a squirrel or rabbit infected with *Yersinia*. "Test the meat," McCoy said. "Dr. Sparks, immediately."

"Yes, *sir*," she said.

Fleas from a dog belonging to Dudley's proximal neighbors had also been collected, and Karl wanted her to test those as well.

"No problem," she said.

There was no trace of the sarcasm she reserved for McCoy. "Anything else?" he asked.

"Should we try and trap rodents by Dudley's house?" Charlotte Lane said.

Jeff Tuttle twisted his diamond stud and said he'd set traps that afternoon.

No one else had anything to add and McCoy declared the meeting over. "Dismissed. We'll meet here tomorrow at oh-eight-hundred hours." By then the window would be repaired, the painter would be finished, hopefully the dog would be found, Carol Dupuis would be located, and the source of *Yersinia* shown to be an infected sample of meat. Was it too much to hope for?

Apparently. He could not even close the meeting. King was objecting to the crowd invited to attend.

"I mean, do we need researchers whose specialties are toxicosis and histoplasmosis? Visitors to the department? If we need extra manpower, we'll ask, but otherwise there's no reason to waste everyone's time. The *Yersinia* specialist should be help enough."

McCoy didn't miss the beaming smile the CDC man shot Dana Sparks. He stared at the grinning lunatic in wonderment. The CDC agents couldn't find a dog, they couldn't find a student, and here they were turning away offers of help? The only positive development was that no new people were infected with the plague, but at this rate how long would that last?

McCoy held up his hand. "You let me worry about wasting time. I told the university president we'll assist you in every way and we will. Until further notice, this whole department is at your disposal. Meeting dismissed."

CHAPTER SEVENTEEN

At the close of the meeting, people were on their feet, responding to McCoy's order to move out. Dana got caught behind the lumbering Charlie Lane and the jovial Karl King. Far ahead, Nick left with McCoy, flanked by Nellie and Michael.

Karl fell into step with her. "Can you come to Headquarters and get the samples?" He had small teeth and a wide smile that showed them all. His hair was a white-silver streaked with blond and his eyes were brown, the color of mud. Despite his smile, he seemed deeply sad.

They went down the hall together. He was walking too close, kept bumping her elbow with his arm. She increased her pace. Nick was already out of sight.

"I hear you worked with Nick," Karl said.

She wondered how he knew, if Nick had told him. "For a while."

"Congratulations on your vaccine."

She nodded in acknowledgement. He knew about that too.

"He said you were good."

"He did?" Dana slowed down, and forced herself not to ask what else Nick said. Instead, "Have you known him long?"

"Since medical school."

Dana looked at Karl with renewed interest.

"He was the best man at my wedding." There was a pause. "Now I'm divorced."

"Sorry." She guessed that explained his sadness.

They reached the end of the hall and Karl lunged ahead, threw open the door, and there was Nick, looming before her, an arm's reach away. She was close enough to smell his sweat, a scent she had forgotten. How could she forget?

He nodded hello, took a step back, and turned around.

They'd been given a small office that was packed with furniture. It held three desks and an over-sized fridge with an orange biohazard sign. Karl opened the fridge and grabbed an orange plastic bag. He pulled out a small vial. "Fleas." She saw black flecks floating in fluid. He held up a capillary tube. "Dog's blood." Then a Ziploc bag. "Meat." He offered her the biohazard bag.

The bag was heavy. She folded down the top and stared at Nick. He still had his back to her and was leaning over a desk, madly typing at a laptop.

"If you're busy, I could Fed-Ex the samples to Atlanta," Karl said.

"This is a priority. I have my orders."

Karl laughed loudly. "I appreciate the help," he said, and smiled a wide smile.

"I should have the results in forty-five minutes."

"I can help you if you want," Karl said.

Dana wanted to be alone. She needed time to think. "I can do it." She looked at Nick, enthralled with his screen. He was already gone, focused on work. "I'll let you know the results when I get them."

"I'll be waiting." Karl flicked his eyebrows up and down and beamed at her.

She slowly backed toward the door. Nick acknowledged her departure with a lift of his head.

She went to her lab, began the assays, rationalizing Nick's vast distance. This was the way he was at work—preoccupied on the task at hand. It signified nothing. He could compartmentalize. He built strict boundaries. It allowed him to focus, and made him good. It was what enabled him to leave.

She'd learned much from him. At the beginning she didn't want him as her supervisor. When she relocated to the vet school and her supervisor quit, she requested Phillip Becker. He wouldn't take her on. He was making noises about retiring and didn't want the responsibility. She was stuck with Nick. It was as if she recognized the danger in advance but in the end was powerless to do anything about it.

He wasn't happy either. She was his only student and he made it clear from the start that she couldn't expect much help. He was busy fine-tuning a computer program that used chaos theory to predict the course of infectious disease. And this from a man who believed that life was a series of random accidents—essentially a mistake.

He didn't do much benchwork and he traveled a lot. He warned her that she'd be on her own. It was he who pushed her toward the monoclonal antibody technology; he who helped her sacrifice the mice. Dana couldn't kill them. She never expected the mice to fight back. Even research mice wouldn't die willingly. Nick had no trouble with them. He had a way with animals. They would walk into his hands and he would calmly snap their necks, dislocate their spinal cords. The mice never knew what hit them, never saw him coming. She could have learned a lot from them.

The antibody work got complicated fast. When she was ready to give it up, he pushed her on. She learned that every unexpected result had something to teach. When things went awry, Nick didn't turn away. He delved deeper, probing for answers to explain what went wrong.

He was that way in his personal life too, with his wife and her schizophrenia. Nick hung in there, refusing to give up, always ready to try the latest treatment. There would be a cure, she would get better; he would wait.

Then Rachel-Anne slipped into a coma after she tried to poison herself with carbon monoxide. She would likely have died if the car hadn't run out of gas. Frank, paddling in the pool, near the point of exhaustion, would have died too if Nick hadn't arrived home early. When Rachel-Anne recovered, she was committed to an asylum and Nick started to travel. In his absence, Dana realized what he meant to her. When he was gone, something big was missing from her life.

Four months after they started working together, they went to a meeting in Galveston. Nick was the keynote speaker and they drove down to the coast together. They had planned to go for the day, but his pickup broke down and they had to stay the night. All the rooms at the Grand Hotel were taken, but two of Nick's colleagues doubled up to give him a room. He gave her the bed and took the floor, as a gentleman would.

It was late September. The windows were open, and a gentle ocean breeze smelled of salt. The moon was full and filled the room with a magical silver light. He fell asleep quickly. She lay alone in the king-sized bed willing him to awake, but he slept on. Finally she went to him, quietly removed her clothes, and crept beneath the sheet beside him. He wore boxers. She laid against the length of him; he radiated heat. When he didn't flinch, she placed her hand on his waist. He stirred and threw his arm around her.

He woke before dawn, his body tensing completely. Then he was up and pulling on his pants. He needed coffee. He would be right back.

It was a long drive home. He said he was married and there was nothing left to say. It was a gray cold day. The air was filled with rain that did not fall.

He started traveling. The very next day, he accepted a last minute invitation to a meeting on HIV and took off for Vancouver. Then over to Europe, Africa, and the Far East. He came and went without notice, making it clear that Galveston was a topic they would not discuss.

Then, one Friday night he appeared on her doorstep, red-faced and furious. He waved an envelope in her face. "What the hell is this?"

She took the envelope, pulled out the letter. It was from the *Journal of Molecular Immunology* acknowledging the acceptance of an article she wrote. She had put Nick as the second author. Months earlier, she had put the article on his desk and when it reappeared unmarked on hers, she assumed he approved and mailed it off.

"How could you do it?" he said. "Without asking? Without my knowledge?" He raised his hands. "Just do it."

"I thought you knew."

"I had no idea."

"I'm sorry."

"Don't do it again."

He stormed out. Dana watched from the porch as the gravel hit the underbelly of his pickup as he reversed up the drive. She wondered if it was the paper they were really discussing.

An hour later he was back looking sheepish and contrite. He was nervous, pulling at his hair, whistling a tune, unable to meet her eyes. He apologized for losing his temper. "I don't know what happened."

"Would you like to come in?"

"No." He handed her the letter from the journal. "I liked it."

"I thought you would."

"I guess it was the surprise."

"I should have been more forthright."

"You couldn't be more so." He blushed when he said this, a red sheen burning beneath his five o'clock stubble. "I wasn't asleep you know. In Galveston." He finally looked in her eye.

"Come in."

"I'd like to stay, but—"

"Then stay."

She took his hand and pulled him inside.

It was dinnertime, and he insisted on cooking. That night she learned among other things that he could cook, sing, and dance. He made a killer spaghetti sauce while Beethoven's Fifth Symphony played. He hummed along, conducting with a spatula.

After dinner and a bottle of wine, he got a Robin Wheeler CD from his car and they danced. He sang songs in her ear she had never heard before and would know by heart before long. At midnight he said he had to go, but he never left. He kicked off his shoes. Before long he removed his shirt. They made love on the living room floor as the CD played. Then again in the shower before he was going to leave. Then at dawn when the birds began to sing, and later, after breakfast, when he said he really had to go.

He left her his Wheeler CD and the sock he couldn't find. He stepped into his shoes. His ankles were bare, his laces untied. She bent down and tied them up. He reached for her hand and pulled her up. He had changed his mind about leaving.

It was like he was two people. The man who went to work was serious and somber, while the other man kicked off his shoes and had songs in his heart. He brought music and love into her life.

The mild winter passed and the spring turned to summer and the abundant time ran together; endless nights when music played and wine never ran out. It was a season of excess, as if they both knew it would never last, that their time would expire, as it had. A promising new treatment in Washington for schizophrenia called him away. It was over. He would not call. She could not call him. They would never see each other again.

He left behind one tangible gift. It was a red plastic poppy he picked up in Montreal to honor Remembrance Day and those killed in war. It was appropriate—fitting for the carnage he left behind. Now he was back. Why did he come? There was so much left unsaid.

The timer rang. The assay was done. The results were negative. There was no *Yersinia* in the meat, fleas, or the neighbor's dog's blood. Dana washed her hands and left the quarantine room.

She reached her lab and stopped short. Nick stood in the doorway of her office. Her heart began to pound and her stomach tightened. She caught the light in Nick's eye before he looked away.

She walked toward him. His same old scent wafted toward her as his familiar bulk filled her space. He was half a head taller; the top of her head came to his nose, and her mouth reached the indent of his clavicle. Two parts of a whole.

"It's been forty-five minutes," he said.

"That long already?"

"I could come back later."

"That's a change."

"Do you have the results?"

It sounded like he was losing patience. "Negative," she said.

He looked puzzled. "What?"

She stared away from his eyes. They were blue, the color of the ocean, and as changeable. Their shade varied in the light. Right now in the lab they looked green. "There's no exposure. The samples are clean. As in testing negative."

He took a step backwards, putting distance between them. "I thought as much."

When it came to work, Nick possessed an uncanny intuition that didn't translate to his personal affairs. "Where do you think *Yersinia* originated?" she asked, seeking neutral ground. When studying disease, the origin was of paramount importance. As his mathematical models showed, the situation at time zero defined the course of an outbreak.

"My guess is the forest."

She gave him the printout with the ELISA results.

He studied the paper and she studied him. His dark hair had begun to turn gray. He still wore it long, and it curled at his neck. It was receding on top, but he took no pains to hide this. His eyebrows were thick, his nose straight and sharp, and his lips pale and pink. There was a dimple in his chin and one by his cheek that appeared when he smiled. He always cut himself shaving and was cut now, though it didn't stand out—it was covered by facial hair. Nick's five o'clock shadow came early.

"I'll take these to Karl." Nick looked up, took a step toward the door.

Don't go, Dana thought. She wanted to move in front of him, block his way, throw her arms around him, and make him stay. She said, "Would you like some coffee?"

He paused, ran a hand through his hair. His tie was gone and the collar of his shirt was unbuttoned. His chest hair was going gray. She remembered how he looked in the morning, or coming home after a long trip. How could she have forgotten the power he had over her? "Coffee would be great," he said.

They went to her office. A full pot was waiting. She poured two cups of coffee with a shaky hand and carefully handed him one. "What now?" she said.

"We'll start with where we are."

"Which is?"

"Rather in the dark."

"Exactly." She took a small sip of coffee.

"I'll go to the hospital. See what Dudley's sister has to say. So far, the state has no other cases. It could be an isolated incident. We may never know where it started. The important thing is that it ends."

"I don't think that's the important thing."

"What do you mean?"

"*Yersinia* shouldn't be here. It's too far south. What brought it?"

"If it's contained, it's inconsequential."

"What if it's not?"

"It will be."

He was always so certain of himself, until he wasn't. She took another sip of coffee. "How long will you be here?"

"Not long. Until we're done. I've got a lot going on back home."

How is work, she meant to say, but she slipped. "How is Rachel-Anne?" She looked at her coffee, took another sip.

"Dead."

Coffee flew from Dana's mouth as she choked. The coffee spilled on her hand, ran down her arm to her wrist. She put the cup down on her desk. "*What?*"

"In August. She'd been on life-support three years."

"That was seven months ago."

Nick stared at his coffee cup. "I thought you knew. I was surprised I didn't hear from you."

"When you left, you said don't call. You expected me to?"

He shrugged. "My secretary sent out death notices."

"I didn't get one."

He shrugged again. "There was an announcement in the *Duane Eagle*. Did you stop getting the paper?"

"I don't read obituaries."

He smoothed down his hair. "I assumed you knew."

She shook her head. "You were always the one who said assume nothing."

There were footsteps in her lab and Betty rushed in. "Oh, good, you're here. I got a call from the clinic." She paused, as if just seeing Nick. She patted down the sides of her stiff hair, blinking heavily. "Frank is in bad shape. You need to get down there."

She had forgotten her dog. Dana was out the door with Nick at her heels. He pounded down the stairs beside her. "*Frank?*" he said, "My Frank?"

He was her dog now and she found him alone in Tim Sweeny's animal room, sitting on the cold cement floor, long pink tongue hanging out, body trembling. She bent down and threw her arms around his neck.

Nick knelt beside her, holding out his hand. "Hey buddy."

Frank's tail began to wag. He rested his head on her shoulder and looked past her, at Nick, his first master, whose wife had tried to kill him. Nick, who left him behind—who left everything behind.

Frank strained toward him and Dana let him go. He lurched sideways toward Nick and licked his face with a sweep of his tongue as he fell. Nick caught him as he went, breaking his fall. Frank's tail wagged again, he let out a loud sneeze, and his trembling stopped. The room went silent as his breath went still. Drops of frothy blood trickled from his mouth and nostrils.

CHAPTER EIGHTEEN

Death was an unpleasant consequence of life and war that could not be avoided. Although McCoy had experience relaying bad news to grieving family members, he never got used to it. Standing in the hospital basement outside the all-denominational chapel, McCoy rehearsed the words of comfort he would say to Dudley Shaw's sister, Tabitha Tott, who sat at the head of the chapel, head bowed in prayer.

McCoy had missed her at the airport. Her flight landed early and she was gone by the time he arrived. He thought she'd go directly to the hospital but she did not, and McCoy had been waiting for some time. He was about to leave, honor his promise to Margaret for another driving lesson, when a nurse informed him Mrs. Tott had arrived.

Normally, notification of mortality was a job for the attending physician, but Dr. Taversham was in surgery, as he had been all afternoon, and McCoy could not waste time waiting for him. He was prepared to do whatever it took to learn where Dudley Shaw had acquired his infection.

There was nothing to gain by further delay, and he entered the chapel. The room was small and comforting. Near the door stood a marble stand filled with holy water, and McCoy blessed himself. He said a small prayer as he walked up the aisle. He turned down the front pew and Mrs. Tott looked up.

She looked about ninety. If Dudley was sixty-five, his sister was considerably older. Her eyes were red and puffy, and her white hair was done up in an untidy bun. A pillbox hat on her head lilted to one side. She clutched a rosary in arthritic fingers, and a heavy gold cross hung from her neck. Catholic, McCoy thought. At least she had faith to support her.

He sat down beside her. "I'm Dr. McCoy. I'm afraid I have bad news."

The old woman stared straight ahead at an altar overflowing with bright plastic flowers. "I'm aware that Dudley is dead."

How did she know, McCoy wondered. Who had she been talking to? How much did she know? "I'm sorry for your loss, ma'am."

Mrs. Tott crossed herself. "What killed him?"

"A bacterial infection," McCoy said. "The hospital is still running tests." Though McCoy did not wish to be less than truthful in the house of the Lord, McCoy and Taversham agreed this was the way they would handle the nature of Dudley's disease. A conclusive diagnosis would not be made for at least a week. McCoy moved quickly on. "We can talk outside if you wish."

Mrs. Tott said nothing. She made no effort to stand.

"Or here is fine."

"When can I see him?"

McCoy hedged. According to Taversham, Dudley had exhibited classical symptoms of the plague—his extremities were black. McCoy did not want the sister to see the body. "You'll have to ask the doctor," McCoy said. He watched the candles flickering in unison at the side of the chapel. Nearly every candle was ablaze. He tried to steer the conversation to Shaw's last days. "We know your brother visited you at Easter. How long did he stay? For the weekend? Longer?"

She sighed. "The weekend."

"Did he come straight back to Duane?"

"Where else would he go?"

She was going to be difficult, McCoy saw. He pushed on with his inquiry. "Do you know if Dudley had recent visitors?"

Mrs. Tott bowed her head. "What did he die from?" Her lip quivered and her voice trembled.

"Ma'am, I'm sorry. He died from a bacterial infection." McCoy spoke staring up at the ceiling. If there was anything worse than a woman who cried, it was a woman who wanted to cry but would not allow it. He heard a sniffle, then another, and dared glance at her. A single tear tracked down her cheek.

McCoy gazed helplessly at the candles. He rose and walked toward the altar, pulling coins from his pocket. He tossed them in a small basket, picked up a book of matches, and lit the three remaining candles. He returned to the pew.

Tabitha Tott was wiping her eyes with a crumpled tissue. "I'll be fine," she said.

McCoy silently applauded her effort at self-control. "When did you talk to your brother last?"

"A week ago. I talk to him every week. He's always home. When he didn't answer Saturday, I knew something was wrong and I called the police. I came as soon as I could. He was strong. I didn't think he'd go so fast." She swatted her damp swollen face with the tissue and sniffled loudly. "To think this happened just before his big trip. What kind of bacteria got him?"

"You'll have to ask his doctor," McCoy reiterated. "We won't know more until the hospital finishes running their tests. As I said, it could take a week."

"A week!" Mrs. Tott cried. "How could you treat him if you didn't know what he had? What about antibiotics? Who dies from a bacterial infection these days?"

"Bacterial infections are more serious in the elderly. And we don't know how long your brother was infected. Can you tell me, when you talked to him, did he mention he was feeling under the weather?"

"Elderly? He was only sixty-five. He shouldn't have died first. I was supposed to go before him."

"I'm sorry. Now I must ask, did he have any out-of-town visitors?" McCoy hoped if Shaw hadn't contracted the plague elsewhere, then someone had brought the bacteria from elsewhere to him.

But according to Mrs. Tott, Dudley wasn't a visitor sort of man.

McCoy tried to hide his disappointment. "We need to know all we can about your brother's habits. Where he went, what he did. Who were his friends, his doctor and dentist. Where did he shop and hunt?"

"Oh, Dudley hasn't hunted for years," Mrs. Tott said.

And McCoy's high hopes that Dudley was infected when hunting were immediately dashed.

"The only company he needed was his dog. I—"

McCoy interrupted her. "Yes, the dog, ma'am. Do you have any idea where we can find the dog?" He thought of the hapless dogcatcher, unable to locate the animal.

"Any idea?" Mrs. Tott straightened her hunched shoulders. "Well I've got him, haven't I?"

She had the dog? "Ah." McCoy was afraid to ask how she managed to find him, though he found great solace in the fact. Finally, a breakthrough. Neither the CDC nor the dogcatcher could find the animal, but the sister could. One of their biggest problems was solved. Things could turn out fine after all. McCoy silently listed the positive developments. The dog could be tested. Thirty-six hours had passed since the disease appeared in Duane and no other victims were identified. It appeared as if Dudley *was* an isolated case. They were fortunate he wasn't a visitor kind of man. His disease was an aberration, an anomaly, an exception.

"May I see the dog?" McCoy asked gently, for in truth, the question was not completely forthright. McCoy would have to do more than see him; he would have to confiscate him.

"Bingo?" Mrs. Tott said. "You want to see Bingo? What on earth for?"

"There are some infections people get from animals," he said.

"You mean rabies? You think Dudley has rabies?"

"If I could just see the dog, ma'am," McCoy said.

She wouldn't budge. "There's nothing wrong with him. Well, he's lame and old, and nearly blind, but take my word for it, he's not foaming at the mouth. He's not vicious. There's nothing wrong with him."

McCoy couldn't take her word for it, but he couldn't tell her that. "There may be symptoms we can't see," he said.

She frowned at him. "What kind of symptoms can't you see?"

McCoy stood up and offered his arm. "Ma'am, if there are any, believe me, I'll point them out to you."

She wound her rosary into a ball and slipped it into an oversized purse. "Point out things you can't see," she muttered, but at least she stood up.

She shrugged off McCoy's offer of assistance. Holding her head high, she tottered up the aisle toward the door. McCoy wondered where she had the dog.

Outside in the hallway, the fluorescent tube lights were blinding. It was the dinner hour and candy-stripers were pushing carts laden with food trays toward the elevator. The air smelled of stew and reminded McCoy of the time. His daughter was awaiting her driving lesson.

They reached the elevator and McCoy impatiently punched the button. The doors opened and Karl King stepped out. He wore a self-satisfied smirk on his face that matched his tone, "I've found Bingo. I notified the dog-catcher."

"You did what?" Tabitha cried. Her voice was shrill and harsh.

Karl scratched the back of his neck and looked at McCoy helplessly. McCoy had recently read that ninety percent of people weren't fit to hold their jobs, and believed at least in the civilian setting, it was so.

"The pound is down the street and I called the dog-catcher on my cell phone." Unbelievably, Karl worked his phone out of his pocket and held it up.

McCoy shot him a furious look. "How do you know you got the right dog?"

"He was in Dudley's car." Karl said. "The one parked at his house is now out in the lot."

McCoy's heart suddenly squeezed tightly in his chest. In this investigation, anything that could possibly go wrong was going that way. The CDC couldn't find a lame, blind dog, and now Tabitha Tott had apparently taken her brother's car. "That car is under quarantine," he said.

The sister glared at him. "It's my car. You can't take it."

Karl explained that Tabitha couldn't use the car or the house because of the contagious nature of Dudley's bacterial infection.

"What contagious bacteria?" Tabitha asked. "I thought the tests would take a week."

Karl King stroked his dirty goatee and looked at McCoy for help.

"Until we're absolutely positive the bacterium is not contagious, we have to assume that it is," McCoy said.

Karl mercifully changed the subject and asked if the car was a fifty-five Thunderbird.

"Fifty-seven," Tabitha said.

"It's a nice car," Karl said. "Would you be interested in selling it?"

McCoy could not believe what he was hearing. Apparently neither could Tabitha Tott.

"No," she said, sharply. "It's my car now and I want it. I want my dog. I want to stay in my brother's house. I want to know what killed him."

McCoy felt sweat stream down his body. Tabitha Tott had been in contact with the dog and was now potentially exposed to bubonic plague. She would need prophylactic antibiotics and he didn't think she'd take them easily. What if she brought infected fleas into the hospital? How could an investigation go so wrong?

The elevator doors opened and Dr. Taversham came out. He was thin, balding and appeared exhausted. In his late-thirties, he was too young in McCoy's mind to be the hospital specialist in infectious disease. Taversham nodded to McCoy. "I'm glad I caught you. We just got our second case."

"Second case of what?" Tabitha Tott demanded.

Taversham looked at the old woman as though noticing her for the first time. McCoy introduced her.

Over a substantial tan, Taversham's face burned red. He offered Tabitha a slender hand. "I'm sorry to keep you waiting. I'm Dr. Taversham. I was treating your brother."

"I want to see him," Tabitha Tott said. "I want to know what killed him."

"Let's go to my office," Taversham said.

But Tabitha Tott shook her head and insisted on going to the morgue.

CHAPTER NINETEEN

Frank's still body lay stretched out in the backseat, swathed in sunlight. He looked peaceful to Dana, as if he had died with a smile on his face. His pain was gone, but she could not shake her sense of guilt that she had been in part responsible for it. Would he have lived longer if she had just left him alone? Would he have lived long enough to see Nick, who came back in time?

Nick sat beside her, twisting knobs on the radio, as if afraid of the silence. He insisted on helping her bury Frank, said he was too heavy for her to carry, and that it was his responsibility. Frank was his dog first.

Dana didn't argue. She adjusted the rearview mirror so she could see Frank. Sunlight dappled his graying coat. He could have been sleeping. It was too beautiful a day to die. She wanted him home, waiting by the porch, or lying in his basket, wagging his tail. She missed him already.

Nick found a radio station he liked and listened to a weather report. There was a high probability that a tropical storm would strike Texas before the weekend. Other than that, the weather for graduation on Friday and Saturday looked great. Highs in the low eighties by Saturday, and nineties on Sunday.

"That will save us," Nick said.

She glanced at him. They could be saved? "What?"

"The heat. Temperatures above eighty-two degrees kill plague epidemics. No one knows why."

"Oh." He was talking about work.

"There were three incidents of the plague last year in New Mexico," Nick said, as he stared out the window. "Five in Arizona the year before that. Your vaccine should help."

He knew about the vaccine and was aware of her research. He'd kept up—he wasn't as detached as she thought.

An ad ended and headline news came on. A Somali warlord warned there would be repercussions against America if compensation was not made for the dead. "We're not the terrorists here," the warlord claimed.

The U.S. said otherwise, and incoming intelligence reports seemed to verify the American assertion that a weapons and ammunition warehouse had been targeted, and not a hospital or mosque. Nonetheless, the U.S. conceded that nearby buildings may have been unintentionally damaged in the strike.

Nick was leaning forward, listening intently, until she turned down the dirt road leading to her house. He sat up straight, peering out the windshield. "You still live here?"

She glanced at him. "It's my house. I bought it."

"I didn't know."

He would have been able to find her had he looked. All this time he could have picked up his phone and dialed her number and she would have answered, but the call had never been made.

She drove down the rutted driveway and parked. There was no sign of Anthony or Judy. Dana whistled loudly and caught Nick's puzzled glance.

"I think we're going to have to carry him," he said.

"I have two other dogs."

"Oh." He sounded surprised once more, as if he hadn't expected her life to change in seven long years.

He got out of the car, retrieved Frank, and followed her across the field toward the trees and what would soon be a grave. He lay Frank gently down in the shade and she got a shovel from the shed.

Soon he was digging, bent double, dirt flying. Sweat ran down his face, his shirt was soaked, sticking to his skin. She got Frank's red blanket from his bed and covered him up. Nick refused her offer to help, and she sat down against a white pine in a bed of soft needles.

Frank lay beside her. She would never again come home to find him waiting. She would never scoop Alpo into his bowl, or feed him by hand when he wouldn't eat. She would never see him in the car again with his head hanging out the window and the wind blowing back his ears. He was gone, gone for good, poor Frank, left alone for most of the day, on the last day of his life. Dana lowered her head. She missed him. He left behind too much empty space. Dana remembered well the feeling of overwhelming emptiness. It swamped her when Nick first moved away. He had become threaded into her life, woven into the fabric of her being that had been ripped to shreds when he left. It had taken a long time to stitch the remnants back together. Now, Nick was here and Frank was gone, leaving a ghost to fill the places he left behind forever.

A lump grew in her throat. She wiped her face and hugged her knees. A sudden wind swept down from the north and bent the tall blades of grass. The wildflowers bowed to the grave.

With a start, she realized Nick was staring at her, standing near a too-big hole, leaning on his shovel. His face was streaked with dirt. He'd rolled up his sleeves and tied his handkerchief around his forehead to catch the sweat.

"I think the hole is big enough," she said, staring at dark earth. With Nick, there was excess or nothing—no middle ground.

A snapping and cracking came from the woods and he turned. Branches shook as Anthony and Judy sprang from the forest. Anthony ran for the blanket and nosed it to the side, exposing Frank's flank. Judy barked loudly, as if trying to rouse him from his sleep.

Dana watched Nick make friends with the dogs. He threw a lump of dirt for Anthony to fetch, and scratched the spot on Judy's belly that always itched. He found the special places, his hand drawn to them as if they ached for him.

The sun was sinking behind the trees when he laid Frank in his grave. Dana could not watch the dirt fall on the blanket. She took the other dogs up to the porch. She knew she never would have been able to bury him alone. Nick was right; she needed help. He made things easy for her.

And now Rachel-Anne was dead. The unthinkable was real, what she never dared wish for.

Nick came up to the porch, wiping his hands with his handkerchief.

"Would you like a beer?" she asked, the first item on a long list of things she had to offer.

"No." Then, as an afterthought, "Thanks."

"Is that a yes or a no?"

"No, thank you. I should get to the hospital. Talk to Dudley's sister."

"I'll drive you. I'd like to talk to her."

"As you should."

"Maybe after, we could have dinner."

"I have a lot of work to do."

He was blowing her off. "Me too," she said, inanely.

He looked at his watch. "Karl will wonder what happened to me. My cell phone's in your car." He was already heading up the driveway.

She turned to the dogs. "Stay." But they followed behind, bouncing at Nick's heels.

She ran after him, wondering why he couldn't stay for half an hour. Did he find her that objectionable? The investigation would go on without him. He could be here with her; his wife was dead, there was no more conflict, but he was in a rush to go.

Dana fell into step beside him and found the nerve to ask the question that was on her mind all day. "Why did you come?"

He reached the car and stopped. His eyes were deep blue now that the sun was gone. The whites of his eyes were bright. "You really want to know?"

"I do."

She heard him exhale and held her breath.

"Between you and me?"

"Of course." She waited for his answer listening to the loud beat of her heart in her ear.

"*Yersinia* at this low altitude—it's strange, atypical. But you already know that."

Her heart stopped, her breath stalled, hope died.

"I didn't have a choice," Nick said. "I had to come. I knew it would be awkward."

She tried to keep a straight face. He hadn't come because his wife had died and he was free. He had no choice. "Is it the VP's visit?"

"I'm sworn to secrecy." Nick said.

"I'll take that as a yes. You think there's a connection between the two?"

He opened the car door. "I didn't say that. I'm here to rule that possibility out."

"Can I ask you something?" She didn't wait for him to answer. "Why didn't you take the job when Brian died? I know it was offered to you."

He gazed across the field to the woods. "I didn't want to intrude." He slowly turned his head and met her eyes. "You had your life. You'd moved on. You—"

From inside the car, his cell phone rang. He opened the door, pre-empting the conversation. It didn't matter why he came, Dana thought, as he answered. The important thing was that he was here; the effect mattered, not the cause.

Karl was calling. She listened to Nick's end of the conversation: "Oh. Okay. Which hospital? Right now? No. Yes. I don't know. No, I can make it. I'm on my way."

Nick closed his phone. "There's another case of the bubonic plague. A senior at the university. I've got to meet McCoy at the hospital. He wants to know where you are. He wondered if you did the assay." Nick looked maddeningly contrite. "Already I'm causing you trouble."

"You're not to blame."

"I shouldn't have come."

"As you said, you had no choice."

"I'm sorry."

She drove to the hospital. He sat as far away from her in the seat as he could get. There was no sign of the man who sang in the shower and danced barefoot in the grass. The cool detached professional was in full attendance and back on topic, reeling off statistics. A second case of bubonic plague in twenty-four hours bode badly. Where were the rats and infected fleas? There was a disconnect. "Something's quite wrong," he said.

She did not disagree.

CHAPTER TWENTY

The hospital lights were muted at night, but the hallway seemed bright to McCoy. He stood with Karl outside a makeshift quarantine room, waiting for Nick before they interviewed the latest patient. McCoy heard the low murmur of a television and imagined a late-breaking news report. A ringing phone evoked fear of the hungry press corps. There was another case now—a student, a popular football player with many friends—and undoubtedly a cell phone. Was it lunacy for McCoy to think he could keep this quiet any longer?

He checked his watch. Where the hell was Nick? Karl had no idea. Nick went to Sparks' lab and disappeared. Sparks vanished too, and McCoy was furious. How did it look to the CDC to have a plague specialist who couldn't be reached in the middle of a—situation? According to Nellie, she left without a word, leaving her lab wide open and her quarantine room, with its contagious material, unlocked. She left no word of the results of the test she was supposed to run that afternoon. Such was his expert! Inside his quarantine gear, McCoy felt rivers of sweat streak down his skin.

He felt better when he saw Nick hurrying down the hall. Less so when he saw Sparks in tow. She mumbled something about an emergency.

"This is the only emergency I'm interested in," McCoy said. "We've got a new case. What did the assay show?"

"Clean. There was no *Yersinia* in Dudley's meat or the neighbor's dog's blood or fleas."

"I'll be damned." Karl King frowned and tapped a clipboard across his thigh.

It was a quandary McCoy didn't like. How in hell was Shaw infected? The *Yersinia* had to come from somewhere. Would the football player know?

Nick and Sparks were suiting up. She did not have to be here. "Dr. Sparks, you may go."

"I'd like to talk to the student."

"She is a plague specialist," Nick said, taking her side.

"Suit up," McCoy said, though she was midway through the process. They were dealing with a Class 3 contagion and anyone entering a quarantine area had to wear scrubs, double gloves, paper boots, hair-covering, and mask. They weren't his rules. Under these circumstances, she seemed to take no issue with compliance. Perhaps because Nick was here. According to Nellie, they had a history—but that was gossip McCoy was determined to ignore.

As they dressed, Karl summarized the case. Jack Dowel was an elite athlete, twenty-two years old. He had driven himself to the hospital late that afternoon, presenting with nausea, headache, high fever, and swollen glands, primarily in the groin. Karl had examined him and clinically verified a presumptive diagnosis of bubonic plague. The disease was in the early stage. The patient displayed no signs of hemorrhage, circulatory collapse, respiratory distress, or organ failure. He was being treated with the triple antibiotic cocktail and his prognosis was good. He'd been given a sedative but it was wearing off and Taversham said he'd be able to answer questions.

When he was through reciting the medical report, Karl positioned the mask over his face, clicked the end of a pen, and opened a door that bore the sign: RESTRICTED AREA. AUTHORIZED PERSONNEL ONLY. CLASS III CONTAGION. They all traipsed into the room.

From his bed, the second victim took one look at them and screamed. He kicked his food tray and it careened toward them, smashing into the wall. "Get out," he yelled. "Take your goddamn masks and suits and get the hell out." He yanked at his IV line. "Don't tell me I have the fucking flu dressed like that."

Karl tried to explain. "I'm Dr. King, I'm here to help. I'm a—"

Jack sprang up and heaved a chair. It flew across the room, forcing Karl to leap out of its path. Even sick, the football player was a powerful man. Dangerous. McCoy tried to speak gently.

"Mr. Dowel, have you left town recently or had any visitors from—"

Jack Dowel hurled a water bottle at him. McCoy quickly ducked. The bottle hit the wall, bounced off and rolled across the floor.

King tried again. "It's not exactly the flu. It's a bacterial infection."

"What kind?" Jack asked.

"The kind that your immune system has trouble—"

Dowel flung his cell phone at him. The toss was half-hearted and the phone clattered to the floor. McCoy thought perhaps they should abort the interview and sedate the patient. They were getting nowhere.

Of course, Dana Sparks had to give it a go. McCoy watched her saunter toward the bed. His mouth dropped open when she dropped her mask. McCoy knew her acquiescence had been too good to last. Straining to stay calm, McCoy said in a sharp tone, "I will remind you, Doctor, of the quarantine regulations of this hospital."

She ignored him. Keeping her back to him, she said, "Hi, Jack. I'm Dana. Can I ask you a few questions?"

"Not dressed like that you don't," McCoy said.

Dana Sparks whirled around, her mask dangling at her neck. "This gear is unnecessary."

"These are hospital rules," McCoy said. "They must be followed without question." Rules were rules, and policy was policy. When people ignored protocol, standards deteriorated, and anarchy and chaos reigned. Under no circumstance would he permit this insubordination to pass. "Replace that mask or leave this room at once."

"We're not dealing with an aerosol contagion. I don't need it."

From the bed, Jack said, "Dana and me can talk. Everyone else can leave."

Karl didn't like it. "Jack, I'm from the CDC." He removed his mask as well. "My name is Karl. If you don't mind, I'd like to conduct the interview."

Jack minded. "I'll talk to her and no one else."

CHAPTER TWENTY-ONE

The door slammed and Dana was alone with Jack Dowel. His hands were clenched, his body tight, like a spring waiting to snap. She crossed the room, retrieving the things he had thrown. Then she dragged the chair beside his bed and sat down.

There was a sour odor in the room. The scent of adrenaline was the smell of fear and rage. It was an apt reaction, Dana thought, of someone being lied to. To extract information, they couldn't pretend they were dealing with the flu. The gear was ridiculously superfluous. They were all vaccinated against the plague. Besides, bubonic plague was transmitted by fleas, not people, so the strict quarantine protocol was unnecessary. The suits sent a message of danger that Jack had read correctly. His response was appropriate.

"I know you," Jack said.

She looked at him. He had short white-blond hair and delicate features that were at odds with his hulking body. His head seemed disproportionately small, but that may have been because his body was so huge. He had round blue eyes and crooked nose. She had never seen him before.

"You gave a special lecture in my bio class in the fall. It was good."

"Thanks."

"I'm a football player."

She smiled at him. "I heard."

"I don't usually get sick," he said. "Well, last week I had the flu, but it was nothing like this." He pushed himself upright and stared in her eye. "What do I have?"

He had the right to know. "We think bubonic plague."

Jack blinked. His eyelashes were long, thick, and blond. "The plague?" He shut his eyes.

"It's a bacterial infection. You're taking three antibiotics. You'll feel better soon."

He opened his eyes. "I feel like I'm going to die. Like there's a boiling hot snake crawling through my body."

Dana checked his medical chart. He was on morphine and past due for another shot. "You could have more pain medicine if you wanted."

He did, and she rang for the nurse.

In a few minutes, Jack's eyes were glazed and he was staring off into space. Dana wanted him to talk about himself and apparently that wouldn't be a problem. He was a local kid, hailed from Brenham, and had been in Duane four years. He was supposed to be finished now, but wouldn't graduate for another year. He had courses to make up on account of football. He was a tight end, a good one. He recounted one of his spectacular plays she may have missed. It was a tie game. Bucky, the quarterback, threw him a lateral toss that Jack caught in an underhand grab. He dodged the defensive line and started running from the sixty-yard line. It was the last play of the game. The clock was running out. Jack was tripped, stumbled, almost fell. He heard the fans screaming out his name and caught his balance, went on to cross the finish line as time ran out. He smiled at the memory, folding thick arms across his huge chest. "Did you see the game?"

Dana tried to look appropriately impressed. She didn't understand the football mania that gripped the town. "I may have missed it. Sounds like a nail-biter. Do you have any pets?"

"Nope. They don't allow them where I live."

"Where is that?"

"The Tremblant Apartments."

She swallowed her surprise. The Tremblant Apartments had a pool, tennis court, and maid service. The building was owned by the university and primarily reserved for honorable guests and visiting scientists. Apparently some football players lived there too. "Have you seen fleas in your place?"

"Nope." Jack said the landlord sprayed for cockroaches every four months and he had seen no fleas. He hadn't got any flea bites. "But I've got a fire ant bite on my ankle."

"Can I see it?"

He threw off the sheet.

His ankle was as thick as her thigh. The bite had turned necrotic and black. Around that was a raised red swell. She touched the bite. It had turned hard. She did not think it was an ant bite.

"Have you seen any mice or rats in your place?"

"Nope."

"Do you know anyone else who is ill?"

He knew lots of people who were sick. There was a bad flu going around.

"Can you tell me who you've seen recently?"

Jack shrugged. That would be a problem, for he was a popular guy. He was taking five classes, went out drinking with his football buddies, and had multiple dates.

Dana copied down the list of his classes. She made a note of his friends and acquaintances, and the girls he dated the previous week -- Bobbi-Sue, Candy, and Lolita. He didn't know their last names.

"I mean, they're not serious," he said.

"Did you have sex?" Dana returned his stare. It was a question she had to ask. If Jack had the bacteria in his blood, boisterous intercourse could rupture small vessels and facilitate the blood to blood transfer of the bacteria and cause septicemic plague.

"Of course," he said.

"Did you use condoms?" A condom would prevent the transfer of bacteria.

"Of course."

"Good for you. When did you first feel sick?"

"Yesterday."

Sunday. Since the incubation period of bubonic plague was around seven days, Jack had been infected the previous week. "Have you gone anywhere?"

"No."

"Do you live alone?"

"At the moment."

"And before now?"

"I roomed with Bucky Finch."

"Who?"

"The quarterback."

"Right. Where is he?"

"He went to San Antonio last week and got married. Shhh." Jack raised a finger to his lips. "He eloped. Big secret."

Bucky would have to be found. "Do you know a man named Dudley Shaw?"

"Who's he?"

"Someone … well … someone who was sick like you." She wouldn't mention Dudley had died.

"I don't know him."

"When were you last home?" Brenham was a small town sixty miles away, famous for cotton and ice cream. Vast grassy fields spanned the distance between the two towns. It was not an unreasonable habitat for rats.

Jack hadn't been home since Christmas. He didn't have time. He was in spring training.

"Have you had any visitors?"

"My mom came last week. She was passing through on her way to Houston."

This was something. "Is she sick?"

"Not that I've heard."

Dana made a note of her phone number. "Did she leave you anything?"

"Lots of advice. Find a nice girl. Settle down."

"Right," Dana said. "Did she stay with you?"

Jack shook his head. "No. When she comes she stays at The Lone Star Heritage Hotel."

"Does she have any pets?" Dana asked.

"Sure. We've got dogs and cats on the ranch."

"Ranch? What kind of ranch?"

"We raise horses."

And where there were horses, there was feed, and where there was grain, there were rats. It was their first lead. "Do you hunt?" she asked.

"You mean animals?" He raised an eyebrow.

"Yes, four-legged animals."

"Sometimes. Not recently."

"Do you eat wild meat?"

"Wild meat? He smiled rakishly. "What kind of wild meat?"

Dana thought that was enough questions for now. "I'll go and let you rest."

He looked at her with open eyes. "Am I going to be okay?"

You're going to be fine, Dana almost said, before remembering she'd said the same thing to Dudley.

CHAPTER TWENTY-TWO

Out in the corridor, Dana saw no sign of her colleagues. She tore off the protective gear and went to the bathroom and washed her hands. She wondered what connected Jack and Dudley, who were both bitten by fleas infected with *Yersinia*. Jack had no pets, yet there appeared to be a flea bite on his ankle. Did his mother bring an infected flea with her from Brenham? And where was Dudley exposed? He was the first to be affected, and likely the first infected. But where? And where had Carol Dupuis trapped those rats? Could Jack, Dudley, and the rats be linked to one place? But what place? To stop the spread of the disease, they had to find out.

In the hospital lobby, Dana heard loud, pitiful sobbing, and saw an elderly woman sitting alone, crying. Dana stared long enough that the woman looked her way. Dana walked tentatively toward her. "Are you Mrs. Shaw?"

The woman shook her head and Dana was mortified.

"I'm Tabitha Tott. Dudley is my brother. My younger brother. My only brother." She stabbed a stray bobby pin into a bun.

Dana winced at her use of the present tense and introduced herself. "I'm helping with your brother's case. I'm so sorry."

She sat down beside Tabitha on an orange scratchy couch that was hard and uncomfortable. There were plastic flowers in a vase on the scarred coffee table in front of them and too much artificial light overhead.

Tabitha dabbed a tattered tissue at her eyes. She looked twenty years older than Dudley. "What is going on here?" she asked. "Why can't I see my brother? Why do I have to wait until the diagnosis is confirmed? Why will it take so long? *A whole week?"*

She had a strident tone, much stronger than her brother's, but their eyes were the same—watery, bloodshot, and brown.

"I want to bury him, now, but I can't do that either. He's got to stay in the morgue, here in the basement. He can't even go down the street to the undertaker's. They're talking about cremation, but he wanted to be buried. Who are they to tell me what to do? What kind of infection did he have? Why can't I stay in his house? Why can't I drive his car?" She paused and stared in Dana's eyes.

Dana felt Tabitha's outrage as if it were her own. *A week to identify the bacterium?* How could McCoy get away with such a blatant lie? It was preposterous. If he expected her to lie like this, he could forget it. Dana told a small one. "There are some diagnostic tests we have to run to absolutely confirm the infecting organism."

Tabitha looked at her skeptically.

Dana lowered her voice. "In confidence, we think it was bubonic plague."

Tabitha closed her eyes.

"It's a disease spread by fleas," Dana said.

Tabitha covered her mouth with an old shriveled hand as tears streaked down her quilted cheeks.

"Which is why we're looking for Bingo," Dana said.

Tabitha opened her eyes. "I found him. They took him."

So, they found the dog. That was something. "Bingo needs to be checked. You'll get him back. I know Dudley was worried about him."

"You met Dudley?"

"I saw him yesterday," Dana said. "He was sick but at peace. He was well-medicated. He asked me to feed Bingo and I went out to his place. I left food, but I couldn't find the dog."

Tabitha shifted in her seat and faced Dana. "It's just so sudden. When I saw Dudley at Easter he was planning his big trip. He was very patriotic, always wanted to see his country. Go off with his dog and his car. It ruined his marriage, you know. Dudley liked the car better than his wife. If you knew Nancy, you'd know why."

"Where is Nancy? Is she around?"

"No, she remarried long ago. He hasn't seen her in years."

"She wouldn't want Bingo?"

"Lord, no. I'll take him."

Dana was happy to hear that. She had a few more questions. "Do you know Jack Dowel?"

"Never heard the name."

"Did Dudley follow football?"

"Hardly."

"Did he hunt?"

"Not in years."

"Did he walk in the woods?"

"Not him. Bingo."

"Does Bingo have fleas?"

"He was scratching mighty bad and that was one dog who hated to be bathed."

Dana wondered what his fleas would show. Had Bingo been infected in the woods? Had the bacteria expanded their range and moved south? She stood up, prepared to leave, and then realized Tabitha had no car. "Can I give you a lift?"

Tabitha pulled a fresh Kleenex from under her sleeve and folded it. "I reckon. If I can't stay at the house, guess I'll go to the Lone Star Heritage."

"It's on my way. I'll give you a ride."

They drove through the quiet streets to the hotel. Dana was going to drop her off—but when she saw McCoy's bulletproof Mercedes in the lot, she parked and led Tabitha inside.

CHAPTER TWENTY-THREE

The Starlight Room was the bar in the Lone Star Heritage named for the domed glass ceiling that showed the sky. Tonight, there were no stars, just fast-moving clouds and a bloated, lopsided moon. Sitting at a crowded table, Nick checked his watch for the third time in as many minutes. Where was the waitress? They would accomplish nothing in this bar.

Twenty minutes had passed and the waitress was yet to come. The room was small and claustrophobic and Nick's party was crammed into a bleak corner. They had grabbed the last table, one meant for four, and six people sat huddled around it. McCoy had seen Dean Duncan's Cadillac in the hotel parking lot and had to stop. Now here they were, along with Nellie and Michael Smith, wasting time.

From the opposite corner, a piano player hammered out a John Denver song on a badly tuned piano. The pianist had a gravelly voice and sang off-key. Nick sunk deeper into his chair. Everything in Duane was off-key. It was a mistake to come, he saw that now. He thought that time had left him hardened, wrung out, squeezed dry, and over it all. Long ago, he decided it was best to go his own way, dedicate his life to work. He loved his job—the endless education, travel, and life-and-death challenges. He had friends, colleagues, and music, and that was enough. Life was full. He didn't want more. He was happy. Though it was a sad Robin Wheeler verse that came to him: *I stood alone and watched the sea roll out, and knew again that what I craved was forever gone.*

Nellie's loud complaints caught his attention. "The service in this entire hotel is abysmal. Even the Caprice was appalling. We wanted to show Mike the best cuisine this town had to offer. I mean, if the Caprice was a dump, and if it was cheap, then you could accept inferior service, but come on." She sat forward, her lips pursed tight. "They even mixed up Mike's dinner and gave him pork chops instead of steak. We waited so long he was loath to return the food even if it was inedible. They better get their act together before the VP comes."

The dean agreed. "This is totally unacceptable." He got up and a minute later returned with a harried waitress who apologized endlessly about the delay. They were short-staffed because it was exam week and people were out with the flu. She took their order. Karl asked for two Coronas, which raised McCoy's eyebrows.

The waitress looked at Karl. "Two?"

"It's after five, isn't it?" Karl said.

McCoy glanced at his watch. He was no drinker.

The waitress left and a cell phone rang. Everyone reached into their pockets. "That's me." Karl stood up, holding the phone to his ear. He headed for the lobby.

Nellie filled the silence. "Despite the service, we did have a lovely dinner."

This was followed by more silence. The pianist was taking a break.

"Did you know Mike's from West Point?" Nellie said, looking at Nick.

"No," Nick said.

"At the moment, I'm in Iowa," Michael said.

"Are you married?" Nellie asked.

For a moment Nick thought Nellie was talking to him. She had a bad habit of interrogating people about their personal lives. But no, she was addressing Michael who pulled out his wallet and passed a dog-eared photo around the table. Yes, Michael was married and had twin baby daughters.

"Nice," Nick said. "What's your area of research?"

"Anthrax."

"Pretty wide area."

"He can't talk about it. Top secret." Nellie put a finger to her lips.

Karl returned bearing news of Carol Dupuis. The undergraduate trapper of rats was in Methodist Hospital in Houston, infected with bubonic plague. "Her doctor reported the infection to the CDC. I called her physician, but he won't discuss the case over the phone. I called Jeff. He'll take the next flight to Houston. It seems the hospital is already receiving calls from reporters."

"Reporters!" McCoy placed his hand over his heart. Nick noticed he had broken out in a sweat. His face was cherry red and the veins on his neck looked like chords of rope. His heart attack had aged him. McCoy didn't look well.

The waitress finally arrived with a drink-laden tray, and Karl stopped speaking. Everyone was silent as the drinks were dispensed. In error, Karl was given only one Corona. "Oh, you wanted two, didn't you." The waitress shifted the empty tray to her hip. "Shall I get it?"

"If it's not too much trouble," Karl said tersely.

The waitress flounced away and the dean said, "What's the fallout here? Will the VP be able to come? We've already spent a fortune on the visit."

McCoy looked pained and turned the question over to Nick.

Nick took a sip of whiskey and considered his answer. He did not believe in coincidences, and did not like their inability to trace the origin of the bacteria. Still, that was often the case in these kinds of investigations. You couldn't pinpoint time zero. He gave a guarded response. "At this point, no one has pneumonic plague. If we don't reach the contagious phase, we should be fine. It's not unusual to see one, two, even three cases of bubonic plague in a given area. Sometimes we can't find the source."

"If there are no sick rodents here, doesn't that mean the bacteria came from somewhere else?" McCoy said. "This is too far south for *Yesinia*, right?"

Karl opened his mouth, as if to respond, and then smiled broadly. He raised his hand in a wave. Nick turned and looked in the direction he was staring. Dana was heading toward the table. She was light on her feet and moved fast. Her shiny blond hair was bouncing at her shoulders, and her sparkling blue eyes gleamed brightly.

Nick reached for his glass and downed it in a gulp. Despite loud internal objections, he studied her approach. She wore cowboy boots with pointy toes that were rapidly advancing. She was tall and slender and wore tight beige chinos that hugged her hips. He raised his eyes. She was looking at him and he looked away.

Immediately, McCoy was complaining about her behavior at the hospital. "What were you thinking? How could you breach quarantine and flagrantly violate hospital policy?"

Nellie's mouth dropped open and she stared at Dana wide-eyed.

"We needed the information," Dana said. "You can't just order someone to talk."

'What did he say?" Karl asked.

"Jack's mother was here last week. She has a ranch in Brenham. Maybe she brought the bacteria with her by car."

McCoy liked it and nodded his head violently. It made sense to him.

Except that it didn't, Nick thought. There was no incidence of the plague in Brenham. At the moment, the only infected wildlife was in Duane. When he mentioned this, McCoy frowned deeply.

"That's not to say there aren't infected rodents elsewhere," Karl said. He thought the State Extension Service should begin trapping animals in the fields between Duane and Brenham. "Maybe if we look in the right place we'll find what we're looking for."

And McCoy perked up again.

Dana was still standing beside the table and Karl jumped up, offering her his seat. "Here, sit down. We'll get another chair." He snapped his fingers at the waitress.

Staring at his clasped hands, Nick cursed himself for not taking action. He remembered this was the way he was when he was near her. As he weighed the appearance of his actions, he was paralyzed. Would he give himself away by offering a chair, or by doing nothing? He could never tell. He caught Nellie looking at him quizzically and picked up his drink. Empty. He put the glass down.

"I can't stay," Dana said. "I came to give you Jack's contacts." She pulled a crinkled sheet of paper from her back pocket and passed it to Karl. "Here are the names of Jack's many friends."

"We'll give that to the local health department," Karl said, as he tossed the paper on the table. "Are you sure you have to go?"

She did. "I was just giving Tabitha Tott a ride to the hotel." She turned to McCoy. "Tabitha would like to know when she can get her car back."

"Look, I've got the VP on his way to a town contaminated with *Yersinia*, and Tott is the least of my worries. She took that car without authorization and she's lucky she's not in jail. She should not have gone out to that house. A person commits an offence if they refuse to comply with a federal quarantine, Doctor."

Dana stared at him and McCoy stared back.

He said, "If that's all, you're dismissed."

Dana did not move. Nick knew from experience she hated being told what to do.

Karl was still trying to get her to stay. He was adamant she have his chair and take his beer. "I have another one on the way. I insist."

Now Dana was leaving. She backed away from the table and stalked from the room, moving slowly, back straight, head high.

Nick watched her go. The pianist was back but another Robin Wheeler line rang in his head: *When you go, I will follow, wait for me. In the space you leave behind I am emptied.* He wrung his hands. Despite her emotional volatility, she was dedicated and professional. Yes, she was too passionate, too sensitive, too stubborn, but he admired these things about her too—the depth of her emotion, her compassion, and her warmth. Despite his promise to stay detached, he found himself drawn to her, and longed to go after her. But that would be madness, and he did not move. Instead, he caught the eye of the waitress, raised his hand, and ordered another drink.

APRIL 28TH

CHAPTER TWENTY-FOUR

On Tuesday morning, Dana awoke to the sound of an alarm. She thought it was a clock, but she didn't have one. It took her a moment to realize it was the phone. She picked up to hear Sheryl's hysterical voice.

"Penny's sick. I don't know what to do. She's got a fever of a hundred and four. She's coughing so hard she can't breathe."

In the morning gloom, goose bumps broke out on Dana's skin. "Take her to the hospital."

"I'm there," Sheryl shrieked.

"I'm on my way."

Ten minutes later Dana arrived at the hospital and roared into a parking space next to a low-slung black convertible with the license plate FB-JOCK. Sheryl streaked toward her. She looked a mess. Her face was swollen and her long curly hair was loose and in tangles. She wore dirty jeans and her husband's old Duane University sweatshirt. She smelled of vomit.

"I waited too long," Sheryl wailed. "I should have brought her in earlier. All night long her fever kept getting higher and higher and Tylenol did nothing." Sheryl clasped the sides of her head with her hands. "She held her head like this and was rolling back and forth in her crib. Then she started coughing and couldn't stop. As soon as I got her here, they whisked her away. They won't let me see her."

Dana grabbed her arm and pulled her toward the building.

"What if she needs a transfusion?" Sheryl said. "She has a rare blood type. Richard is the only person I know who is AB negative. How are we going to find him? What if he has to donate blood? What if he won't? It would be just like him."

Dana was thinking along other lines. *Don't let Penny have the plague. Don't let her have the plague. Let it be tonsillitis, an ear infection, please not the plague.*

With Sheryl on her heels, Dana barged through a door that read Medical Personnel only. She tore through the area, yanking open curtains that covered examining rooms. There was no one. She went to reception and found the same woman who gave her Dudley's blood on Sunday.

"I'm Dr. Sparks. I'm working with the CDC and looking for Penny Paige."

The redheaded woman with nicely filed pink nails tapped on her keyboard. "Room 104," she said pleasantly. "Down the hall, just before ICU. It's a quarantine room."

Outside the door stood a cart laden with plastic bags containing protective suits. These were cloth and yellow and came with hoods. They suited up and went in. A man hunched over an examining table said they had to leave. He turned around and Dana saw through the face panel of the hood, a round black face. It was the nurse she'd met on Sunday. "Sam, is that you?"

It was. He smiled at Dana, and glanced suspiciously at Sheryl. "Who's that?"

"My assistant," Dana walked to the examining table. "How is the baby?"

"Not good," Sam said, and Sheryl sobbed into her gloves. "We can't bring down her temperature and she's badly dehydrated. Her respiration is poor."

Dana felt weak, and could barely bring herself to look at Penny. The baby was naked. Three IV lines fed her body. There was a line to each wrist and one to her ankle. A cannula in her nose fed her oxygen. She coughed constantly. Her lips were blue, her small body so pale it looked green. Her eyes were closed and blue veins snaked across her chest. Sam was icing her down with a sponge, trying to bring down her fever.

"Is it the plague?" Dana said.

Behind her, Sheryl choked.

Sam nodded. "The most contagious form. Pneumonic plague."

Sheryl gasped.

"What are you treating her with?" Dana asked.

"Acetaminophen for fever, the standard antibiotic cocktail for *Yersinia*, plasma for fluid replacement, and gamma globulin as a shot in the dark," Sam said.

Dana reached down and stroked Penny's cheek with her glove. Suddenly, she too had trouble breathing. She had been in the delivery room when Penny was born, had seen Penny fighting to breathe, saw her fighting now.

Sheryl was crying louder and Sam said they had to leave. "Put the clothes in the tub."

Dana pulled Sheryl to the bathroom. There was a biohazard bag in the bathtub and Dana pulled off her gloves, hood, and then the suit. Sheryl tore off her clothes, turned on the faucet, and washed her hands as if she would never get them clean. "How did it happen?" she cried. "How could Penny get pneumonic plague?"

"We'll find out."

Sheryl rinsed her hands under the tap. She threw water at her face and it slopped down her shirt. "Was it me? Did I infect her? Did I bring something home?"

"How could it be you? You're not sick."

"I've been vaccinated."

"No," Dana said. "You're not up to date. You took one shot and you need six. You should start taking prophylactic antibiotics."

"I may have residual protection. I could be a carrier. I could have given it to Penny and not be infected myself."

"Unlikely. What about the boys?"

"As far as I know, they're fine. They're still in Houston. What about the lab? What if Penny was infected in the lab?"

"She picked this up two or three days ago. Saturday or Sunday. Was she in the lab on the weekend?"

"No."

"Is anyone at her day care sick?" Dana asked.

Not that Sheryl knew.

"What did you do on the weekend?"

Sheryl had done a lot. She went to Houston, dropped off the boys, and spent the rest of the day with Penny. They went shopping at the

Giant supermarket, had lunch at the Pizza Garden, and played in High Park. Sheryl got a flat tire going home. Tim saw her on the side of the road and changed the tire. On Sunday they went to church and then to the mall. Sunday night, Penny was fussy and Sheryl thought it was her tooth. She kept her home Monday, and at midnight her fever spiked. "I should have brought her in then. What if I left it too late?"

"She's healthy, she'll be fine," Dana said, but she was worried herself. Treatment had to start within twenty-four hours after symptoms appeared or there was no cure. Since they had entered the pneumonic phase of the disease, time was critical. Exposed people had to be found and found fast. Without treatment, mortality from pneumonic plague was close to one hundred percent. They had to find out where she was infected. They had to retrace Sheryl's steps, go everywhere she went, talk to everyone she saw. Dana also wanted to check on Jack, and did not want to be late to McCoy's eight o'clock meeting.

She left Sheryl in the hallway and ran upstairs. Jack was sleeping. Dana peered in the room from the doorway. He lay on his back, eyes closed, rolling his head side to side as he moaned. Dana grabbed his chart. His condition had deteriorated during the night. His fever had soared to 105 degrees and he had been delirious. Acetaminophen and morphine reduced his fever and calmed him down, but his condition was listed as grave.

Grave. Dana flipped the chart closed. *Grave.* How could his situation be grave? He was in good shape, a strong, healthy football player. He should have been better by now, only he was worse. What strain of *Yersinia was* this? Why had Dudley died? What did it mean for Jack and Penny?

CHAPTER TWENTY-FIVE

After a long and sleepless night, McCoy arrived early to work on Tuesday morning. Sitting at his desk, he unraveled the *Houston Chronicle*. The day's headline featured the Somali bombing and the UN team that was examining the incident. There was no mention of Carol Dupuis. McCoy opened the *Duane Eagle*. On the front page was a spread about the VP's visit, nothing on the plague. Reporters had not picked up the story.

Keeping this quiet was critical. After the anthrax attacks in the wake of 9/11, mass hysteria resulted in copious but meaningless tips that seriously hindered the FBI's investigation. It was imperative to keep the press out.

McCoy scanned the article about the VP's visit. The fundraising dinner alone would raise one million dollars. Additional pledges and money was expected from alumni and the business elite. Unofficially, the VP would kick-start his presidential campaign.

McCoy tapped his finger on the paper. If nothing else happened, if the outbreak was contained in the bubonic phase, and the origin of the bacteria identified, the VP could come. McCoy would do everything in his power to make it happen.

He turned the newspaper over and studied the weather map on the back page. A tropical storm was swirling in the gulf. That morning McCoy noticed a vicious wind. It was eighty degrees at six-thirty in the morning. While high temperatures could stop the advance of the bacteria, there were other ways.

McCoy had a contingency plan. Last night after leaving the bar, he called his former superior at the Pentagon and requested help in procuring a potent pesticide. The chemical he had in mind required a special dispensation from the EPA—and this had been requested. While DDT was primarily an insecticide, it was also an effective rodenticide. If *Yersinia* spread, one aerial spray of DDT and the fleas and rats in town would be history. One way or another, the problem would be solved. But it would not happen with this wind.

McCoy bowed his head and prayed for good weather. He reassured himself that things weren't so bad, and indeed could be worse. There could be dead rats with fleeing fleas everywhere. The FBI could be on the case, and the VP scared away. They could be hit with the more contagious pneumonic plague and have tens or hundreds of people sick. Under the circumstances, things were going well.

Then he remembered Dr. Sparks. McCoy had spent a great deal of his night formulating a battle plan for her. She would have to learn to take orders and behave professionally, or else. There would be no more temperamental outbursts like the one last night. Was it McCoy's fault that Shaw's sister placed herself at risk? He had to consider the populace at large and could not concern himself with the comfort of one individual. As a scientist, Dr. Sparks should know that.

He saw the line and he drew it. He wanted her at departmental meetings on time and he wanted her in a lab coat. She would comply with all regulations whether she found them offensive or not. She would increase the security in her lab. She would keep her door locked at all times. Last evening her laboratory had been left unattended for hours. Who knew where she went or why? She had not bothered to tell anyone. It would not happen again. From now on, she would sign out. There would be no more gallivanting to the hospital. No more interviewing patients. She was confined to her lab where she would run diagnostic tests and stay out of trouble.

He heard his stomach rumble and realized he was hungry. He regretted leaving home without breakfast. He should have listened to his wife and taken the time to sit with his daughter. Margaret was giving him the silent treatment after her latest missed driving lesson. When the week was over, McCoy would take her to Austin to tour the University of Texas campus. She wished to return to Virginia, but McCoy wanted her here. He put a hand on his heart. He didn't know if he was up to the task of letting her go.

Just before eight, McCoy headed for the conference room. Christ Almighty, who messed with his room? The air conditioning was off yet again, the curtains were open, as were all of the windows. God damn it! McCoy cranked the air conditioner. He closed each and every window with a slam, and then drew the curtains to blot out the light. At least the window had been repaired, and that was something. He turned around as the door opened, and a young woman carrying a can of paint burst into the room.

"I'm here to paint the place," she said sprightly. "Got to get ready for the VP's visit you know. Orders from General TJ McCoy."

The former and familiar use of his title brought him comfort. McCoy told the painter they were having a meeting and to come back in an hour.

"Yes, sir."

She left and McCoy wiped his brow and went to his chair. If only his other problems could be solved so easily.

At eight sharp, McCoy began his meeting. Becker was absent and Sparks had not arrived, but he wasn't going to wait. Charlotte Lane was already watching the clock. Nellie Duncan doodled on a notepad. Bob Fairway examined his fingernails. Karl King appeared to be asleep, and Nick rubbed his eyes. Only Michael Smith, McCoy's forgotten visitor, sat with rapt attention.

McCoy began by warning his staff to stay clear of the media. If any reporters came poking around, refer them to him. No one was to make as much as a comment. He asked Nick for a report on Shaw's dog.

"After gross examination, the dog appears healthy and not infected with *Yersinia*. We need the blood work to confirm."

"Dr. Sparks will do it." McCoy's pique at her tardiness was offset by Nick's good news. The dog wasn't infected and out spreading *Yersinia* through wildlife populations. He turned to King. "Did you catch anything in the traps by Shaw's house?"

"Three mice and a rat. They look healthy. But rodents aren't our biggest problem." King exhaled dramatically. "We've got our first case of pneumonic plague."

McCoy's chest hurt immediately. Not pneumonic plague. Not the contagious form. McCoy thumped his chest to catch his breath. "Who is sick?"

"A year-old baby, Penny Paige. Her mother works in this department. The child was hospitalized early this morning. Russ Taversham just confirmed *Yersinia*."

McCoy gripped the sides of the chair. Penny Paige was the daughter of Dana Sparks' technician. Had the mother infected the child? It was the worst case scenario. Lethal bacteria maintained in a lab under his jurisdiction had escaped, infecting the town.

Just then Dana Sparks came in. McCoy stood up and faced her across the table. "Penny Paige has pneumonic plague."

"I know." She pulled out a chair and sat down.

"Is your lab the source of this?" He could see it now. An accidental spill of *Yersinia*. The bacteria were picked up by one of the dogs she was always bringing to the lab and somehow fleas were infected and then a baby.

Dana Sparks shook her head. "Sheryl isn't sick, and since she's breast-feeding she can't work with the bacteria. She didn't infect Penny. Besides, the timing isn't right. The rats, Dudley, Jack, and Carol, were all infected before Penny, which indicates another source."

McCoy glanced at King. "Do we know where Carol Dupuis trapped her rats?"

"We know," Karl said. "It's not good."

McCoy waited. His heart thumped so loudly he wondered if everyone in the room could hear it.

"It would have been nice if the rats came from the woods near Dudley Shaw's house, but they didn't," Karl said.

McCoy groaned loudly. Why all the theatrics? Why not just state where they were found? "Where?" he said in a high voice he hated.

"Down the street. In High Park. Across from campus."

McCoy loosened his collar. It was coming closer. Dudley Shaw lived far from campus, but High Park was right here, down the street, across from the university and the Lone Star Heritage Hotel, deep in the heart of town.

"Penny's day care is across the street from the park," Dana Sparks said. "And she was in the park on Saturday."

"Was she in your lab?"

"No."

McCoy wiped his forehead and his hand came away soaking wet. This new outbreak changed everything and introduced a new urgency. He listed what had to be done and who would do what. Each of Penny Paige's recent contacts had to be notified, and he assigned Karl and Nick to the job. Doctors Lane and Fairway would fan out in town and assist with the trapped animals, retrieve the blood samples and bring them to Dana Sparks to test. She would remain in the lab and assay samples. If she left, she was to notify his secretary. Becker would do the autopsies.

But McCoy had forgotten Becker was out with the flu, as Nellie now reminded him.

"Dr. Sparks will do the autopsies."

Her hand was raised and waving. "Since we don't know the source of the bacteria, shouldn't we advise people to bathe their pets and get rid of fleas?"

"We advise nothing," McCoy said. "We're dismissed."

Sparks continued undaunted. "We could have a flea dip at the vet school. People in the community could bring their pets. We could advertise in the local paper and on the radio. Run ads telling people how to minimize exposure to rats and mice."

McCoy could only stare at her in amazement. "We will keep this quiet." With all the announcements she had in mind, at the end of the day, who would there be left to tell? "We have a campaign to control the local population of both fleas and rats. This meeting is adjourned." He rose from his seat.

Sparks was still objecting. "What campaign? What controls both fleas and rats? Only DDT. You can't use that. It's banned."

"It can be used in an emergency," McCoy said.

"DDT?" Sparks was up out of her seat. Did McCoy know it had a half-life of fifteen years? DDT got into the soil, water, and food chain. It mimicked estrogen, thinned eggshells and killed fish, not to mention insects. "DDT is banned, and for good reason."

"You can use it in an emergency," McCoy said, clenching his fists. He could hear every single one of his loud, strained breaths. "And whether you realize it or not, this is an emergency." His voice was high and vibrating with anger. His actions did not require her approval. He was the boss. He was in charge. It was his call and he had made it.

He would take the responsibility for the act. The risk was his and his alone. "I said, dismissed."

McCoy stalked to the door. He had to call his cardiologist. His face was purple and he knew his blood pressure was off the charts. He needed stronger medicine for his heart, perhaps something for his nerves. He needed the wind to stop so that he could spray.

CHAPTER TWENTY-SIX

The meeting ended, and Dana raced after Nick. Spraying DDT was lunacy. Where was McCoy going to spray? The rooftops and trees? Why not have a flea dip? Go after the vector, not the host. She caught up with Nick in Headquarters. "I can't believe you sanction McCoy's plan to spray DDT."

Nick stopped rifling through his briefcase and turned around. His face was already darkened with a five o'clock stubble, which meant he'd been up early. "It's not my decision."

"Or your city? So you don't care where he sprays? In the park? The woods? My house?"

Nick loosened his tie and shook his head disapprovingly. "McCoy's no fool. He'll take appropriate precautions. Don't overreact."

"Overreact? He shouldn't use DDT at all. If you objected, he'd listen to you."

Nick ran his hand through his hair. "McCoy is in charge of the investigation. I'm here as an observer."

"And observing madness is okay with you?"

Nick exhaled slowly. "We have a serious problem. If we don't act, we'll have a city of corpses. One way or another we need to stop the bacteria."

"There are other ways." Dana stared out the window. The wind that had been raging that morning was raging still. "This is like amputating your foot when you stub your toe."

"This isn't a toe. It's a deadly disease. Instead of going off half-cocked, focus on the disease."

"Half-cocked? What does that mean?"

He returned to his briefcase. "Nothing."

He meant emotional, over the top. "I am focused on the disease. On saving lives. But there are other lives to consider here too. DDT lasts for years. A warmonger shouldn't be making biological decisions."

Nick looked up. "He's in charge. He's not a warmonger. He's trying to stop an epidemic."

"Tell that to the birds."

She left the office and was in the hallway when he called her. "Dana."

She took a few steps before she turned.

"Maybe test Frank's blood. He could be the source."

She remembered Frank's labored breathing. She had not considered he might have the plague.

"Perhaps call Becker. Confirm he has the flu."

She nodded.

"With this wind, McCoy can't spray."

She nodded again, feeling better. Nick knew how to talk to her; he offered suggestions, never barked orders. Even nature was against the general.

"Oh, and can you assay Bingo's blood and test the rodents trapped overnight? There's only four of them." He opened the fridge and got a biohazard bag.

She left Nick and went down the hall to Tim's lab. Sheila was there, and Dana asked for a tube of Frank's blood.

"Why?" Sheila asked, looking at the biohazard bag in Dana's hand.

Did the gag on truth extend to Sheila too? Dana assumed so. "I'm thinking of cloning him."

Sheila lifted an eyebrow, but went to the fridge and got a tube of blood from a box in the door.

"Have you heard from Tim?" Dana asked.

"No. He's supposed to be back tomorrow. Sorry about Frank."

Dana returned to her lab and went to the biohazard room and opened the bag. There were ten tubes of blood. She picked up a tube and saw a number. The assay would be done blind. Each sample was identified only by number. Dana did not know what type of animal blood she had, or where the animal had been trapped. Her job was to determine if the blood was positive or negative for the bacteria and pass on the results.

She did the assay. Only the positive controls tested positive. Every blood sample was negative. Frank and Bingo did not have the plague, nor did any of the rodents. Whatever they were and wherever they were trapped, they were not carrying plague antibodies.

Still, the bacteria came from somewhere. Four rats were infected, as were four people: Dudley, Jack, Carol, and Penny. The bacteria were in Duane, but where? Every time Dana considered the problem, she hit a dead end. The facts didn't make sense. There wasn't enough information. How did Nick solve epidemiology cases? How did he live with loose ends and uncertainty?

Well, she knew how. He kept himself far removed from the emotional aspect of his work. He refused to let himself feel, and was therefore able to remain objective and rational. At the moment, his logical self was dominating the Nick that she preferred—the one who sang and skipped and knew how to laugh and make love.

She emptied the tubes of blood into the biohazard waste and began the disk test to assess antibiotic resistance. She went to the incubator and grabbed the agar plate that contained Dudley's lymph nodes that she had plated yesterday afternoon. She remembered him jumping when she felt under his arm. The pain from the pressure of the swelling alone must have been enormous, yet he didn't mention it. He didn't want anything to interfere with his trip.

She took the plate to the hood. The bacteria that killed him dotted the culture plate, looking like little white bumps. The bumps were clumps of bacteria that arose by cell division from a single cell. In the disk test, she would assess the ability of the antibiotics to kill the cells.

The antibiotics she tested were the ones normally used to treat the plague: streptomycin, chloramphenicol and tetracycline. Dana prepared the antibiotics. She used a pair of straight tweezers to draw a line in the agar and divided the plate in half. On a filter paper the size of a dime, she pipetted a drop of each of the three antibiotics in the standard cocktail. She carefully laid the filter paper in the center of one sector. On another filter paper she dabbed a dot of distilled water, which would serve as the control.

It would take twenty-four hours to see a response. During this time, the antibiotics would diffuse from the filter paper into the agar. If the antibiotics were effective, the bacteria would die and leave a clear area.

If the drugs didn't work, there would be no clear zone. Dana returned the plate to the incubator. All she could do now was wait.

Sit in the lab and receive samples, according to McCoy. Sign in and out with his secretary. Forget that. Dana shrugged off her lab coat, washed her hands, grabbed her keys, and left the vet school. She went to see Becker. Though he lived within walking distance of campus, Dana drove, down College Avenue and left on Duane Way to High Street. Phillip lived on the corner, up the street from the park, in a tiny bungalow with a well-kept lawn.

The front door opened as Dana pulled into the drive. Becker stood in the doorway, wearing khaki pants and a lime green polo shirt. He smiled as she crossed the flagstone path, but held up his hand in warning to keep her distance when she reached the porch. "I'm infectious. Don't come too close."

His face was shiny, as if it glowed with an inner light. He looked tired, but other than that, healthy for someone his age. "Okay, we won't kiss or shake hands," she said.

"Come in. This is a pleasant surprise."

"How are you feeling?"

He coughed into his fist. "Better."

"You're sure it's the flu? Not the plague?"

"I told you I've been testing my blood. I've got the flu. It's going around town. Even my doctor has it. Come look at the slide."

She followed him into the house. It was immaculate and comfortable. Becker had lived alone since his wife died, ten years back. He had a microscope set up on his dining room table, and he flicked a switch that turned on a light. A slide was set on the stage and Becker peered through the eye-piece. "Yep." He got out of the way so Dana could take a look.

It was a blood smear. She looked at the white blood cells. In a bacterial infection, neutrophils were the predominant immune cell in the blood. Through the scope, she saw very few. He didn't have *Yersinia*.

He was hovering over her. "See?"

She stood up. "I see."

He invited her to stay for a cup of tea and she followed him into the kitchen. He put a kettle on the stove to boil. "What's going on?" he said. "I wish I was there." He took two flowered china cups with matching saucers out of a cupboard. He sat on a stool at the kitchen counter, and she sat down next to him.

"McCoy's talking about using DDT and no one says a word. When I do, I'm overreacting. Emotional." She heard her voice break. "Maybe it's true."

"There's nothing wrong with thinking with your heart."

"It's been a bad week. Frank died yesterday and Penny is sick. She has pneumonic plague."

Becker clicked his teeth. "How did she get that?"

"The suspicion is my lab. I don't see how. But I'm the only one in town who has the bacteria. What if it did come from my lab? Aside from the four rats, there is no natural source." The kettle was nearly boiling and she jumped up, poured the steaming water into the teapot and brought it to the counter.

"The rats weren't lab rats, were they?" Becker said.

"No. Wild rats. *Rattus rattus.*"

"The worst carrier. You would think the bacteria would be every-where. Dead rats lying in the streets."

"I just checked four samples of blood, and there was nothing." Dana poured two cups of tea.

"Weird."

"Nick thought maybe some animals increased their range due to population pressure."

"The bacteria shouldn't be in this climate or at this elevation. It's strange." Becker lowered his face into the steam and took a loud sip of tea. "Perfect. The peppermint is good for calming the nerves." He put down his cup.

Dana took a sip. She didn't feel calm at all. "I need to do something. This is my disease, my bacteria, and I'm being shut out. I'm supposed to stay in the lab and do assays like I'm a student?"

"Do the assays. You're good at them. There are a lot of specialists here. Everyone has a job."

Dana took another sip of tea. "I'm under strict orders not to leave my lab. I'm supposed to sign out."

Becker stirred his tea with the small spoon. "Did you?"

"Of course not."

"You make trouble for yourself. You know, that don't you?"

"I do what I have to."

"You're in a battle with McCoy. I don't see how you'll win."

"He's trying to take my power. I won't give it up. If I get a new grant, there's nothing he can do."

"He can make your life miserable."

"I thought he was temporary."

"Maybe he likes the job." Becker changed the topic. "How is Nick?"

"His wife died."

"I didn't know."

"He didn't tell me either."

"I'd think you'd be the first he'd tell."

"He wants no reminder of the past. It's like it's gone, never happened."

Becker stirred his tea. "He's working. Nick is serious. His gift is focus. Wait till this is over. It's good that he's here."

"So he can solve the case?"

"So he can solve his past."

But from what Dana could see, it was already solved—buried deep and forgotten. She finished her tea. "I should get back."

Becker followed her to the door and wished her luck. "Bottom line," he said, "do what you think is right. If there are decisions made you don't agree with, speak up. Don't allow yourself to be silenced." He pushed open the screen door and she stepped outside. "Call me if you need anything."

"You know where to find me."

CHAPTER TWENTY-SEVEN

Nick rode shotgun, slumping low in his seat as Karl drove down University Drive toward Penny Paige's day care. They were moving slowly, traffic was bad, and they hit every red light. Nick watched the wind gust across the campus lawn. The tropical storm was on its way.

He regretted mentioning to McCoy the spectacular record of DDT in curbing outbreaks of the plague in third world countries. McCoy jumped on the bandwagon and would not hear of newer pesticides that had a lower environmental impact. McCoy would never use a bullet when a cannon was nearby.

Still, the situation had taken a serious turn. They were now in the pneumonic phase and did not know the bacterial source. This was the strangest outbreak of the plague Nick had ever seen. It made him unsettled and uneasy. Though that may have been Dana.

He couldn't put her out of his mind. In D.C., when she hovered at the edge of his thoughts, he was able to push her away. Though she came to him in his dreams, usually naked. He banished the thought from his mind. It was madness. He had forgotten how dangerous she was. She could figuratively disrobe without warning, expose herself, bare it all. As soon as this was over, he would leave. Robin Wheeler, singing in his head, agreed: *The moon was gone, blood pooled the ground; you stood on the wasteland, shattered; you had to go, there was no other way.*

Stopped at a light, Karl turned on the radio. He found the classical station and Vivaldi's *Four Seasons* was playing the tract of 'Winter.' Nick watched a crowd of students cross the street on their way to campus, ignorant of the crisis unfolding around them. They had to stop it.

In order to contain pneumonic plague, they had to locate Penny's contacts and get them on prophylactics. Anyone she was in contact with over the past three days had to be found. In Nick's mind, epidemiology was an exercise in collecting and assembling facts. In any investigation, the most important piece of information was identifying the first person to fall ill. That person was the index case, the person from whom all subsequent infections could be traced. Right now they were dealing with two outbreaks of *Yersinia*—bubonic and pneumonic plague. Because fleas spread bubonic plague, identifying the index case was not critical. With pneumonic plague, it was imperative.

At the moment, Penny Paige was the source and they had to determine where she was infected. Her day care was in a private home on Front Street, which was across the street from the Lone Star Heritage Hotel and alongside High Park. Karl swung into a driveway.

The babysitter, Christine Grey, lived in a small house on a large lot that was surrounded by a chain-link fence. The yard was full of kids, bikes, a Toys-R-Us wagon, and a convoluted jungle gym. A determined-looking gray-haired lady stalked toward the fence. "There's no parking here. Move that car."

Karl pulled out his business card and passed it over the fence. "I'm with the CDC." He introduced Nick. "Penny Paige is ill. We're investigating the source of her infection."

Toddlers followed Christine to the fence. One of the kids raised her hands to be picked up and Christine swung her up on her hip. Another child gripped her leg. His nose was running and when he coughed, Nick winced. A single exhalation released a million bacteria into the air. All it took to infect another person was one breath and a few days' time. He reached over the fence and felt the child's forehead. No fever. It couldn't be pneumonic plague; probably just a cold.

"At the moment, Penny is sick with a very bad cough and high fever," Karl said. "Do any children have similar symptoms?"

"Peter has a cold," Christine said, patting the head of the boy wound around her leg. "But he's getting better, aren't you. Everyone else is fine."

"Then Penny Paige wasn't ill last week?" Nick said. They had to pinpoint precisely the day she was infected. It would be difficult, because of her age and because she was still being breastfed by a mother who had been vaccinated. Her course of infection would be skewed from the normal curve.

"Penny was fine on Friday, the last day I saw her," Christine said.

"How many kids do you watch?" Karl asked.

Christine had five kids, which was all she would take. She gave them breakfast, lunch, and wholesome snacks. She abided by the food groups and watched the kids' nutrition. In a few minutes there'd be snacks, and then naps. Later on in the day when the sun was past its peak, they'd go to the park and take a nature hike, pick leaves, or look for bugs for their collection.

"And feed the squirrels and chipmunks?" Karl asked.

Christine looked offended. "Of course not. Squirrels and chipmunks can bite."

The girl on Christine's hip jammed her thumb in her mouth and stared at Nick. He smiled at her and thought of his son, who was put in day care when he was a month old. Rachel-Anne was suffering from postpartum depression, and could not care for him. Two months later when he died, she couldn't forgive herself. A week after his son was buried, she made her first suicide attempt.

The young Peter started to cry and Christine shifted the child she was holding in order to pick him up. Karl was trying to assuage her worry. "You're in no danger. We notified the health department. They'll visit you today and arrange for everyone to begin prophylactic antibiotics."

Across the fence, Christine demanded to know what kind of infection Penny had that required a visit from the health department and antibiotics.

"It's an infection that can be treated if we catch it in time," Karl said obliquely.

Nick wondered about the strategy. On one hand, you didn't want to overreact and terrify people, but on the other hand, you couldn't assume a 'wait and see' approach that could leave many dead.

Two other kids joined the fray and hid behind Christine's skirt. "What kind of antibiotics did you say?"

"Prophylactic," Karl said. "Precautionary, protective, preventative antibiotics. Free of charge, of course."

On the grass, another child raised her arms, but both of Christine's hips were taken. She patted the child on the head as she returned to her effort of ascertaining the name of the disease. "I mean, what kind of sickness is this?"

"Between you and me, it's caused by bacteria called *Yersinia pestis*," Karl said, in a lowered voice.

"Is that like chicken pox?" Christine asked.

"Not really," Karl said. "Now, we do request you try to keep this as quiet as possible. Both for your own protection and the protection of those that may panic and try to leave town."

"Panic and try to leave town?" Christine said. "Because of *Yer* — what? I've never even heard of it."

"Don't worry. We're prepared to deal with this problem, but doctors elsewhere may not be so adept. If you have any questions, call my cell phone anytime."

With a few additional assurances that antibiotics would take care of the problem, Nick and Karl left Christine to her children.

They returned to the car and Karl cranked the air conditioner. "She reminds me of Helena," he said, as he pulled onto the street.

Nick was surprised by the statement. He hadn't found Karl's ex-wife maternal or nurturing in the least. She had been a lot like his own wife.

"She should have put the kids in day care," Karl said. "She would have been happier, not so resentful. Four were too much. Eight in the morning and she was already wasted."

"It was long ago," Nick said. Karl's kids were grown up, and the decision not to do day care had been made a long time ago and couldn't be revisited. At the moment, Nick was concerned with things that could be changed.

They drove around the block. Jack Dowel lived in the Tremblant Apartments, which was diagonally across the street from High Park. The white clapboard complex had steep red roofs with elaborate trim that reminded Nick of a doll's house. Karl parked in a visitor's parking spot. *The range is getting smaller*, Nick thought as he got out. A focus of infection was coming into sight.

They interviewed the superintendent, and learned Jack had lived in the building for two years. Except for a few loud parties, he was no trouble. He had a two-bedroom apartment he shared with another football player. The apartments were fully serviced. A maid cleaned twice a week and the complex was sprayed for insects every other month. The building and grounds had been fumigated the previous week. Pets weren't allowed in the building, and fleas and rodents weren't a problem.

The landlord gave Karl a key to the second floor apartment. It looked clean. There was no sign of fleas or rodents. No sign of the roommate who was out of town and would have to be found.

Nick stepped out onto the narrow balcony. It faced south, towards the university campus. Farther down, past the railroad tracks, Nick saw the yellow brick facade of the veterinary school. Christine Grey's house was on the left and the front yard was empty now. Across from her was High Park, which was adjacent to the back parking lot of the Lone Star Heritage Hotel. Across the street from that was the University Plaza, with the supermarket, movie theater, car wash, dry cleaner, and coin laundry. Except for Dudley Shaw, everyone infected could be traced to this area.

In an epidemiological investigation, identifying the epicenter—the source of the bacteria—was as important as establishing the index case. Was he looking at the epicenter? Did the bacteria spread from here? But how did it get here?

Nick watched the students on campus. An exam must have just ended, for the streets and sidewalks were packed. The park was busy. The wading pool was crammed with kids, and edged with mothers and nannies. A large black dog loped across the grass. The park filled a city block. There was a playground on one end and a wooded area on the other. At the verge of the trees, he saw two technicians dressed in white coats, laying cage-traps. He watched squirrels leaping in the trees and chipmunks scurrying on the ground. His heart nearly stopped when a young boy held out a crust of bread to a black squirrel. It was close interactions like that which facilitated the movement of fleas from wildlife to humans.

"Would you look at that stupid kid," Karl cried. He yelled out, but was too far away to be heard.

A park employee shooed the child away. A mother came running. Nick watched the exchange: the frown on the woman's face, the park official shaking his head, and the child crying as his mother dragged him away.

"It could have happened like that," Karl said. "Penny Paige played in the park and got too close to an infected rodent. She got bubonic plague that was somewhat contained by her mother's antibodies. When the bacteria reached her lungs, she developed pneumonic plague."

Nick agreed it was a plausible. If Penny was infected here, he did not like what he saw. There were too many people in the vicinity of the proposed epicenter. People had to be warned. Nick disagreed with McCoy and Karl's policy to dispense as little information as possible.

In the past, Nick managed to contain epidemics with forthright honesty. He preferred to deal with people openly rather than keep them in the dark. He did not like watching kids play in a park, oblivious to the threat around them. He did not like watching students going to school, thinking that the only thing they had to worry about was an exam. Until they could pinpoint the source of the disease, everyone in town was at risk. "This news blackout is wrong," he said. "People have a right to know what's going on."

Karl disagreed. "You were involved in the anthrax investigation. You know what happened. The hysteria screwed everything. This is a college town. If students catch wind of what's happening, they'll be gone. We make an announcement and Duane will become a ghost town. We could spread the plague throughout the whole of Texas. The whole country."

Nick watched kids swing on the swings. "No. Give people the truth and ask them to behave responsibly. Tell them to stay home, not leave town, minimize outside contacts. Tell them to call a doctor if they have flu-like symptoms. Let them take steps to protect themselves."

Karl leaned against the balcony railing. "There's already a flu epidemic in this town. What will happen if everyone with a sniffle runs to their doctor? How many doctors do they have here? Imagine the chaos if everyone thinks they have the plague?"

Nick flung his hand at the direction of High Park. "We know four rats collected in the park were infected with *Yersinia*. How can we justify keeping the park open?"

"Close it and you'll have a lot of explaining to do."

Nick exhaled heavily. "Maybe we need to start explaining. Hold a press conference."

"No way," Karl said. "I won't do it. We need these people here so we can trace this thing. We go public and the road out of Duane will turn into a parking lot."

Nick shook his head. "We keep this quiet and the town will turn into a morgue."

CHAPTER TWENTY-EIGHT

That afternoon, Dana began the autopsy on the four rodents trapped overnight at Dudley's house. In light of the negative blood tests, she thought the autopsies were unnecessary, but McCoy ordered them, and Nellie had delivered the bodies.

At the hood in the quarantine room, Dana opened the biohazard bag and pulled out three mice and a rat. The rodents had been identified and tagged. The mice were *Peromyscus attwateri* and the rat, *Dipodomys ordii*. The names meant nothing to her, except that they weren't the typical species that spread the plague.

Starting with the rat, she arranged him on his back on a tray. His body was cold, but soft. His fur was brown and smelled of the ether that had been used to kill him. Dana grabbed the loose fur by his stomach and cut into it with a pair of sharp scissors. The intestines began to spill out, a twisted gray slimy gelatinous mass. She pushed them to one side with a finger, pulled back the skin, and peered inside. No bulbous lymph nodes. The liver was a bright reddish brown and the lobes were firm. She examined the spleen and thymus, two organs of immunity. The tissue was neither swollen nor enlarged; there was no sign of an intensive immune response. She saved the organs for Phillip Becker, dropped the body into a biohazard bag, and grabbed the next victim.

Dana finished the autopsies in an hour and all of the animals appeared healthy. They in no way resembled the sick rats Carol had given her Friday afternoon. The rodents out by Dudley's house were clean.

Before leaving the quarantine room, Dana checked the progression of the disk test. There was no clear zone. The bacteria were still growing flush against the filter paper. There seemed to be more colonies now then there had been earlier. Were the bacteria still dividing? The antibiotics should have put a stop to that by now.

Still, it was too early to expect a response. Only four hours had passed. The test took time and she couldn't expect conclusive results in less than twenty-four hours. Each *Yersinia* strain was different. She often ran disk tests to assay new strains for antibiotic resistance. It was her policy to never use bacterial strains that were resistant. In case of an accident, Dana wanted an effective antidote. Generally, with non-resistant *Yersinia*, a lethal effect of the antibiotic cocktail was visible early, within four hours. While some strains had a delayed reaction, Dana had never seen a non-resistant strain continue to divide after exposure to antibiotics. She wondered if this was an antibiotic-resistant strain. She told herself it was too early to tell.

But a quiet voice in her brain nagged on about resistance. Over the years she had learned to pay attention to that voice. Another thing she had learned was to never underestimate bacteria. Because of rapid cell division, they evolved quickly. Bacteria devised a variety of strategies to deal with antibiotics. They could block the antibiotic's entry into the cell, actively pitch it out, or chemically modify it so that it no longer worked. Some bacteria used more than one mechanism. These were the super-bugs, and *Yersinia* was in that category.

In Madagascar, Dana told herself, on an island far off the coast of Africa, not here.

The phone was ringing when she reached her office. Once more Sheryl was on the line and screaming. "Penny's worse. The antibiotics aren't working. Her temperature is a hundred and six. She's convulsing. She's dying."

Dana struggled to breathe.

Sheryl's voice turned quiet. "How much of the monoclonal do we have?"

Dana closed her eyes. "The monoclonal vaccine? We sent it to Fort Troy." She wasn't telling Sheryl anything she didn't know already.

"We didn't send everything. We're still feeding a few cells. How much do we have?"

"It doesn't matter," Dana said. "Penny can't take it." Morally and ethically it was unthinkable. "Sheryl, give the antibiotics time."

"Don't tell me that," Sheryl screamed. "I saw what the monoclonal antibody did to the mice. It saved their lives. But you have to give it early. It's already late. We have no time. Penny can't breathe. She's burning with fever. She's had seizures. And you can do something," Her voice grew calm. "Dana, you can do something. You can't let her die."

"Remember the guinea pigs." Forty-five percent had allergic lung reactions, thirty percent suffered systemic shock, twelve percent had renal failure and eight percent died. Only five percent had suffered no untoward effects.

"Rabbits, dogs, and monkeys responded well," Sheryl said. "We have to try."

In her mind, Dana ticked off potential side effects: kidney failure, lung infection, shock, death. It was too big a risk. "I can't do it."

"You owe me," Sheryl said. "On Friday you said you owed me. I'm calling in the favor."

Dana pressed the receiver on her shoulder and stared up at the Van Gogh print. Injecting herself with an experimental vaccine was one thing, but injecting someone else was another. She touched her muscle, the site of Friday's injection. That was another thing she had forgotten—yesterday she was supposed to take blood and assess whether or not the active vaccine induced protective antibodies.

She had taken an antigen, which was a piece of the bacteria, and different than the monoclonal. The monoclonal was a human protein, a pre-formed antibody. As they saw in the guinea pig, a foreign protein could act in bizarre and unexpected ways and provoke a massive auto-immune response. How the monoclonal vaccine would work in people was still uncertain. The army wouldn't start widespread testing for two months. Penny couldn't be the guinea pig. She was a soft, sweet baby with four teeth and fine hair that was beginning to curl at the ends. She smelled like baby powder and was just beginning to talk. What if something went wrong?

In humans, the monoclonal antibody could work in ways they could not predict or imagine. It could do more harm than good. The monoclonal antibody could bind to a cellular protein and cause a widespread allergy. It could clot the blood, cause a stroke, or a heart attack. They weren't dealing with a guinea pig here; this was a baby, her godchild.

Still, there were no side effects in mice, rats, dogs, or monkeys. And what was the alternative if antibiotics didn't work? Dana looked at her watch. Penny had been on antibiotics for eight hours. If the bacteria were resistant, the antibiotics would never work.

What about Penny's life? Dana had put on her best clothes, gone to church, and swore on a bible that she would do everything she could to protect the baby. But what if she made things worse? How could she live with herself? What if the antibodies worked and Dana gave her a monoclonal that killed her?

Was it best to sit around and wait? Give the antibodies a chance? But if they left it too long, it would be too late and there would be no chance of recovery. Time was against them. Dana glanced at her watch again and heard loud ticking.

Life without Penny. Dana saw in her mind a small casket and a gravestone. What clothes did Penny have to be buried in? What would happen to her crib, her toys, her books? She would never touch them again. Her small comfortable room would forever be empty. Like Frank, she would be gone and leaving behind too much space. No, Sheryl was right. Waiting was the wrong approach.

She stared up at the van Gogh print. *Go with what you think is right,* Phillip Becker advised earlier. She would go with her instincts. She raised the receiver to her ear. "Hold on. I'm coming."

Dana went to the cell culture room trying to empty her mind and blank out the consequences of what she was about to do. She opened the incubator and stared at the neatly stacked immunological plates that contained the monoclonal antibody vaccine.

The technology to produce the monoclonal was simple. Antibodies were made in specialized immune cells called plasma cells. One plasma cell made a single type of antibody. Once they knew the antibody they were looking for, they could identify the cell that produced it, and isolate that cell from the rest. They then fused that cell with a tumor cell and created a hybrid. The hybrid divided indefinitely and produced a single antibody: a monoclonal antibody.

When the production stage was at its peak, they had a hundred plates and collected a total of one milliliter of the monoclonal antibody a day. For six months Sheryl had done little but mass-produce the vaccine. A month ago they had shipped enough to Fort Troy to test sixty thousand people. They had frozen the remaining hybrid cells and less than a half a milliliter of the monoclonal remained.

Using a glass pipette, Dana transferred one-tenth of a milliliter to a vial, which she slipped inside a protective sleeve. She grabbed a needle and syringe and put them in her briefcase. Though it might be unethical, she thought it was more unethical to do nothing. Dana locked her lab and headed out.

Texas Avenue was clotted with pre-rush hour traffic. The sun was bright, but to the south the clouds were building. The wind was still blowing. It swung the traffic lights, kicked a cereal box along a gutter, and whipped through the open window of the car tangling Dana's hair.

On the radio, the four o'clock news began. A senior state department spokesman was defending the U.S. strike against Somalia. Yes, a hospital may have sustained damage in the air-strike, but it was not the target. A warehouse stuffed with ammunition and explosives was targeted and bombed. The hospital was inadvertently damaged when the warehouse exploded. The spokesman reiterated that overseas citizens take security precautions. He downplayed the possibility of a terrorist strike on American soil. He was confident the UN investigative team would completely exonerate the U.S. from all wrongdoing.

Dana reached the hospital. Outside the world was going crazy, but inside nothing looked amiss. At the reception desk, the secretary with the pink nails sat reading her magazine. There was no one rushing in the hallway, no alarms beeping. From all outward signs, it was as if nothing were wrong and life was progressing as usual on a routine Tuesday afternoon. It seemed impossible that down the hall a baby was dying from the plague.

Dana reached Penny's room and pulled on quarantine clothes. The door opened and Sheryl, dressed in a biohazard suit, yanked her inside.

"Hurry, hurry, there's not much time. The nurse just left." Sheryl pulled Dana across the room toward Penny.

A slant of sunlight shone down upon the crib. Penny's golden hair was soaked with fever. She was naked and waves of heat seemed to radiate off her. Beads of sweat dotted her forehead. Her pearly fingernails were black. Her lips, eyelids, and skin were tinged in blue. She lay uncrying, unresponsive, except for the shuddering of her chest as she grasped for breath.

She was as blue now as she was at her birth. After a long and hard delivery, her Apgar score had been zero. The doctor wondered if she had broken Penny's shoulder during the delivery, and when she was an hour old, Penny had her first x-ray. It was a bad start, but from then on, things got better. Aside from tonsillitis and a few earaches, Penny was healthy. Dana wasn't prepared for a life without her. How Nick survived the loss of his son, she didn't know. Where was the God that Sheryl believed in? How could this happen?

Sheryl clutched her arm. "Come on, come on. Hurry, hurry. The nurse went to finalize arrangements for Penny in ICU. She'll be right back."

With trembling fingers, Dana pulled the vaccine from her pocket. She ripped the paper cover off the syringe and fastened it to the needle. She uncapped the glass vial and pulled back the plunger to draw the monoclonal into the syringe.

"Want me to do it?" Sheryl asked.

Dana shook her head. She would take responsibility. She twisted the IV tube from the needle in Penny's foot and stemmed the flow of plasma with her thumb. She had trouble because the gloves were too big and the polyethylene made her hands sweat. Her whole body was sweating. She could barely keep her hand from shaking.

As carefully as she could, she shoved the syringe into the base of the IV needle tapped into Penny's vein and slowly depressed the plunger. She wanted to hurry, she was terrified the nurse would return, and it was hard to go slow. But if she pushed too hard, there would be a back-flow of liquid and the monoclonal would leak out. She could not hurry. *Slow down, slow down*, she told herself.

The monoclonal was finally in. Dana withdrew the syringe and examined the IV needle in Penny's foot. No liquid dripped down the side. She fitted the tubing back onto the end of the IV needle. Plasma dripped out, blotting the sheet.

The door opened and a gargantuan nurse burst in. She looked at Penny and yelled at Sheryl for moving the crib. "I am already telling you to keep her from sunlight. We must keep her cold." She spoke in a strong German accent, scowling deeply. "There are to be no visitors," she added, glowering at Dana. "This is quarantine room and she is having to leave. Immediate family only." She walked to the crib and rolled it away from the window.

Dana backed up, listening to her heart slam as the nurse examined Penny. Would she see the blot on the sheet? Would she call Taversham? No. She pulled the IV bottles down from their stands and looped them over the rail of the crib.

"I am moving the baby to ICU. The mother may enter only." The nurse rolled the crib toward the door, which Dana hastened to open.

When the nurse was gone, Sheryl sagged against the wall, hands pressed against her throat, uttering her thanks. Dana was already worried she'd made a mistake. This was not some small thing she could take back. The step taken could never be undone. If it was the wrong thing to do, Dana had just administered a lethal injection to a twelve-month old baby. It would be murder.

CHAPTER TWENTY-NINE

The day had been long and frustrating, McCoy thought as he sat in the conference room awaiting the start of the five o'clock meeting. He had managed to squeeze in a visit to his cardiologist, who had increased his heart and hypertension medication. Now his heart rate was normal, as was his blood pressure, but McCoy was experiencing unpleasant side effects. His ulcer, dormant for five years, was active again. His stomach burned. If he stood up too fast, he felt faint. He wondered at times if his thinking was clear.

He had spent most of the afternoon out at the airport, clearing the pesticide that had arrived from DC. A spray plane had been loaded and a pilot was on standby. As soon as the wind let up, the pilot would fly.

Earlier, McCoy received a call from the *Washington Post*. Some nosy reporter wanted to know what the DDT was for. McCoy, begging an emergency, hung up. He promised to call back—and he would—perhaps next week. At least there were no queries from local reporters.

McCoy massaged his temples and felt a headache coming on. Whether it was another side effect of his medication or the paint fumes, he did not know. He looked across the room at a half-painted wall. The painter gave her word the job would be finished by lunchtime, but by the look of it the job was barely underway. He could see where the strokes faded as the paint ran out. At lunchtime, the painter had gone to get more paint, but she had not returned.

Not that it mattered. Given the current situation and the case of pneumonic plague, it was doubtful if the VP could come. There were too many unanswered questions, too many things that didn't add up. At the moment, the only thing he could do was wait and see what happened. There was a sense of helplessness that McCoy could not stomach.

He closed his eyes. He was very tired. At least no additional people were infected with *Yersinia*. McCoy had the results of the blood tests from the rodents trapped by Dudley Shaw's house, and all were *Yersinia*-free. So was Bingo and his fleas. It would be good news for Barry Ackerman, the FBI agent who at that moment sat in McCoy's office, waiting to speak with him.

Somehow the FBI had learned Nick Biget was in town on government business and wanted to know the nature of his visit. McCoy said they would talk after the meeting.

McCoy's researchers were filing in. He nodded hello to Michael Smith, again just remembering his visitor. Smith's seminar was scheduled for the following morning and McCoy had neglected to post notices of the talk. He would ask Betty to do that the moment the meeting was through.

Nick and Karl arrived, each lugging a large carton containing the prophylactic antibiotic tetracycline shipped from a Houston factory. Everyone in the department who was not vaccinated against *Yersinia* would begin taking the drug. No one would get sick on his watch. For a change, Dana Sparks was on time and in a lab coat. Phillip Becker was still out with the flu, and everyone else was accounted for except Nellie, who had gone home early to prepare for a dinner she was hosting that night.

McCoy began his meeting. He stood up, felt faint, and immediately sat back down. He looked at the blackboard, saw an empty space, and remembered the painter had cleared it out. Well, he only had a few words to say and he said them. "We've got no new cases. No sign of a rodent infection in Duane."

He thought it was good news, until he saw Nick frown. Sparks raised her hand. Ignoring her, McCoy asked Dr. King to bring them up to date.

The CDC agent scraped his chair away from the table and stretched out his legs. He had spoken to state extension officials. During the last twenty-four hours, three hundred and fifty-two rodents had been trapped. Their blood had been tested in the state lab. Eight animals had *Yersinia* antibodies. Five of the animals were trapped in the Panhandle near Amarillo and three near Plains, just east of the New Mexico border. The animals appeared healthy.

Here was the first sign to indicate the bacteria *were* in Texas, McCoy thought. Perhaps the epicenter *was* far away. "We should shift our focus to West Texas. Trap more animals there."

Nick objected. He thought they should continue to focus on Duane. "The epicenter is near High Park."

McCoy's stomach burned. "Only four rats in town are infected. The wildlife here appears fine."

"That may be," Nick said. "Except all infections but one can be traced to High Park. That's where Carol trapped the rats, where Jack lives, and where Penny goes to day care."

It was too close, McCoy thought, as his heart thumped too loudly in his chest. It was too close to home. McCoy wiped sweaty palms on his slacks.

Nick wouldn't let up. "If we suspect the park *is* the epicenter, it should be closed."

McCoy looked at him. At the moment that was out of the question. Closing the park would mean going public and McCoy wasn't prepared to do that. For the time being they would take no overt action. "It's possible the source is West Texas. Parks and Rec are monitoring the park. We keep it open. We'll test the rodents." McCoy turned to Karl. "Are we setting traps?"

They were. In fact, they had caught some chipmunks and squirrels and taken blood to assay.

"Give it to Dr. Sparks," McCoy said. He would wait for the results before deciding what to do next. "That's it for now."

No, Sparks had something to say. "Is it possible the bacteria are resistant to antibiotics?"

"I suppose *anything* is possible," McCoy said. "Maybe you can tell me. You're the one doing the disk test."

"It's only been six hours," she said.

"Let's give the antibiotics time to work."

"What if we *are* dealing with resistance?" she asked.

But McCoy hated the game of *What If*, and wouldn't play. He closed the meeting. When he jumped to his feet, he almost fainted. Orthostatic hypotension was a side effect of his medicine. McCoy took a deep breath and slowly walked toward his office and the waiting FBI agent.

CHAPTER THIRTY

Dana sat through the meeting worrying about Penny. Under no circumstance were babies ever included in drug testing. Their growing bodies, high metabolism, and rapid rate of DNA synthesis made them unusually sensitive to drugs an adult could easily tolerate. And what about the dose? Dana extrapolated from a mouse to a baby. What if Penny needed more because her immune system was incompetent? Or less, because of low body fat? And what about unique developmental proteins with which the antibody could interact? Dana could easily envision a multitude of horrifying complications: shock, cardiac suppression, lung deflation, circulatory impairment, neural intrusion, mental retardation, or a full-blown allergic reaction. Halfway through the meeting, Dana decided to seek medical advice. Nick was a physician and would know what drugs could treat an impaired immune system.

He would want to know why she needed the information and she wondered what to say. He played by the rules; he wasn't one to break them. But he had lost an infant son and ultimately would understand the need to do all that could be done.

When the meeting was through, she followed him to Headquarters. She opened the door as she knocked and caught him knotting a tie. He looked tired—his five o'clock shadow was a rough stubble, the beginning of a beard.

She closed the door behind her. "I have a question."

Looking down, he finished tying his tie. "Ask Karl. He's in charge." He slipped the knot up to his neck. He was cutting off his heart, pushing her away, increasing the distance between them. It didn't matter what steps she took; for every advance she made, Nick was retreating until he would be gone.

"It's a medical question."

"I'm in a rush. I've got to go." He turned his back, gathering up papers strewn across the desk.

No matter how busy he was before, he always had time—or would make time. She backed up toward the door, and then jumped out of the way when it opened and Karl came in.

"Dana," he said. "Pleasant surprise."

Why couldn't Nick respond like that?

"Everything okay?" Karl studied her face. "You look a little—off."

"Do you have a minute? I have a few questions."

Karl sat on the top of a desk. "Shoot."

"If the kidneys stop functioning, what are the clinical signs?"

Behind her back, Nick's shuffling of papers ceased. Karl said, "A blood test will show the presence of urea."

A blood test? "Isn't there a change in urine output?"

"A decrease. If you smell the patient's breath you can detect the scent of urea. It's quite distinctive."

Dana paused before asking the next question. If Nick knew the guinea pig response, he would know why she wanted the information. "Is there a way to tell the difference between pneumonic plague and a lung allergy?"

Nick turned around and answered. "Look at the blood. The level of basophils. Or more specifically, the level of IgE. Why do you want to know?"

"Just curious."

"You can treat allergy-impaired respiration with epinephrine," Karl said.

"How would you treat systemic hypersensitivity?"

"Dexamethasone," Karl said.

She nodded. A steroid.

"What's this about?" Nick asked.

"I like to be prepared," she said. "What about infants? Do they usually get more or less of an equivalent adult dose?"

"Dose of what?" Nick said, sounding suspicious.

She couldn't say what she really wanted. "I'm speaking in general."

"You have to be specific," Nick said, with narrowed eyes.

She looked at Karl.

"I wish I could answer," Karl said, smiling his wide smile. At the end of the day, strands of hair had slipped free from his ponytail and his goatee looked tangled. "I like it that you like to be prepared."

"Do you think the bacteria are resistant?"

"I don't know. We'll have to wait and see," Karl said.

He had Nick's patience. How did he live with uncertain outcomes? Dana couldn't stand ambiguity. "What will we do if it is?"

"Deal with it," Karl said. He tucked a loose strand of hair behind his ear.

"I don't think Penny was infected in the park," Dana said.

"Let's see what the park residents have to say," Karl said. He went to the fridge and grabbed a large biohazard bag. "Here are some rodents trapped in the park."

Dana took the bag. It was heavy.

Nick crossed the room, sat on the edge of Karl's desk, and folded his arms across his heart. "The park seems to be the epicenter."

"Penny got too close to an infected animal," Karl added.

"I know Penny. She hates animals. She's terrified of my dogs. To her, all animals are different sized dogs. She wouldn't go near one."

"How do *you* think she was infected?" Nick said. His voice had softened, but there was still an edge to it.

"Someone infected her. She's not the index case."

"Usually the index case gets sick first," Nick said. "Right now Penny is the only one with pneumonic plague."

"What if there are others we don't know about?" she said.

Nick shrugged and glanced at his watch.

Karl stood up, as if on cue. "I'm ready." He looked at Dana. "Are you coming?"

"Coming? I don't think so."

Karl hooted his inappropriate laugh. "I meant coming to the dean's for this big dinner."

"Um. No." She was being deliberately excluded. *And the local Yersinia specialist was largely ineffectual during the outbreak ...*

"Pity," Karl said.

"We should go." Nick picked up his briefcase.

Karl followed him out, flashing his white teeth and crinkling his eyes as he bid her a hearty goodnight.

CHAPTER THIRTY-ONE

The dean lived in the valley on the south side of town, where the roads were winding and wide and the streets were dark. Karl drove while Nick, slouching beside him, gave directions. If he had his way, he'd skip this dinner altogether.

It had been a long and stressful day, and Nick was tired and on edge. He had a headache, and despite four aspirins his head was still throbbing. It was the case. Nothing about it made sense. Where were the rodents that were spreading the bacteria? Why were infected animals in West Texas? Where were people being exposed? Protecting people against exposure was of paramount importance, but Karl wouldn't go public.

While Nick understood his reasoning, he didn't agree. They had too little information at the moment to predict the outcome of the infection. It could either explode in their faces and become a widespread epidemic, or blow over and die out. The computer models supported either scenario. While Nick anticipated the worst, Karl hoped for the best. In the end, Karl was in charge and these decisions were his to make.

The most worrying factor in Nick's mind was the inadequacy of treatment. What if they were dealing with a resistant strain? It had occurred to Dana, and she had an accurate sense about these things. She raised the point in the meeting, and then later in her line of questioning to Karl. Renal failure, systemic hypersensitivity, and pulmonary depression were the side effects of her monoclonal vaccine in the guinea pig. Was she thinking of using the vaccine in people? Nick was appalled by the thought. It was an untested treatment and a preposterous idea. They had other options which were far less extreme.

Beside him, at the wheel, Karl said, "What's wrong? You seem distracted. Is it the case?"

"Of course." Nick combed his hair with his fingers. They were driving down a wide road lined with huge post oaks and houses set far back from the curb. They shot past Sassafras Drive. "You should have turned there."

Karl slowed and made a sweeping U-turn. "Is it dinner? Why isn't Dana coming?"

"I don't know."

"It would be a lot more fun if she was," Karl said, as he maneuvered the corner.

Nick said nothing.

"I don't think Nellie Duncan likes her," Karl said. "Do they have a problem?"

"How should I know?"

"What's your problem with Nellie? I get the feeling you're trying to avoid her."

Nick shrugged and chose not to answer. He was wary around Nellie, that was for sure. She knew about his indiscretion and he felt guilty about it. Still, what had happened was his fault, not hers. As Robin Wheeler sang: *It was me, I was to blame, I paid the price and sacrificed my heart.*

"My wife reminds me of her," Karl said. "Minding everyone else's business."

Nick had nothing to add. He liked Helena, thought Karl was being unnecessarily harsh. He always thought Karl's marriage was strong, and guessed you never really knew what was happening in someone else's life. Perhaps his wasn't as transparent as he feared.

"I like her," Karl said.

"Nellie?"

"Dana." Karl shot him a withering look. "She's not your average scientist."

"No."

They drove down the street, Karl idly running a finger across the steering wheel. "I'm tired of being on my own. I don't like it. It's different for you—you're a widower and you're used to it, but after being with someone for twenty-two years, it's a bitch to be on your own."

"I don't mind it," Nick said. In fact at the moment he longed for it. His own space, with a door he could close, and a phone he didn't have to answer.

"It's time I started dating again," Karl said. "This time I'm not eighteen. I know what I want. Someone open and upfront. Someone who doesn't hide what they think and who isn't afraid to be who they are. I want someone like, well, like Dana."

Nick started, nearly gasped.

Karl pulled into the dean's circular driveway and parked. "I'm going to ask her out."

"It's a bad idea," Nick said.

"Not now. After this is over. I've got vacation time. Maybe she wants to see Atlanta."

"I doubt it."

"Why do you say that?"

Nick opened his door. "She's got dogs. She hates to go anywhere."

"I'll talk her into it. Pour on the old charm." Karl smoothed down his goatee.

"She won't go for it."

"How do you know?"

"You forget. I know her. Quite well."

Karl narrowed his eyes. "Is there something you're not telling me?"

"Don't get your hopes up."

"Why not?"

"You're not her type."

"Oh?" Karl raised his eyebrows. "What's her type?"

"Someone she doesn't work with."

Karl threw open his door. "That's me when this is over." He punched Nick lightly on the shoulder. "Lighten up. It's not like you want her."

"Right," Nick said, sounding unconvincing even to himself. He got out of the car and headed slowly to the house.

The front door swung open, and Nellie Duncan swept out onto the porch. She wore an inappropriately tight, shimmering dress designed for someone thirty years younger. She gave Nick a tight hug, leaving the scent of heavy musk perfume all over him. She said he looked nice, but he felt under-dressed in his blazer and a tie with benzene rings. His face itched, and he wished he had time to shave.

The dean came out dressed in a tux that clashed with cowboy boots and a ten-gallon Stetson that all but buried his face. Duncan crushed Nick's hand giving it a shake.

Duncan took them to a study off of the living room, while Nellie went to check on dinner. In the dark office an unnecessary fire blazed. The head of a moose with impressive antlers poked out of the mantle. The black marble floor was covered in animal skins. There was a sweeping bar in one corner burdened with rows of bottles and heavy glasses. The room smelled of wood smoke and leather.

McCoy was sitting at the end of a low couch. Beside him, in a chrome-frame chair, hulked the university president, Mitchell Marshall. He was a tall, substantial man, with white hair and a large ruddy face. A lazy southern accent belied shrewd intelligence. He had been at the university twenty years and was gradually bringing it into the modern age. It was his baby, and he ran it as if he owned it. There was another man present Nick didn't know, and he guessed FBI before Duncan introduced Special Agent Barry Ackerman.

Duncan served the drinks and then cleared his throat. "I'm glad everyone could make it. I asked Barry to come because there's a late-breaking development." He leaned forward and said in a somber tone, "There's a possibility the outbreak is deliberate."

The room fell silent.

Duncan deferred to the special agent. Tall and thin, with short dark hair and dark eyes, Ackerman looked young, about thirty. He was too tall for his chair, and his knees nearly hit his chin. Dangling knuckles grazed the fur-tipped fringe of the zebra pelt beneath his chair. "Our bureau has received a threat against the life of the VP," he said.

No one spoke. The glass-eyed moose stared. A log in the fire sparked. Karl reached forward and took a large handful of cashews from a bowl resting on a leather-topped table. He munched loudly.

Ackerman cleared his throat and folded together long, spidery fingers. "As you have probably heard, following the strike in Somalia, varied militant Arab factions have issued a new *fatwa* against us."

"It's been on the news," McCoy said.

Drake tipped back his oversized hat. "According to the BBC, Islamic fundamentalists plan to extract payment for their dead with American blood."

Ackerman nodded his head. "We have evidence to believe the current outbreak of the plague in Duane is intentional and in protest against the upcoming vice-presidential visit."

"What evidence?" Nick said.

Ackerman pulled a paper from the breast pocket of his dark suit. "'We will strike you down with bugs in your own backyard.' It's translated from Arabic, of course."

Nick replayed the words in his mind. He wondered if there was an error in the translation. Perhaps the original message was meant to mean 'strike you down *like* bugs', not '*with* bugs'. In any case, calling bacteria 'bugs' was western slang. "How do you know the threat is serious and not a joke or a college prank?"

Karl, with his mouth full of nuts, agreed with a vigorous nod of his head. He spoke with his mouth full. "The threat does sound particularly vague."

"The timing doesn't fit," Nick said. "The rats were infected with the plague before Somalia was bombed."

Ackerman's face was set. "The validity of threats to the VP's life is our jurisdiction, not yours." He smiled thinly. "Here we have an outbreak of the plague in a region of the country, which in my understanding is too far south, too hot, and at a too low elevation for the bacteria. We have evidence the epicenter is near the hotel where the VP is scheduled to stay. These are factors we cannot ignore."

Nick was surprised by the extent of his information and guessed McCoy had brought him up to speed.

"The VP knows the situation, yet insists on coming," Ackerman said.

"That's our boy." Mitchell Marshall raised a fist and nodded to McCoy.

Ackerman stood up, his long arms hanging like sticks by his side. He had said what he came to say and now his presence was required elsewhere. He reminded everyone the information was confidential and not to be repeated. "We will keep in touch as our investigation unfolds. This is a heads-up in the hope you will reciprocate. Good night, gentlemen."

The discussion began the instant Ackerman left. Could it be an act of terror? McCoy, who long seemed intent on proving the outbreak was elsewhere, was suddenly ready for war.

Karl found the allegations outlandish. "What evidence is there?" he asked. "A dubious note? The outbreak is too random to be deliberate. How can you dump bacteria and expect to target a specific person who's not even here?"

"It is an abnormally hardy strain of *Yersinia*," Nick said. "The treatment isn't working as it should. We have one dead and three people responding poorly. We could be dealing with resistance. We know that former USSR researchers genetically engineered a multi-drug resistant strain of the plague. We know a plant in Kazakhstan can produce ninety-six pounds of freeze-dried plague bacteria in a week. We also know their funding was cut, and half the people in the plant lost their job. Where are they now? Afghanistan? Iraq? Somalia? We don't know."

McCoy fervently nodded his head. "All along we've seen abnormalities in this outbreak."

"We should bring in the antibiotic trimethoprim," Nick said. "It was used in Madagascar to treat a resistant strain."

Karl agreed it would be good to have on hand and said he would order it. But McCoy was worried the request would raise questions and generate unwanted publicity. "Is it really necessary?"

While the discussion raged, Nick wondered what to tell Washington when he called to make his report. There was still a paucity of facts with no clear picture of the epidemic. They needed more information, but a solid epidemiological assessment of *Yersinia* could take days. Nick doubted the information would be complete by Friday. He privately believed the VP's determination to keep his appointment in Duane was insane. The bacteria were unusually virulent, and while the VP was vaccinated against the plague and would be placed on prophylactic antibiotics, if this was an act of biological war then Rich Rutherford needed to keep out of harm's way. In the meantime, the most effective way to contain the outbreak was to identify those at risk. Despite McCoy's aversion to publicity and Karl's fear of hysteria, the easiest way to reach people was to go public. Nick pressed again for a news release.

"If the FBI are treating this outbreak as deliberate, and in view of the fact we haven't identified the source of the bacteria, in the aim of human safety, shouldn't we warn people of the risk?"

"No," McCoy, Karl, and Mitchell Marshall answered in unison. McCoy added, "Bad press is the last thing we need. If we're dealing with a kook, we don't want to give him any publicity."

Nick disagreed. "If news leaks to the press, we're going to have to defend our position and our secrecy, which will be difficult if more people get sick."

"There's already a flu epidemic in town," Karl said. "We won't solve this case if everyone absconds."

"If we're clear on that, let's go eat," Duncan said, as if the matter was decided. He removed his hat and threw open the door.

Nellie stood in the doorway and laughed nervously. "I came to tell you, dinner's ready."

"Wonderful." Duncan waved the crowd out of the study.

Obediently, they all trooped to the dining room and sat down at a long table. Overhead, a heavy crystal chandelier hung low and sparkled on polished silver and flowered china. The food kept coming, but Nick had lost his appetite and could do no more than cut his food and shove it around his plate as Nellie ran a monologue about a myriad of topics that at one point included her regrets about his poor dead wife.

Nick was barely listening. He heard Robin Wheeler singing in his head: *What's gone won't go; it persists, remains in the blood that flows like wine.*

CHAPTER THIRTY-TWO

Dana's stomach was rumbling as she finished testing the blood from the animals trapped in High Park. The results were negative. In the park, only the four rats Carol trapped had the plague. No other rodents were infected. It was beyond bizarre.

She checked the disk test. Still no zone of inhibition. At least it looked as if the bacteria had stopped growing and there were no new colonies. Maybe the antibiotic just needed time to work.

She called the hospital. Her heart raced as she waited for Sheryl to answer. When she did, Sheryl wept as she spoke. "The doctors don't know if she'll make it."

"I'll be right there."

"You can't come. Visiting hours are over. I don't want to make the nurse more suspicious than she is already."

"Does Penny have any new symptoms? A drop in blood pressure? Shock? Impaired breathing?"

"No." Sheryl sounded horrified.

"Does her breath smell like ammonia?"

"Why would you ask?"

"If there's a change in symptoms, call me. If she goes into shock, tell the doctor to give her dexamethasone. If her breathing gets worse, give her epinephrine."

"I've got to go," Sheryl said.

"Wait!" But the phone went dead.

Dana left the veterinary school. A three-quarter moon hung high, staring out of the clouds like a malicious eye. A heavy wind rattled the trees and the air felt electrified, though there was no lightning. Still, there was no doubt a storm was coming.

APRIL 29TH

CHAPTER THIRTY-THREE

On Wednesday morning, McCoy rose early after a restless night. He was unable to fall back asleep after a midnight call from Agent Ackerman, who was eager to dispense free advice. Until they identified the terrorist, McCoy was warned not to trust anyone. "You could be led astray. Your inquiry intentionally derailed."

Ackerman was, of course, referring to Dana Sparks. According to Ackerman, who had done some checking, she had both opportunity and motive. In the previous months, she had placed catalogue orders for numerous strains of *Yersinia pestis*. With her university contract set to expire, she was under tremendous academic pressure. She had no tenure. She needed a grant, which had not yet been approved. If she could show the research was necessary, she would keep her job.

McCoy listened quietly to Ackerman's accusations with growing skepticism. The possibility she was behind a deliberate outbreak of the plague was frankly absurd. Dana Sparks was naïve, and ignorant of warfare and politics. McCoy could not fathom her jockeying with Islamic fundamentalists in an international scheme of terror, and told Ackerman as much.

"It's always the person you expect the least," the FBI agent said.

When his back began to ache, McCoy rose from bed and dressed in the dark. He kissed his sleeping wife goodbye and tiptoed down the stairs. He reached the kitchen breathless and faint. He had to sit down and breathe deeply to stop his head from spinning. He stared longingly at the coffeepot. He had given up coffee after his heart attack and could use a cup now. What if he wasn't up to this? What if he failed? If this was a terrorist attack, it happened on his watch and he bore the responsibility. Would a younger, healthier man do a better job? McCoy felt a lump in his throat he tried to clear. It began a coughing fit he could barely control. Once again he was fighting exhaustion, though his day had barely begun.

At six in the morning he called Greenlee Hospital for an update on admissions. The shift was changing and he had to wait to speak to Dr. Taversham, who came on the line sounding irritable and whiny.

"I just arrived," Taversham said. "Call me later."

"That won't be necessary if there are no new admissions."

But it seemed there were.

"We've got an eleven-year-old boy with bubonic plague," Taversham said. "And five from the Lone Star Heritage Hotel have pneumonic plague."

McCoy placed a hand over his heart. The hotel was hit after all. Perhaps it was the intended target. The strike was less random than the pony-tailed Karl King surmised. "Anything else?"

"Not here. At the north hospital, your veterinarian Tim Sweeny was admitted during the night, as were two high school students and a university sophomore, all with pneumonic plague."

McCoy's heart tightened as if held between the pinchers of a vise-grip. "What?" he said in a whisper.

"I said your veterinarian Tim Sweeny has pneumonic plague," Taversham shouted in his ear.

"No, the high school students."

"Two seniors from Duane High have pneumonic plague."

McCoy heard no more. His daughter Margaret was a senior at that school. She could have been in the same classroom with the infected students, *breathing the same air*. McCoy's chest was badly constricted. He lost his breath, and began coughing so hard he couldn't stop. Something was caught in his throat, clogging his esophagus, blocking his air. He pounded his sternum with his fist and the phlegm cleared. Breathing hard, he pushed the receiver against his ear.

"Are you there?" Dr. Taversham said. "Are you all right?"

"Yes, yes, fine," McCoy answered sharply, though his voice was high and vibrated as if he needed oxygen.

"If there's nothing else," Taversham said.

"There is," McCoy said, fighting for control and winning. His voice sounded normal when he added, "As a precaution, tighten security at the hospital. Restrict visitors and post security guards at the door. Keep out the press."

"If you think it's necessary," Taversham said.

McCoy did. He dropped the receiver and stared out the kitchen window at the back yard. The tent was still there from the garden party that now seemed so long ago. He saw the jungle gym he carted down from Virginia. In his mind's eye, he watched a younger Margaret scrabble across the rungs of the high horizontal ladder, as her mother cringed for her safety and begged her to take care. It was the job of parents to protect their children and provide a safe environment. Now Margaret's health was in danger. He'd keep her home and out of harm's way, and leave antibiotics for her and his wife. What about the other people in town? Was it ethical to deny other parents a chance to make a similar choice?

Yet the alternative meant calling the press and going public. In all likelihood the university would have to close. Rich Rutherford would cancel, and the anticipated and much needed revenue from his visit would be lost. McCoy's new department of human health that would specialize in war would be put in jeopardy.

But Margaret's school was hit!

McCoy always swore that the sacrifice to one's country was the greatest, most noble sacrifice one could make. But what of his family? The VP's trip could be put on hold, postponed, or rescheduled. Margaret was only sixteen; she had a long life ahead of her. She had to be protected. The town had to be closed.

McCoy called President Marshall and uttered the words he never thought he'd say. "I think we should go public."

"Excuse me?" Marshall said.

"It appears the hotel is a target after all. We need to call a news conference."

"I got it the first time. I thought it was a joke. TJ, you can't be serious."

Keeping his eye fixed on the jungle gym, McCoy confirmed that he was. "We need to warn people there are contagious bacteria in town. Ask everyone to stay home."

"What do you mean, stay home? In two days time we have parents and alumni who make sizeable donations to our institute coming for convocation. We've invited political heavyweights—senators, congressmen, the governor, not to mention the VP. We can't close the university."

"We'll go a little public," McCoy said. "If we close the town now, for maybe a day, minimize exposure, we may contain this."

"The press will blow it up."

McCoy stared out the window, where the wind was blowing hard. "As soon as weather permits, we'll spray DDT. That should stop this in its tracks. In the meantime, we minimize casualties."

He paused, but there was no response, so he went on. "Alternatively, if we do nothing, if we pretend all is well, and if more and more people fall ill, then this thing will escalate, and an outside quarantine will be imposed upon us. No one will come."

Marshall exhaled heavily. "I hope you know what you're doing."

McCoy hoped so, too.

He hung up the phone and rose from his stool like an elderly man carrying an impossible load. He couldn't recall a morning when he felt so weak, so impotent, and so uncertain of victory.

Skipping breakfast, but remembering to take his multitude of medications, McCoy left the cool air-conditioned comfort of his house. Outside on the porch, a whistling wind rushed against him. Across a sweep of manicured lawn, McCoy saw the orange sleeve wrapping of the Houston newspaper blowing in the wind. The blue-sleeved *Eagle* hung tangled in the branches of a prize rosebush. McCoy retrieved his newspapers and stalked to his car.

Sitting in the Mercedes, with the engine running and the air conditioner cranked, McCoy opened the *Houston Chronicle*. Taking up half the front page was a picture of the VP and a reminder of his impending visit. The other half of the page was a report on the UN investigation into the Washington strike against Somalia. The UN confirmed that a hospital and mosque had been hit. There was no warehouse full of munitions. The U.S. was protesting, adamant their bombs alone could not have caused the extensive damage that ensued. It was possible that the terrorists bombed their own hospital and mosque to frame the U.S. Needless to say, the investigation was ongoing.

Taking up a bottom corner of the front page was the warning of a tropical storm. It was expected to make landfall sometime that morning. McCoy peered up through the windshield. Thick clouds skipped across the sky. He pounded his fist on the steering wheel. They were fighting even the weather. It reminded him of his last days in Vietnam, of typhoons and endless rain, of a time when the deck was stacked against him, and he led his troop to a battle that had already been lost.

CHAPTER THIRTY-FOUR

After a nearly sleepless night, Dana was up before dawn and on the way to the hospital. A pale sun was rising and a hard wind was blowing. She had tried calling the hospital, but all she got was a taped recording and no news from Sheryl. She didn't know if Penny had made it through the night.

At the hospital, a tall gaunt policeman blocked the entrance. "I'm sorry, ma'am. There are no visiting hours today."

"Why not?" Dana peered through the glass of the automatic doors into the hallway and saw no bustle of activity that would explain the barring of visitors.

"Temporary hospital regulations, ma'am. You can call. The phone lines are open."

What was going on? Why the security? Did the hospital know she injected Penny? But Sheryl would have called her. Dana gazed across the dew-soaked grass. Should she press her case or go? She smiled at the policeman and he smiled back. In her nicest voice, she said, "I'm working with the CDC on a current case. I need to follow up on some patients." She had to see Penny for herself, smell her sweet breath, take her fast pulse, and touch her warm skin.

The policeman wanted to see ID, and she produced a laminated badge that bore a bad picture and a university ID number. The cop checked the picture, copied down her ID number, and let her pass.

A few moments later, Dana stood outside the ICU staring through the window. The room was vacant. The crib was empty. There was no Sheryl, no nurses, no other patients. Dana knocked on the door. No answer. She tried the knob. Locked. She jogged down the hallway to the reception desk. No one there. Where was the lady with the pink nails? She went to the lobby. Empty. Then to the main bathroom, where she found Sheryl.

She was hanging over a sink, splashing water at her face. Through the mirror, Dana saw Sheryl's eyes lined with dark rings. Her face was pale and tight, and she smelled of sweat and vomit. Dana gripped her arm. "Where's Penny?"

Sheryl turned around. "Upstairs. She's fine."

Dana released Sheryl's arm and hugged her tightly, "She's fine?" She exhaled slowly, relief flooding through her. "When I saw you, I thought ... I thought ... I thought ..."

"I think I've got it." Sheryl said.

Dana's euphoria vanished.

"I started feeling bad last night. I started taking antibiotics. They're not working."

"And Penny is fine? No side effects? No shock? No organ failure? No allergic reaction? Nothing?"

"The doctors are amazed."

"And Jack?"

"He may not make it," Sheryl said.

That was it, then. For Dana, the evidence was strong enough to convince her that humans would not mimic the guinea pig response. She told Sheryl to wait, she would go to the lab, get the monoclonal, and come back.

Twenty minutes later, Sheryl was injected.

Dana went to see Jack. He lay in bed twisting and turning. He was puffy, his cheeks were swollen, and his skin was marbled with purple lines. IV drips fed each wrist and a cannula in his nose delivered a steady stream of oxygen. Dana did not try to wake him up to ask if he wanted the experimental vaccine. As she had with Penny, she injected the monoclonal directly into his IV.

She was leaving the hospital when she saw Sam, looking exhausted and worn out. "I have no time to talk," he said, slowing down nonetheless.

Dana thought the hospital looked eerily empty and quiet given the seriousness of the situation. The ICU appeared to be closed, and there were no medical personnel or auxiliary people in the corridors. No candy stripers and cleaners, no smell of breakfast cooking, no flower delivery people. "What's going on?"

"It's a nightmare," Sam said. "The hospital itself is under quarantine. No one can come or go." He fixed his gaze on her. "What are you doing here?"

"I came to see Jack Dowel. How many are sick?"

"We've got six new cases, and St. Joe's has four. The hospital is turning the ICU into a quarantine room for people with pneumonic plague. They've cleared out half the patients and sent non-critical patients home. We've called in all medical staff. I was due for a four-day break, and now I have to work straight through. We're on day and night." Sam lowered his voice and looked around the deserted hallway. "This is a bad strain." He added in a whisper. "It may be deliberate."

"Why do you say that?"

"Off the record? There's a terrorist loose, or something. That's why cops are at the door." He looked over his shoulder. "Federal Agents were here last night. The FBI is asking questions. The VP is due Friday and this has something to do with his visit. It may be an extremist from Somalia. You need to stay away from crowds, watch where you go, watch who you trust."

He left and Dana digested his words. He must be mistaken. Had he confused the CDC with the FBI? Karl and Jeff were the only federal agents around. And the policeman at the door was there to keep visitors away, not terrorists out. They couldn't take any chances with pneumonic plague, and closing the hospital was a step long overdue. Now there were fourteen cases of the plague. Fourteen people infected in three days. One person was dead. At least Penny was better.

Though now there was a new question. Was she saved by antibiotics or the experimental antibody?

Dana returned to the lab and examined the culture plates. The disk test had been running for twenty hours and there was no clear zone on any of the five plates. The antibiotics weren't working as they should. They were dealing with a resistant strain.

CHAPTER THIRTY-FIVE

The painter was hard at work when McCoy entered the conference room. To his horror, once again the room was an oven. The windows were shut, the curtains were gone, and the room was bright. The paint fumes were suffocating—almost as bad as the hot humid air that was choking him. Lacking the energy to be pleasant, McCoy roared at the painter. "God damn it, you were supposed to be done yesterday."

The fool of a painter smiled vacuously and removed her paint-splattered cap. "I just got the paint."

"What's wrong with the air conditioner?"

"Nothing. I turned it off. It will help the paint dry."

McCoy turned it back on and began opening windows.

"I have strict orders not to open them, sir."

McCoy opened the last window and turned around. "I've got a meeting. Get out." He strode to his chair. He had to sit down.

"Another meeting." She looked at him in dazed wonderment. "When should I come back?"

"When we're through. When you're done, bring back my blackboard."

"I could get that now."

"Perfect."

After she left, McCoy raised his hands to his head. He was sweating profusely. His shirt was soaking wet. Behind his scalp, his head was tightening. McCoy had not felt this weak since his heart attack. Here was a potential terrorist threat, a war on his soil, an attack against his country, and what he wanted more than anything besides cold air was sleep. He closed his eyes and must have dozed off, for he awoke when the painter returned and excused herself for waking him. He looked at his watch. The meeting was about to start.

Staff arrived and when all were present, he began with an announcement. "I'm afraid we have a situation on our hands." He was appalled by the indolence in his tone, but his energy was gone and he could not revive himself. To looks of surprise, he declared the university and town were closing. "The mayor will make a statement shortly."

Nellie gasped loudly.

"There will be information centers." He held up three fingers. "At St. Joe's, Greenlee, and the campus health clinic. We'll service these centers ourselves. I drew up a timetable." He passed it around the room, caught sight of Michael Smith. "I'm afraid we will have to reschedule your lecture, Dr. Smith."

"That's no problem," Michael said.

McCoy smiled at him. "Fine. Now I want everyone to remember, when dealing with the public, discretion is the word." To his own ears, McCoy sounded like a record stuck on a slow speed. There was nothing he could do about it. "The goal is to alleviate fear and promote early detection. Speak in vague or oblique scientific terms. No one is to mention the word plague. Call it an infection if you will, a bacterial infection if you must. You may talk about lung infections, prophylactic antibiotics, excellent chances of recovery, et cetera, et cetera. Appeal to people's reason, request they remain in town. Doctors here are prepared to deal with the situation, while outsiders won't have a clue. Assure everyone all is well." McCoy ended his monologue and slumped in his seat. Just speaking wore him out. He could not in his life ever remember being this tired. He wondered if he had been drugged.

Beside him, Karl asked if he was all right.

"Fine, fine. What have you trapped?"

"We snared thirty rodents in and around Duane last night. I'm afraid we didn't collect any more rats or mice in the park."

Of course he would miss the target.

"We did catch a few more squirrels and a chipmunk. They appear healthy, but we'll have to confirm that with blood work."

McCoy looked at Dr. Sparks. "Did you test the samples from the park yesterday?"

She had, and the results were negative.

Karl stretched out his legs. "Besides Carol Dupuis and Jack Dowel, five guests from the Lone Star Heritage are ill, as are a vet, two high school seniors, a car wash attendant, and an elementary school boy. That's a total of thirteen if you count Dudley Shaw. Though there's likely more we don't know about."

McCoy didn't count dead people, he didn't count people in Houston, and he didn't count people that weren't diagnosed. "We're dealing with eleven."

"I spoke to the kid last night," Karl said. "Travis Levine has bubonic plague. For an eleven-year old who's sick, he's quite lucid. He's recently been to High Park and the Lone Star Heritage Hotel. He also has a cat that's been missing for over a week. All he talked about was the cat."

"I saw Travis this morning," Nick said. "He isn't doing good. Not lucid at all. His doctor said his condition deteriorated rapidly. They're pumping him full of antibiotics, but his prognosis is not good."

Dr. Sparks raised her hand. "Could the bacteria be resistant to antibiotics? It's been twenty hours and there's no clear zone in the disk test."

"You made a mistake," McCoy said. "We have clinical evidence the antibiotic works. Penny Paige recovered. Repeat the test. Michael, lend her a hand."

"I don't need help," she said. "There is no mistake. This eleven-year-old boy got worse over night. Jack almost died."

"Jack's fine," Karl countered. "I just spoke to the hospital. Frankly, they're astounded. They didn't expect him to make it. So, we know the antibiotics *are* working."

"Carol isn't responding," Nick said. "I talked to her doctor and she's critical."

"Yet people are recovering," McCoy said. "It takes time."

"The antibiotics aren't working," Dana said. "It's the vaccine."

McCoy heard a sudden, insistent pounding in his head. No, it was the door. The painter was back with the blackboard. McCoy stood up and waved her away. What did Sparks just say? "Excuse me? What vaccine?"

In a small voice, McCoy thought she said, "The monoclonal vaccine."

He couldn't have heard her correctly. McCoy leaned forward, bracing his hands on the table. "What?" he said, in a desperately high voice. Had she tried her experimental monoclonal vaccine on people? Was she out of her mind? There were regulations to follow. New treatments were employed only after the most rigorous of testing that the army had not yet started. She could not have injected people with an experimental vaccine. It was not possible. Especially not after the guinea pig's poor response. McCoy breathed deeply and placed his hand on his solar plexus. He said slowly, clearly, "Tell me you did not inject the monoclonal vaccine into sick people. I have misunderstood, correct? When you say vaccine, you mean the regular vaccine. The one you take routinely."

She shook her head.

He tried to stand up. The room began to spin. He blinked his eyes to clear his sight and prayed his ears would stop ringing. He wondered if he would faint. He pressed hard on his chest to calm his racing heart. He faced the window and fresh air seemed far away. The room was turning. McCoy staggered, trying to keep his balance as blackness fell upon him. He called out for help, but he had no breath. A vice clamped his lungs together and an unbearable force pushed his body to the floor ...

CHAPTER THIRTY-SIX

Dana heard a clunk as McCoy's head smacked the table. There was a loud thud as his body slammed the floor. Karl leapt out of his seat and was on his knees, loosening McCoy's tie and yelling for an ambulance. Nellie pulled a cell phone from her purse. Nick straddled McCoy's chest and administered CPR. Dana, hovering over them, covered her mouth to hold back her screams.

Fairway was pushing people back, herding them to the door, trying to make room. Dana couldn't move. What if McCoy didn't recover? What if she killed him? What if she was wrong? What if the antibiotics worked and she didn't have to use the monoclonal?

The shrill sound of a siren drew near. Footsteps pounded in the hall and attendants in white rushed in. McCoy was lifted to a stretcher, a respirator placed over his mouth. Dana turned away from his ashen face and sweat-soaked skin. Bile rose in her throat and she leaned against a wall, needing support. She bowed her head as McCoy was swept from the room with Nick in close pursuit.

Would McCoy die? Dana pressed her hand over her mouth. She wondered if she would throw up.

Karl draped a heavy arm across her shoulder "Let's get out of here." He led her from the conference room, through the head office, and into a hall filled with curious veterinary students confused about the delay of their morning exam.

Karl steered her down the hallway. Her feet felt wooden and numb and she was weak and dazed. Her mouth was dry and her throat was sore. She was sweating and her shirt stuck to her skin. Doubts assailed her. What if the antibiotics worked? What if McCoy was right, and she'd erred on the disk test? Maybe the antibiotics had expired. Maybe she hadn't formulated them correctly. She wasn't absolutely sure the monoclonal explained Penny and Jack's recovery. They were young and healthy, their infections had been caught early, and maybe the antibiotics took time. Time Dudley didn't have. Maybe she gave the monoclonal without justification, and a man had a heart attack for no reason, and she had sacrificed her reputation for nothing.

With a squeeze of her shoulder, Karl ushered her into her lab. He poured two cups of coffee and handed her one. Caffeine was not what she needed. Her hand trembled so badly that coffee slopped over the side of the cup. She put it down.

"What happened wasn't your fault," Karl said. "McCoy's a heart attack waiting to happen." He took a sip of his coffee, stared at her over the rim of the cup. "Did you really use the monoclonal vaccine?"

She nodded slowly.

"That took guts. I admire that. I'm sure you wouldn't have used it if you didn't have to."

"I plated the bacteria. Added the antibiotic cocktail. Nothing happened. The bacteria keep growing."

She took him to the quarantine room, turned on the hood, and got out Dudley's culture plate. He stared at it thoughtfully. "Maybe we're seeing outside contamination."

He was grasping at straws, as McCoy had done earlier. Hoping for a mistake. "It's *Yersinia*," she said.

He rubbed his chin. There was something different about him today. He seemed less scruffy. "Here's the thing," he said. "We've got people on prophylactic antibiotics. If there was resistance, we'd see more people ill."

He had a point. Tetracycline was the antibiotic used both as a preventative and in the cocktail as treatment. She took the plate from him. "There's a seven to ten day incubation period for bubonic plague. Two to four days for pneumonic. It's possible the prophylactic has failed and we don't know it yet."

"Let's repeat the test."

He helped her prepare agar, prep another culture plate, and she wondered if he was watching her, keeping his eye on her. Did he not trust her? She began to think that was the case when he insisted on helping her test the blood from the rodents collected during the night.

"It's no trouble," Karl said. "I don't have anything else to do. It's my pleasure, really."

"It's not necessary. I can do it."

"It'll go faster if I help," he said.

They began the assay. Karl talked constantly. Despite everything that happened, he looked happy. His face was shiny and Dana realized what was different about him. He'd shaved off his goatee. He looked better without it.

He invited her to come to Atlanta, tour the CDC and see the town. It was more culturally advanced than Duane, and if the weather and traffic weren't better, the restaurants and bars were something to see. "L-l-let me know if you want to come and I'll s-s-set it up."

Dana heard the stutter and wondered if he was more nervous than he appeared. She changed the subject so she didn't have to answer. "You said you went to the hospital last night. Did you speak to Tim?"

"The vet? Tim Sweeney? No. He was unconscious. Not speaking."

"He was supposed to be in D.C. this week."

"He got what he thought was the flu and didn't go. He drove himself to the hospital on Monday night and was sent home. He went back yesterday and crashed in the ER as he was filling out forms."

"When did he get sick?" she asked.

"We're not sure," Karl said, shoving a yellow tip on the end of the small Gilson pipette. "He apparently decided to treat himself. He'd injected himself with gamma globulin and six different antibiotics."

"He could be the index case. He could have been exposed by an animal. It wouldn't be the first time."

"Does he come in your lab?"

"You think he was infected here? He came in and was inadvertently exposed?"

"Something like that."

Dana passed him the rack with the diluted sera, which he pipetted onto the plate. "It's not possible. He doesn't come back here. It's more likely he was infected in the clinic. We should check the records. See the cases he was treating."

"Do you keep this room locked all the time?"

She pulled a face. "It should be. Not always."

Karl said nothing, and Dana wondered if he thought the origin was her lab. "This isn't the epicenter. I test every strain of *Yersinia* I order. I only use antibiotic-sensitive bacteria. I won't touch anything resistant."

"In case there's an accident, and someone's exposed?" Karl said.

It was the exact reason, and she nodded.

"Good policy," he said.

They finished the assay and the results were negative. Thirty rodents collected in and around Duane the previous evening weren't exposed to *Yersinia*. The squirrels and chipmunks trapped in High Park were healthy. "The epicenter can't be the park," Dana said.

Karl agreed.

"It's strange there's no wildlife infected. What if the bacteria were brought in by someone who came and went? We ruled out Jack's mother, but there are other possibilities. Like someone who stayed at the Lone Star Heritage. Both Penny and Tim were there on the weekend."

"The hotel makes more sense," Karl said.

"Maybe a guest was infected."

Karl nodded his head. "It's looking more and more like it came from somewhere else."

His cell phone rang. Nick was calling. McCoy was stable, and the mayor was about to make his statement. Dana switched on the radio. There was a *beep, beep, beep* sounding the alarm that preceded a severe weather warning, and then the mayor came on:

"We are afflicted at this time in the city of Duane with a severe form of influenza that is highly contagious and invasive. While there is no need to panic, in an effort to minimize the spread of disease we are at this time closing all schools. Parents are asked to retrieve their children immediately. Any individual who experiences flu-like symptoms, which include: fever, chills, muscular aches and pains, lung congestion, or difficulty breathing, are to proceed directly to hospital. I repeat, there is nothing to fear, no reason to panic, no reason to leave town. Local physicians are equipped to deal with the health emergency and have all the necessary medical and pharmaceutical supplies on hand. As a precaution, the governor is sending in the National Guard for reinforcement. They will be in position at all access roads leading in and out of town. They will remain on standby

in case of emergency. As a final note, any individual who may have been in contact with anyone exhibiting these flu-like symptoms may commence a course of prophylactic antibiotics that may be collected, free of charge, from either hospital, or the health center on campus. There are sufficient drugs for all. I repeat, we are in no danger of running out of medicine. If you have any questions, any problems, information is available at any of the three medical centers. I thank you for your attention and repeat there is no need to panic."

"That sounded pretty good," Karl said, when the message began to repeat.

Dana turned off the radio and stared at him dumbfounded. The mayor sounded alarmed himself. He was out of breath and his sentences were choppy. The way he kept repeating there was "no need to panic" made it seem as if people were already panicking. When he assured people there were enough drugs, she wondered if he was worried they would run out.

Karl looked at his watch. "I hate to leave you, but I have to make a few calls. Update my office."

CHAPTER THIRTY-SEVEN

Dana was scheduled to help staff the health center on campus from ten to one, but she had things to do and was going to be late. University Drive was clogged with cars. The sidewalks were empty. There was no one out on the street inhaling contaminated air. Dana drove with the windows closed. The wind was gusting, swirling in from the north and the temperature was dropping. The sky was gray and the air was clammy and cool. Five days ago it was in the eighties, and now it was in the low sixties. Gone was the heat Nick said would save them. According to the weather report on the radio, a front was moving up from the gulf and would meet the cold front in Duane, causing a tropical storm. A flood warning had been issued.

The car crawled along. The deserted campus was on her right, shrouded in gray. To the left stood the Lone Star Heritage Hotel, shining brightly in the morning gloom. She drove past the University Plaza, which was usually buzzing, but not today. There were few cars in the parking lot, and no line up at the car wash where another victim of bubonic plague was employed. Beyond the Plaza was the park where four diseased rats were trapped. Dana wondered why more rats and mice weren't trapped in the park. Where were the traps laid? Up in trees?

Dana made an abrupt left turn. She pulled into the University Plaza and took a shortcut through the parking lot to the park. She saw a young man carrying two animal cages and stopped the car and jumped out. She rattled the chain on the park's locked gate trying to get the kid's attention. He finally turned, and she waved him over. He wore overalls and had a bandanna tied around his face like a bandit.

The kid reached the gate. He was young, about twenty, with stringy black hair.

"I'm working with the CDC," Dana said. "Who are you?"

The young man extended his hand. "Howie Dryer, Parks and Rec."

As Dana got older, everyone else seemed to get younger. "Are you setting the traps?"

Howie admitted he was. "Must have laid out thirty last night. Didn't catch much." He stroked the skin over his lip. It looked like he was trying to grow a moustache. "I think the bait's no good."

"Why do you say that?"

"We're looking for rats and field mice. I know they're around, but we're not catching them." Howie shrugged deeply. "I don't think the animals like Ritz crackers and peanut butter."

"Really?" Dana was surprised, for her research mice loved peanut butter.

"When you're used to dining on Lobster Thermador and Steak Diane, crackers don't cut it," Howie said.

"Lobster?"

Howie pointed to a dumpster at the edge of the University Plaza. "That's where Caprice throws their leftovers. That's where the rodents go to eat."

It made sense. The traps used food bait. They weren't enticing the rats and mice with food, because the rodents weren't hungry.

Dana had one more question. According to Sheryl, the park was notoriously clean of fire ants and most insects. So much so, the kids in the day care had trouble finding bugs for their collection. "Do you use pesticides?"

"Twice a month," Howie said. "Every other Monday. We're due for a repeat next week."

Which meant the park had been sprayed recently. Howie didn't know the name of the chemical, but he thought it was likely effective against fleas.

She thanked him for the information and headed for the dumpster. Did the pesticide explain why more rodents in the park weren't infected? If the pesticide killed fleas, it would also kill the bacteria. It was McCoy's pending aerial campaign on a smaller scale.

Dana reached the rusted dumpster and lifted the warped, squeaky lid. The smell of rotting trash assailed her. The dumpster had been recently cleaned, but it still stank. Flies buzzed loudly. She saw no steak or lobster, but banana peels, flattened strawberries, droopy lettuce rinds, and a flattened birthday cake were in evidence.

Dana wondered what they would find if they laid a trap here. She dropped the dumpster lid and headed back to her car, wiping her hands on her slacks.

She drove around the corner, heading for Phillip Becker's house. She wanted his take on the outbreak. His front door opened as she pulled into the drive. Phillip came out in safari pants and a yellow polo shirt. "Well, this is a pleasant surprise." He ushered her into the living room and pointed to a couch covered in a pink crocheted blanket. "Sit down, sit down. Tell me what's happening."

Dana sat down, surrounded by the presence of Becker's dead wife. She smiled out from a wedding photo, was there in the doilies and the petite point pictures hanging on the walls. "Feeling better?" Dana asked.

"Lots. What did I hear on the news? A cryptic message for people to leave town?"

"Or to start panicking. That we're about to run out of drugs."

"Too bad if we do, now the roads in and out of town are sealed and the National Guard is coming to make sure everyone stays put. I hope someone informed the wildlife not to stray."

Dana ran her hand across the blanket. "That's the problem. The wildlife doesn't seem to be infected. The CDC thinks Penny is the index case and was infected in the park. I don't see how. I can't figure out a scenario that makes sense. It's too confusing. I don't get it."

"How about some tea?"

She had to decline. She didn't have the time.

"Live with the confusion," he said. "It's like muddy water. Wait for it to clear."

"I don't know how epidemiologists stand this. There's too many unanswered questions."

"Because too many pieces are missing. Or one big one. Just wait."

"There's no time to wait." She smoothed out the blanket. It had been made by sewing together hundreds of little crocheted circles. Becker's wife must have been a patient woman.

"What about you?" Becker asked. "You okay? You're not looking well."

"McCoy had another heart attack."

"Well, he would, wouldn't he. War or not, that man lives in one."

"It was my fault. I think this strain of *Yersinia* is resistant. I injected Penny with the monoclonal antibody. I thought she was dying."

"How is she doing?"

"Better."

Phillip sat forward in his easy chair, elbows on his knees. "Then I fail to see the problem."

"I injected her with an experimental unapproved drug."

"After what happened to the guinea pig, that took some nerve."

"I was desperate."

"Of course you were. You did what you had to do. And I say good for you. You made a hard choice, but it was the right one. If you follow your heart, it will show you the way. The adage is not restricted to clandestine affairs alone."

Dana blushed, unable to hold his eye. She left a few minutes later and saw him watching through the window as she drove off. Intermittent drops of rain splashed at her windshield. On the radio she heard a weather update. The front from Galveston was moving fast. People as far north as Dallas were supposed to take precautions against flooding. This was the last thing they needed.

On the main campus, Dana parked her car in the biology building lot and went on foot to the health center. She heard the racket before she turned a corner and saw the crowd that swarmed the clinic. There must have been two or three hundred people, more than she could count. They were jostling one another, pushing, shoving, and yelling.

Charlie Lane and Michael Smith stood outside the clinic under the portico dispensing boxes of antibiotics. Dana tried to push her way to the front. Her clothes billowed in the wind. Overhead came the rumble of thunder. The rain was picking up under darkening skies.

She was midway through the crowd when Michael clambered up on the table. He was dressed for his seminar that had been cancelled, and looked dapper in a three-piece beige suit and white pointy shoes. He raised his hands.

"We are out of antibiotics," he yelled. He went on, but the roar of the crowd and a loud clap of thunder drowned out his words.

Beside him, the eight month pregnant Charlie Lane scrambled up on the table and tried to talk to the crowd. "Do not worry," she said, when the thunder stopped. "We're going to get more. We'll be back shortly."

Get down, get down, Dana silently urged her. *Go home*. It wasn't so much of a crowd as a mob. With renewed vigor, Dana pushed forward, enduring the elbows and jeers of those rightly protesting her progress.

Suddenly the sky turned black, as if a light had been switched off. There was an abrupt and shocking silence. The wind stopped blowing. A jagged line of lightening cracked the sky and thunder peeled. Rain pelted down and people began to run.

They pushed against her, pushing her farther back. In seconds she was drenched, rain dumping from the sky. She could not see three feet in front of her. Charlie and Michael had vanished. She stopped fighting the crowd and raced back to her car. What would happen if they were out of prophylactic antibiotics? Was it the clinic or the whole town? If the roads were closed, how would they get more drugs?

Did it matter if the drugs didn't work? The antibiotic tetracycline was used both for treatment and as a prophylactic. If the drug didn't work as a cure, it wouldn't work as a preventative—not if the bacteria were resistant.

She reached the vet school. The parking lot was empty, only a couple of cars in the lot. The clinic was closed and the main doors were locked. She found the correct key and unlocked the door. The building was empty and her footsteps echoed off the walls. The doors to classrooms, offices, and labs were locked. Her lab door was open and she went in. Karl was there, pacing. He was soaking wet too. His limp ponytail was dripping.

"You're here." He shook water off himself. "We have a problem. I think you're right. The prophylactics aren't working. Betty is sick. So is a lady friend of Jack Dowel's who we put on antibiotics yesterday morning. I suspect everyone exposed will get sick. It's just a matter of time."

"We could use the monoclonal vaccine. But first we'd have to get it back from Fort Troy."

Karl stopped pacing and rubbed his chin where the goatee used to be. "It's too risky. We're going to have to try other antibiotics. Trimethoprim for example. We used it in Madagascar."

"Some strains are resistant to that. We'll have to test it on this strain."

"Culture another plate and test it. In the interim, we use it."

"Do we have enough for everyone?"

There was a loud crack of thunder. Rain slogged at the windows. "Nick flew in a load this morning from Houston."

"Then he must have also suspected resistance," Dana said.

"There's a lot about this outbreak he doesn't like." Karl looked at his watch. "Have you seen him?"

"No."

"He's not answering his phone. Tell him to call me if you see him. I'm going to the hospital to let the doctors know to switch antibiotics."

Karl left at a jog, leaving Dana more worried than ever. Up until now he had treated the outbreak like a joke, but he was no longer smiling. She knew why. They were working blind, dealing with a strain of resistant *Yersinia* they knew nothing about. A strain that was resistant, contagious, and deadly.

CHAPTER THIRTY-EIGHT

The rain caught Nick by surprise. He had stopped to rest on a rickety picnic bench under a grove of trees outside the vet school when the storm hit. At first he welcomed the cool relief, but now he was freezing and unable to summon the energy to move. He had a fever and shivered as icy water ran down his skin and waves of rain swept across him. He lowered his head to the picnic table and hugged his shaking body with trembling hands. He seldom got sick. When he did, he tried to ignore it. He worked when he had typhoid, malaria, and cholera—but there was no way he could work with this.

He had the plague. It wasn't possible, yet he knew it was so—despite twenty years of vaccinations that were supposed to last a lifetime. Three hours ago, he'd taken a double dose of trimethoprim and was waiting for it to work. It was a folic acid inhibitor, a bactericide rather than a growth inhibitor. He knew to be this sick he had to have a high concentration of bacteria in his body. Maybe he should have taken more of the drug. Or were the bacteria resistant even to this?

Did Dana suspect as much? Is that why she used the monoclonal vaccine? She had tried to talk to him last night and he brushed her off. He should have listened to her. Her questions made sense now. He should have paid more attention. He should have done something to stop her.

He was simultaneously awed and exasperated by the risks she took. She reacted emotionally, though in this instance, correctly. She'd been lucky. What if the baby responded like the guinea pig? The girl would have died and Dana would be responsible. Did she know something they didn't? From his vantage point, there were less drastic options on the table. They had newer antibiotics to try. If not trimethoprim, then other experimental drugs that were at a late stage of human testing.

That morning Nick spoke to the Secretary of Homeland Security, Don Stodgecraft, who wanted an update. Nick said to seal the town. Do whatever was necessary to contain the bacteria. Close the roads. Cancel air service. Send in the National Guard. No one should move in or out of the city until the outbreak was contained.

Don wanted to know if it was the work of terrorists, and Nick didn't know. What he *did* know was that the bacterial strain was more virulent than any he had ever seen. Was it genetically engineered to be so? He had no answer, but the pattern of the outbreak was not right. It could be an act of war.

Nick thought he would throw up and folded his arms around his head. His stomach cramped, his head throbbed, and rain poured down. Robin Wheeler sang to him: *It would never be easy, just didn't think it would be this hard, or feel this bad.*

Wheeler must have sung him to sleep. Time passed, one hour became two, and still he could not move. His head was too heavy to lift from the table. His brain felt like it would explode. His whole body ached. He was either on fire with fever or shaking with cold. He was in the freezing phase now and his teeth were chattering. His stomach cramped tighter and he threw up a violent spray of frothy clotted blood. That told him what form of plague he had. Septicemic. The worst kind. The bacteria were in his blood. It explained the severity of his response. He was carrying too high a bacterial load and his immune system was overwhelmed, despite multiple vaccines. He knew there were bio-engineered strains of *Yersinia* developed specifically for antibiotic resistance, and he guessed this was one of those strains.

He tried to pry open his eyes, lift his head, but it was not possible. Wheeler sang on: *Through it all I knew, down on my knees, I would go on, do all I could do.*

The words spurred Nick on. He had to raise the alarm, get someone to analyze the *Yersinia* DNA. He tried to lift himself up off the bench. He could not move. His energy was gone. He gripped his arms, holding himself together, as the rain struck and something hard and cold pressed against his face. Then, something soft and warm covered him, bringing shelter from the storm.

CHAPTER THIRTY-NINE

"Nick, Nick, wake up." Dana leaned down, threw an arm around his back, and jostled his arm. She thought he was at the hospital with McCoy, until she saw him out her window at the picnic table, shrouded in pounding rain.

She tried shaking him, calling his name, but there was no response. He felt floppy, wasted, spent. His body burned as he shivered. *He was sick too.* He had the plague. *And he was vaccinated. He had received vaccinations for decades.* He should have been immune.

She felt sick herself. *What if he died?* She began to shiver and could not stop. Beneath them, the rackety bench tottered. Nick groaned and opened his eyes.

"*You have Yersinia,*" she said. She thought he would deny it, but he did not.

"Septicemic," he said in a thin weak voice.

Dana shivered again. His blood was infected, which meant all his organs. Even with effective treatment, he could die within twenty-four hours. "You have to get to the hospital. Take trimethoprim."

"Doesn't work. I tried. Hours ago."

"The monoclonal vaccine then. It works."

"No. Use new antibiotics. The fluoroquinolones."

They were promising new antibiotics that altered DNA confirmation and three-dimensional shape. The fluoroquinolone Ciprubocin was being touted as the new wonder drug, though it was still in the testing phase. They didn't know it would work now and they had no time to test it. "We have to use something proven to work."

"No, you're in too much trouble."

She had to convince him the monoclonal vaccine was the only way. They were dealing with a super-resistant strain of *Yersinia* and she knew the monoclonal was effective. Penny proved that. The only problem was that the army had the experimental vaccine. On hand she only had enough for one injection. "The monoclonal is in Fort Troy," she said. "Call General Schwartzke and tell him to send it back."

"No way. It's not been tested."

"We could get it just in case."

"No."

"We don't have to use it, just have it."

"No."

The wind turned, blowing hard against them. Dana lowered her head, saw a pool of blood on the bench. There were blood stains on Nick's shirt and arms. There was no time to argue. Nick had no time. "You need something that works. I'll give you the vaccine."

"No."

"Stop saying no!"

It was the wrong thing to say.

Nick roused himself, shaking his head back and forth. Rain sprayed from his hair. He threw back his shoulders and inhaled sharply, as though summoning energy stored deep in his core. He wiped the blood on his face. "You have no authorization. Do not use the monoclonal antibody. If anything goes wrong, you are accountable. Even if it goes right, you will lose your job. You will never work in science again. Do you understand?"

He was talking to her as if she was four years old. And more concerned for her future than his own. "It doesn't matter. You'll die."

"You're out of your field. You cannot inject people with an experimental drug. Period." He held her eye. His were bloodshot and heavily hooded, as though he could barely keep them open. "Promise me."

They were wasting time he did not have. She knew when it came to regulations, whether they were in his best interests or not, this Nick followed the rules. The other Nick was far away, or perhaps had been vanquished long ago, and was no help now. "All right. But you've got to go to the hospital."

Nick argued no further. A few minutes later, in the car on the way to the hospital, he passed out. His head fell forward, cracked on the dash. She pulled over and straightened him. His body was burning, slack and limp. Dana drove sobbing through the rain slogged streets.

There was a traffic jam outside the hospital. A line of ambulances and taxis blocked the emergency-parking bay. The parking lot was packed. Dana ditched her car at the side of the road and dashed across a flooded flowerbed. A policeman guarding the emergency door refused to let her pass. Two attendants in biohazard suits came for Nick, and lumped him on a stretcher as if he were already dead.

Dana was not allowed in the hospital. She returned to work, sliding through streets turned to rivers as the rain stormed down and the wind stole her screams.

CHAPTER FORTY

Back in the lab, Dana called Karl and learned he was in the hospital with Nick. "How is he?"

"Moving in and out of consciousness," Karl said.

"The trimethoprim may be ineffective."

"Not maybe. Is."

She could barely hear him. The line was bad and crackled in her ear.

"Carol Dupuis' been treated with it all along," Karl said. "She went into a coma this morning. She's not expected to live."

Dana felt a catch in her throat. What if she had autopsied her rats earlier? Could her life have been spared? Five days ago Carol was in class, taking notes, listening intently, and now she was dying. They had to do something. "We need to change the treatment," Dana said. "Use the monoclonal vaccine."

"We'll find an effective antibiotic."

She wanted to bang the phone on the table. Hammer it on his head. "Clinically, we know the monoclonal antibody works."

"It's not approved. No can do."

"But it works!"

"In Penny and Jack. Two people. For now. You don't know the intermediate or long-term effects. Hell, you don't know the short-term effects. Imagine the malpractice suits if something went wrong."

He was worried about lawsuits? "There'll be no lawsuits if everyone dies."

"There are other experimental drugs. Drugs the bacteria have never seen. We're going with Cipruboxin. It's close to being approved."

Dana heard a great roar of thunder. The lights blinked off and came back on. Karl's words faded in and out. "What if it doesn't work?"

Karl was firm. "We hope for the best. We go this route and there's no personal liability. Not to you, not to anyone. It's the only way."

"It's the safe way," she said, but she knew in her heart it wasn't the right way.

Karl hung up and Dana lowered her phone. Karl was wrong. This was not the time to worry about lawsuits or try nearly approved antibiotics. Nick needed the vaccine and he needed it now. Yet she had promised not to use it.

What if someone else authorized it?

She eyed her phone. Two hours away, in Fort Troy, there was enough of the vaccine for sixty thousand people. It was her vaccine—she made it, she shipped it, and she could call the general and ask him to send it back. Not to her, but to Dr. Taversham at the hospital. The decision to use it or not would be his. If there was nothing else, they'd at least have something. The vaccine contained pre-made antibodies that would work immediately.

Dana took a deep breath and picked up the receiver. The line was bad, spitting and buzzing with interference from the storm. It took time for the call to move through the army hierarchy. Finally, General Schwartzke, the man in charge of the biological warfare program at Fort Troy who was overseeing the vaccine trials, came on the line. "What is it? I'm very busy."

Dana had met the general once, and found him cold and intimidating. "I'm calling about the vaccine."

"Your call is premature. We're testing in June as arranged. Why do you ask? Did you get your letter?"

"Letter?"

"Your proposal was approved. Phase 2 is a go."

Dana closed her eyes. *Her proposal was approved?* A minute ago she had nothing to lose, but now she had her grant. Her excitement was brief. After what happened today with McCoy, the approval may not matter.

"Are you there?" Schwartzke demanded.

Dana opened her eyes. "Yes, I'm here. Thank you. Thank you very much."

"If there's nothing else, I'm—"

"There is," she said. "We may need the vaccine. Can you ship it back?"

"What's going on there? Is there a plague outbreak? Do you plan to use the vaccine?"

"Not me. Not unless it's necessary."

"Why would it be necessary?"

"In case of antibiotic failure. We're dealing with a highly resistant strain."

"Are we talking biowarfare?"

"That's a possibility."

"Put McCoy on the line."

"Uh . . . he's not here. He's at the hospital."

"Let me speak with the CDC agent. Who is it? Karl King?"

"He's not here either."

"Then Nick Biget. Get him."

"Everyone is at the hospital. We're dealing with a full-blown epidemic. None of the antibiotics are working. The prophylactics have failed. Even the newer drugs don't seem to work. The vaccine could be our last hope."

"Why didn't you say so? When the weather clears, I'll ship."

They didn't have that long. "We need it now."

"I'll see if any trucks are available."

"The town is closed. Can you fly it to Greenlee hospital?"

"Send a chopper? It's not possible in this weather."

"The storm is moving fast."

"I'll see what I can do. It will likely be tomorrow, first light."

"Can you address the monoclonal to Dr. Taversham? He's the physician in charge at Greenlee."

"I'll ship to McCoy. Over and out."

The phone went dead. Dana exhaled with difficulty. He was going to ship the vaccine to McCoy. There was nothing she could do about it. Nothing she could do about the weather. It was out of her hands.

Except for Nick, there might be no tomorrow. He could die tonight waiting for the storm to clear.

There was enough of the monoclonal left for one more shot.

He said no, he didn't want it, and he wouldn't take it. She gave him her word she wouldn't use it. She couldn't force medical treatment on someone who refused it.

But he could die.

Nick was worried about her, about the consequences of giving an untested drug. Medical doctors would lose their license, face a malpractice suit, and a court of law. He was worried about her career.

But she was no medical doctor, and *he could die.*

There was no choice to make. Life came first before everything. Nick would hate her for it, though. He would probably never forgive her. At least he would be alive. She couldn't bear a world without him in it.

She went to the cell culture room and grabbed the vial with the remaining monoclonal antibody. There was so little left. Was it enough? She had no experience with septicemic plague, a much more serious disease than the other two forms. What if he needed more of the monoclonal antibody?

It was a moot point, it didn't matter, there was no more left. That was another decision that didn't have to be made. She tucked the ampule in her bra. At least it would buy Nick some time. She shoved a syringe into the pocket of her jeans.

Seconds later she was splashing through puddles to her car. With the storm, an early night had fallen. The skies were black and the wind swept waves of water across the flooded road. Thunder roared and lightning pulsed. A loud boom and a scream from the sky made her jump. The town went dark as the power cut out. From behind her, a generator roared. She turned around, and the lights of the vet school flickered and then blazed as the emergency generator kicked in.

Dana jumped in her car and drove off. The windshield fogged immediately and the wipers couldn't keep up with the rain. At first she went slowly, fighting the drag on the tires, and leaving a high spray in her wake.

Out on the main road, hers was the only car. She fiddled with the radio and got static. The university station and local public station were off the air. An Austin station gave a weather update. The tropical storm had moved inland faster than predicted. There was a great danger of widespread flooding. Another reminder that the roads in and out of

Duane were closed. The airport was shut. Planes were grounded and all incoming flights were suspended. The National Guard had secured the town, and the Governor of Texas had declared a state of emergency in the county.

Cognizant of the passing time, Dana accelerated and sped up. She shot through an intersection and saw a light ahead. She was trying to make out what it was, when she realized it was another car in her lane.

She slammed on the brakes. The car careened through water, turning sideways. She let up on the brake and spun the steering wheel as the car slid off the road. The wheels lost contact with the ground. There was a hard slam and darkness as the dashboard lights cut out.

CHAPTER FORTY-ONE

The car was stuck in the ditch. Dana got out and was pummeled by rain. It came like hail, pouring from the sky as loud as a waterfall. She pushed on the fender as hard as she could, but it wouldn't budge. The wind howled, shaking trees, swinging power lines, and rattling streetlights. Rain flowed in icy rivers that gushed along the roads and sidewalks. She was standing in three inches of water. Her boots were soaked through to her socks.

She wanted to be home in her warm house, with a glass of wine in her hand and the dogs by her side. But Nick was dying. Moving in and out of consciousness, according to Karl. Dana would have to go to the hospital on foot.

She started walking, head bowed, as the rain streamed down her hair and got under her clothes. The wind raged and screamed and time slowed. It took longer to cross campus than she expected.

She reached the hospital. The generator lights were blinding and harsh. She climbed the hospital steps. A policeman in a mask and suit leaned against the main door. It was the same emaciated policeman that had been on guard that morning. He groggily came to attention and folded his arms. "The hospital is closed."

She'd left her purse with her identification in the car. "I'm Dr. Sparks. I was here earlier. I'm working with the CDC."

"Wait here." He used a key to unlock the door and pushed the automatic door open manually. He came back with a clipboard and flipped through it. "You're not on the list." He shoved the clipboard her way.

They had a list of people they were admitting? She scanned the names. Between McCoy and Taversham there was nothing. Sparks wasn't there.

"It must be a mistake," she said. "I was here earlier." She smiled her most charming smile. "It was you, you let me in. This morning. Don't you remember?"

The policeman stood unmoved. "Believe me, you don't want to be here."

It was true, but there were times when there was a vast difference between doing what she wanted and what was necessary. "I'll just be a few minutes."

He took out his radio. "You need to leave. This town is under curfew. You shouldn't be out."

"I'm going."

She turned around and walked down the stairs. She was going nowhere. She crossed the parking lot and then doubled back. Creeping along the side of the building, she was on the lookout for an emergency exit or open window. She went down the length of the building. Everything was locked up tight. She went around the corner and found the windows along the building's width shut. She turned another corner and went down the other side. There was a gray emergency door with no handle. The door was flush with the door jam. She couldn't get it open.

She kept going. She reached the front and wondered, what now? She didn't know. She waited, shivering, huddled under the overhang of the roof as the rain streamed down. She waited and waited and time passed and she wondered what to do, when there was movement in the street. She saw what looked like an injured animal, crouched low and lumbering. A dog hit by a car? No, a man.

At the curb, he stopped by a row of low bushes and vomited. Dana saw his shoulders heaving, heard his convulsions, and watched as the bushes were sprayed with blood. He wore a beige suit and white shoes. *Michael.*

Dana ran toward him, calling his name. He wiped his mouth and stared up.

He had it too. His dark eyes had lost their glitter and he looked afraid, like a deer caught in the glare of a headlight. He was shivering, rose shakily, reaching out his hand. She helped him up and led him toward the emergency entrance.

There was another policeman here, but he did not ask for ID. He opened the door and waved them inside.

The emergency room was crammed full with the sick. Over the sound of coughing, a baby wailed loudly. There was blood on the walls and patients lying scattered on the floor, reminding Dana of archangels launching poisoned arrows, letting loose a curse upon the land.

The nurse was sleeping at a desk, her head encircled in her arm. Dana touched her hand and woke her up. The nurse pointed to the waiting room. There was a line-up to see the doctors. "End of the line."

It snaked down the hall. Dana helped Michael to the end and lowered him to the floor. How many people were ahead of him? A hundred? He was shivering and she wished she had something warm to cover him with, but she did not.

He closed his eyes, fell back against the wall.

"I'll be back," she said.

She walked quickly down the hall to the nurses' station. There was no one there. She ran around the counter and typed Nick's name into the computer. He was in the ICU.

She went down the hall, grabbed a package of quarantine clothes from a pile, and went to the bathroom. She took off her clothes, rolled them into a ball, and placed them behind the trashcan. Her skin was splattered with mud and she washed her hands. She threw on sunny yellow quarantine clothes and hurried to the ICU. She pounded on the door and waited. She inhaled deeply, felt detached, uninvolved, as if what was happening wasn't real. She'd had dreams that were more authentic than this.

The door opened. Sam. In this strange dream it couldn't be, but it was. He pulled off his hood. He was still working, dressed in a dirtied, bloodied yellow suit and holding an unlit cigarette in his hand. "Oh, it's you," he said.

Dana greeted him with enthusiasm she didn't feel. "I'm here to assess the situation. What do we have?" Would he send her away? Call the cops? Her indifference to the outcome surprised her.

Sam leaned against the door, yawning. A gray gristle of a beard had sprouted on his coffee-colored face. "I thought you guys gave up. You were too scared to make your nightly assessment." His voice was flat, like a talking computer. "I'm sorry to say your treatment doesn't work." He shoved the cigarette in his mouth. "But I guess you know that."

Sam lit the cigarette, though the hospital was a smoke free zone. You couldn't even smoke in the cafeteria. Sam stuffed the match in his pocket and exhaled smoke at the ceiling.

"You're okay?" she said. "You didn't get sick?"

"I appear to be protected." He let smoke drift out his mouth and inhaled it through his nose. "And you?"

"I'm fine too."

"Have you given blood? We need antiserum from everyone who hasn't got sick. For the critically ill patients. I've given three pints."

"I'll go when I'm through here. Can I come in?"

"The CDC never asked permission." Sam dropped the cigarette and crushed the burning ember with the tip of his shoe. He bent down and retrieved the long butt.

She went in. The room was crammed with beds arranged row-by-row against two walls. It reminded Dana of an orphanage dormitory she saw on an elementary school trip years ago. There were no doctors or other nurses in sight. Sam passed her a clipboard and told her to sign in. "New regulations. Like we need more red tape."

She scribbled her name, a scrawl she hoped no one would recognize. She surveyed the room. The overhead lights were off and the room was illuminated by the electrostatic glow of a multitude of monitors. There must have been forty beds, forty men, coughing, retching, sobbing, wailing amidst a background of machines that were rhythmically pumping and clicking.

"How is everyone doing?" she asked, though a moron could see no one was well.

"You came at a bad time," Sam said. "Karl made the same mistake and I can tell you he didn't make it again. I'm dispensing medication. Useless antibiotics for grins. Morphine for sedation."

"Do you mind if I look around? Peek at a chart or two?"

"Be my guest."

"Are we in danger of losing anyone?"

"Oh yes," Sam said, without hesitation. "Everyone."

"Nick Biget?" Dana could barely speak his name.

"He's not good," Sam said. He pointed to a bed. "He's the epidemiologist on the case. Should have known better than to let it go so long. He's in trouble."

Dana looked at Nick and drew a sharp breath. He lay on his back, tossing back and forth, covered in a tangle of wires and cords and tubing. He was moaning, as he did sometimes in his dreams.

"I'll give him morphine," Sam said.

"Please."

Dana stood out of the way while Sam grabbed a bottle from a cart and filled a syringe. He gave Nick an IV injection and turned to the next patient.

Dana sank to her knees by Nick's bed. He wore a yellow smock that made his skin look green. She worked off her hood and dropped it on the floor. The morphine worked fast and within seconds his breathing slowed. Beside the bed, a monitor showed rhythmic snaking blips. Dana leaned her elbows on the bed and studied Nick's face. His eyelids fluttered, his face was white, and his lips were pale and pink. He had a round red bump in the middle of his forehead where he'd banged his head on the dashboard of her car. The shaving cut on his chin near his dimple had begun to heal. She reached out and ran her finger lightly along his cheek. His skin was soft, for once no five o'clock shadow, as if his follicular cells were too sick to function. She leaned into him and jumped when he opened his eyes.

Go back to sleep, she told him with her mind.

He closed his eyes. She breathed with relief, and then gasped when he took her hand. He closed his fingers around hers and bent his elbow, curling their hands over his heart. She could feel it beating, a slow weak pulse. He rolled towards her and she eased up on the bed and lay down beside him as she had often done a lifetime ago.

The wheels on the cart wobbled as Sam moved on. She would wait until he was farther away and then give Nick the inje—

She shot up. She didn't have a syringe. She left it in the pocket of her slacks that were in the bathroom. She scanned the room. There must be a syringe here. She glanced at Sam. He had a syringe in his hand. On his cart stood a row of bottles, each with their own syringe. And why not? Everyone was hooked up to IVs and receiving the same drugs. A single syringe could be used for each medication.

She went to the front desk. There was a computer, phone, a canister filled with pens, a stack of forms, but no syringes. She looked in the garbage and saw paper. Syringes weren't left lying around.

An alarm began to beep. The one by Nick's bed. She ran to him and scanned the monitor. His blood pressure had fallen. His heart had stopped. A straight line cursed across the screen. She screamed for Sam who was already sprinting toward her.

"He's gone." Sam reached down and pulled a sheet up over a man in the adjacent bed. It wasn't Nick. Dana had been staring at the wrong monitor. The alarm screeched on and a red button flashed. Sam punched the power switch with his fist bringing silence. He detached wires and hoses from the body and then wheeled the bed to the door.

Sam left, and Dana sprinted down the length of the ICU to the medicine cart. She yanked a syringe from a bottle. How much time did she have? Sam wouldn't be gone long. He couldn't leave all these patients unattended. She raced back to Nick, working the ampule out of her bra.

He was asleep.

She sucked the solution into the syringe. Sweat rolled down her underarms. A drop of monoclonal antibody remained in the vial and she drew it up. Every bit counted. She lifted Nick's arm.

With her mind screaming to go slow, she worked the syringe onto the free end of the IV and depressed the plunger. Nick did not move. His eyelids fluttered and he dreamed on. His shirt was damp and spotted with mud. Her clothes were filthy, her hair still dripping. She couldn't worry about it now. She counted *one thousand and one, one thousand and two, one thousand and three*, and then the plunger met resistance. She disengaged the syringe and heard a pop.

No, that was the door. Sam was back, rolling an empty bed.

She hid the syringe in the palm of her hand and waited as Sam made the bed. He fluffed the pillow, slipped it into a case, threw open a sheet and smoothed down the corners, making precise envelope tucks.

He was back at his cart. Dana tightened her grip on the syringe. She had to get it back. Sam was peering at a laptop on the cart, reading intently. She approached him, saw a box of swabs perched precariously on the cart edge, and knocked it with her elbow. The box clattered to the floor. Sam bent down to pick it up and while he was down, Dana thrust the syringe into the vial. Sam stood up and she apologized.

"Sorry about that. Guess I'll go make my report."

Wide-eyed, she watched Sam pick up the vial with the syringe she had just returned. She headed for the door and had the handle in her hand when he called her.

She froze, wondering if she would faint. Should she run for it, or turn? She swiveled, wondering if at that distance he would notice her distress.

"You forgot to sign out."

"Right." She went to the desk and scribbled on the page.

CHAPTER FORTY-TWO

Dana went to give blood. Though she neglected to test her own antibody concentration, she presumed that like the monoclonal vaccine—the active vaccine that Sheryl had given her five days previously—was protective. Anyone receiving her blood would get antibodies effective against the plague.

The serology lab was being serviced by the gigantic German nurse who had watched over Penny in the ICU. Her name was Herzog and she demanded to know why Dana was so late in answering the call for blood. "There are many people sick. They will die. Antiserum is all we have." She was taking two pints of Dana's blood, instead of the usual one.

Dana lay on the cot, hooked up to a drip, trying not to watch the pint fill with blood. It was almost midnight and she was exhausted. She watched the hulking German nurse fiddle with the flow rate of the bag, trying to speed it up.

"How many people gave blood?" Dana asked, feeling nauseated. Presumably, all those who were exposed and healthy had one way or another developed the protective antibodies that could be given to others.

"With you, there are five. Myself, I have once been ill with *Yersinia enterocolitica*. There appears to be a cross-reaction. Dr. Taversham, a patient's mother, and another nurse are all fine for reasons we do not understand. And yourself?"

"I've been vaccinated many years," Dana said.

"As are others who are ill," the nurse said.

"Each person is different." Dana closed her eyes, hoping her blood would flow quickly and she could leave. It took forty minutes, and though the nurse wanted her to stay and rest, Dana bolted.

She moved too quickly and immediately felt faint. Out in the hall, she leaned against the wall and caught her breath. To get home, she had to find Sheryl and borrow her car.

After a quick check of an unattended computer at the pediatric nurses' station, Dana determined that Penny was in the Lollipop wing. Dana found the room and eased open the door. She saw a crib and a rocking chair with a snoring Sheryl. Dana tiptoed into the room and tapped her shoulder.

Sheryl awoke with a start and a gasp that woke Penny. Dana jumped to the crib and scooped Penny up in her arms. Penny wrapped her legs around Dana's waist and laid her head on Dana's shoulder. Penny was warm and soft, and smelled of talcum and baby shampoo. She shoved her thumb in her mouth. Dana stroked her fine sparse hair and wound a finger around a gentle curl.

"What are you doing here?" Sheryl asked, yawning as she stretched.

"I need to ask a favor."

"What are you wearing?"

Dana had traded the quarantine clothes for green surgical scrubs. "My clothes got wet," she said. She had to remember to pick them up before she left. "I need to borrow your car."

"Why?"

Sheryl already thought Dana was a bad driver, and now she had to confess she drove her car into a ditch. "It wasn't my fault. A car came into my lane. I had to swerve out of the way."

"And you want to borrow my car?"

"I'll return it tomorrow. I'll leave the keys under the seat."

Sheryl worked the keys out of her pocket.

Dana hugged Penny tighter. "How is she doing?"

Her mouth was closed in a smile around her thumb.

"She's doing fine, which is great, but a problem. Taversham wants to know why she recovered. I said I worked with *Yersinia* and that I'd been vaccinated and because I'm breast-feeding, Penny was protected."

"McCoy knows," Dana said. "I had to tell him."

Sheryl clasped her hands to her head. "What did he say?"

"Not much, actually." Dana wasn't going to mention his heart attack.

"He didn't tell Taversham. I got the third degree. He went on and on, he and this other guy, a tall man in a suit. They said the antibiotics failed totally. Every single one that's been tested. And here I was healthy. And my baby recovered. They wanted to know why. They asked about you. Why didn't you get sick?" Sheryl looked at her closely. "Did you take the monoclonal vaccine?"

"No, the antigen vaccine you gave me on Friday. It must have worked and induced the protective antibody. That's why I'm not sick."

Sheryl frowned despite the good news. "Then you're in trouble, too. You can't test bacterial fragments on yourself. You'll lose your job."

For more reasons than one, Dana thought as she hugged Penny again and kissed her soft cheek. She knew that given the same circumstances, she would do what she did again. Though whether that made it right nor not, she didn't know.

Sheryl was studying her, examining her through narrowed eyes. "What are you doing here?"

Dana sat down on the nightstand. Penny melded into her and seemed to have fallen asleep. She felt loose and floppy in her arms. "I came to give blood."

"And?"

Dana hung her head. "I injected Nick. He had septicemic plague. I gave him the last of the monoclonal. It's all gone."

"If he took it, that proves it had to be used. You're in the clear."

Dana stared at her feet. "He doesn't know."

"Fuck."

"He said not to use it."

Sheryl clicked her teeth with disapproval. "He'll never forgive you. He'll hate you when he finds out."

"Maybe he won't."

Sheryl shook her head dubiously. "Of course he will. You thought no one would find out about Penny or me. Wait till the doctors question you. What makes you think you can get away with this?"

Penny was stirring and Dana passed her to her mother. "I had to do it."

Sheryl patted Penny's back. "There's always a choice."

Dana didn't answer. She knew that wasn't always the case. "I've got to go."

Sheryl went to the crib and laid Penny down. Soon she was fast asleep, breathing lightly.

Dana hugged Sheryl and left. She headed for the fire exit marked with a sign that warned of an alarm if the door was inadvertently opened. Dana punched it open anyway and ran. An alarm rang out in her head, but whether it was real or not she could not say.

APRIL 30TH

CHAPTER FORTY-THREE

During the night, Nick's fever broke. His muscles stopped aching and doubt began to override his certainty that he would die. His immune system was finally functional. He felt stronger with each breath. He was stoned on morphine he knew, and he felt disengaged from the world. He was no longer a participant, but an observer. The distance brought relief. He was deliriously high.

Around him, machinery buzzed and the labored breathing of the sick filled the room. The male nurse slept in a chair by the door, feet up on the desk, snoring loudly. Nick alone was awake and aware of the passing night. He glanced at his watch. Five minutes to three.

He stared at the ceiling, hands under his head. When he thought he was dying, he had looked back on his life—and the review surprised him. Instead of finding satisfaction in work and marital sacrifice, Nick thought of what he had missed, what was left undone, and roads not taken. He thought of his father and their estrangement, and his death that precluded reconciliation. He thought of his son and three months that were not nearly enough. He thought of Dana and the life he left behind. He was humming along with Robin Wheeler, who was serenading him: *You had to go, thought it would lessen the loss, make the ruin seem not as great.*

Nick lowered his hands and clasped them together. He studied the arch of his fingers, the mirror-image fit of his hands. He turned them over. When he was in medical school, he knew the names of every bone in a hand. He couldn't remember any of it now. There was much he had forgotten. Much he could not forget.

He checked his watch. Three o'clock now. Soon he'd lose his morphine high. He was already worried about coming down. He closed his eyes and drifted. He was in the country, surrounded by trees, red and white pine, dripping with smilax. He was swinging a machete, clearing a path. Sticks and leaves were flying above him, and Dana was in front of him, swearing. She was unlike anyone he knew. She was one step ahead from the start. She followed some desultory instinct he couldn't fathom. She ignored logic, preferring hunches and signs. He would have thought it lunacy—except for her, it seemed to work.

He had dreamed of her tonight. She was fresh from the shower, as he liked her best. Slick with water, hair streaming. She bent over him, and the water fell from her hair onto his skin. He held her hand and felt the heat of her by his side.

She felt so real that Nick opened his eyes. Of course, he was alone. She wasn't here. How could she be? The hospital was closed. Karl told him that. Karl who lay in the bed beside him, inhaling oxygen as he snored in a troubled sleep. Nick couldn't remember when he arrived. At some point an old man had occupied that bed.

Nick checked his watch once more. Five minutes after three. The drugs slowed time. He closed his eyes and began to drift once more.

CHAPTER FORTY-FOUR

The rain stopped during the night, and when Dana awoke the birds were singing. She could remember no dreams, though it seemed to her as if the previous day had been a dream. In the morning light, recent events were hard to believe. It did not seem possible she had done what she did.

She thought of Nick and jumped from bed. Questions flew at her. Did he live through the night? Did the monoclonal vaccine work? Would the vaccine come? Would McCoy discover an order he had not made? Now that she had her grant and had confirmed she was on the right track with the active vaccine, would she lose her job?

The electricity was still out, as it had been all night, and she could make no coffee. She gulped milk that was beginning to sour. She picked up the phone, but the landline was dead. Her cell phone had no service. She fed her dogs, forgetting again that Frank was gone. Without him, the house seemed too big, too bleak, and too cold.

The other dogs followed her up to Sheryl's car. After Anthony peed on every tire, Dana sped off, slipping and sliding on the muddy road. In the morning haze, she saw what she had missed the previous night. On the bypass, she maneuvered around cars abandoned in the middle of the road. Electrical poles were down. The trees had been ravaged and branches laden with new leaves lay plastered on the muddy grass. A cat carrying a rat slunk low, tiptoeing along high ground.

At the hospital, it took three tries to parallel park Sheryl's car and return it to its place. She tucked the keys under the driver's seat and got out. The air was cool and crisp. Overhead, the clouds were breaking and ribbons of blue sky shone through.

She headed for the hospital. There was no policeman at the door. She pushed against an automatic door and it slid sideways. She entered the hospital without effort. It was too easy.

She walked the length of the hallway. The patients from last night were gone and the floors were vacant, though filthy with dirt and mud. She went to the ICU and suited up in quarantine clothes. She pulled on the hood and then knocked on the door.

There was no answer. She peered through the window and saw only shadows. What if they were all dead? She tried the knob and it turned in her hand. She opened the door and went in.

Her face panel fogged up with her breath and she could not see. She pulled the hood off her head and heard the sound of air whistling, people moaning and rustling, a low voice talking. Nick was on the phone.

She blinked her eyes. He was sitting up, had his back to her, phone by his ear. He had made it, he lived through the night. She walked toward his bed.

He turned and looked at her, through eyes that were glassy and huge. His cheeks were darkened by a five o'clock shadow. He closed the cell phone. The strawberry bruise on his forehead had turned blue.

"You look better," she said,

"I feel good." He smiled broadly. "It took a while for my immune system to kick in."

She sat down on a rolling stool and scooted to the bed. He didn't know about last night. For once, he seemed happy to see her. This was what she had been waiting for. Here was the familiar Nick who was relaxed, connected, and accessible. After a long retreat, he had returned.

He gave her an update on the situation, and she tried to read between the lines to learn if the vaccine had come. Nick had been speaking with Carol's doctor in Houston. Dr. Frost had no luck with the Cipruboxin and was testing new antibiotics. One that showed great promise, CK-202, was a drug that Dana had never heard of before.

"It inhibits DNA twisting," Nick said. "If it works, we'll fly it up. We need something." He scratched at his beard.

"When will we know?"

"Within the hour."

"That's great." She smiled into his eyes.

He smiled back. "It is. I tell you, being sick is hell." He smoothed down the yellow doctor's smock he wore in lieu of pajamas.

She saw spots of mud on his shirt which looked like fingerprints, and gasped out loud.

He noticed too. He pulled the shirt away from his chest so he could study the stain. He slowly raised his head. His eyes narrowed and he frowned at her through the dark troubled eyes of the cold professional. "You were here last night." It was no question.

"I did the nightly assessment," she said.

"You injected me. You promised you wouldn't, but you did."

His voice was loud and angry. It stirred the man in the bed next to him, and she realized with a start that it was Karl. He was sick too.

"How could you?" Nick said, slashing the air with his hand. "After I told you *no*. What if something went wrong? What if I responded like the guinea pig?"

"I thought you would die."

"There were other options. We could have a new antibiotic in an hour."

"For you, it was too late."

"So you injected me. As if it was your decision. You had no right. You cross lines you shouldn't cross. You always have."

"I'm sorry." She paused. "No, I'm not."

"Have you considered the repercussions?"

"Not having you in this world? Yes. I considered it. I considered it a lot."

"You put your career and who knows what else in jeopardy."

"It was worth it." She looked in his eyes. "You're worth it." The words hung in the air. Too loud and unable to be taken back.

The ICU door burst open. Sam leapt up. The German nurse from the blood bank marched into the room, waving a slip of paper aloft. "Nick Biggay. I am looking for a Nick Biggay."

Nick identified himself, and the nurse informed him that a shipment of drugs had arrived by helicopter for Dr. McCoy. He was unable to respond. Could Nick receive the drugs in his place?

Nick could. He jumped out of bed and jammed his bare feet into his shoes.

"Go to the roof," the nurse said.

The nurse left and Nick turned to Dana. "See, the drug is here." He spread open his palms, as if to let her know that what she'd done had been in vain.

CHAPTER FORTY-FIVE

The morphine high vanished in an instant, leaving Nick feeling listless and feeble as he dragged himself up the stairs to the roof. The hospital was filled with sick people who needed treatment immediately. He had not experienced a late-acting immune kick. His health was Dana's doing. She had not been in his dreams as he presumed. She had come to the hospital and administered the monoclonal vaccine he explicitly forbade her to give him.

Nick reached the rooftop as a green and beige army chopper lifted into the sky. It was eight o'clock and the sun was rising, reflecting off the revolving gunmetal blades. The noise of the engine filled the air and the blades sent a vast breeze gusting across the rooftop. A policeman stood in its wind, holding a small Igloo cooler.

Nick relieved him of it, went inside, and downstairs to the executive staff lounge. He opened the cooler. Chilled air rose and Nick shivered. The cooler was filled with liquid nitrogen that would keep the drug frozen. There was an envelope in a plastic bag and he ripped it open. It was addressed to TJ McCoy from General Schwartzke at Fort Troy: *Here is the monoclonal you requested. Dilute concentrate 1:100. God speed. Fred.*

Nick closed his eyes and ran his hand across his face. No songs played in his head now; no timely advice from Robin Wheeler came. The words were silent, the chords were gone. After too little sleep and too much morphine, his brain wasn't functioning properly. He was tired and reality seemed distorted. He still had a headache, though not nearly the intensity of the one he had yesterday.

Nick reread the note stupefied. Obviously McCoy had not requested the vaccine. Did Dana think ahead? Did she consider what would happen if McCoy intercepted the letter? What had she told Schwartzke that compelled him to send a chopper? Whatever it was, it had been a lie. The vaccine was untested and could not be used. Newer drugs, further down the pipeline, would have priority. If her vaccine had side effects, if any harm was caused by its use, she would be responsible. Her use of the vaccine thus far was unconscionable. She put everything she worked for at risk. Again. Nick ripped up the letter. He tore it into tiny pieces that he crammed into his pocket.

The audacity of it. Like removing her clothes and lying with him on the floor of a hotel room. It scared him to death. He wanted to shake her. Protect yourself, put on your clothes, cover yourself.

He was heading back to his ward when his cell phone rang.

Diane Frost was calling from Houston with the result of the promising CK-202 antibiotic. "It doesn't work," she said. "It's something about this strain. The bacteria have mutated. The cell wall contains modified transport proteins that have enzyme function. As soon as the transport proteins pick up the antibiotics, they're inactivated."

Nick stared at the cooler. Transport proteins did not just acquire enzyme function. He remembered a conversation with a Russian dissident who was working at a biological warfare facility in Moscow. The man was splicing different proteins together, deliberately designing resistant bacteria.

"I'll keep trying new antibiotics," Diane said. "I'll call Paris and see if the Pasteur Institute has something."

"How's Carol doing?"

"Still comatose."

Nick hefted the cooler in his hand. If there was widespread antibody failure, and if the monoclonal antibody was effective and without side effects, in an emergency, it could be used. With the right authority. "We've got a vaccine we can try," he said.

"Send it down for Carol," Diane said.

Nick said he would. He closed his cell phone.

Dana could not be the one to authorize the vaccine, but McCoy could. It was less than ethical, but as Dana recognized, it was necessary.

Doing the right thing at times meant doing the wrong thing. He went to see McCoy.

He had a private room and was being closely supervised by a nurse who told Nick to come back later. "He has just had a sedative and he is very sleepy."

She meant McCoy was stoned. "I need to see him now," Nick said. "It's urgent."

The nurse reluctantly admitted him into the room.

It was bright with sunshine and hot with light. McCoy lay in bed gazing out the window, eyes glazed. He wore an oxygen mask, which he lifted. "The sun is there. Would you look at that color of orange."

"Yes." Nick sunk into a chair. "We're in a quandary."

McCoy continued staring out the window, inhaling oxygen. He lifted the silicone mask. "I don't know when I last watched the sun rise. I don't know if I've ever seen that color of orange before. It's glowing, don't you think?"

Nick dragged the chair around to the other side of the bed to block McCoy's view. "We have evidence this strain of *Yersinia* was genetically engineered for resistance. No available or experimental antibiotics we have are working. Most of the vaccines have failed. I'm going to call the Secretary of Homeland Security and explain the situation."

McCoy nodded and craned his head around Nick to ogle the climbing sun.

Nick pried the cell phone out of his pocket and called the personal number of Don Stodgecraft. When he came on the line, Nick updated him on the situation in Duane, as McCoy waxed on about the unusually vibrant color of the sky.

"You're telling me we have no treatment," Don said, when Nick was through explaining.

"No antibiotics," Nick said. "There is an experimental monoclonal vaccine."

"How experimental?"

"Very. We have nothing else."

"Use that if you think it will work."

"I'll let you speak to General McCoy." Nick handed McCoy the phone.

McCoy removed the oxygen mask and took the phone. He listened intently, nodding his head fervently. When he snapped the phone closed, he said, "Call Fred Schwartzke at Fort Troy. Tell him to ship the monoclonal. This is biological war and all rules are lifted. Don has the impression the vaccine will work." McCoy fitted the oxygen mask over his nose and inhaled deeply, gazing out the window. "Right here. A war. Can you believe it?"

But Nick was on his way out the door.

CHAPTER FORTY-SIX

Before leaving the hospital, Dana went to the bathroom to retrieve the wet clothes she had left behind the night before. She walked slowly, weighed down by guilt and a sense of irrevocable loss. Sheryl was right, Nick would never forgive her. He would hate her. Dana caught sight of her reflection in the grainy bathroom mirror. She looked pale and wasted, forsaken and alone.

She washed her hands and scrubbed her face. The hospital was conserving water that was running at a trickle. There were no paper towels left in the dispenser. She wiped her hands on her jeans and her face with an arm. She bent down to get her clothes. Gone. She moved the trash can. There was nothing behind it. She looked inside. It was filled with crumpled paper towels. She stuffed in her hand. No clothes.

She left the bathroom, hurrying for the exit. At the side door, where previously no policeman stood, was a very tall man. Dana tried to go around him, but he moved and blocked her way.

He was over seven feet tall. He had a folded shopping bag he slipped under his arm so they could shake hands. "Barry Ackerman, FBI. You must be Dana Sparks."

She looked up at him. He was at least two heads taller than she, but younger, maybe in his late twenties. He had small beady eyes, thin lips, and a ski-jump nose. He didn't look like an FBI agent to her.

"Do you have a moment? I'd like a word with you." He smiled a congenial smile. "I'm investigating the outbreak."

Sam had been right—in addition to the CDC, the FBI was on the case. "Why is the FBI involved?"

As if she had not spoken, Ackerman said, "May I ask what you're doing here?"

"I came for an update."

"On whose authority?"

"Well, my own. Everyone else is incapacitated."

"Yes, but not you."

"No."

Ackerman folded his arms across his chest. He wore a black suit that was too big for him. It hung off his shoulders and was too wide at the sides. "I understand you talked to Dudley Shaw. What was your impression of him?"

"He was a nice man."

"Did he bear a grudge against the government?"

"Dudley? What makes you think that?"

"You spoke with Jack Dowel. Does he know microbiology?"

"He's a football player. What do you think?"

"But you knew him."

"No, I didn't. He was in a seminar I taught." Dana folded her arms, matching Ackerman's stance. "What are you getting at?"

"Carol Dupuis was in your class."

"One class. That's it."

"You know Penny Paige. Where do you think she was infected?"

"I don't have a clue." Dana stared down the hallway. She was distracted by a clackety sound and a squeaky wheel. She saw Nick in a white lab coat followed by the German nurse and Sam. He was carrying a small cooler. The experimental antibiotic CK-202 must have arrived. They disappeared into a room.

"Was Penny infected in your lab?" Ackerman asked.

"That's absurd."

"You *do* deal with the plague."

"I don't have bacteria like this."

He stared intensely in her eyes. "Yet you have a vaccine against them."

"What the hell is this?"

"We're dealing with virulent bacteria that exhibit outstanding resistance. We have evidence the resistance is a result of genetic tampering. Yet you have the antidote to the newly mutated bacteria."

"Genetic tampering? Are you a molecular biologist? You don't know what you're talking about. This is a natural outbreak."

"Hardly. We are in fact quite sure it's deliberate."

"That's ridiculous."

He lowered his eyes and studied her carefully. "There have been severe cutbacks in scientific funding recently. It has affected your position, your research, and your future. Whether or not you make tenure is dependent upon federal funding. You seek a military grant. No one could blame you for begrudging the government for your unpleasant predicament. Or is it the VP's trip? He was due to come tomorrow. Perhaps you saw this as an opportunity to show the necessity of your work."

"*Me?*" She returned his stare, but she blinked first. "You think *I'm* behind this?"

"Why were you here last night? What were you doing? A policeman said you were at the door. You were in the ICU. In serology. Why?"

"I came to give blood."

Ackerman considered it for a moment and then dismissed it with a shake of his head. He opened the shopping bag and slowly pulled out her wet clothes from the previous evening. "Would these be yours?"

She didn't answer, but her knees went soft.

He fiddled with her clothes, turning them over in his hands. "The thing that is most strange about this outbreak is that there is no origin of the bacteria. It came from nowhere." He stopped rearranging her clothes and stared at her. "What if the origin was a syringe?"

She knew what he would pull out of her wet clothes and he did so then, holding it high to make his point.

"I work with syringes," she said, and took a step away from him.

"Yes, you do."

"Excuse me, I must go." She turned around and walked steadily away from him. Her ears were ringing and her skin burned as if with a fever.

"This interview is not over," Ackerman called out. "I am not finished. This hospital is under quarantine. You are confined to these premises."

But Dana heard no more. She turned a corner and was gone.

CHAPTER FORTY-SEVEN

Nick was shaving when there was a sharp knock on the bathroom door. It flung open and Barry Ackerman burst in. "Do you have a moment?" asked the FBI agent.

Nick continued shaving and did not reply. He couldn't have five minutes to himself. There was no privacy in this place. Not even in the bathroom. It was like being in a prison.

"I just spoke to Sparks," Ackerman said. "She's hiding something. She's defensive and highly agitated. Something is upsetting her."

"This whole outbreak is upsetting," Nick said, as he continued shaving. "In case you hadn't noticed, she's not the only one upset." He soaped his face and ran the razor across his skin, carefully avoiding the healing cut on his cheek.

Ackerman watched him through the mirror. "Lucky for her, she had the antidote."

"Lucky for us. All of us," Nick said. "If you'll excuse me, I've got to go inject people with her vaccine."

"I need to ask you a few questions. Explain to me how come she has a vaccine to newly mutated bacteria?"

"The whole bacterium didn't mutate. As long as critical surface antigens remain the same, the vaccine will be effective." Nick dropped the razor, lathered his hands with antiseptic soap, and vigorously washed his face.

Ackerman pulled a syringe out of his pocket. "I found this in the pocket of her slacks. She left them in the bathroom last night."

The syringe was covered in a paper wrapper. "It hasn't been used," Nick said.

"Why did she have it?" Ackerman tucked the syringe back into his pocket. "What if Carol Dupuis' rats were deliberately injected with *Yersinia*?"

Nick turned to face the man. "Unlikely. The rats were wild. They would bite." He picked up a can of rose-scented air freshener from the counter. "It would be easier to place the bacteria in a can and spray it as an aerosol. But then the pneumonic infection would be the first to appear."

Ackerman wouldn't give up. "Do you think the epicenter is the hotel where the VP was scheduled to stay?"

Nick turned the cold faucet on full. Just a few drops of water. The hospital was rationing water and electricity. He cupped his hands, collected water. "It could be the park across the street." Nick splashed water on his face.

"But why no *Yersinia* trail?" Ackerman spoke like Rachel-Anne's psychiatrist, with calm but attentive indifference.

Nick straightened and combed his hair with his fingers. He punched the button on the hand dryer. It didn't work. Probably only essential machines were hooked into the generator. "It could have been an out of town visitor who came and left. Perhaps an infected hotel guest."

"We're checking the hotel registration," Ackerman said.

"It's a smarter use of your time than checking out Dana."

Ackerman pointed to the disposable razor. "Can I borrow that?"

"Go ahead."

Staring in the mirror, the special agent foamed his face with soap. He dragged the razor across his cheek, leaving a sharp stripe. "So, you don't think she's behind this?"

Nick shook his head. "No."

Ackerman stared at Nick through the mirror. "Why?"

An open-ended question. It was Rachel-Anne's psychiatrist's favorite type. "If you knew her, you'd know."

"How well do you know her?"

"She worked for me when I worked here. Seven years ago."

The eyes in the mirror stared hard. Nick looked back as if he had nothing to hide.

Ackerman finished shaving and wiped his face with the sleeve of his dark jacket. He leaned against the counter. "What's she like? Political? Left Wing? Religious? Any dalliances with mercenary boyfriends?"

"No," Nick said.

Ackerman smiled. "Just no?"

"She's not a terrorist. She can't kill a mouse. Her methods may not be sound, but her aim is honorable."

Ackerman looked at him.

And Nick knew he had said too much. The silence was loud and made him uncomfortable. He felt he should say something and added, "Do you think she'd put her own life at risk if she were behind this?"

"I really don't know what she's capable of," Ackerman said. "I'm learning a lot." He shot Nick a significant look.

"What about other suspects?" Nick said. The best defense was offense—he learned that from the psychiatrist, too.

Ackerman seemed to deflate. "Our investigation has been compromised by the storm. The power is off in town, cell towers are down, and email is out. The fact that the hospital is under quarantine doesn't help."

No, it doesn't, Nick thought. He hated the idea of being incarcerated another night.

"And yet, Dana Sparks is coming and going like the wind. She was here this morning and she left. I haven't finished questioning her."

"She's probably at work."

"Where does she live?"

"You'll find her in the lab."

"I want to check her house."

Nick knew she had nothing to hide. "She lives off the bypass on an unnamed dirt road."

Ackerman pulled out a pen and a notepad and passed it to Nick. "I'd like a map."

Nick picked up the pen and drew hasty scribbles. A circle for the bypass. A spoke for her access road.

While Nick was drawing the map, there was a knock on the door. It opened and Michael Smith peered in. "I have been waiting so long," he said.

Ackerman waved him toward the toilet. Michael came in and stood with his back to them, urinating.

"Are we done?" Nick asked.

Ackerman said, "For now."

CHAPTER FORTY-EIGHT

Dana left the hospital using the emergency exit, which, despite the warning, issued no alarm. It must not have been wired to the generator. In the parking lot, she looked for her car and when she didn't see it, she thought it may have been stolen. Then she remembered the ditch.

She trudged to the veterinary school on foot. The clouds were thinning; the sky was bright. There was water puddled everywhere. Underfoot, the streets and sidewalks were littered with garbage and debris. Branches torn from trees lay on the ground. Windblown newspapers plastered the shrubs. Plastic bags hung on wind-stripped trees. Bluebonnets were trampled in the mud. The spring landscape was in ruin.

Dana crossed campus and saw no one. The curtains on the dorm windows were closed. Not a window or door was open. The houses were shut tight. It was the same on the streets. No moving cars, no people. Dana imagined throughout history the reaction to the plague had been just like this.

She reached her car and saw it inclined in the ditch. The night rains had not swept it away. She would call AAA when she reached the vet school. She passed the Lone Star Heritage Hotel and saw the front doors closed, the proud flags gone. No doormen guarded the mirrored entrance. A red and white gingham tablecloth from the Pizza Garden floated in the gutter. There was an electrical line on the ground.

She reached the vet school. The parking lot was empty. The generator roared loudly in the morning silence. Inside, the halls were vacant and laboratory doors were locked. In her office, Dana picked up the phone and was happy to hear a dial tone. She called AAA and got a recording. She went to make coffee, but her can was empty and she headed to the main office for Betty's private stash.

She reached the office, saw Nellie Duncan, and her sour morning got worse.

"Oh, Dana, great you're here." Nellie put down the coffeepot. "With the boss out, I assumed you took off." She threw herself into a chair. "I'm dying for java. Can you make it? I never get it right."

Dana took the pot. She wanted a decent cup and was glad to make it herself. She filled the pot with water.

"You're looking a little hangdog this morning," Nellie said. "Feeling under the weather? Something the matter?"

"No." Dana spooned coffee into the filter while Nellie spun around in Betty's chair like a little girl.

Nellie stopped spinning suddenly. "Don't make the coffee too strong. I'm feeling weak myself this morning." She lifted her bangs with a small hand.

Dana added an extra scoop.

"I hope I'm not sick. Almost everyone is. Except you." Nellie wrinkled her nose and stared at Dana.

"And you." Dana said.

Nellie changed the subject. "You got a phone call. From an FBI agent. You are to report immediately to the hospital."

"Right." Dana turned on the coffee pot. In a few seconds the machine began to hiss.

"I wonder what he wanted," Nellie said.

Dana shrugged and watched a stream of coffee shoot into the pot.

"The FBI agent thinks this outbreak is deliberate."

"I know."

Nellie lowered her voice. "I probably shouldn't warn you, but in confidence, the agent thinks it's you."

Dana walked to the cupboard and got a cup and wiped the inside with her finger. She wouldn't dignify the accusation with a response.

"As Nick said, you *are* the only one with the bacteria."

Dana stared at the dripping coffee, keeping her back to Nellie.

"I would have thought Nick would try to keep you out of the fire, not throw you in."

The coffee was still dripping, but Dana filled her cup. She wasn't going to listen to any more of this.

"You probably didn't notice, but they're watching you. They think you're out of step with the investigation. You're being deliberately misleading."

Dana shoved the coffee pot back in place. Was that why Karl insisted on helping her with the assays?

"For what it's worth, I told them it was beyond your capability."

Dana gave her an icy smile. "How nice to have you on my side." She gripped her cup and left the room.

In her office, she sat at her desk gulping deep breaths of air, and tried to stop herself from shaking. The outbreak wasn't deliberate. Nellie was wrong, and Ackerman was insane. It was a natural phenomenon; roving wildlife extending their range after a rainy spring, and carrying the bacteria farther south than they would otherwise go.

There were strange things about the outbreak, though. The *Yersinia* were extremely virulent and highly resistant. The rodents around Duane weren't infected and the bacteria appeared to come from nowhere. They appeared in an environment they had no business appearing in on a week that the VP was coming to town. Ackerman said the bacteria were genetically engineered, but how would he know? This wasn't a deliberate act of terror. The *Yersinia* came from somewhere, and she would find the source. She finished her coffee and got to work.

CHAPTER FORTY-NINE

Dana was no epidemiologist, but she'd watched Nick in action and knew the first thing to do was correctly identify the index case. From that starting point, she had to trace the infection forward to people who caught the disease, and then back to rodents that may have carried it.

First, she needed her car. She called AAA again and got the same recording. She decided to try and free the car herself. She left the vet school. The sun was rising and the air was steamy and hot. The lakes and puddles on the ground were drying. The sky was bright, and leaves that remained on the trees shone as if they'd been scrubbed and polished.

She reached her car, and studied it from all angles. She pushed on it and nothing happened. The car was lilting to the right, nose down, the belly stuck on the vertical decline. The front right wheel was half covered with water. It was the only wheel that made contact with the ground; the other three wheels were in the air. Dana would not be able to drive forward, which meant she had to drive backwards—try to get all tires on the ground.

She opened the car door and climbed inside. The interior was damp and smelled of mildew. The windshield was steamy and fogged up. She wiped it clear with her hand. She cranked down the window, turned the key, and the car jumped to life. She eased off the emergency brake and the car remained immobile. She paused for a moment and read the car manual to learn how to engage four-wheel drive. *Push a button.* She pushed it. Then she thrust the gear into reverse, depressed the accelerator, and felt the backward shift of the car. A loud scraping sound made her close her eyes.

She accelerated backward and heard mud pelt the car. The front right wheel began to slide and a back wheel made contact with the ground. She opened her eyes. The angle was wrong and the car lurched to the right. She leaned left and spun the wheel counterclockwise as the car began to tip. A warning alarm sounded, and Dana let go of the steering wheel and slammed her body against the door. The car stalled, rocked back on forth on its wheels. All four wheels. All now in contact with the ground.

Dana straightened and looked out the window. She brushed the hair out of her eyes and saw the car was parallel to the ditch. She cranked the key once more and pressed on the accelerator. The car slid sideways at first, like a boat, before her momentum picked up and the car moved faster and faster, and then she was cutting across the ditch and up the embankment. She bounced over the curb and hit the road. She was out. The investigation could begin.

CHAPTER FIFTY

In the middle of a day he didn't think he'd live to see, McCoy lay in bed, watching a nurse inject morphine into his IV line.

"You'll feel better now," she said, though McCoy had not been feeling bad. The nurse was perky and smiley and reminded him of his wife, who, along with his daughter, were in the north hospital. Except for the fact that he was isolated from them, McCoy felt fine. He knew in a minute he'd feel even finer.

He stared out his window. The sun was high and bright and rays of light beamed down upon the trees. There were no clouds, and the sky was a clear bright blue. Limpid. The word was correct, but not apt. Brilliant was more appropriate. The sky reminded McCoy of summers he spent as a child on the Chesapeake Bay. He inhaled deeply and could almost taste the salt air. These were sights and smells he had not expected to experience again in his lifetime.

Was it the morphine? Finally McCoy understood how the boys in Vietnam became addicted to heroin. He understood how an opium ban in China precipitated a war. *Papaver* something was the scientific name of the opium poppy. Funny he could remember a genus name, and not a conversation with the VP he apparently had an hour ago. The nurse told McCoy he had spoken to his wife as well, and he couldn't remember that either. A conversation with the Secretary of Homeland Security was another blank. McCoy closed his eyes as a wave of morphine swept him away.

It seemed only a few minutes had passed when the nurse shook him awake and informed him the men had arrived for the meeting.

Meeting? It was news to McCoy. He fought his IV lines, struggling to sit up. Who called the meeting? It wasn't him, was it? What did he have to say? Nothing that he knew of. His brain felt muzzy and pillowy, like a sagging mattress. He glanced out the window. He was in no condition for a meeting.

But Ackerman, Nick, and Karl flounced in anyway. The nurse hurried to arrange chairs around the bed. Then Ackerman sent her out. When the door closed, the FBI agent called the meeting to order. Good, so he ordered it. All McCoy had to do was listen and appear attentive. He stared back out the window. The leaves on the trees looked like emeralds glinting in the sunlight. Marge had earrings that color. He smiled at the image, until he intercepted the FBI agent's stare.

"How do *you* feel?" Ackerman said.

McCoy dragged his sight from the window. "Just fine, just fine. And you?"

He must have already inquired for Ackerman said sharply, "I said I was fine."

McCoy ordered himself to concentrate. Nick got up and closed the curtains. Still, it was hard for McCoy to focus. He fixed his eyes on the FBI agent. Jesus, he had long arms. Like a chimpanzee or a gorilla. Was it normal for your arms to reach the floor when you sat on a chair? Nick and Karl's arms were crossed in their lap, so he couldn't compare. McCoy extended his arms and disconnected something that triggered an alarm that brought the nurse. McCoy closed his eyes as she re-hooked a tube. When the door closed he had to fight to pry his eyelids apart. He was suddenly very tired.

"Okay," Ackerman said, "we've got twenty dead. Everyone else admitted is recovering. We seem to be over the worst."

Karl was in apparent agreement. "The National Guard will disband this evening and the airport will reopen tomorrow."

"Admitted patients will be kept overnight," Nick added. "The vaccine works as a preventative as well as a treatment, so there's no danger of new infections. Tomorrow we can all go home."

Great, McCoy thought. He expected the meeting was nearing its conclusion and was sorely disappointed when Ackerman changed the subject again.

"We're dealing with an unusual strain of *Yersinia*."

"The CDC confirmed it appears to have been genetically engineered for resistance," Karl said.

Nick explained. "Membrane transport proteins have acquired an enzyme function. The change occurred at the level of the DNA. The length of the transport protein gene is double what it should be."

Ackerman stared at McCoy. "That's twice as long."

McCoy, struggling to keep his eyes open, wondered if the FBI agent had just defined the word *double* for him.

Karl began talking about transport proteins, oxidative enzymes, and other things McCoy couldn't follow. He wasn't a geneticist. Why did he have to listen to this tripe? Why couldn't they go away and leave him alone?

"We're lucky we got through this as well as we did," Ackerman said, when Karl stopped for a breath. "There could have been devastating repercussions. Ordering the antidote from Fort Troy was an acute call."

McCoy started. Ackerman was addressing him. Here was another call he made he couldn't remember making. When had he spoken to General Schwartzke? He turned to his window. Someone had closed the goddamn curtain.

"We know the Russians developed resistant *Yersinia* strains to use as agents of war," Nick said.

"They also developed an antidote," Ackerman added.

Well now McCoy was listening. He faced the agent.

Ackerman sat back in his chair and folded his impossibly long fingers together. "Perhaps, in bankruptcy, the Russians sold the bacteria for a price."

McCoy waited for him to continue, but Ackerman was staring at him. Was *he* supposed to say something? "Very interesting." McCoy tried to look thoughtful.

"To whom did they sell it to, is the question," Ackerman said. "We're looking at suspects now. Despite the lack of power and inoperable cell phone towers, we're making progress."

Karl agreed the breakdown in communications was hampering the investigation. Cell phone communication was awry. He was trying to call Atlanta and make a report.

Ackerman said to try the *woof*.

"Woof?" McCoy said. Were they talking about a dog? The dead guy's dog? What was his name? Puddley? Muddly? Was the conversation jumping around or was it just him?

"Roof," Ackerman said, shouting loudly. "I said roof." He rubbed his eyes. "Look. Now that the health concern is past, we can concentrate on finding the culprit."

He pulled a sheet of paper from his suit pocket and unfolded it. God, his fingers really were long and skinny. Like tree branches. He had a long list of suspects.

In the manner of a child learning to read, Ackerman used his finger to follow words on his sheet. McCoy remembered reading to Margaret when she was a child. She loved the book *Night Moon,* and before she was two years old, she had the words memorized and used to say them out loud. *Night spoon. Night moon.* McCoy used to know the whole thing, but that was all he could remember now.

Before him, Ackerman was listing his suspects. Dana Sparks was still top on his list. But there were others. The old guy with the dog. The violent football player who threw chairs. Tim Sweeny from the vet school. Any of the first cases were possibilities. As were people who didn't get sick, which included two nurses, a doctor, and three of McCoy's employees.

Ackerman said they were paying special attention to the local hotels. "We're running the names through our computer."

"It's possible the epicenter is the hotel and not the park," Karl said.

"The VP," McCoy said, and saw bobbing heads. It reminded him of a toy Margaret once had, a game of wobbling fish with snapping mouths and ...

Ackerman was shaking him, his long fingers like talons on his arm. "McCoy, are you with us?"

McCoy opened his eyes. "I'm here."

Ackerman continued. The investigation was not confined to Duane. No siree, Ackerman's long reach extended across the state. There was a Russian couple in Dallas who once worked in a chemical plant in Vanova and were given political asylum. As for the airlines, Ackerman had information that a well-known Arab terrorist had flown to Houston two weeks ago. The FBI was searching for him. Meanwhile, McCoy, Karl, and Nick were in the clear. Even the visiting Michael Smith had been ruled out.

Christ almighty, McCoy had forgotten all about him. Where was he? He was supposed to give a seminar on Wednesday. Had he given it? Did McCoy miss it? Had Michael left?

What day is it?" McCoy said, and received horrified looks.

"Thursday," Karl said.

"Maybe we should go," Nick said. He stood up and opened the curtains and the room turned bright.

McCoy tried to argue, but felt himself sinking into a vast abyss. A strange distant feeling crept over him. He felt like he was shrinking.

The next thing he knew, he heard the sound of a chair scraping across the floor and his wife and daughter were there. Marjorie moved the chair to the head of the bed and sat down next to him. Margaret sat on the bed, and as she did when she was little, tested the springs, bouncing up and down. She was looking robust and healthy.

McCoy's heart pulsed in and out as she bounced. His chest felt tight again, but in a good way, as if his heart were too big for him. He held her hand, moved by the softness of her skin.

There were tears in her eyes. "I didn't think you'd make it."

Her tears looked like diamonds and made her eyes sparkle. "It'll take more than a heart attack and the plague to get rid of me. We've got driving lessons, a trip to Austin, maybe a trip up north?"

Margaret smiled through her tears, the sun shining on her young, fresh face. For McCoy, at this moment, all was well.

CHAPTER FIFTY-ONE

Dana drove to the University Plaza and headed for the dumpster, armed with an animal cage. According to Howie of Parks and Rec, the dumpster was where local rats and mice went for lobster and steak. The lot was empty and she drove to the back. The dumpster had more trash, and she managed to lean down and place a trap atop a flattened moving carton.

She turned around and saw a car at the car wash. If the place was open, she'd clean her car. She pulled up beside a black sports car and jumped out. A young man pounding on the front door turned. He was young, blond, and muscular. He would have been handsome, except for a glistening white scar that snaked down his cheek from his eye to his mouth. "You work here?" he said.

Dana tried hard to look at him without looking at the scar. "I was hoping *you* worked here. Is the place closed?"

The man raised his fist and pounded the door again. The door shook. A rounded biceps popped out beneath the tight sleeve of his T-shirt. "Everything in town is closed," he said. "I can't buy beer. I can't get the blood out of the rug. I can't wash my car."

Dana stood there. *Blood out of a rug?*

"You don't have gas to spare, do you?"

Dana shook her head. "I'm nearly out myself."

"You take a honeymoon and look what happens." The man sat down on the stoop. He traced the line of the scar with his finger. "I just got back this morning from San Antonio. Cut my honeymoon short. I heard on the news the town was closed. I didn't believe it."

"How did you get back?" Dana knew the roads were closed, as was the airport.

"I rented a car. Said I was going to College Station. Took the back roads. No problem. Except for this freaking blood stain." He flung an arm at the black MG.

Dana looked at the car and read the license plate: FB-JOCK. It was the car parked at the hospital all week. Dana looked at the man with the scar. "Are you ... uh ... uh ..."

"Yep. Bucky Finch." He held out his hand. "The football star. I see you recognized me. I suppose you want an autograph."

"No." Dana shook his hand. "You're Jack Dowel's roommate."

Bucky Finch smiled and flicked his eyebrows up and down. "You a friend of Jack's?"

Dana introduced herself. "I met him at the hospital. How's he doing?"

"Fine. They sprung him yesterday."

"So, this is your car, but Jack borrowed it. You were out of town." She remembered now. "You eloped."

"He told you."

"It's a secret. My lips are sealed. You were telling me about the blood. It's in the car? What bled?"

"A cat. It's been there a week. The blood, not the cat. See, we were going to the airport, Kimberly and me. That's my wife. Well, this was last week and back then we weren't married. Anyhow, the plan was to leave the car at the airport, see."

"Okay."

"But we pass a cat that's been hit by a car." He pointed to North Street, a busy road. "Kim says we can't leave it. It's a bad omen or something. It's bleeding and mangled and when I get it in the car it bleeds all over my white carpet. I called Jack. I asked him to pick it up and get it washed. The car, not the cat. He did, but the blood didn't come out."

He went on, but Dana stopped listening. The hair on the back of her neck was raised. This was it. This was what she had been looking for. The missing piece.

While Bucky talked about his honeymoon, and a play he had seen at an outdoor theatre that sounded like *Romeo and Juliet,* Dana surveyed the car wash. The wash was automatic and arranged in an assembly line fashion. The vehicle passed through the wash on a motorized track. The washing bay was fitted with high-pressured nozzles that cleaned the car's exterior. Mechanized polishers buffed the body. The interior was manually vacuumed with a powerful suction hose.

Dana eyed the vacuuming station. The debris from a car would be sucked into a vacuum bag. And dumped where? She stared at the dumpster. The place where lucky rodents went to dine.

Bucky was looking at her. "So *do* you know how to get a blood stain out?"

"Try club soda. What did you do with the cat?"

"I dropped it at the vet."

"Which one?"

"The vet school. It was the closest."

"When was this?"

"A week ago Monday."

"What did the cat look like?"

"Big. The size of a small dog."

"Was it orange?"

"Do you know whose cat it is?"

Dana thought she did.

She thanked Bucky and crossed the parking lot heading for the Pizza Garden. The outdoor restaurant was closed and in disarray. Checkered tablecloths floated in the swimming pool, along with leaves and branches. But the Sequoia cactus stubbornly held the notices impaled to its thorns.

Dana tore off a flyer. *Please bring Pumpkin home. Call Travis Levine.* It was the eleven-year-old with bubonic plague. Dana knew what happened to his cat.

CHAPTER FIFTY-TWO

The animal clinic was locked and Dana used her key to enter a hall-way from inside the building. An appointment book lay on the front counter and she went back ten pages to Monday, April 20th. According to the book, a male calico was dumped at the clinic and Tim signed on as the attending veterinarian. The diagnosis was a damaged spine and crushed front leg. Dana remembered the orange cat with the bandaged stump in his animal room. Now she knew his name. Pumpkin.

On Saturday, Pumpkin developed pneumonia and Tim put him down. On Monday, Phillip Becker mentioned in the meeting that he wanted to autopsy the cat and McCoy told him to forget it. If only he had autopsied it. The cat didn't die from pneumonia. It had *Yersinia*. The cat was the index case. It infected Tim.

Dana went upstairs and let herself into Tim's lab. It took her less than five minutes to find a sample of the cat's blood in his freezer. She took the tube to her lab.

She grabbed the tube with Frank's blood. Since it tested negative for *Yersinia* antibodies, she assumed he died from lung cancer. Now, she was no longer so certain. Frank had been in the room with Pumpkin, inhaling *Yersinia* with each troubled breath. He was on an immuno-suppressant drug that would have blocked an immune response. If he was exposed, he wouldn't have been able to make antibodies and his ELISA result would be misleading. He would have bacteria in his blood, but no antibodies.

Dana went to the quarantine room and began an antigen capture assay to look for the bacteria directly. In a little over an hour, she had the results. Two positive samples confirmed *Yersinia*. Pumpkin and Frank had the plague. She had taken her dog to the clinic for treatment at the worst possible time. Wanting to help him live, she hastened his death. Doing the right thing turned out to be wrong.

She washed her hands and went to her office. There was still one loose end. Dudley. Except for him, the pieces fit. But where was he infected? She returned to the clinic and examined the appointment book more carefully. Did Dudley use the vet clinic? Had he brought in Bingo the same time Pumpkin was dropped off?

The answer was no. Dudley's name wasn't in the book. So where was Dudley infected? Did he know Pumpkin's owner, Travis? Had Dudley taken Bingo to High Park? Did he stop to pet Pumpkin? Did the dog and cat fight and transfer fleas? Or did Bingo get into garbage that came from the dumpster? Anything was possible, she thought, and the man she needed to ask was dead.

She headed home. The bright sunshine had faded, giving rise to a cloudy afternoon. She was on the bypass when the answer to the question came to her. Dudley had used the car wash. She knew that he had. At the hospital, when he drew her a map to his house, he had drawn it on the back of a car wash receipt. The receipt was still in the pocket of the jeans she had worn that day.

She guessed that someone drove the bacteria to town. Someone used the car wash and went on, but not before leaving behind infected fleas that initiated a sequence of events that would affect many, and likely cost her her job.

Dana turned on the radio looking for music, and got the news. There was no mention of Duane, not even a reminder the roads into town were closed. The lead story was the situation in Somalia. UN investigations revealed that the damage inflicted on the mosque and hospital far exceeded the damage expected from a cluster bomb. The evidence indisputably supported the U.S. claim that the buildings were used to store munitions. The Somalis had put their own people at risk. It was an accusation the Somalis denied. If munitions were present in the mosque and hospital, they blamed the U.S. for putting them there.

Dana switched off the radio. Overseas things were a mess, but what happened here was nothing more than an innocent outbreak, started at a car wash by a cat. She knew she should probably go to the hospital and tell Ackerman what she found out—but she wasn't in the mood.

At home, Dana found the receipt Dudley had given her. The car wash receipt placed him at the epicenter. He had taken his car to be washed on Monday, April 20th, the same day Pumpkin was hit. They were both in the wrong place at the wrong time, and, like Frank, had paid with their lives.

Dana envisioned a scenario where Jack took the MG to the car wash and tried to clean Pumpkin's blood off the carpet. He was bitten on the ankle by a flea. When the rug was vacuumed, fleas were sucked up and ended up in a dumpster. Other fleas jumped to safety on the vacuum hose. When Dudley arrived, the fleas jumped again, ending up in Ladybird. One must have bitten him, causing the infection that made his lymph node swell the size of an egg.

She crumpled the car wash receipt, opened her last beer, and sat down at the kitchen table. Dudley was likely exposed on Monday when he washed his car. He started feeling sick on Thursday, three days later, and was dead within a week. It was an uncommonly rapid progression for bubonic phase, and an indication of the strain's extreme virulence. She had to call Karl and tell him what she had learned.

But the landline was still dead, as was her cell phone. The electricity was not yet restored. Notifying Karl would have to wait until morning.

She went to the porch and sat down on the swing, watching darkness fall. She felt uneasy and cold, as if the warmth of the place had leaked away. It seemed as if everything she had was slipping away. As soon as McCoy learned she impersonated him, tenure would be out of the question. The grant would be rescinded. Her life here would be gone. Maybe her career as well. She had tried to save lives and lost everything, as Nick and Karl warned that she would.

Nick said it all earlier at the hospital. *You cross lines you shouldn't cross. You throw your life away.* That's what she'd done, wasted seven years waiting for him. Earlier that morning she thought they had a chance, but that was impossible now. The man she knew was gone. If he thought she was behind this, he didn't know her at all.

Night fell, leaving a starless sky and dark shadows. The wind had died and the air was still. There was no sweet scent of jasmine or honeysuckle. No chirping of crickets or frogs. No night birds sang.

Dana finished her beer and crumpled the can. She was hungry, but she had nothing to eat. From far away she heard the low rumble of a car engine. It grew louder and before long, she saw two headlights shining through the trees. A car door slammed.

She followed the barking dogs up the drive.

Michael. He emerged from a rental car. Dana saw the Hertz sign on the windshield before he cut the lights. By her side, Anthony snarled and Judy barked.

Michael used the door as a shield, crouching behind it. "Dana? Is this you? I have been lost."

She wondered how he found her house.

"I was worried when you did not show up last night. I borrowed Karl's car. You said I could see where you lived."

Long, long ago, she remembered saying that. She felt a pang of guilt when she remembered deserting him at the hospital. She said, "How did you find my house?"

"Nick drew a map for that FBI agent, Ackerman. He is saying this is deliberate."

So, Nick really was working with the FBI.

"That Ackerman is an ass."

Dana's thoughts exactly. "Would you like to come in?"

He was worried about the dogs, and stood pressed between the door and the car. "Will they bite?"

Dana yelled at Anthony to quit barking. He was growling and looked ready to strike. Judy hid behind Dana's legs, shaking. "I'll put them in the car." Dana shut them in the Raider, where Anthony flung himself at the windscreen and Judy yapped shrilly.

She invited Michael to the house. Inside, she lit a candle and offered wine, forgetting he didn't drink. She found a box of apple juice, poured herself red wine, and sat with him at the kitchen table.

"You have a nice house," he said. "Very private. You live here alone?"

Dana conceded she did.

"It is very secluded. No neighbors nearby?"

"One down the road. Far away, but close enough." She picked up her glass and took a sip. Red wine was supposed to be served at room temperature, but she liked her drinks cold. The wine left a sour taste in her mouth. She could almost taste the vinegar it would become. She put down the glass.

"And you are fine?" Michael said. "You didn't get sick?" He brushed the end of his moustache with a finger.

Dana shrugged. She wasn't going to give him any details. "Lucky, I guess."

"There is no luck," Michael said. "God smiled upon you."

Hardly, Dana thought, as she threw back more bad wine.

He patted the breast pocket of his shirt. "Mind if I smoke?"

"Yes. You should quit."

Nevertheless, he took a package of Winston's from his pocket. He also removed a guitar string and a flashlight. The latter was small and purple, the kind given away free with batteries. He turned it over in his hand. "Ackerman is checking everyone. At the hospital, they are saying the strain is new and genetically engineered, that the outbreak is deliberate."

"So I heard."

"I should not tell you, but they find it strange you have the antidote."

He averted his eyes at this declaration. Lifted his glass of apple juice and drank thirstily. His sleeve fell down his arm. She saw the scratches on his forearm. Three deep parallel crimson tracks that had not healed. He tugged at his sleeve, dropped his hand, and covered the guitar string. In the silence, Dana heard Anthony howling and Judy's frantic bark. A strong gust of wind rattled the window. The candle flickered and nearly went out.

Dana jumped up.

"What is wrong with those animals?" Michael asked.

Dana went to the door. "I heard something." She opened the wooden door.

Michael glided to the window. Crouched low, he peered out the glass. "I do not see anything."

Dana stepped onto the porch. She heard the screech of an owl. Her heart was pounding and her ears filled with blood. "Something's out there."

CHAPTER FIFTY-THREE

After dinner, Nick accompanied Ackerman to the basement morgue. The agent had received a fax from Quantico that bore a grainy photograph of the terrorist sighted in Houston two weeks ago. Ackerman wanted the bodies checked. According to his latest theory, the terrorist was likely the first infected and therefore presumably dead and in the morgue awaiting identification. They were looking for a slight man with dark hair, dark eyes, and a moustache.

There weren't enough body bags. The dead were covered with sheets and laid out in rows on the floor. With his nose to his sleeve, Ackerman pulled back the sheets one by one. The air conditioning was functional, but to conserve generator power it was barely working. A rotting stench hung in the air. Holding his handkerchief over his nose, Nick examined the faces of the plague-infected dead.

They went down the rows. There were twenty bodies, twenty black and bloated bodies with tight, screaming faces. Nick could have been one of those bodies. He came that close. If not for Dana, he would be in this room, on this floor. Ackerman dropped the last sheet. "See anything?"

Nick shook his head. No face resembled the image in the photograph. And none of the dead men bore a moustache, though it could have been shaved.

"I'm going to go through it one more time," Ackerman said.

Nick had seen enough. "I'll be up on the roof.

A few minutes later he was outside, looking over the town, gulping clean, cool air. An austral wind was blowing, and the air was salty and wet. The sky was ridden with cirrocumulus clouds, scuttling fast. Occasionally a sweep of headlights flared on the streets below. Behind him, beside a satellite dish, Karl was talking on his cell phone.

Karl had lost faith in the FBI and was conducting a parallel investigation of his own. The first person he checked out was Ackerman. He was disgusted the FBI agent was trying to pin the outbreak on Dana. Karl thought Ackerman could have been trying to take the heat off himself, but a call to Quantico verified the FBI agent was on staff and currently in Duane on assignment.

Nick believed any terrorist was either dead or long gone. Who would unleash an agent of biological war and wait around to get ill? Unless they had the antidote. Dana obviously had taken the vaccine. She had given it to him, Penny, Jack, and Michael Smith.

Nick paused. *Even Michael Smith?* He was amongst the last to get sick. He was fine, asymptomatic, when Dana said she had enough for one last shot that she used on him. "What do we have on Michael?" Nick said.

Karl flipped through his notes. "Ackerman called his university in Iowa and confirmed he's on the faculty. He's got tenure and apparently is highly ethical. Ackerman ruled him out."

"How old is he? Thirty? Why is he looking for a job here if he's got tenure there?"

"Good point. He's pretty young to have tenure. I'll request a photo." Karl began typing into his phone.

Nick gazed over the dark city, wondering about Michael. He never had anything of relevance to say. He refused to talk about his research, acting as if it was completely classified, which was absurd. Nick thought of something else that made him pause. Michael was in the bathroom when Nick drew the map to Dana's. He knew where she lived. He opened his phone and called Dana's cell phone. The phone didn't ring. He called her landline. Dead. He grabbed Karl's arm. "We need to check on Dana."

Hurling questions, Karl followed him down three flights of stairs. In the parking lot, Karl searched for his keys, turning his pockets inside out.

"Hurry up, hurry up," Nick said.

"The keys are gone." Karl pointed to an empty spot in the crowded lot. "So is the car."

CHAPTER FIFTY-FOUR

Dana had lied. There was no one outside. She had heard nothing but her howling dogs, trying to warn her of the danger she had not seen. She had to get away from Michael. The scratches on his arm were too deep and too vicious to be caused by a vine. He had been clawed, clawed by poor Pumpkin who got hit by a car and was left on the road to die.

The outbreak *was* intentional. The man who deliberately started it was here in her house. And she was alone in the country with the electricity out, her landline dead, no cell phone service, and the closest neighbor half a mile down the road.

"What is it?" Michael came to her side. "I do not see anything."

Dana walked to the edge of the porch and stared up the driveway. "I thought I heard something." The bawling of the dogs was louder now. They were her only hope. Michael was terrified of them.

He took hold of her arm. "It is only the animals. Let us go inside." He pulled her toward the door.

A voice in her head screamed: *run, run, run.*

She ran. Leapt across the porch, vaulting over the stairs, and tearing up the drive. Heavy footsteps on the porch pounded behind her. Michael yelled out in a foreign tongue, *"Bara nek!"*

A shadow passed overhead and Dana screamed as Michael took a flying dive off the porch and tackled her to the ground. He grabbed her arm, yanked her up, and dragged her up the porch steps. The veins in his forearm bulged like cords. He was stronger than he looked. He towed her across the porch and shoved her into the house, slammed the door, lifted the chain, and locked them inside. "Sit."

She did as he said. Sat at the table in the eerie orange candlelight. He lit a cigarette off the flame. She felt surprisingly calm and was shocked by her reaction. Her heart was barely beating, yet she was alert, on edge, with her thoughts focused, distinct, and clear.

Car keys. She needed her car keys. She would not get out without them. Where were they? Briefcase? Jeans? No, there, in the living room, on top of the TV. She had to get past Michael to get them and get out.

He was in good shape for someone who smoked so much and was recently sick. He was hardly breathing. After what he had done, he would be desperate.

She looked at the wine bottle. She could use it as a weapon. *No. No. No.* She couldn't hit him hard enough to knock him out. A knife then. *To stab him with?* No, she could never do it—there would be too much blood.

Run. Run. Run.

Yes, it was the only answer. But she needed her keys. Help was her dogs, shut in the car, crying themselves hoarse in warning. She had to distract Michael. Make him think she'd given up, was no flight risk. She said, "Where did you get the cat?"

He sucked on his cigarette, contemplating the smoke. "I took it. Found it in a driveway two weeks ago. Injected it. Bastard scratched the hell out of me."

That's what he cared about? Scratches? "You killed people. You almost died yourself. I saw you last night. Puking your guts out, unable to stand. I met the man you killed. How could you do that?"

"It is how you say, what goes around, comes around. Fair is fair."

"I say it's murder. You almost killed a baby. What if it was one of your twins?"

"You are an idiot. You know nothing." He got up, grabbed a plate from the dish drainer, and crushed his cigarette into it.

Dana turned around in her chair to look at him. She wasn't striking the tone she wanted, but she couldn't help herself—she had to know. "Why did you do it?"

He checked his flashlight, turned it on and off, and then on again. "To let you know. We have weapons too. As deadly as yours. We can fight back. You are the terrorists." He turned off the flashlight.

"Where did you get the bacteria?"

"We bought it." He lit another cigarette.

"From Russia?"

"Does it matter? It was guaranteed to be drug resistant. This vaccine of yours was unfortunate." Michael threw open a cupboard. "I am starving. What is there to eat?"

"Not much."

He pulled out a can of tuna. "Fish in a can. Disgusting." He made a spitting noise and grabbed a can of Alpo. "Lamb chunks. Now, here is something."

She stared at him.

"Where is the can opener?"

She pointed at a drawer and heard the dogs again. She had to get out. This was her place. She knew the terrain. Her dogs were in the car and she'd drive to the hospital. Police were at the door. All she needed were a few seconds to get to her car. First, she had to get her keys.

Michael had the can opener. She watched his arm working as he turned the knob. "Knife?"

She pointed to the utensil drawer. A stupid response. He pulled out her sharpest knife and ran his thumb along the blade. A thin line of blood beaded on his skin. He dropped the knife and turned on the tap. Dry.

"Water. I need water." He looked at his thumb with horror.

She stood up. "I've got a napkin."

"Sit down," he screamed. He grabbed a towel from the counter and wiped his thumb. "Bread?"

She pointed to the cupboard. "Crackers. They're stale."

He carried a box of garlic flavored Triscuit crackers to the table and sat down. With her sharpest knife he speared a chunk of Alpo and shoved it in his mouth. "Mmm, great." He chewed with his mouth wide open.

She looked at the table. He was a heavy smoker. In a race, who would win? Was she fast enough to get to the car? Would the dogs protect her? If Michael charged, would Anthony attack?

Michael smeared Alpo across a cracker and popped it in his mouth. Brown sludge trickled down his chin. The candlelight flickered on the walls. She had to get around him, grab the keys, slip the chain, and get out. But she was frozen in place. "*Do* you work in Iowa?" she asked.

He chewed loudly, like a cow. He had no West Point manners, no manners at all. "Of course not," he said contemptuously.

"Where did you meet McCoy?"

"I sent him an email. He was thoroughly impressed and wished to meet me."

"*Are* you a scientist?"

Michael sneered and spread another cracker. He didn't answer.

"You injected the cat. Then what?"

Talking with his mouth open, Michael said, "I waited. There was no news. I thought I had failed. Then, the old man got sick and I knew the plan worked. I did not know the cat was hit by a car, that a good Samaritan took it to the doctor. You Americans and your pets. They are treated better than most people in my country. We are bombed and the world turns their back."

"What is your country?"

"It does not matter."

"That story about your wife and twins? Did you make it up?"

He pointed the knife at her. "That was true."

He had a wife and daughters to live for. She recalled his photo with the twins who were just babies. He had a reason to stop and not go any further. "Where is your family?"

He used the rim of the can to clean the knife blade. "Dead." He reached for his cigarettes.

Dana's rising hope fell fast.

Michael leaned into the flickering candle. It was burning down, the wax running out. He inhaled sharply. "Your president blew them up when he bombed my neighborhood five years ago. I was at work. My family was killed. Their bodies burned to black tar. My wife's head was identified by her teeth. We never found her body. My daughters had no teeth."

Sweat rolled down Dana's side from under her arms. "I'm sorry."

Michael impassively blew smoke rings. They sailed across the table in front of her. There was Alpo caught in his teeth. He pointed his cigarette at her. "What do you say? Do not get upset, get even? What happened could not be changed. It was fate. There, as here."

"What happened here wasn't fate. It was *you*. You did it."

"It had to happen. What is, must be. Whether you believe it or not, makes no difference. It is so."

"This wouldn't have happened without you. These people would still be alive. All those people you killed—"

He banged his fist on the table. "There was a plan greater than ours. Nothing went the way we thought. We did not know the bacteria were so bad. We did not know it would spread so fast, that the town would close, and I would be stuck. That the antidote would not be strong and I would be sick. That you would have a better cure. This was not our plan. There was another plan at work."

The candle flickered and died. The room went dark. Michael snapped on the flashlight. "Get a candle."

There was a package on top of the fridge. Dana stood up and began pulling out kitchen drawers. "I can't remember where they are."

He passed her the flashlight.

Now she had the light. Bad move for him. "I think the living room."

She held her breath as she walked behind him. He reached up, grabbed her wrist, and squeezed it hard. "Quickly."

She passed him, wondering if he could hear her heart knocking against her ribs. The flashlight beam was shaking on the floor. Her hands were sticky and sweaty. Her breaths were sharp, short gasps. The adrenaline she needed to run was in full force.

She walked past the door, heading for the TV. Her car keys were within reach. She grabbed them as she pretended to peer behind the TV in search of a misplaced candle. She could undo the chain, twist the lock on the door, and shut him inside. Buy a few seconds of time.

She stood frozen. What if she couldn't make it? What if he caught her? He had her sharpest knife with Alpo stuck between its serrated teeth. He could stab her to death. He had his wire. A guitar string, or a garrote? What if he had a gun? What if he had more bacteria? What if he tried to inject her? Could her immune system stand such an assault? She suddenly felt weak, unable to move.

But the words ran out in her mind like an order that could not be denied. *Run, run, run.*

She ran. Lifted the chain, opened the door, turned the knock to lock, slammed the door, and sailed across the porch.

Inside, the door handle rattled and Michael screaming again. *"Zub ur omak!"*

She tore up the driveway. Anthony was howling, forepaws up on the dashboard. The windshield was fogged with his breath. She cut the light.

Behind her came thudding footsteps. Michael was out. Ahead the car was tilting. Were the tires sunk in the mud? She reached the car and realized the tires were flat. She opened the driver's door and the dogs tumbled out.

Michael came bolting up the slope.

She took off up the driveway with the dogs by her heels. Her only hope now was her neighbor. She hit the dirt road running, nearly tripping over Judy, who was too close to her feet. Ignoring Michael completely, Anthony surged ahead.

She sped up, her arms pumping, legs flying. Both dogs were ahead, and her neighbor's house was a dark shadow on the curve of the road. Small pebbles and stones flew under her feet as she sped across the pitted road.

Michael was gaining on her. His breathing grew louder.

She sprinted down the road, scanning the neighbor's house. There were no lights, no pickup in the drive. Was it in the garage? Was he home? Out of candles? Or sick? At the hospital? If she turned down his drive, she'd be trapped.

A kicked pebble ricocheted off the back of her calf. Michael had caught up. His hand fell on her shoulder, and she cried out and lunged forward in a spurt. She'd never get away, he was too fast, too close. Close enough to smell the garlic on his breath and hear his words. *"Allah el akbar."*

He came again. His hand slapped her shoulder and fell. Now a grasp for her hair. It slipped through his fingers.

She whistled for Anthony and made no sound. "Anthony," she cried, as a hand seized a clump of hair and yanked back her head.

Anthony stopped and turned. The white stripe of his nose and whites of his eyes flashed, and then he came galloping toward her.

Michael gasped, and Dana jerked her head and broke free. She scrambled forward as the headlights of a car brightened the road. Her neighbor's pick-up? The *we* working with Michael?

The car came toward them, lights too close to the ground for a pick-up. She was trapped between the car and Michael. She veered left, leaping across a ditch, and then scrambling across a field toward the trees.

Behind her, brakes squealed and headlights lit up the night. She ran faster through the field, feet barely touching the ground, heart on fire, air gone from her lungs, as she followed the dogs across the soft marshy ground.

They were coming after her, coming closer, gaining ground. Someone new. She heard easy breathing, water splashing, muck gurgling, and branches snapping. She hit the forest, dodging tree trunks and bushes as smilax grabbed at her clothes. Ahead, thick brambles and brush blocked the path. Anthony stopped and Judy ran into him, crying as she rolled. Behind her, Dana heard a rush of air and her name, and a scream as she went down.

CHAPTER FIFTY-FIVE

Dana sank into the mud. A shadow passed over her and she closed her eyes, and the world went dark. She heard loud screaming she wished would stop. When she held her breath, it did.

"Dana, look at me. Open your eyes."

A familiar voice. She opened one eye.

Nick. He was down in a crouch beside her, brushing hair out of her eyes. "It's okay, you're all right." He paused. "Are you?"

She shuddered, gulping air. Her heart was jumping, her throat ached, and her mouth was dry. She hugged Judy to her and caught her breath.

Ahead on the road, two headlights shone. In the bright light, Dana saw Ackerman wrench Michael's hands behind his back and slip on handcuffs.

She straightened and stood up. Her legs were weaker than she thought and she lost her footing. Nick steadied her with his hand.

"He stole Karl's car," Nick said, as they crossed the marshy field.

Ackerman helped Michael into the car and slammed the door. The spindly agent leaned against the car, eyeing their approach. Before they reached the road, he was already firing questions. "What happened? What did he say? Who is he?"

"According to him, Michael Smith," Dana said.

"Except he's not," Nick said. "The real Michael Smith is in Iowa. This is an imposter."

Ackerman threw open the front door of the car. "I need you to make a statement, Ms. Sparks. Come with me."

She saw Michael in the back seat, head resting on his knees. She shook her head.

"It's not a request," Ackerman said. "We need to know what happened. The man is a cold-blooded assassin. A terrorist."

"I thought that was me."

Ackerman reached in his pocket and pulled out the garrote. He snapped it between his fingers, pulling it tight. "You're lucky you're alive."

Michael was close enough to strangle her if he wanted to. He never intended to kill her. "He's a victim, too. The U.S. bombed his house, killed his twin daughters and his wife."

Ackerman's eyes gleamed and he leaned down, his face in hers. "Who's he working with? What are his goals? What did he hope to achieve? *Jihad*?"

The rapid fire of questions again. "Ask him," Dana said. "You bomb his town, he bombs yours. When does it stop?"

"Dana, not now," Nick said in a warning tone. He turned to Ackerman. "Barry, she's tired. Can't you leave this for later?"

"I need a statement."

Nick argued on her behalf. Ackerman had his suspect and Karl was waiting at the police station. Dana could make a statement in the morning.

Though Ackerman insisted on interviewing her immediately, she refused. "I can force you," he said, but in the end he chose not to. "All right. Tomorrow. First thing." He tossed Nick a set of keys. "I found these in his pocket." Ackerman jumped in his car and drove off in a burst of flying pebbles.

Dana and Nick stood in the road as the dust billowed and the lights disappeared. "How did you know?" Dana said.

"His age." Nick kicked at a pebble. Anthony pounced on it, then picked it up and dropped it at Nick's feet. "I should have known. Everything about him was wrong."

"I should have known too. I saw the scratches on his arm Saturday night. He said it was smilax, but it was a cat. Pumpkin. He injected it with *Yersinia* that he bought. It was guaranteed to be antibiotic resistant. Pumpkin belonged to the eleven-year-old you saw at the hospital who you called less than lucid. After Pumpkin got sick, he was hit by a car. Jack's roommate dropped it off at the vet school. Tim operated on him. At some point, Pumpkin developed pneumonic plague and infected Tim. He's the index case. He had dinner at the hotel Saturday night and infected the hotel guests. He helped Sheryl change a tire and must have gotten close to Penny."

Nick whistled. "I'm impressed. How did you figure it out?"

"I went to the epicenter. The car wash. Jack took his roommate's car to get it washed. The cat must have left behind infected fleas. They bit Jack, the car wash attendant, and Dudley. Infected fleas must have been vacuumed and ended up in the dumpster where they infected Carol's rats."

Nick clucked his teeth. "What about me?"

"Frank. He got it from the cat, or from Tim when he was in the clinic. The antibody test was negative because he was on the immunosuppressant. His blood tested positive for *Yersinia*."

Nick rubbed his cheek and the place where he cut himself shaving. "Septicemic plague. I knew it was bad."

"It was bad because it was engineered to be bad. I guess the terrorists didn't know about the new antibiotic CK-202."

"It was junk," Nick said. "It didn't work. We used your monoclonal vaccine. We had it shipped from Fort Troy." He looked into her eyes. "But I think you already know that. McCoy authorized its use. You're in the clear. We injected ten thousand people."

It took a moment for it to sink in. "How did it work? Any side effects? Cross-reactions? Allergic responses?"

Nick smiled. "No side effects reported. It was as quick and effective as you'd expect ready-formed antibodies to be." He stared off into the forest. "Dr. Taversham did have a question. He treated the worst patients with antisera. For some reason, people who received your donated blood recovered the quickest."

Dana folded her arms over her heart. "What are you saying? You think I was involved?"

"Of course not." Nick dismissed the accusation with a sweep of his hand. "What I think is, you found an active vaccine. I talked to General Schwartzke. He told me your Phase 2 proposal was approved. I think you've already done the work. You found a promising antigen and you tested it on yourself. Your own white blood cells made your antibodies, and they're better than the monoclonal antibodies you made in the lab."

There was a rustling in the woods and Anthony took off, hurtling through the underbrush. Dana whistled for him. "I'm going home."

She began walking down the road. She felt exhausted, too tired to deal with Nick. She stared at the sky. The clouds were gone, the moon was out, and stars were shining. Anthony returned and Nick was shuffling beside her, kicking stones that Anthony chased.

"Why did you do it?" he said. "Why take that risk? What if something went wrong?"

"Would you care?"

"Of course. Just because I left doesn't mean I'm gone."

"Is that a new Robin Wheeler line?"

He stepped toward her, put a hand on her arm. "I realized something last night. Too many years have gone by."

"Just last night you realized that."

"Come on, Dana." He looked into her eyes, holding her gaze. "I thought you'd moved on. I didn't want to intrude. I thought you found someone more suitable and were happy."

"Why would you think that?"

"I heard things—gossip."

"What things? From whom? Nellie?"

He stared off into the darkness, lifting his hand. "I wanted to come back. I didn't in deference to you. I turned down the department chair. For you."

"For me?" She stared at her dogs, shaking her head. "You could have asked." She raised her eyes and looked at him. "You could have called. Do you think everyone I met was like you? That I would feel the same way?" She stepped toward him. "You know what? I found someone suitable who made me happy and he left. I always thought if I held him in my heart, he'd come back. I've been waiting."

Nick exhaled slowly and returned her stare. The whites of his eyes were shining, and his pupils were as big and black as the night. "This long?"

She put a hand on his. His skin was electric to her touch. "I knew you would come."

He took her hand, slipped his fingers between hers. The old Nick was back. "I don't know how it would work."

She stepped toward him, closing the space between them. "Yes you do. A wise man once said: *follow your heart, it will show you the way.*"

"Did Robin Wheeler sing that?"

"He should have. Maybe then you'd have come long ago."

"I'm here now."

She moved into his arms and kissed him. He kissed her back, as the night closed in around them.

MAY 1ST

CHAPTER FIFTY-SIX

Dawn broke and the stars vanished quickly. Staring out the window at the horizon, Dana saw a gold band light up the trees. The first bird began to sing and another joined in. She tried to remember her dreams, and could not; perhaps she was still dreaming. Nick was back in her bed.

He started in his sleep, his eyelids fluttering, breath catching, hold tightening. She put her hand on his arm and he closed it around her. She kissed his cheek and his lips and as the night left off, a new day began with a slow making of love as the sun filled the sky. Nick's doppelganger was back. The better half who was impassioned by music and wine; in tune with old rhythms that shattered physical boundaries and captured the radiating pulse of the sun. It shone down upon them. His sweat bathed her skin, his five o'clock shadow burned her cheeks, and his heart beat in time with her own. There was no division where his body left off and hers began. The two parts were back together, once again whole.

Then Nick slept, as he would, and she thought of this moment, this place, this time, and the events that led them here. It was like a warp in time—an influence of the future on the present—tomorrow affecting today. A result necessitating a cause. Like something ahead in time, reeling you forward to itself. A strange form of causality that worked in reverse.

Dana closed her eyes. It was too unreal. Nothing seemed as it was. The world was sharper, more defined, and more alive. Something vital in the empty spaces was making things more clear. She was experiencing her own renaissance. Only the Duane plague wasn't showing the failure of God, but of empirical science. The world had become more like Van Gogh's vision—a world where things were more than they appeared to be; a world where substance went beyond physical definition; a world of hidden forces and unseen connections that brought things together in non-causal ways.

Outside, a car door slammed and the dogs barked. Nick threw his arm over his eyes. Dana leapt up, pulled on a sundress, and left the room. Through the front picture window she saw McCoy on the porch, standing straight and impeccable in his military suit. She flung open the door and the dogs roared out. She followed them.

"You didn't show up for work, and I came to see if all was well," McCoy said. "Ackerman said there was trouble last night."

"Everything is fine. I'll be in soon." She wondered what time it was. "Is Nick still here?"

In the past, they had to hide; nothing could be out in the open. She stood in the bright light wondering how to answer when Nick appeared. Barefoot, he buttoned his shirt, making a statement.

The men shook hands, congratulated each other on their health and recovery. The sun beat down and sweat broke out on McCoy's forehead. Dana, remembering the mess inside, was loath to let him in—but Nick did so. "Come in, TJ. Let's get a drink." He clapped the general on the shoulder and waved at the door. Nick winked at Dana. He was making himself at home.

They went inside. Shoes and socks and other items of clothing were strewn across the living room. There was an empty bottle of wine on the counter and two half-filled glasses on the dining room table. Dana removed them as McCoy sat down. Nick got him a bottle of cold water. The electricity was back.

"The town is open," McCoy said, unscrewing the cap, his back to the living room. "The VP is coming after all. He'll be here by noon." He paused and sipped water. "Karl will inject him with the monoclonal vaccine as a precaution." McCoy held up his hands, fingers framing an invisible picture. "Do you think the headline, 'VP GETS SHOT,' is too sensational?"

Dana thought it was. "The caption is misleading."

"Yes, Dr. Sparks, perhaps you are right." McCoy took another sip of water. "I talked to General Schwartzke this morning."

Dana gulped.

"He called to applaud my order to use the experimental monoclonal vaccine."

"It saved numerous lives," Nick said. "It was a good call."

McCoy shrugged, and looked at Dana. "Sometimes I surprise even myself."

She wondered what to say. He knew what she had done and was letting it slide.

"I have decided to retire," he said. "There is something about facing the abyss that makes one prioritize. I suspect Nick knows what I mean."

"Seize the moment," Nick said, and moved on to safer ground. "What about your new warfare unit?"

"It is time to go. Heads up? The dean would like you to replace me. Nellie said you wouldn't consider it, but I hope that you will."

Nick looked at Dana. She lifted her eyebrows. "I'm interested," Nick said.

"Good." McCoy turned to Dana. "General Schwartzke informed me your proposal was approved. You got your grant for Phase 2. He needed my letter of support and I told him it was in the mail." McCoy held out his hand. "I am confident tenure is yours. You deserve it. We are in your debt."

Dana took his hand and endured a bone-crushing shake. "Thank you, sir." For once there was no bite in her tone.

"I owe you an apology," McCoy said. "I made a critical error in calling the suspect."

"Yes," Dana said.

Nick cleared his throat.

"I'm sorry, too," Dana said. "I could have been more of a team player."

"We're fortunate you weren't." McCoy stood up. "I should go. Leave you two to—" He didn't bother finishing. He went to the door, stepped onto the porch, and looked at Nick. "There is a reception at the dean's at thirteen hundred hours. Can you make it?"

"I'll be there," Nick said.

McCoy turned to Dana. "And you too, Dr. Sparks. Would you be available?"

It was a request, not an order. "I'm free."

McCoy went to his car. Nick took Dana's hand and they watched him leave, waving goodbye as he drove off. A new day was dawning. What had long been buried was brought to light, making the whole world more luminous. The sky was bright, leaves shimmered, and the green grass shone. Wild azaleas were blooming and the morning glories were turned to the sun.